"Desai is masterful at character banter and will have readers laughing out loud."

—Sharon C. Cooper,
USA Today bestselling author of *In It to Win It*

"Dripping with banter, this action-packed and hilarious romp will keep you at the edge of your seat. Simi and Jack's sizzling chemistry leaps off the page, and their hard-won HEA feels so satisfying. But what really shines is the amazing, talented ensemble of misfits working together to pull off a daring jewel heist while simultaneously planning a wedding. You don't want to miss this brilliantly crafted heist story!"

—Farah Heron,
author of *Jana Goes Wild* and *Accidentally Engaged*

"A wickedly fun and wildly engaging romp, led by a strong female protagonist whom readers can't help but root for through all her schemes and hijinks." —Kyla Zhao, author of *The Fraud Squad*

"A jewel heist, an engaging heroine, a wedding, the pitch-perfect banter, and a mysterious guy—*To Have and to Heist* has it all! Grab this engaging and funny mix of a caper and a romance and get ready to be charmed."

—HelenKay Dimon, author of *Moorewood Family Rules*

"The next time someone asks for a rip-roaring action rom-com, I'm pointing (read: shoving) them to Sara Desai's *To Have and to Heist*. Desai strikes the perfect balance of high-stakes plot and relatable main characters. The zany and irreverent crew are peak millennial chaos, and I am so here for it! The crew's skill sets are particularly interesting, especially our action man's endearing love of horticulture. From the very first page, I was swept away faster than a getaway driver. With breakneck pacing, antics that don't let up, and a spunky heroine that just won't quit, Desai's *To Have and to Heist* will easily steal away your afternoon."

—Lillie Vale, author of *The Decoy Girlfriend* and *The Shaadi Set-Up*

"Sara Desai's voice pulls you in from the first page in this fun caper with sizzling chemistry."

—Namrata Patel, author of *The Candid Life of Meena Dave*

"Romantic comedy meets *Ocean's Eleven*."   —*USA Today*

"*To Have and to Heist* is what happens when you take *Ocean's Eleven*–style capers, turn the sexiness up to eleven, and slather it in some good ol' fashioned Desi family drama."

—*Good Housekeeping*

"An action-packed heist story that delivers a fun hit of romance."

—*Woman's World*

"Come for the crime; stay for the sizzling chemistry."   —*Parade*

"*To Have and to Heist* by Sara Desai is a wonderfully fun and thrilling read. If you are looking for a beach read, this is absolutely perfect."   —*Culturess*

"Lots of secrets and plot twists will keep readers turning the pages. Don't miss this one!"   —*Fresh Fiction*

"Fans of *How to Lose a Guy in 10 Days* will enjoy this South Asian romantic comedy about a bet between two enemies with lots of chemistry. Indian culture plays a key role in the story, from the mentions of dishes to apparel. Between these cultural glimpses and the sparks between the couple, everything about this book is vibrant."
—*The Daily Star*

"Desai . . . fills the pages with wry observations . . . and allows her heroine some steamy romance with a thief who's 'gorgeous but in a devilish way.' You can practically start casting the movie already."
—*The Seattle Times*

"Sara Desai's *To Have and to Heist* is the perfect hilarious and action-packed rom-com for fans of *Ocean's Eleven*. . . . Fast-paced, fun, and full of all the makings of a great beach read, this book will steal your heart!"
—She Does the City

"This caper is perfect for those who love rom-cozies—books that blend cozy mystery and rom-com tropes."
—Book Riot

"Desai perfectly balances the lighthearted romance with a fun and twisty heist plot enacted by a kooky cast of indebted millennials. Romance lovers will devour this unputdownable treat, and even readers generally wary of the genre will be swept away."
—*Publishers Weekly* (starred review)

"This unputdownable novel will fly off shelves, and readers will clamor for Desai's backlist."
—*Library Journal* (starred review)

"A beautifully told rom-com that's full of laughs, heart, and scorching sexual tension." —*Kirkus Reviews* (starred review)

"Outrageously funny, meltingly hot and tender, and wrapped up in heartwarming community, this book will warm you in the best ways. Daisy and Liam are just the kind of sexy joyful magic we need in the world right now."

—Sonali Dev, author of *Recipe for Persuasion*

"A smart, sexy read. If you haven't done so already, prepare to mark Sara Desai as your new fave author!"

—Sajni Patel, author of *The Trouble with Hating You*

"A writer to watch."

—Bustle

"Geek-chic Daisy makes an endearing heroine, and the dysfunctional Murphy family provides believable tension. Desai's fans will be thrilled to reconnect with the eccentric Patels, and new readers will be hooked. This is a gem."

—*Publishers Weekly* (starred review)

"This novel has all the funny banter and sexy feels you could want in a romantic comedy—and, of course, a terrific grand gesture before the happy ending." —NPR.org

"Desai's delightful debut is a playful take on enemies-to-lovers and arranged marriage tropes starring two headstrong Desi American protagonists. Rom-com fans should take note of this fresh, fun offering."　　　　　—*Publishers Weekly* (starred review)

"*The Marriage Game* is the most delicious read! From the humor to the heartwarming family bonds to the off-the-charts chemistry, it's impossible for me to love this book any more. I can't wait for more from Sara Desai!"　　　　—Alexa Martin, author of *Intercepted*

"I fell hard for *The Marriage Game* from the moment I read Layla and Sam's dynamite meet-cute. It's a hilarious, heartfelt, and steamy enemies-to-lovers romance."
　　　　　　　—Sarah Echavarre Smith, author of *Faker*

TITLES BY SARA DESAI

The Marriage Game
The Dating Plan
The Singles Table

To Have and to Heist
'Til Heist Do Us Part

'TIL HEIST DO US PART

SARA DESAI

◆ ◆

BERKLEY ROMANCE
NEW YORK

BERKLEY ROMANCE
Published by Berkley
An imprint of Penguin Random House LLC
penguinrandomhouse.com

Copyright © 2024 by Sara Desai
Excerpt from *The Marriage Game* copyright © 2020 by Sara Desai
Penguin Random House supports copyright. Copyright fuels creativity, encourages diverse
voices, promotes free speech, and creates a vibrant culture. Thank you for buying an authorized
edition of this book and for complying with copyright laws by not reproducing, scanning, or
distributing any part of it in any form without permission. You are supporting writers and
allowing Penguin Random House to continue to publish books for every reader.

BERKLEY and the BERKLEY & B colophon are registered
trademarks of Penguin Random House LLC.

Library of Congress Cataloging-in-Publication Data

Names: Desai, Sara, author.
Title: 'Til heist do us part / Sara Desai.
Description: First Edition. | New York: Berkley Romance, 2024.
Identifiers: LCCN 2023052666 (print) | LCCN 2023052667 (ebook) |
ISBN 9780593641316 (paperback) | ISBN 9780593641323 (ebook)
Subjects: LCGFT: Romance fiction. | Novels.
Classification: LCC PR9199.4.D486 T55 2024 (print) |
LCC PR9199.4.D486 (ebook) | DDC 813/.6—dc23/eng/20231113
LC record available at https://lccn.loc.gov/2023052666
LC ebook record available at https://lccn.loc.gov/2023052667

First Edition: August 2024

Printed in the United States of America
1st Printing

To John
For never saying no to an adventure

'TIL HEIST
DO US PART

ONE

◇ ◇ ◇

JACK

I magine you are a smokin'-hot dude. You have a new Ford F-150 truck, a great job traveling the world to steal and repatriate priceless art and antiquities, a collection of rare succulents that you have left in the care of your plant nursery owner / black market arms dealer cousin Lou, and money in the bank after pulling off an almost impossible heist with a bunch of rank amateurs. You have a girlfriend, Simi, who is not only beautiful but fiercely intelligent, and you have a new BFF, except you don't call him that to his face because chances are he'll punch you in the gut—Gage is all about repressed emotions. You've finally avenged your dearly departed grandmother, and your boss has promised that your next gig will be the chef's kiss of heists. Life has not been kind to you, but finally things are going your way.

Or so you think.

It starts out small. What was supposed to be your last job ever—the theft of a collection of stolen Cambodian antiquities—is a bust when you discover that the antiquities are fakes. Your boss sends you to Colombia instead and you somehow wind up as the unwilling guest of some local drug lords who don't care that your new girlfriend has been waiting for you to return to Chicago. After that, it is one country, one job, and one disaster after another that keep you and Simi apart. You are pushed out of a third-story window in Rio, and for two weeks you can't remember your own name. Then there's the remote hillside town in Italy where they don't sell burner phones, but they do have thugs with automatic weapons who take issue with people who steal from their boss. The rural doctor who finds you in a ditch keeps you sedated while you recover, and you miss all Simi's calls. Her messages become fewer and farther between. You just can't catch a break. Who knew there would be no cell service underwater when you board a submarine to retrieve lost treasures from a sunken ship? Or that you aren't allowed a phone call in an Afghan prison? Your boss seems determined to keep you away from home. You miss Simi's birthday, her father's sixtieth, her mother's fifty-ninth, her cousin's thirty-third, another cousin's engagement party. You miss Thanksgiving, Christmas, Diwali, Easter, and Memorial Day. Simi begs you to come to a family reunion so she can introduce you to everyone, and you miss that, too.

Each time you do manage to connect for a video chat, Simi is a little less warm, her smiles a little less bright. And then one night after you outdo yourself in the sexting department—as you always do—she says the words you knew were coming but don't want to hear: "I'm not getting what I need out of this relationship. Let's take a break."

You promise it won't happen again. You'll buy a new burner phone. *She* is the priority and screw your boss and national security and all that jazz. When she calls, you'll be there with the sexy talk she likes so much, and hey, Thanksgiving is coming again and this time you'll bring the turkey. But it's eight months too late. You lose the girl of your dreams, and your so-called perfect life shatters.

To make matters worse, as soon as you are out of the picture, Detective Garcia moves in.

Garcia is Simi's police friend. He's been crushing on her since the day he tried to arrest her as an accessory to the theft of a $25 million diamond necklace. By the time the bad guys were caught, you and Simi had hooked up and Garcia didn't have a chance. But he was waiting, watching, ready to pounce.

And pounce he does. In the history of time, no man has pounced faster and harder than Garcia when he finds out Simi has dumped you.

Deli lunches. Pizza dinners. Walks in the park. Every time you call her office—she blocked your cell number after the breakup—she is out with Garcia. Her receptionist, Janice, offers herself in Simi's place. She tells you that she is freshly divorced, and fifty-eight is the new thirty, especially since she's now on HRT and has the libido of a woman half her age. She doesn't mind long-distance relationships, and she just bought a new phone with a giant screen.

You realize you have no chance with Simi if you continue in your current line of employment, but money is an issue. You tell your boss you are done with excitement, adventure, and international travel, but you are willing to do *one last job* before you leave the business for good. Horticulture has always been your passion and Lou needs someone to handle the plant nursery side of the business, so he can focus on the more lucrative arms dealing that goes on behind the flowering plants and shrubs.

Luck is finally with you, and your boss approves a juicy piece of work in your hometown. So, there you are in Winnetka, the most exclusive suburb of Chicago, after spending the afternoon casing a billionaire's mansion with your BFF. Gage is ex-military. Black ops, or maybe even something more secret and sinister. He doesn't talk about his past, but there isn't a weapon he can't handle. You've personally witnessed him beating six men in single-hand combat without breaking a sweat. He likes to break bones, noses, and spirits during torture times. He is over six feet of solid muscle and hard raw power, but he's a big softie inside. You couldn't imagine a better heist partner than Gage. He makes you feel safe.

Your mark, tech billionaire Peter Hearst, has managed to uncover the long-lost Florentine Diamond, which has an estimated value of $200 million and has been missing for over one hundred years. Through incredible skill and stealth while disguised as a waiter, you have just discovered that he keeps it in a secure museum in a bunker beneath his multimillion-dollar mansion and shows it only to his billionaire friends. Your mission, if you choose to do it—and you do because it's your job and you need the cash to get out of the business and win Simi's heart—is to liberate the diamond and repatriate it to Austria, where it rightfully belongs. You like the word *liberate* because it doesn't have any criminal connotations, even though your life has been pretty much one criminal connotation after another.

But you digress. After this last heist, you will be a changed man—a man of whom your soon-to-not-be-ex-girlfriend will be proud; a man so straight—in all senses of the word—that she will be desperate to get back together with you and won't be tempted by squeaky-clean police detective Garcia, who gave her a Boston fern as an office-warming gift when she opened her new event-planning business in the Loop.

A Boston fern. Even now it makes you laugh. If Garcia had done even the most basic research, he would have discovered that there is nothing a *Nephrolepis exaltata* likes less than a south-facing office with low humidity and an owner who is unlikely to appreciate its sensitive watering routines. Simi could do so much better.

You are laughing to yourself about Garcia's total lack of plant knowledge when Gage decides to take one final look around as the high-society types stumble out of the party. You tell him to be careful. You had an unfortunate encounter with a former associate, Clare, at the party, and she was up to no good. He tells you to stay alert. You tell him you've been doing this kind of work for much longer than him and "alert" is your middle name.

You take off your waiter disguise and relax in the seat of your new truck. Too late you realize "alert" doesn't involve resting your eyes. The rear passenger door opens and Clare climbs into the back seat. The same Clare you just outed as a thief at the party because she was after your score. The Clare you thought had been taken to jail. The Clare who was your shadow, and then your girl, and then your ex, and now your nemesis. That Clare.

You blame Clare for your mutual enmity because you can't blame yourself. After all, you didn't make her any promises. How could you? She worked for some people. You worked for some other people. Those people didn't get along. Your paths crossed. One thing led to another, led to seduction in a hotel room in Istanbul, led to someone being handcuffed to a four-poster bed and robbed of a valuable antiquity that had just been stolen from a Russian oligarch's Siberian mansion. Not Clare. Obviously. You are a gentleman and would only handcuff a woman if she gave her consent.

After you escaped the handcuffs, it was weeks of chase, seduction, cross, and double cross. You got your antiquity back. She followed you to Egypt. Totally ruined your Nile cruise. Instead of seeing the sights and retrieving a few antique necklaces along the way, you got to spend three weeks in an Egyptian prison. Then there was Vegas. Don't worry. You shot to wound. Her bullet just missed your heart. After that fiasco, you and Clare called a truce. She even did you a favor when she was working a scam as a personal shopper at Bloomingdale's, helping Simi find a glamorous outfit for a charity ball. Back then you and Simi weren't together because she suspected you were a thief and didn't trust you. You won her over once. You can do it again.

Do you know who doesn't trust you? Clare. Not after you told the security guard at the billionaire's mansion that you'd seen her stealing someone's wallet—a wallet you had just dropped into her fancy designer handbag. All's fair in love and thievery.

You turn and force a smile. Clare leans back in the passenger seat and crosses her legs, all cool and casual like she was just in the neighborhood and decided to drop in for a visit. Your skin prickles with warning. Maybe it's her aura of menace. Or maybe it's because she's got a lit cigarette in one hand and a butcher knife in the other. Ash falls on your shiny new seats.

You extend a polite, pleasant greeting. She does not reciprocate. Instead, she says mean things like "you bastard," "the truce is over," "this is my score now," and "if you don't give up this job, I'm going to destroy you." She drags her knife over your admiral blue multicontour bucket seats, slicing through the high-end leather like butter. Then she tells you she's got a room at the Plaza and a fresh set of handcuffs calling your name. As if you would fall for that trick again. Your heart belongs to only one woman, and *she* doesn't smoke.

You wonder where Gage is. Protection and security are his thing. Why didn't he spot Clare lurking outside? With her long platinum-blond hair, piercing blue eyes, high cheekbones, and heart-shaped face, she doesn't exactly blend into a crowd. The short, tight white dress, gold stilettos, and show-stopping ninety-three-carat cabochon-cut Colombian emerald necklace from Bulgari's Magnifica high-end jewelry collection are an unusual choice for a recon mission. You are pretty sure it's the same necklace Zendaya wore for the *Dune* premiere. You are also pretty sure the jeweler who loaned it to Zendaya doesn't know it's missing.

Clare slowly uncrosses her legs. She pauses just long enough for you to suspect she's not wearing underwear. Then she crosses her legs again. You are immediately reminded of *Basic Instinct*, a

1992 neo-noir erotic thriller featuring Sharon Stone as a psychopathic serial killer. You tell Clare she'd be perfect for the role.

Wrong thing to say. Clare stubs out her cigarette on the back of your seat, leaving an angry black hole. The acrid scent of burning leather makes your nose wrinkle. Before she opens the door, she warns you again to stay away from the billionaire's mansion. This time when she uncrosses her legs, you look down at the floor mat, color coordinated with the carpet. You went all out on your truck purchase, paying extra for the limited edition. What a mistake.

"When I'm done, you'll have nothing left. No job. No truck. No girlfriend named Simi." Her sinister laugh sends a shiver down your spine. With a cold sneer, Clare climbs out of the vehicle and drags her butcher knife along the side of your truck, scratching the smoked-quartz-tinted clearcoat metallic—a $450 extra—as she walks away. The shriek of metal on metal twists your gut, but not as much as the fact that the truce is over, Clare is after your score, and she knows your greatest weakness: Simi.

Moments later you are burning rubber down the street. Gage can look after himself. If he could survive three months alone in the jungle living off rainwater and insects, he can find his way home on the Chicago L train. You text Simi and tell her you need to see her as a matter of urgency. You are shocked when she agrees to meet you the following day at Bloomingdale's, where she'll be helping her goddaughter find a dress for prom. It has been two months since the breakup. Ten months since you've seen her in person. Your heart pounds in your chest, and not just in anticipation of seeing her again.

Simi is in danger.

TWO

◇ ◇ ◇

SIMI

Some people have trouble with boundaries. They say "no" but often find themselves doing the very thing they didn't want to do. They set rules and allow people to break them. They have a moral code but will throw it out the window when their best friend, Chloe, is being framed for a crime she didn't commit. They say they need to take a relationship break but then they agree to meet their ex at a department store just because he said it was a matter of life and death.

My name is Simi Chopra, and I'm one of those people.

"You know it is likely not 'life or death,'" Olivia said as we walked down the sidewalk toward Bloomingdale's. "He just wants to see you again." Chloe's fifteen-year-old daughter was nothing if not practical. Even though Chloe had raised Olivia on her own after getting out of an abusive relationship and had read her countless fairy tales with happily-ever-after endings, Olivia didn't share her mother's love of romance or her rose-tinted outlook on life.

"Given what Jack does for a living, she can't take that risk," Chloe said. "Also, they still love each other. Maybe she wants to give him another chance."

"I've had enough heartbreak and disappointment," I said, skirting over the whole who-loves-who issue. "I need a man who is going to be there for me. I need someone I can call when my new business is floundering, and my parents are desperately trying to find me a husband because I'm single and—gasp—thirty years old, and the ceiling of my new condo cracked, and water is dripping on the kitchen floor because my upstairs neighbor left the bathtub running, and the condo association now wants everyone to pay $100,000 to have all the plumbing redone because they've discovered it's substandard."

"You don't need a man," Chloe said. "You have me."

"You have me, too," Olivia piped up, pushing back the thick blond hair that, along with her gently rounded face and slim build, made her an almost identical copy of her mother.

I shared a look with Chloe. She'd had Olivia when she was in her teens and sometimes Olivia forgot that we weren't all just friends. "That's sweet, honey. But you're too young to understand real-world problems."

"I know more than you think."

"What exactly do you know?" Chloe pulled open the door to Bloomingdale's. "Drugs? Sex? Alcohol? Do you have a boyfriend you didn't tell me about? Are you being safe?"

"Mom! Cringe."

Chloe didn't respond with her usual motherly admonition. She was staring straight ahead, a frown creasing her forehead. "Is that Jack?"

I followed her gaze and recognized Jack right away. I knew every inch of his broad shoulders, his strong back, and the long legs that were always clad in jeans that hugged his muscular thighs. He moved with a fluidity that belied his strength, every motion conveying the message that he was a man who knew what he wanted. And what he wanted in that moment clearly wasn't me.

"Who is he kissing?" Olivia said. "Why is he kissing someone else? He's supposed to be Simi's boyfriend."

"We broke up two months ago," I told her. "He can kiss who he wants."

"But he was supposed to be meeting you," she said. "I secretly thought you were going to get back together."

Despite what I'd just told my girls, in my heart of hearts I'd thought that, too. For some reason, I'd convinced myself that Jack was going to beg my forgiveness and give me a legitimate explanation as to why he'd barely stayed in touch for eight months. We would kiss and make up, and then get back to long, hot, sweaty nights between the sheets, and days full of laughter and adventure. With those fantasies in mind, the sight of him kissing another woman was like a punch to the gut. Pain, betrayal, and disbelief hit me all at once.

His absence had been a test of my patience and trust. His infrequent messages as he traveled around the globe on one dangerous job after another were like breadcrumbs, barely enough to keep my hope alive. I'd held on as long as I could, believing in him, in us, until finally I'd called a break. I hadn't heard from him in the ensuing two months until the message last night. And there he was. In the arms of another woman.

Not just any woman: Clare.

Clare was a personal shopper at Bloomingdale's. Jack had sent me to see her last year when we were working a heist together. I know. I know. Me? Dutiful daughter? All-round good girl? Owner of an up-and-coming event-planning company? Killer of plants and unwed at thirty? *Pulling a heist?*

Guilty as charged.

I'd never been the type to engage in law-breaking behavior, but when your best friend is facing jail time for something she didn't do, you would be amazed at the lines you will cross and the depths to which you will descend, including hooking up with a professional jewel thief slash amateur botanist slash now cheating bastard.

Not being rich, I hadn't even had Bloomingdale's on my radar when I realized I needed a ball gown for a charity event, but Jack had whipped Clare's card out of his wallet and sent me to see her for the full *Pretty Woman* experience. Chloe and Olivia had come with me for moral support.

Clare had started off snooty but turned on the charm when she found out Jack was paying the tab. Then it was all fawn, fawn, "let me bring you a rack of five-figure dresses," and "go with the Louboutins and not the Chanel," and "who would like a glass of champagne?" It had been a fun afternoon. So fun, I'd tucked away the inkling of suspicion I'd had about Clare's past relationship with Jack. Yet another mistake come back to haunt me like a late-night curry.

Or a kiss on the pouty red lips . . .

"OMG!" Olivia's gaze stayed off her phone for a full twenty seconds. "What a freaking bastard."

"Language," Choe warned.

"Language?" Olivia gave an exasperated groan. "Mom, there are bigger issues here than words. This is yet another example of the insidious systemic misogyny that permeates our world. But what do you expect in a patriarchal society? Men can do whatever they want and they aren't judged, but women are constantly subjected to sexual double standards."

"How do you know what men are like?" Chloe asked, missing Olivia's point entirely.

Usually, I would have been down for one of Olivia's lectures about the evils of patriarchy, but I was distracted by the evils of one man in particular—a man who had his hands on Clare's ass. More importantly, they were still kissing, and he wasn't throwing up in disgust, which told me everything I needed to know.

"Why would he arrange to meet me here and then do this?" I winced as Clare twined herself around Jack like the silent killer kudzu. *And damn Jack for filling my head with useless facts about invasive vines.* "Is he trying to punish me for breaking up with him? Is he showing me he's moved on? It's not like him."

"Maybe Janice told him that Detective Garcia kissed you after you and Jack broke up."

Ah. The kiss.

When I'd first started my new event-planning business, I had naively hired Janice, a fifty-eight-year-old receptionist who had worked for a big event-planning company in New York. I thought I could benefit from her experience. I hadn't realized her experience was primarily gossip related. When I found out she'd warned prospective clients that my business was struggling, I had to let her go.

On her way out, Janice casually dropped the bombshell that Jack had called several times after our breakup and she'd told him I was out with my new man, Detective Garcia.

I first met Garcia when he arrested me in connection with the theft of the Wild Heart necklace. We spent a lot of time together during his investigation, mainly because I was his prime suspect. After the dust had settled and I'd been cleared of any crimes, he asked me out, but by then I'd hooked up with Jack, and Garcia had to settle for being friends. At least until the breakup.

"It's still no excuse to throw his new relationship in my face . . . if it is even new." My chest tightened. "Maybe he's been seeing her all this time."

"Can we throw something at them?" Olivia asked, reaching for a glass vase on the counter beside her.

"We can't afford to pay for anything we break," Chloe said gently. "We've got a mortgage now and an education savings account. I

wouldn't want your future to be compromised because some frick-
ing deadbeat son of a bitch can't keep his dick in his pants."

I tuned them out, still trying to process what I was seeing.
This wasn't the Jack I knew. Had I really hurt him so badly that he
felt the need for revenge?

"I say march on over there and give him a piece of your mind,"
Chloe said firmly. "If you want to rough him up a bit, I'll back
you up."

"Can I back her up, too?" Olivia asked. "I want to take a blow
at the patriarchy."

"Absolutely not," Chloe said. "I need you outside waiting for
our getaway Uber." She turned her attention to me. "How are we
handling this? Evisceration, obviously, but do you want it to be
physical or verbal?"

Chloe was my ride-or-die. One time, when I mistakenly thought
I'd killed a man, she showed up with a bottle of bleach and a tarp.

"I'm a professional now," I said. "I have my own failing business. I've resisted all my parents' attempts to get me married. I've
pulled off a heist. I've gone to therapy to deal with my abandonment issues. I was even able to tell Garcia after he kissed me that I
wasn't ready to jump into anything new."

"So . . . physical," she said, understanding.

"What's the heaviest thing you've got?"

Chloe pulled opened her giant tote bag and displayed a cornu-
copia of patriarchy-pandering beauty supplies, her laptop, a pair of
flip-flops, a change of clothes, baby wipes, assorted snacks, and
three library books. I'd given her the bag, embroidered with a giant sun, when she graduated from college with a computer science
degree because she was the sunshine of my life.

"What's that one?" I pointed to the largest book.

"*War and Peace*. Olivia just took it out of the library for a school project. They're having a competition to find out who can make the tallest tower using the least number of books. It's got 1,225 pages."

"Too bad it's not the hardcover copy." I hefted the book in my hand. My mother had made me read *War and Peace* when I was sixteen. An English professor at Northwestern University, she had made it her mission in life to ensure that at least one of her four children was well versed in the classics before leaving high school.

"Olivia, go outside." Chloe pointed to the door as I wound up for the pitch. "I don't want you to be part of this. I don't condone this kind of activity and I never want to hear that you've resorted to violence after your ex-boyfriend sets you up to see him with his new girlfriend in a high-end department store."

"No." Olivia folded her arms. "I'm not leaving you."

"No?" Chloe's angry voice rose to a high pitch, attracting the attention of the people around us. "Did you just say 'no' to me?"

Jack stiffened and pulled away from Clare, turning to the sound of Chloe's voice. Clare looked over his shoulder and met my gaze. Her sly smile told me she'd known we were here all along.

I knew the exact moment Jack saw me because his jaw tightened and his face smoothed into an expressionless mask. Or maybe it was a mask of shame. I didn't care. The moment our gazes locked, I threw the book as hard and fast as I could. Then I pushed my girls toward the door and shouted, "Run!"

Detective Garcia had a funny way of showing up whenever I was in trouble, so I wasn't surprised when he walked in the door of the Bloomingdale's security office a mere fifteen minutes after I'd been caught by the security guard. Chloe and Olivia had been weighed down with shopping bags, and when I realized all three of us were in danger, I'd slowed down and volunteered myself as tribute so they could get away.

"Garcia." I had to fight back a smile, especially since the security guard who was holding me prisoner was already frowning at my less-than-respectful greeting. "Fancy meeting you here. Did you just happen to be in the neighborhood, maybe looking for a shirt, having coffee, or buying gifts for your nieces?"

"Actually, I was a few blocks away when dispatch called out a disturbance at Bloomingdale's. You mentioned you were coming here with Chloe when I stopped by the other day. It was only logical to assume you'd be involved."

"I'm both hurt that you think so little of me and happy that you think of me at all."

"So, what happened this time?" Garcia leaned against the doorframe, arms folded over his thick, muscular chest. He was a looker, and he knew it. With those big blue eyes, square jaw, and broad shoulders, he was quite the catch, and I could easily have fallen for him if I wasn't still hung up on Jack.

"She threw a book at one of our customers and then attempted to flee the scene." The guard who had caught me on my way out was one of those officious types, pleased as punch he'd seen some action and likely salivating at the possibility of testifying in court and sending me to jail.

Garcia laughed as I knew he would. "You threw the book at someone?"

"I knew you'd like it."

"What does the other party to this alleged crime have to say?"

"The victim has disappeared," the security officer said. "There was a woman with him, but she also left before I could speak to her."

Garcia lifted an eyebrow at me. "Do you know this person?"

"If I was involved in this incident, which I can neither confirm nor deny, it is possible that an individual who may or may not have been my ex-boyfriend was kissing another woman." My voice wavered the tiniest bit as I relived that terrible moment all over again. "And if that were the case, which again I can neither confirm nor deny, I may have suffered a shock, and my copy of *War and Peace*, which I carry around for light reading, may have slipped out of my hand." Chloe and Olivia had made it out safely. No way was I getting them involved.

"It's a big book," the security guard said. "I'd call it a weapon."

Garcia wasn't interested in the book; he was more interested in Jack's reappearance in my life. I knew this because he said, "Ah, the boyfriend you broke up with because his itinerant lifestyle triggered your abandonment issues," and not something like, "Let me see the alleged weapon." Garcia had never met Jack and sometimes I wondered if he thought I'd made Jack up as an excuse not to go out with him.

"He's back in town and . . ." I waved my hand vaguely in the air, unable to put the scene into words again.

"Well, since we've got no victim . . ." Garcia's hands dropped to his hips, where he kept his police belt. It was filled with dangerous and exciting things like the handcuffs he'd already used to arrest me three times—including once at my parents' house after I begged him to help me convince my parents' friends that I wasn't marriage material. ". . . I think we can let this one slide. Unless, of course, any store property was damaged."

"She had good aim," the guard said. "Got him smack on the side of the head."

Garcia waved me up, and a ghost of a smile appeared on his face. "I'll walk you out just in case you happen to lose control of something else."

"I'll need my copy of *War and Peace*." I held out my hand to the security guard. "It's a long train ride back to Evanston."

Garcia walked me out of the store and down the street. "So . . . he's back?" I knew what he meant, but I didn't know how to answer. Clearly, Jack hadn't come back for me.

"He's in Chicago. That's all I know. He messaged me yesterday and asked to meet up. He also said I should spend the night at Chloe's house because I was in danger. She's seeing this ex-military guy who installed a kick-ass security system for her after she was threatened by her abusive ex, Kyle . . ." I trailed off only seconds before revealing what had happened when Gage finally got his hands on Kyle. Crimes had definitely been committed in the service of justice—and not just by Gage. Chloe had finally had her revenge.

"Do I need to track down Chloe's ex?" Garcia's face had gone all serious. I liked him better when he was smiling.

"No. That problem has . . . uh . . . gone away."

"And what about your problem?" he asked softly.

I looked back over my shoulder at the department store where my fleeting hope of getting back together with Jack had just been dashed to pieces. "I guess he's gone away, too."

THREE

◇ ◇ ◇

think a part of me knew Jack would show up at my apartment. I just hadn't expected him to wait a full three hours. He was the kind of guy who liked to have the last word, and I was now 1,225 pages of words ahead. In anticipation of his unwanted presence, I had poured coffee into the pothos plant he'd given to me when he left on what was supposed to be a quick work trip to Cambodia but had turned out to be an eight-month relationship-ending adventure instead.

Jack's "work"—I always thought about his "work" in quotation marks because I still didn't really know what he did except that it involved some Robin Hood–type shenanigans in which he stole illicitly acquired art and jewelry and returned it to its proper owners—had taken him away for the better part of the last year, and I'd finally grown tired of having a nonexistent boyfriend. Sure, the sexting was great, but I missed having someone to talk to about the little day-to-day things—the struggles with my new business, my parents' incessant desire to see me married, and the total inability of the owner of the nearest hot dog stand to remember to refill his mustard.

I was in my living room talking through some last-minute details

with a client when Jack appeared on the balcony outside my sliding glass door. My event-planning business had initially been set
up as a cover for the heist we'd pulled off together, but I'd enjoyed
the experience so much, I'd made the business permanent. I'd used
my share of the reward money we'd received for "finding" the
Wild Heart necklace to rent a small office only a few blocks from
Olivia's school, and I'd leaned heavily on my family and my connection with Simone, a high-society friend I'd met at a charity
ball, to bring the first few clients in the door.

Incensed that he would climb the three floors to my apartment and deny me the pleasure of slamming the door in his face, I
grabbed the curtains and pulled them closed.

"Simi. I need to talk to you. You're in danger." He knocked on
the glass door, calling my name. I heard footsteps upstairs and
knew my neighbor Mrs. Gunter would be down soon to tell me the
noise was upsetting her cat.

Unable to conduct a professional conversation with him bang-
ing and shouting outside, I ended the call. I was contemplating
whether to call the police or leave him to Mrs. Gunter when I
heard the glass door slide open, a reminder to never again go out
with a professional thief. Moments later, Jack pushed the curtains
aside and walked into my apartment.

"You are breaking and entering," I told him. "That's a criminal offense."

"I wouldn't have had to pick the lock if you'd let me in," he
said. "I came to protect you."

Jack walked across the room to inspect the plants he'd given me
to brighten up my new apartment. He was big into horticulture and
had carefully selected various houseplants and flowers that would
do well indoors and with my southeast-facing windows.

My stomach twisted in a knot as his strong hands gently lifted
the leaves on the wilting African violet. I thought I'd be able to

handle the sight of him after my rage book throwing, but all I wanted to do was throw something else. Ten months ago those hands had caressed my skin, stroked my hair, and given me mind-blowing pleasure. He had held me in his arms and made sweet promises about getting out of "the business" so we could be together forever. To be honest, I wasn't down with the "forever" part. Forevers were scary. They meant commitment. They meant vulnerability. They meant you were running the risk of opening your heart to someone who might walk away. Just as he had done.

"I don't need your protection. Just tell me why I'm in danger and then get out." It was hard to see him standing there looking breathtakingly roguish in his retro Rolling Stones T-shirt, battered leather jacket, and worn boots. His dark hair was thick and casually mussed like he'd just jumped out of bed. Maybe he had.

Jack sniffed the pothos. "You gave it some coffee. Great job. I was going to tell you that the *Epipremnum aureum* loves the occasional watering with black coffee. You can also add coffee grounds into the potting soil while transplanting and watch it thrive in the long term."

"Seriously?" I picked up the snow globe he'd sent me from India. I didn't think it had ever snowed over the Taj Mahal, but I appreciated the sentiment. "After what you did with Clare, do you really think I care about the damn plants? They're all going in the trash except for the Boston fern in my office." I knew that would get him. Garcia had given me that fern, and Jack hadn't been pleased.

"It was an ambush," he said, eyeing the snow globe in my hand. "She found out I was meeting you there and—"

"I don't believe you."

"She set me up." His face grew serious. "She knows about us—"

"There is no 'us,'" I said, cutting him off. "Not anymore. Why didn't she know that?"

"I didn't tell her."

"So, you let her think we were together when you kissed her in front of me?" My voice rose in pitch. "That's low even for you. But congratulations. You deserve each other."

"Simi . . ." His face tightened. "I don't want her. I want you."

"I didn't see you making any effort to push her away." My voice cracked, broke. I couldn't stop the painful mental replay of the Bloomingdale's scene. It was on a permanent loop in my mind.

"She had a gun in her pocket," Jack said.

"Are you sure that wasn't you?"

He gave me a pained look. "She threatened to shoot me if I didn't make it look good."

"You could have won an Oscar with that performance."

Jack scrubbed his hand over his jaw. "She's dangerous, Simi. Very dangerous."

I snorted in derision. "What's she going to do? Dress me in the wrong clothes? Sell me last season's Gucci? Shop me to death? Overcharge me?"

"She's not really a personal shopper." He crossed the room and settled in one of the peacock blue side chairs I'd just bought for my living room. I loved color. The brighter and bolder, the better. "The personal shopper gig was just a cover for a scam she was running. She's a . . ." He trailed off, his fingers drumming an offbeat rhythm on the mirrored side table. "She does what I do except for the wrong people. We have a history together."

"Apparently." I traded the snow globe for my phone. I was seconds away from texting Chloe and asking her to bring her bleach and her tarp. "Did you sleep with her?"

"We worked together and then . . ." He opened his hands in a helpless gesture. "It was a long time ago and it didn't mean anything. We parted ways and wound up on opposite sides. She's been making my life miserable ever since."

"You didn't seem miserable in Bloomingdale's."

"She was trying to hurt me by hurting you." He gave a heavy sigh. "She showed up at a high-society party where I was doing recon for a new job. We were after the same score. I outed her as a thief, and the police came and took her away. She escaped and came back to trash my truck and threaten to destroy my life."

"Too bad for her you managed to do it all on your own." I didn't want to hear his explanations and excuses. I wanted him gone.

"I know you're angry," he said. "Clare is good at what she does, and she knew just how to twist the knife." He fiddled with the frayed friendship bracelet on his wrist. I'd been helping Olivia make them for a school fundraiser and, on a whim, I'd made one for Jack. I'd jokingly told him it was the sign of everlasting friendship, and he was supposed to wear it until it rotted off. I never imagined he'd take me seriously.

"I can handle Clare. She tried to convince me to buy jewelry as well as shoes when I went to see her about the dress for the charity ball, and I managed to resist." I grabbed one of the plants he had given me and shoved it into his hands. "Take it. I killed it. Just like you killed our relationship by never being there when I needed you. Just like you killed it again by asking me to meet you so you could get your revenge. Good-bye."

"It's not dead," he pointed out. "It just needs a little love."

"Then give it to Clare."

"She's not a loving type. She's an evil, using, betraying, double-crossing type. Not like you, sweetheart."

"Don't sweetheart me," I snapped. "Your fake seduction won't work here. Clearly, the only thing that is a danger to me is you."

I was done playing games. It hadn't been easy to drop my guard and let Jack into my heart. Although my parents had done their best, I'd played second fiddle all my life to my sports-mad brothers. I was used to being overlooked, to having my needs go unmet. Jack was the first person besides Chloe who I thought had seen the real me. He'd made me feel loved and wanted, which was why the blatant rejection hurt even more.

"What do you want?" he asked as he reluctantly made his way down the hallway. "What else can I do?"

"I want to be loved, Jack. Loved by a person I can trust, and who I know in my soul won't hurt me. I want to feel like I'm good enough, that I'm deserving of love and respect. I thought I had that with you, but I was wrong. I thought I was over my abandonment and trust issues, that they didn't define me or control my life, but you've made me realize I was wrong about that, too."

"You know me," he said quietly. "Do you really think I'd hurt you that way?"

"I *thought* I knew you, but—"

"I'll prove it to you," Jack said. "Give me a few days and I'll prove that Clare set me up. I want you back, Simi. I miss you, and I think you miss me, too, because otherwise you would have thrown the plant at my head."

I did miss him. I hadn't realized just how much until I'd woken up that morning looking forward to our meeting, only to be absolutely crushed to see him with Clare. I picked up a tiny succulent and held it aloft. "Maybe I should throw something at your head."

"Where did that come from?" Jack asked, frowning. "I didn't buy it for you."

"Garcia gave it to me. He's been a good friend. I mentioned that the plants you gave me were high-maintenance, so he bought me a cactus. He said it was strong, hardy, and impossible to kill."

"Garcia doesn't just want to be your friend." Jack crossed his arms in front of his chest. "Janice said he kissed you."

I silently congratulated myself again for letting Janice and her gossiping ways go and just stared at Jack. He didn't deserve to know that the kiss had been unexpected and unwanted and that I'd had to tell Garcia that I wasn't ready for another relationship.

"He also gave you a succulent," he said when I didn't respond.

"It's just a plant."

"*Just* a plant?" His eyes widened. "There is no 'just a plant.' He was putting down a marker, and now he won't stop. I know his type. He'll probably give you an *Asplenium nidus* next. If you thought my plants were high-maintenance . . ."

I'd finally had enough. He had no right to be jealous after revenge kissing his ex in front of me. "I think you should go before one of us says something we're going to regret."

"I've asked some of my guys to keep watch on your apartment," he said, turning in the doorway. "Don't be alarmed if you see them outside. They'll keep you safe if you aren't planning to go back to Chloe's place tonight."

"What guys? I thought you worked alone doing whatever mysterious job it is you do that you can't tell me about."

"They're just guys I know."

"Guys with guns?"

"They can't protect you without weapons."

For the first time since he'd arrived, I felt a niggle of apprehension. "Jack, what's going on?"

"It was supposed to be one last job," he said, pushing open the door. "One last job so we could be together."

"Beta, so nice to see you." My mother swooped in for a hug the moment I stepped into the kitchen of my childhood home in Evanston. She loved to dress the part of an English professor, with thick-rimmed glasses, flowing tops, and cardigans that had seen better days. "I was just about to send you a message. We've invited guests for dinner on Saturday night. Wear something nice."

"I won't be able to make it. There's somewhere I'll need to be."
I greeted both my parents with a kiss on the cheek and gave my

maternal grandmother, Nani, a hug. I'd come home for food and a visit, not to discuss marriage proposals. My parents enjoyed springing surprise potential husbands on me when I least expected it, and the meet and greets always involved a smattering of my matchmaking aunties. "I had hoped you'd give me some time to get over my relationship with Jack."

"We did," Mom said without even the barest hint of shame. "We waited two days before introducing you to that boy Tariq, and you seemed to be fine."

"I wasn't fine then. I'm not fine now. I don't know if I'll ever be fine." I was still shaken by the Bloomingdale's kiss and Jack's subsequent unwanted appearance in my apartment.

"You just need a new man, and you'll forget he ever existed," Nani said cheerfully from behind the kitchen counter, where she was busy heating enough leftovers to feed an army. Nani had moved in after my grandfather passed away and spent her days cooking huge meals, gossiping with her friends, and trying to pick up men at the local seniors' center.

"How about a pint of ice cream?" I suggested, sitting at the table across from my dad. "Maybe a mother-daughter shopping trip? Most parents don't try to cheer their daughters up by arranging a marriage."

"They don't love their children as much as we do." Mom handed me a CV. "Take a look. He's the nephew of one of my colleagues in the English department. He and his big brother were orphaned when their parents passed away in a fire, so she adopted them. He has a PhD in chemistry but right now he's looking for work and a place to live. He was sleeping on his brother's couch because he has no money, but his brother was just arrested, and the landlord ended the tenancy when the police found a dead body in the kitchen. Something to do with a gang killing."

I stared at my mother, aghast. "Are you serious? You've spent years parading doctors, lawyers, and engineers in front of me. You looked down on anyone with less than impeccable credentials, a respectable family, and a hefty bank account, and now you want me to marry a guy who's orphaned, homeless, destitute, and the brother of a murderous felon?"

It occurred to me that Jack was also an orphan, homeless, underemployed, and, since he'd given up his share of the reward money from our last heist, likely destitute as well. I should have introduced him to my parents when I had the chance.

"He's got a PhD," Mom protested.

"And to be fair," Nani added, "you were arrested, too. I don't think you're in a position to judge."

"I was innocent," I shot back. "Detective Garcia just thought it was me because I happened to be at the scene of the crime, and he didn't have any other suspects."

"You're not getting any younger." My dad looked up from the fashion magazine he had been perusing for inspiration for his next collection. "Many of the young South Asian men having arranged marriages today are wanting brides in their early twenties. They tell me all about it when they come in for their suits." Dad was a master tailor and owner of Chopra Custom Clothiers, a business he'd built with his dad into one of the top custom tailors in Chicago. In contrast to my mother's eclectic ensemble, he was dressed for success in a bespoke suit-and-shirt combination from his Masters line for mature men.

"It would be a kindness if you married him," Nani said. "And you can't complain that he's living in his mother's basement like you did with that boy we invited for dinner last week."

"That guy was thirty-seven years old, and his mother was still cooking his meals and doing his laundry," I protested.

My father gently patted my hand. "Even you lived at home last year."

"I came home for a few months because my basement suite flooded. I've been living on my own as a responsible adult for almost ten years." I didn't see any point in mentioning that water was leaking from the ceiling of my apartment, my business was failing, I'd had to let my receptionist go, and my ex-boyfriend had just rejected me all over again.

Emotion welled up in my chest and I reached for a tissue. Right away, Nani grabbed the plates, and a few minutes later we were sitting around the worn kitchen table passing around my favorite comfort foods. Between bites of coconut curry, channa masala, and my father's special dal, I told my family about Jack and Clare and the kiss I wish I hadn't seen.

"I broke up with him for a reason," I told them, "and seeing him with Clare confirmed it. But when he showed up at my apartment and told me she'd set him up, part of me wanted to believe him. I also wanted to believe all the crazy stories he'd told me about why he'd barely been in touch when he was away. I felt like I was betraying myself for having those feelings, so I threw him out."

All the fear, the insecurity, and the trauma from my past had come rushing back. I'd been ignored and overlooked as a child, so desperate for love and attention I would have done anything to get it. I'd been working on reconciling all that trauma with my parents, but clearly trust was still an issue for me.

Confusion turned to anger and resentment, and I stabbed at the samosas on my plate. "How could he do this to me? How could he disappear for so long, only to come back and break my heart?" Why did it hurt every time I opened myself to love?

"He's a bastard." Dad thumped the table so hard the plates rattled. "If he comes to my store again to buy a suit, I'll only sell him something off the rack."

"Thanks, Dad." I smiled at his fierce expression. For a bespoke tailor, nothing was worse than an off-the-rack suit. "Make sure you give him a polyester tie, too."

"I don't carry polyester ties." Dad sniffed. "What kind of establishment do you think I run?"

"Men are scum," Nani said in an attempt to cheer me up. "Worse than scum. They are scum on scum. But when you're ready, I do know a nice boy who does pole dancing."

"Seriously?" I stared at her, aghast. "Pole dancing?"

"I went with his mother to watch him at his track meet," she said. "He was wearing an orange leotard. It left very little to the imagination, but I can assure you that you will not go unsatisfied in that department."

"Oh God. Nani . . ."

"Do you mean pole vaulting?" Mom asked. "Did he run with the pole and throw himself over a bar?"

"Yes, that's it," she said. "Dancing. Vaulting. Cheating. Betraying. In the end, men are all the same when they're wearing tight clothes."

FOUR

◇ ◇ ◇

was at once relieved and disappointed that Jack didn't try to contact me over the next two days. He wasn't the kind of guy to give up easily, but he hadn't shown up with the proof he promised, so I had to assume what I'd seen was real. Still, that didn't stop me from holding my breath every time the elevator dinged down the hall from my office, or from feeling crushed all over again when someone else walked in the door.

By midweek, I'd let too much slide, so I got to work early and focused on catching up. After letting Janice go, I had downsized to a smaller office on the same floor and had pared down my furniture to a desk and credenza, two chairs, and a small table. I'd kept the same white-and-sage-themed decor and filled the empty shelves with plants. I had just finished my watering regime when Simone Du Post walked in the door.

Simone and I had met last year at a charity ball I'd crashed with Jack. We were hoping to convince Bella Angelini, the daughter of Mafia boss Joseph Angelini, to hire our then-sham event planning company to organize her wedding so we could steal the Wild Heart necklace from her father's safe and return it to its rightful owner to save Chloe from jail.

Tall and slim, with a mass of blond curls and a thick Southern accent, Simone had taken a shine to me at the ball after we'd hit it off over the travesty of our matching handbags. She had kindly offered to introduce me to the Angelinis and recommend my event-planning business to all her society friends. After the ball, she'd thrown her $2,000 bag in the trash—because that's what the billionaire elite do if someone has the same bag as them. I pawned mine to pay Chloe's rent after her deadbeat ex failed to make his support payments yet again.

Simone's word was gold in high-society circles, and when I first started running the company, she'd sent a few clients my way, giving me the false impression that my business was destined to be a success. With the reward money left over after I'd paid off my parents' mortgage and my student loans, I went on a spending spree—high-rent office, experienced receptionist, branding advisor, and even an expensive PR company to spread the word that there was a new event-planning company in town.

You'd think with a business degree, I would have been less naive about the competitiveness of the event-planning business in Chicago, but I just kept spending, confident that at some point, the work would come flooding in. When I'd run the business almost into the ground, Simone had suggested I move into the less-competitive area of funerals and celebrations of life, and she just happened to have a friend who died, so I could make a fresh start.

Funerals were events, too. Just not happy ones.

"Darling." Dressed in head-to-toe pink Dior, Simone blew me a kiss as she settled in the chair across from my desk. She loved slumming it with regular folk like me and always made the driver of her Bentley park halfway down the block so she could enjoy the sidewalk experience. "How are the funeral plans coming along? Martha was such a dear friend. I want everything to be perfect."

"I've taken care of the floral arrangements for the service," I said. "I was thinking something low-key for the celebration of life since it is . . . uh . . . a somber event."

"Don't be such a bore, Simsim." Simone waved a vague dismissive hand in the air. "The service is the sad part. Afterward it's about good food, good friends, good gossip, and good clothes. That's what Martha would have wanted. She was always the life of the funeral after-parties. I want to send her out in style. How about some jugglers and magicians to circulate among the guests, and fireworks at the end? Martha loved fireworks."

"People might think it's in bad taste for a celebration of life," I suggested.

"Maybe your people; not mine."

I made a few notes on my phone. "Are you sure the family will be okay with a more 'festive' atmosphere?"

"They're thrilled she's gone," Simone said. "She had the family fortune tied up in a trust. We're talking eight figures. I'm pretty sure they won't even be at the party. They're too busy planning how to spend her money." She leaned closer. "If you ask me, her death wasn't an accident."

My eyes widened. "You think her family killed her?"

"Oh, they wouldn't have done it themselves," she said. "We hire people for that sort of thing."

"Of course," I said, as if I, too, wouldn't want to get my hands dirty when bumping off a relative for money.

"I think a photo booth might be fun," she mused. "Or how about that elephant you got for the Angelini wedding?"

"I know a police detective," I said, concerned about poor Martha's untimely demise. "If you think she was pushed, I could give him a call. He works in high-end theft, but I'm sure he knows people in homicide."

"Oh God. No." Simone gave a light laugh. "They wouldn't want strangers walking through the house and asking questions. It's a private matter."

"Murder is a private matter?"

"We call it an accident." She reached over and patted my hand. "It happens all the time. The more money you have, and the bigger the family, the higher the chance you might have an unexpected fatal accident. It's an occupational hazard."

"I think I'd choose poor and alive over rich and prematurely deceased."

Simone's light laughter echoed around the room. "You are so amusing, darling. That's why I love you so."

I heard the ding of the elevator and the thud of footsteps in the hallway. I wasn't expecting any other clients, and Chloe and Olivia weren't due to come by until late afternoon, but by the time it had even occurred to me to be concerned, it was too late. Two huge broad-shouldered men in dark suits and sunglasses walked through the door, and behind them was a man who dominated the office through the force of his presence alone.

He was wearing an expensive tailored suit that was unmistakably Italian, the fabric hugging his muscular frame. His jet-black hair was slicked back, revealing eyes so dark and intense they seemed to penetrate my very soul. Menace dripped from every pore of his body, and it took all my effort to stay calm and collected as he made his way across the office toward me.

For the briefest of moments, I entertained the possibility that he needed a wedding planned, maybe a bar mitzvah or funeral. But when one of his goons slammed the door and then stood against it, thick arms folded across his chest, blocking our only way out, I suspected the only funeral in my future might be my own.

I quickly pushed my phone off my desk and onto my lap. Thank

God for Face ID. As soon I saw the messaging screen, I scrolled to Garcia's name and typed, Help. Office. Now.

"Madam." The stranger lifted Simone's hand, his voice rough and gravelly. "I apologize for interrupting your meeting, but I have business that simply cannot wait. Tony Angelini at your service."

"Simone Du Post." Her cheeks flushed when he kissed her hand. "Simi and I were just about done." She moved to stand. "I'll leave you to your business."

"No. Stay." He gestured to one of his megaliths, who dropped a heavy hand on Simone's shoulder, holding her in place. "In a way, this also involves you since you introduced Simi to my brother at the charity ball. It's become a family concern, a matter of honor."

"Your brother?" Simone frowned. "I don't recall . . ."

"Joseph Angelini."

"Why, yes, I did." Simone gave a cautious smile. "And his daughter hired Simi's company to run her wedding. I heard it was a tremendous success."

"The wedding, yes." He nodded. "But unfortunately, something went missing during the festivities. Something very important to my family. Something my brother was holding for a friend."

Bile rose in my throat when he turned those dark eyes on me. In addition to his multimillion-dollar casino and real estate businesses, my visitor's brother, mob boss Joseph Angelini, also acted as a fence, brokering the sale of high-end stolen jewelry for both national and international buyers. Someone had retained his services to sell the Wild Heart necklace after it had been stolen from a museum, and Chloe had been framed for the theft. Jack and I had put together a heist crew to "retrieve" it from his safe under cover of the wedding I had planned for his daughter. I'd always known there was a risk he'd suspect my crew was behind the theft, but after a year had gone by, I figured we were in the clear.

"How unfortunate," Simone said, sparing me yet again the need to put together a coherent sentence. "I also lost something important to my husband's family at the charity ball, so I completely understand how you must feel."

"We've been searching for the culprit since the wedding," Mr. Angelini said, nodding. "Imagine how pleased we were to receive a tip that led us here. Apparently, several of Simi's employees were involved."

Simone gave an exasperated sigh. "Isn't that always the way? I was just telling poor Simi that you can't get good help these days. I spend most of my time dealing with staff issues. It is so aggravating."

"Indeed." Mr. Angelini lifted a bushy eyebrow. "I understand my item found its way into the hands of a man who has a close relationship with our Simi." He nodded at the goon standing at the door, who knocked one of Jack's plants off the credenza. The pot shattered on the tile floor with a loud crack and the room filled with the rich, earthy smell of soil, mingling with the scent of Simone's perfume and my rising fear.

Simone flinched, her hand flying to her chest. "Oh my."

"Where is he?" Mr. Angelini narrowed his gaze, and my mouth went dry.

"I don't know."

"Surely you know where your boyfriend is." He tipped his head to the side again and the goon knocked over two more plants, sending them plummeting to the ground with a resounding crash. The sound echoed through the office and Simone glanced at me, her eyes wide with horror. I could see the panic bubbling beneath the surface of her composed façade, a reflection of my own.

"He's not my boyfriend. I caught him kissing someone else. We broke up."

The goon yanked a picture off my wall and smashed it over his thick thigh. I looked down at my phone again to see if Garcia had received my message.

Mr. Angelini's second henchman pulled out a gun. "Hands where I can see them."

Simone and I raised our hands. The dude came around the desk, plucked the phone off my lap, and tossed it in the trash.

"Is this what people call a setup?" Simone asked me.

"I'd call it more of a shakedown."

"Consider it a friendly request," Mr. Angelini said, leaning back in his chair. "I want Jack Danger and I want the Wild Heart necklace—not the value in cash but the actual necklace. And, of course, the interest that we've had to pay our buyer while trying to locate our stolen goods, and interest on the interest for our inconvenience. That's an additional 28 percent on the increased value of the necklace, which is now worth $30 million. I'll leave you to work out the math. Capisce?"

"That's Italian for 'do you understand,'" Simone whispered. "My mother is Italian."

"Twenty-eight percent?" I stared at him, aghast. "That's what credit card companies charge."

"You're right," he said evenly. "Let's call it an even 30 percent. I wouldn't want anyone to mistake me for Visa or Mastercard."

Simone reached across the desk and touched my arm. "Sim-sim, darling. I think you should quit while you're ahead."

I fully agreed so I moved on to my biggest concern. "Why do you want Jack?" I didn't actually need him to tell me. Jack had not only helped us steal the Wild Heart from Mr. Angelini's brother, but also stolen Simone's necklace at the charity ball and planted it in Joseph Angelini's safe. When the police searched the house, they found Simone's necklace along with evidence linking Joseph

Angelini to multiple crimes, including the death of Jack's grand-mother. Now Joseph Angelini was in jail, and it was clear his Mafia family had come for revenge.

"I think that's obvious," he said.

"But then why do you need me? I don't have the necklace and I don't have Jack."

"You were involved." He lifted his chin again and his goon went back to playing *Smash Bros.* with my plants until the only one left was Garcia's Boston fern. "You and your friends: Jack, Gage, Anil, Rose, Chloe, Cristian, and Emma. I hold you all responsible." He pulled his phone from his pocket. "A new acquaintance gave me a list of their names. I know where they live, where they work, where their families live, where Chloe's child goes to school—"

"Leave her out of this." I shot out of my seat. "If you even go near Olivia—"

Mr. Angelini laughed. "What are you going to do? Call your police friend? I have information about you that I'm sure you wouldn't want him to know, information that would implicate not just you, but all your friends in all manner of crimes." He stood and adjusted his suit jacket just enough that I could see the weapon holstered underneath. "You and your crew, and of course darling Simone, have four weeks to return the necklace and pay the vig."

"'Vig' is slang for interest paid to loan sharks," Simone whispered. "I remember it from *The Sopranos.*"

"What if we can't get the necklace back?" I asked him.

"Then you'll have eight funerals to plan before your own. Your business will go out with a bang." He laughed at his own joke. His henchmen waited a beat and then laughed, too.

"Simone isn't part of this," I protested.

Mr. Angelini shrugged. "She should take care when she makes a referral. It puts her reputation on the line, and in her circles, rep-utation is everything." He smiled through the veiled threat and bent to kiss Simone's hand again as his henchman opened the door. "You truly are exquisite. It's been a pleasure."

I heard the ding of the elevator, the rapid thud of feet in the hall. Moments later, Garcia appeared in the doorway. He took one look around the room and his hand dropped to the weapon holstered at his side.

"I got your message." His eyes narrowed at my uninvited guest as he walked into the office. "Is everything okay?"

Mr. Angelini held up his phone to show me a picture of Olivia in front of her school. My heart pounded in my chest, and I had to take a deep, calming breath before I lied. "Yes, everything's good. I think there must have been a minor earthquake. My plants just fell to the ground."

"Our business is concluded, so I'll be on my way." Mr. Angelini placed a card on my desk with nothing but a phone number on it. "I look forward to seeing you on the big day."

"Simi?" Garcia moved back to the doorway, blocking their way. "Are you sure everything is okay?"

"Yes," I said with a confidence I didn't feel in the least. "Everything is great. I've got some new work to keep me busy."

Garcia reluctantly stepped to the side to allow Mr. Angelini and his henchman to depart. Simone stood and straightened her dress. "I'll get going, too. I must call Moira. She'll die when I tell her about my afternoon. Dead. What a fascinating man. And he said you had a thief on your staff. You really need to take care with your hiring. I just let one of my housekeepers go because I caught her eating a banana. It seems a small thing, but if you let one of the staff eat a banana, then they'll all eat bananas and at the end of the day there will be no bananas left for Richard or me."

"She's high society," I murmured to Garcia as she swept out the door.

"I figured it was that or Mars."

Garcia took a seat in front of my desk and stretched out his legs. "Do you want to tell me what Tony Angelini was doing in your office with his enforcers?"

"You know who he is?"

"Everyone knows who he is. He's the boss of the Eastern Seaboard branch of La Cosa Nostra, aka the Italian Mafia. His brother Joseph Angelini was an underboss. Tony directs a vast network of criminal activity that spans Chicago, Philadelphia, and parts of New Jersey. He sets the rules for all LCN families and collects profits from illegal activities that are siphoned upward through the LCN command structure and back to Italy." He folded his arms behind his head. "He doesn't usually go out in the open because he has so many enemies. It's quite something that of all the times he would choose to take that risk, it was to come here to see you."

"He needs an event planned." I wasn't lying. Not exactly. He did need an event planned: the retrieval of a $30 million necklace currently on display at one of the most secure museums in Delhi, where Jack had repatriated it after our last heist.

"Why don't you tell me what's really going on?" His voice softened. "It was bad enough when you got mixed up with his brother, but this guy, Simi; you don't want to mess with him."

"I can't tell you," I blurted out. "Client confidentiality."

His forehead wrinkled. "Is it Jack? Has he got you involved in something bad again? He's trouble. I told you that before."

"It's not Jack's fault."

"Whatever is going on . . ." His blue eyes darkened. "Tell me you won't have to deal with it alone."

"It's okay," I said. "I have my crew."

FIVE

◇ ◇ ◇

Disappointment washed over me as I stood in the garage where we had planned our last heist, staring at the sea of empty chairs. My former landlady, Rose, an octogenarian with a colorful past as a Broadway performer, had offered the garage behind her Evanston home as a base of operations in exchange for being the "grease woman" in our crew. I could still smell the faint scent of chocolate from the pastries her ex-lover Chef Pierre had fed us during our heist-planning sessions, and the barest hint of her floral perfume.

"Where is everyone?" I asked Chloe. After sending out an urgent message on the secure server we'd used for the last heist, I'd expected the crew to show up on time, even if it was a Friday, excited to get together and catch up for the first time since we'd parted ways. It hadn't occurred to me that they wouldn't show up at all.

"Maybe they didn't get the message." Chloe straightened the whiteboard I'd used to plan our last heist. "We haven't used that server in over a year, and everyone has been busy spending their reward money to make their dreams come true."

"They must think it's a joke. I shouldn't have used the word *whacked*." I grabbed my bag and gestured to the door. "We'll have to go and hunt them down. We're all in this together."

"It is pretty crazy," she admitted as I locked the door. "Gage was stomping around this morning cursing and swearing. He wanted to call some guys he knew from his time in service to help him take Angelini out."

"And where is your secret black ops ex-military boyfriend?" I lifted an eyebrow. "Why isn't he here?"

"He's picking Olivia up from soccer practice." She shrugged. "He's not in town often, and when he does show up, he insists on driving her everywhere. She's got him wrapped around her little finger." She tipped her head to the side. "What about Jack?"

"I haven't heard from him since I kicked him out of my place. He said he was going to bring proof that Clare had set him up, but now I'm wondering if he heard that Tony Angelini is looking for him and he decided to skip town."

"I still don't understand," Chloe said as we made our way down the tree-lined street. "How did Angelini find out we took the necklace? Or that Jack was the one who framed his brother?"

"He said someone gave him a list of our names. We were ratted out."

"Jack?"

"I don't think so. He has the most to lose. I actually can't imagine *anyone* from our crew putting us in danger."

Chloe raised an eyebrow. "Does that mean you believe him about Clare?"

"I don't want to believe him," I said as we headed toward the L train station. "It's easier to tell myself that what I saw justifies my decision to break up with him in the first place. But when I saw Clare's face . . . that smirk . . . I think she knew I'd be there, so it isn't a big leap to accept that Jack was telling the truth."

I'd been tossing and turning all night trying to figure it out. Jack wasn't an unkind person. I'd never seen him be purposely cruel.

Even when he'd disappeared from my life except for a few random messages and the odd sexy-times video call, I'd never gotten the impression he was purposely trying to hurt me.

"Maybe it was revenge for dumping him."

"Then why did he show up on my balcony? He was desperate for me to believe him." My hand tightened around the strap of my bag. I was tired of thinking about it, tired of trying to understand a man I thought I knew.

"Are you trying to convince me or yourself?" Chloe asked.

I was saved from answering that difficult question when my phone finally pinged with a message. Anil, our gadget guy, couldn't make it because he was at the gym training to be an MMA star, but he did have Emma's address . . .

For someone who had just received an $833,333 windfall, Emma was living it rough. We found her crashed out on the couch in a run-down apartment, an empty bottle of tequila in one hand and a lime in the other. Her dark hair had grown to shoulder-length and had been haphazardly chopped and dyed with vivid green streaks. She was lean and gaunt without her curves, but she'd added new designs to her sleeves of ink, a septum piercing, and two new piercings in each ear.

"Emma." I shook her awake while Chloe went to fill a glass of water. "You were supposed to be at Rose's garage for a meeting."

Emma opened one eye and closed it again. "How did you get in here?"

"The door was open."

"Damn lock is still busted from the police raid last week," she muttered. "I told my roomies not to bring their clients into the house."

"This isn't a house. It's a disaster."

"I've lived in worse. Cars, toilet stalls, caves, even a coffin—"

"We don't have time for this." I pulled the bottle from her hand and replaced it with a water glass. "What are you doing here? I thought you were going to use your reward money to train for Formula One."

"I thought so, too," she said. "I did karting as a kid, so it wasn't hard to switch to single-seater vehicles, which is where you make your name and get in the running for the twenty Formula One seats that come up each year. Except I'm thirty-five and competing against kids who are eighteen and at their physical peak. Not only that, but you're also looking at paying $400,000 for Formula BMW races and up to $1,000,000 for GP2 races, plus you gotta have money for mechanical problems and the basics of living. Guess how fast I blew through that reward money? Too fucking fast."

"What about your dad?" Chloe asked. "I thought he was a Formula One driver. Couldn't he help you out?"

"The old man is retired now and living his best life in the Bahamas. He said if I didn't do it on my own, it wasn't worth doing. Same thing I heard from him all my life—school, sports, birthdays . . . He wouldn't even come to the daddy-daughter dances."

"So how are you paying for"—I looked around the utter dive of an apartment—"this?"

"Back to driving an Uber," she said. "Fourteen-hour days."

"What happened to Anil? I thought you two were living together."

"He moved back in with his parents when I moved out." She sighed. "I miss the guy. He was like a little brother, and I got to introduce him to the best parts of life—first time getting stoned, first time getting so drunk he couldn't stand up, first time with a hooker . . ." She trailed off when Chloe gasped.

"Just kidding." She chuckled. "I wouldn't corrupt him that way. Anil is one of the good guys and I wanted him to stay that way. But I did introduce him to a friend of mine who owns an MMA gym. He needed some proper training to make his dream of fighting for UFC come true."

"Let's get you cleaned up and go and find him," I said. "We're going to need him if we have any hope of getting out of this alive."

Anil was lying flat on the mat in the middle of a makeshift octagon when Chloe and I walked into the gym where he did his MMA training. Emma was still in her car trying to get rid of her hangover by playing *Death Magnetic* at full volume. Anil looked more twenty-one than twenty-six years old. His thick black hair had been shaved down to a number two, making his bushy eyebrows the most dominant feature on his lean, narrow face.

"Anil? Are you dead?"

"I wish." He turned his head and groaned when the medic climbed into the ring. "Put me out of my misery. Please."

"Fourth time this week." The medic checked Anil's blackened eyes and put a finger on his pulse. "You need to build up some muscle before you step into the ring. You're too skinny—all arms and legs. Think protein, weight lifting, high-intensity power moves. You're trying to skip steps and that's just not going to work if you want to go pro."

"I can't eat any more," Anil said. "Ever since I moved back home, my mom has been cooking for six. I'm stuffed with samosas."

"You need protein," the medic said. "Not carbs."

"Why did you move back home?" I asked, kneeling beside him. "Why didn't you get a place of your own when Emma left?"

"My parents were desperate to have me back so they could find me a wife after you so brutally rejected their attempt to arrange our marriage." His voice caught, and he drew in a shuddering breath. Anil loved his drama.

"Brutally?" I stared at him, aghast. "I just said we weren't compatible. Our four-year age difference was just too much."

"You broke my heart." He stared up at the ceiling, his dark eyes watering. "I still haven't recovered. How could you pick Jack over me?"

Given that he was still apparently under the mistaken impression I was marriage material, I decided not to mention that Jack and I were no longer together. "I'm sure you'll find your perfect someone. You've got a great job . . ." It occurred to me in that moment that we might need a decoy and Anil, who had made a replica of the Wild Heart necklace for our last heist, was best placed to get one. "Are you still working as an engineer at that 3D jewelry-printing company?"

"Yes, and I got a promotion," he said. "My entire life is going to be a slow, tortuous climb up the middle-managerial ladder until I finally reach the top, and after six months they'll give me a fake gold watch and thank me for my forty years of service. That's what they did to the last middle manager who retired." He covered his face with his hands. "I can't believe this is my life. The reward money was supposed to make everything better, but I'm still living in my parents' basement being pressured to get married, working at the same company, and losing fight after fight in the ring. I can't take the stress."

"I get it," I said. "My parents arranged a meet with a potential husband two days after I broke up with Jack." Damn. I'd let it slip.

"You're not with Jack?" He rolled to his side, resting his head in his hand. "Will you marry me? My parents will forgive you for rejecting me if you give them grandchildren. I paid off their mortgage, so we can live with them as long as we want. We can have the whole basement to ourselves. There's lots of room unless we want to have more than three kids. I'm still a virgin. You could teach me things, mold me to your desires."

Chloe stared at me open-mouthed. Anil had changed in the last year, and not, I had to say, in a good way. What had happened to his joie de vivre? His enthusiastic innocence?

"Thank you for the kind offer, but I'll have to pass."

The medic helped Anil to a bench outside the ring. He was definitely more ripped than I'd ever seen him, but his arms and legs were a mass of bruises and his handsome face bore a few lines and wrinkles I hadn't seen before.

"I can't believe you were planning to blow us off," I said. "The message I sent you wasn't a joke. Tony Angelini threatened us."

"I'm sorry." Anil shook his head. "I wanted to be physically ready in case anyone gets kidnapped again. My performance at the end of the last heist was substandard. This time, I want to beat people up for real instead of just running around in a costume scaring them."

"We need you for your Mensa and gadget skills more than your MMA skills," Chloe said. "Don't tell me you've given up on your pursuit of higher thinking."

"Actually, I just went to a Mensa meeting last week." Anil sighed. "It was debate night, but we spent most of the time debating what we should debate: Gif or gif? Code wars? Who Goku could beat . . . ? Kirk versus Picard? Which comic book character would smell the worst? The theory of time travel? Can a lightsaber cut through adamantium?"

"Do I want to know what you decided on?" Chloe asked.

I shook my head in warning, but there was no stopping Anil once his geek mode had been triggered.

"Balrogs. Did they have wings or not?"

"Maybe we don't need him," she whispered, clearly uninterested in the wingedness of Balrogs. "I think he's off his game, and to be honest, he seems a bit depressed. Let's just go and get Cristian."

"No way. He's our gadget guy. We just need to get him back to Rose's garage and give him something to fix."

Cristian met us outside the TV studio where he was filming his animal show for kids. He was wearing some kind of safari uniform, a far cry from the flashy shirts and designer clothes he'd worn when he worked in my dad's tailor shop by day and ran his "life coaching" escort service by night. His escort side hustle saved us from being caught during the heist when Joseph Angelini's wife turned out to be one of his clients, and Cristian became our "inside man" in every sense of the word.

"What's this all about?" Cristian asked, kissing me on both cheeks. He was half Portuguese, half Brazilian, and all F-boi, with a degree in zoology and a passion for saving the environment. He'd used his reward money to rent a house with a yard big enough for two rescue dogs and to start production on his dream television show.

"Didn't you read my message?"

"Yes, but . . ." He made a vague gesture with his hand toward the studio set. "It sounds like something straight out of a bad movie, and I would know. Apparently, *Cristian's Animal Kingdom* was the worst pilot the studios have ever seen. We're wrapping the second episode tomorrow and then we're shutting it all down. I've got no money left, so I'm going back to my escort and life-coaching business to make ends meet. I even had to rehome my rescue dogs so I could move into a more compact space. They're much happier out in the country."

"I'm sorry it didn't work out."

Cristian sighed. "I thought that money would change my life forever."

"We all thought that. Maybe we dreamed too big."

After a few last-minute words with his director, Cristian joined us in the car, squeezing into the back of Emma's Chevy Bolt EV with Chloe and Anil. He and Emma had often clashed over his views about saving the environment and Emma's determination to fill it with ozone-destroying pollutants from the vehicles she loved to drive.

"I am honestly shocked that you've gone electric," he said after they'd exchanged greetings.

Emma sniffed. "It wasn't by choice."

Cristian leaned back in his seat. "Any of you ladies currently single?"

"Chloe's still with Gage," I said. "Should I call and tell him you just asked her out? He might leave you with one or two working fingers."

"Chloe is out," he said. "How about you? Are you still with Jack?"

"No, but I'm taking a break."

"I'm taking a break, too," Emma said when his gaze slid to her. "I just broke up with a dude who lost a certain body part while operating some heavy machinery. I went to see him in the hospital to tell him it was over for reasons of abject stupidity. I mean, what was it doing out there in the first place? There's a time and a place, is all I'm saying."

"Was there anything left?" Anil asked, his face a mask of horror.

"Yeah, but I wasn't into the whole frankenwiener thing. Size does matter. I learned that from Rose." She looked over at me as she started the car. "What does Rose have to say about this whole thing?"

"I haven't had a chance to share everything with her," I said. "She took an acrobatics-for-seniors class after our heist and landed a job on a cruise ship as the evening entertainment. She's somewhere in the Caribbean with terrible cell service, and all I got in response to my message was permission to use the garage and a promise that she'd call when she got into the next port."

Emma's engine gave a quiet hum as she pulled out of the parking lot. "I hope you're planning another heist with some serious cash," she said. "I need to get rid of this environment-saving piece of tin and get a Hummer."

"No one *needs* a Hummer," Cristian spat out. "Do you know how bad they are for the environment?"

"Yes, I do."

"And . . . ?"

Emma looked at him through the rearview mirror. "You'll get the very first ride."

SIX

◇ ◇ ◇

Jack and Gage were waiting at Rose's garage when we arrived. They'd brought a stack of pizzas, a few bottles of pop, and an organic kale salad and kombucha tea for Cristian.

After everyone had caught up, I told them about Angelini's visit. Jack glared at me while I was talking, his lips pressed tight together, hands shoved in his pockets in his trademark pissed-off pose. I knew he was annoyed that I hadn't called him the minute Angelini left my office, but my trust in him was broken and I couldn't take the risk that he might disappear before everyone had a chance to weigh in about what we should do.

Gage was out of his chair and slamming his fist into random objects in the garage as soon as I was done. He was lean and muscled, with the most sculpted jawline I'd ever seen, tawny brown hair, and sharp blue eyes that only softened when Chloe was around. Gage wasn't a big talker, but both Olivia and Chloe adored him, and there wasn't anything he wouldn't do for his girls. Any threat to them sent him into a protective frenzy.

"I still can't believe this is real," Cristian said, stretched out on one of Rose's folding chairs. "It almost seems too crazy to believe."

"As crazy as stealing a necklace from the safe of a mob boss while organizing his daughter's wedding and then helping her escape a forced marriage to a rival mob boss's son?" I gestured to the whiteboard, which still held the remnants of the plan for our last heist.

"Where is the necklace now?" Cristian asked. "Does anyone know?"

"It's in India," I said. "Jack stole it after we returned it to the museum and—"

"Reacquired," he corrected.

"Whatever." I shot him a glare. He knew there was nothing I liked less than being interrupted when I was meeting with the crew. "He then repatriated it to India, and it is now in a museum in Delhi."

"The simple solution seems to be to go to Delhi and steal it back," Anil said. "Does everyone have a valid passport?"

Jack shook his head. "It's not simple at all. Pulling off a heist in your hometown is one thing. Traveling to a foreign country to pull off a heist when you have no resources, no contacts, no equipment, and no information is something else entirely."

"Maybe we should consider alternatives before we book plane tickets to India so we can break into a highly secure museum, steal a cultural artifact worth $30 million, illegally smuggle it out of the country and into the US, and give it to a leader of organized crime," Chloe suggested. "Just thinking out loud here."

"Garcia confirmed Angelini was who he said he was," I said. "I managed to text him for help, and he showed up while Angelini was still there. From what he said, the mob doesn't consider alternative options."

"You texted Garcia for help?" Jack gritted out. "Garcia? Not me?"

"He has a gun."

"So do I."

"He's steady and reliable," I said. "He doesn't disappear for eight months. He doesn't go on business trips that require burner phones and secret codes. He doesn't refuse to tell me what he does for a living. I texted HELP and I knew he'd come. I wasn't sure about you."

"You don't think I would have come if you'd texted me for help?" Indignation laced Jack's tone.

"For all I knew, you were being tossed out a window in Rio, tortured by the Italian Mafia in Tuscany, or you were in the North Sea trapped in a Russian submarine."

"The Italian Mafia are based in Sicily," he corrected me. "Tuscany doesn't have the port access they need for the drug trade."

I folded my arms and sighed. "You missed the point entirely."

"Listen, as much as I want to hang with you guys and rehash old times and listen to your relationship woes, I'm out," Cristian said. "If you recall, I wasn't involved in the heist. As soon as we found out that Angelini had Mafia connections and I realized I'd slept with his wife, I walked away."

"And then you showed up at the wedding and helped us out by sleeping with her again," Emma pointed out. "You are still part of this."

"Not the part that seems to have pissed off the boss of the biggest Mafia family in town." Cristian grabbed his satchel and threw it over his shoulder. "You really should use those recycle bins I left here during the last heist. We can't do too much for the environment."

"You can't be out," I said. "I told you. He's got your name—"

"Tell him my name shouldn't be on the list because I wasn't part of it," he said. "He's got nothing on me."

"Except the part where you slept with his brother's wife during his niece's wedding," Emma pointed out.

"If he knew about it, I'd already be dead." Cristian pushed open the door. "Sorry, guys. I've got high anxiety and a low danger tolerance, and I'm dealing with too much in my life right now. I lost my house, my dogs, my show, and all the reward money. I just can't with the whole mob-boss thing. I need to look after myself."

We stared in stunned silence as the door slammed behind him.

"I can't believe he just walked out on us," I said.

"Cristian has always been about Cristian." Jack checked the window before pulling the blind. "He did us a favor. When you're dealing with the mob, you don't want people on your crew who aren't fully committed."

"What would Angelini really do if we don't hand over the necklace?" Anil asked. "I have a hard time believing he would kill us all. That's a lot of dead bodies to get rid of, and in the end, he wouldn't get what he wanted."

"Do you know nothing about the mob?" Emma asked. "Haven't you seen *Reservoir Dogs*? *Casino*? How about *Casino Royale*? Killing is too easy. It's the torture they enjoy. Who knows what would have happened in Simi's office if Garcia hadn't shown up?"

"I'll tell you what would have happened if you'd called me," Jack said, sulking. "I would have dealt with the problem there and then. But you didn't trust me."

It wasn't just a matter of trust. Jack would be dead if I'd called him. Angelini wanted his head, and in hindsight calling Garcia had been the right decision. "I didn't text you because I thought you'd probably run in the other direction," I snapped. "Or maybe back to Bloomingdale's for another smooch session with Clare."

"Uh-oh. Trouble in paradise." Emma held out her hand, and Gage and Anil each handed her a twenty-dollar bill.

"You took bets on us?" I stared at them, aghast.

"You gotta admit that you two were always an unlikely couple," Emma said, pocketing the cash. "Bad-boy rogue thief with dubious underworld affiliations and no fixed address. Hardworking cookie-cutter good girl who worked in a candy store, spent her Friday nights watching crime shows with her octogenarian landlady, showed up every Sunday for dinner with the fam, and never refused a meet and greet with a prospective husband because she didn't want to let her parents down."

"I organized a heist," I protested. "I was arrested for trying to break into a museum. I robbed a mob boss. I got so drunk I passed out on the floor. I did bad things."

"In a good-girl way. No selfishness involved."

"What about another heist?" Anil suggested. "We could steal something valuable and then offer to buy the necklace from the museum in Delhi. What rate of interest is Angelini charging us?"

"He said the necklace is now valued at $30 million. He was going to charge 28 percent—"

"So, we owe him $8.4 million," Anil said, cutting me off. "Unless it's compound interest—"

"Actually, it was 28 percent and then I made him angry by comparing him to a credit card company so now it's 30 percent."

"We owe an even $9 million," Anil said. "If he didn't say compound interest, then I think it's safe to assume it's simple."

"I hate it when you do math stuff like that," Emma said. "It makes me feel like I could be doing so much more with my brain."

"That's a crazy amount of money." Chloe shook her head in disbelief. "He can't be serious. We're just ordinary people. Where would we come up with that kind of cash?"

"We barely made it through the last heist," I added. "We can't do another one. Even if we did steal something else, we'd have to sell it on the black market, and then convince the museum to sell us the necklace. Too many things could go wrong."

"I could make another replica," Anil offered. "It worked last time."

"He won't fall for that," Jack said. "He'll have a jeweler with him to check it out. I think our best bet is to leave the country and lay low for a bit while we figure this all out."

"But Olivia is in school," Chloe protested. "I can't just pull her out and go on the run. What kind of life is that for a child?"

"One where her mom hasn't been killed by a crazy Mafia boss." Emma shrugged when Chloe glared at her. "Just keeping it real."

I held up my hand to quiet all the protests. "We can't panic," I said. "We need facts. Would he really whack all of us if we don't give it back, or was that just his idea of a motivational speech? I'll see what I can find out about him. In the meantime, we need to look into retrieving the necklace because that is the simplest solution, leaving the matter of the interest aside."

"Gage and I will do a little digging into the museum in India and see what we can find out on the dark web about their security system." Chloe shared a look with Gage. "Maybe it won't be that hard to steal . . ."

"We still need to be prepared to leave the country in case it all goes sideways," Jack said. "I know a guy in West Englewood who can get us fake passports. We'd be too easy to trace if we use our real ones. I'll need Simi to come with me as a cover for the meet. We can drive out there tomorrow."

"I can't be in a car with you all the way to West Englewood," I said, keeping my voice low. "What if I get the urge to throw something at you when we're on the road?"

"Why doesn't Emma drive?" Chloe suggested. "She's good at staying neutral."

"Why can't you come?"

"Because I would take your side," she said. "Then both of us would be throwing things at him and nothing would get done."

"You're such a good best friend." I smiled for the first time since Angelini had walked into my office, pleased that my bestie would take my side no matter what.

"Until the end."

I just hoped "the end" wasn't four weeks away.

SEVEN

◇ ◇ ◇

We're a couple," Jack said the next evening in the car while we were en route with Emma to West Englewood. "We've been together for years."

"You want me to pretend we're together when I still feel like slapping you across the face?"

"You're good at deception," Jack said. "You fooled Joseph Angelini into thinking you were a wedding planner."

"I grew into the role. If you recall, I did such a good job he gave me a five-star review."

"Now you get a chance to grow into the role of my girlfriend," he said with a warm smile. "If you do a good job, I'll give you a five-star review, too."

Half an hour later, Jack and I were seated at the bar of the Sawmill Pub watching a bachelorette dirty dancing with a complete stranger, both of them unfazed by the guy next to them who was trying to simultaneously pee in a garbage can and order a round of shots as a sweaty group of soccer players flung chicken wings at one another to the heavy beat of Guns N' Roses' "Welcome to the Jungle."

"What do you think?" Jack asked, looking around. "It's great, isn't it?"

"This is the kind of place you visit once in undergrad and wake up with a mouthful of cigarette butts and bile." I had managed to score a shot of whiskey for Jack and a gin and tonic for me after a twenty-minute wait at the bar. I didn't love hard liquor, but when I'd asked for a Long Island, the bartender told me he'd run out of "girly drinks" in the nineties.

"He's here," Jack said, looking over his shoulder.

"What do you want me to do?"

"Act like you're madly in love with me." He ran his hand down my arm, sending a wave of goose bumps sheeting across my skin. We may have broken up, but our chemistry was still insane.

"How? Do you want me to gaze into your eyes?"

"He needs to think we're serious and I have something to lose." Jack moved his stool and ran one hand over my thigh, pushing my little black dress indecently high. "You've already made it easy for me in this dress."

Okay. Maybe I had dressed for revenge seduction and not success, and maybe the neckline of my dress plunged a little low, but dammit, he'd kissed Clare and I wanted him to remember what he was missing.

"Jack . . ." I grabbed his wrist. "I'm not going to let you . . ."

"Let me what?" he murmured, his lips barely brushing against the shell of my ear. He smelled of whiskey and leather, and his breath was hot against my skin. "Touch you? You're my girlfriend tonight. I need to touch you, Simi. Let me touch you . . ."

"Fine." My breath hitched in my throat as his hand moved higher, his fingers brushing the edge of my panties. "But you . . . don't . . . need . . . to . . . touch . . . there."

"You like to be touched there," he shot back, his voice low and husky. "If I moved my finger just an inch, you'd be dragging me into the restroom to have your way with me."

Swallowing hard, I pushed his hand away. "Is someone really watching us, or is this just a wish list?"

"He's watching. Tip your head to the side for me."

I did as he asked and he kissed my neck, his soft lips burning a trail over my heated skin.

"I miss the taste of you," he whispered. "I miss the softness of your skin. I miss the way you feel in my arms. I miss waking up beside you."

Electricity crackled in the air between us. I knew I shouldn't let him go too far, but it felt so right, like I'd found the missing piece of me. And besides, the crew needed fake passports. I wasn't giving in. I was taking one for the team. "Your fake girlfriend also likes to be kissed on the lips," I murmured.

Jack slid an arm around my waist and pulled me out of the chair and between his spread legs. Heat rushed through me like a lava flow, his touch, his deep voice, the feel of his hands on me, lighting me up inside. I inhaled his scent of leather mixed with a hint of musky cologne, a potent mix, and so familiar it made me ache inside. I groaned softly at our connection and pressed my hands against his chest.

"Jack—" I didn't get a chance to finish what I was going to say because Jack cupped the back of my neck and kissed me. His lips were soft and sweet, and his heart thudded strong and steady beneath my palms. I slid my hands over his shoulders, drawing him closer. He deepened the kiss and I lost myself in the sheer heat of him, the chemistry that had sparked the first night we met returning in a tidal wave of desire.

"This had better be part of the plan to get information from your contact," I warned him, "because if it turns out to be a gratuitous make-out session, you're going to be in bigger trouble than you are with the boss of mob bosses."

"It's everything," he said softly and lowered his mouth to mine. This time his kiss was pure seduction. My lips parted on a groan, and he slipped his tongue inside, sending a shiver of arousal down my spine. His body was against mine, hard and lean. With no more thoughts of resisting, I curved my arms around his shoulders and closed my eyes, drowning in sensation.

"Look at me when I kiss you," Jack said quietly as he wound his hand through my hair and then tugged my head back to ravage my mouth. I could feel his heart pounding in his chest, and when I opened my eyes, I saw his desire smolder into a passion that matched my own.

It had been too long, and we were so damn good together. "Jack, I missed—"

"You've got some nerve showing up here after all these years," a woman's voice interrupted, sharp and biting.

I startled, and suddenly Jack was gone, leaving me bereft. I blinked to clear my vision and took in the tall redhead beside us. Dressed in all black, she wore a strappy camisole, skintight jeans, and four-inch heels covered in silver studs.

"And picking up some skank in my bar?" She looked me up and down before giving a sniff of disdain.

"Jesus, Eva," Jack bit out. "Not now."

Stunned, I managed to blurt out, "I'm not a—"

"Shut it." She shot me an angry look. "This is between me and the bastard who walked out on me. No breakup conversation. No good-bye. No nothing. One day he's there, making promises, and then he's gone." Without any warning, Eva slapped Jack across the face. His head turned slightly in the direction of the blow, but he didn't move.

"I've waited a long time for that." She gestured to someone behind me. "Get him out of here. And the skank, too. They're not welcome."

Two bouncers in tight black polo shirts, their biceps bulging beneath ribbed sleeves, grabbed Jack by the shoulders and shoved him toward the door. A third bouncer gestured for me to follow and I grabbed my stuff and hurried after them.

By the time I was able to push my way through the crowd that had gathered outside, one of the bouncers had Jack pinned up against the brick wall. For a moment, I thought it almost seemed like their conversation was more friendly than heated, but then he drove his fist into Jack's stomach. Jack doubled over from the blow, but before he could straighten up, the second bouncer joined the fray, and for the next few minutes the air was charged with the sounds of knuckles connecting with bone, flesh thudding into flesh.

I had just messaged Emma for a getaway pickup when I realized Jack was up again and not just holding his own but doing some serious damage. The first bouncer hit the ground, clutching his stomach, while the second struggled to keep his footing after Jack's fist connected with his jaw.

I had never seen Jack fight, and I couldn't help but be impressed with his skills. He moved with a grace that belied his muscular build, every punch landing with precision and power. He was like a completely different person, his movements fluid and calculated, delivered with a raw, animalistic energy that stirred up feelings I didn't want to admit. I couldn't take my eyes off him, the way he moved, the way he breathed, the way his muscles flexed . . .

"Jack, stop playing with your food," Emma shouted through the window of her sparkly blue Bolt, pulling me out of my haze of lust. "We have to go."

Jack dropped both bouncers to the ground in a flurry of punches, and a few minutes later we were in the back seat and purring away.

"Are we moving?" Jack swiveled around to watch the bouncers.

"It's only got two hundred horsepower," Emma said. "And I

forgot to charge it this morning. We're doing our best. The sarcasm is not appreciated."

"Maybe I should get out and push."

"Another outing. Another ex." I handed him a wad of tissues. "How many of them are out there? Is it even worth trying again to contact your illegal-passport-making friend if your old girlfriends are going to be crawling out of the woodwork to slap and kiss and who knows what with you?"

"It had to be done," Jack said. "I had to let my contact know that I'd finally settled down with a serious girl and I wasn't interested in anything or anyone else."

"It was a setup?" My heart skipped a beat. "She isn't an ex?"

"She is an ex," he said. "The slap was real. I was a different person before I met you."

"You didn't get to talk to your contact," I pointed out. "The whole thing was a bust."

"I did talk to him," Jack said. "He was the big guy who hauled me out of the bar, and he didn't have good news. He can get the fake passports, but he said if that's what we plan to do, we need to leave right away in case Angelini gets wind of our plan. Apparently, he has connections everywhere."

"I can't leave my family," I protested. "My parents are here, my brother and his wife, nieces, aunts, uncles, cousins, second cousins, third cousins . . . We have to find the necklace. I'm not running away unless there is no other option."

My phone buzzed with a message from Chloe. The bad news just kept rolling in.

"Chloe just found out that the necklace isn't at the museum in India." I leaned my head against the window with a heavy sigh. "Someone stole it last week."

"I say we just keep driving," Emma said. "My vote is for Canada, but I'm also open to Mexico if you prefer sand to snow. I'm easy. At least that's what the guys used to say."

"That's not fair to everyone else," I said. "Angelini has all our names on his list. We'll be leaving them to take the fall."

"We are in a kill-or-be-killed situation," Emma said. "I, for one, don't want to wind up on the wrong side."

"There is only one side and we're all on it together. We have four weeks less a few days. More than enough time to figure something out. I've got a celebration of life to run tomorrow, but we can meet up on Monday evening and make a plan."

I tried to sound upbeat, but we had no leads on the necklace and no way of getting the cash to cover the exorbitant rate of interest. And even if we did somehow pull it all off, what about Jack? There was no way I could hand him over to the mob. "Together" didn't mean that one of us would wind up dead.

EIGHT

◇ ◇ ◇

I t was a beautiful service," Simone said, sipping her champagne in the vast back garden of Martha's family's Lake Forest mansion. "And this celebration of life is so much fun. You've really outdone yourself."

"It was a first for us," Chloe said brightly. "We've never done a circus-themed celebration of life."

Chloe helped me with weekend events and we'd been up since five A.M. making sure everything was perfect, from the red-and-white-striped marquee to the authentic center ring complete with clowns, jugglers, fire-eaters, and trained poodles. I'd been worried that the festive party would be too much of a shock after the funeral, but event companies had to be flexible, even if the client's demands were a little extreme, and even if the event planner had other things on her mind. The charade with Jack had brought back a myriad of feelings I didn't want to admit, from the pain of his absence to the warmth of his kiss, and the terrible choice that loomed on the horizon.

"The magician was a great idea," she continued. "He pulled a coin out of my ear, and he guessed the card I had in my hand."

Her words pulled me away from bad thoughts and into the moment. "I didn't hire a magician."

Simone frowned. "Maybe he's a guest."

"I'll go and find him and check the situation out," Chloe said. "We wouldn't want people's wallets and jewelry to disappear."

"When do I get to meet your friends to talk about the missing necklace?" Simone asked after Chloe had gone. "It's so exciting. My friend Moira thinks I should dress in black and wear a mask, so I'm not recognized if we have to engage in any nefarious deeds. I've got a pair of Prada nappa leather gloves that fit over my nails and will ensure I don't leave fingerprints behind. They're as soft as butter."

"As of right now, the necklace isn't where we thought it was," I told her. "Someone stole it before we could get to it. We're meeting tomorrow to try and figure out what to do." I wanted to keep Simone's involvement to a minimum. It was totally unfair that Angelini would include her when all she'd done was make an innocent introduction to help a new friend.

"I just love a good mystery," Simone said. "There was an unfortunate incident on our street when I was young, and a homicide detective came out to investigate. I was fascinated by his work, and he was kind enough to let me follow him around and answer my questions. For the longest time afterward, I wanted to become a detective, but my father was appalled. No one in our family has ever worked. It just isn't done."

"That's very cool, Simone. You never mentioned an interest in criminal investigation before."

"It was a long time ago," she said. "My father made me study art history in college. He thought it would be more useful in our social circle. He introduced me to Richard the day after I graduated. I was surprised my father even knew him and even more surprised he was considering him as a son-in-law. Richard isn't one of us. He's a self-made tech billionaire. Very new money. We went out for dinner twice, and then he proposed."

"That was fast. Was it love at first sight?" I'd definitely felt a spark the first time I met Jack, even though he was holding me hostage in the bushes.

She gave a resigned sigh and shrugged. "It wasn't about love. My grandfather and my father lost most of the family fortune in bad investments and they needed Richard's money. They pushed me into the marriage as a way of saving the estate and the family name. Richard needed someone to guide him through high society and manage all the charity work and social events that go with having wealth. Our marriage made sense. Don't get me wrong. I enjoy helping people, but this world I live in can be stifling at times. Sometimes I just want to do something reckless, something that makes me feel alive."

I understood that feeling. I hadn't felt truly alive until Jack had walked into my life and turned it upside down. "Our current situation should make you feel alive, at least until we're dead," I said dryly.

Simone laughed. "So funny, darling. Only bad guys wind up dead, and that's not us."

After Simone had left to find her friend, I wandered around the reception making sure that the waiters were keeping glasses filled, the trays of food were full and fresh, and the circus performers were entertaining the guests. In the end, I didn't have to hunt down the magician. He found me just as I caught up with Chloe near the photo booth.

"Ladies." He removed his top hat and gave a deep bow. "Magic Mike at your service."

Tall and muscular with cold, hard eyes and a grim smile, the magician wore a black suit and mottled green tie. His neck was fully inked with skulls and roses on one side and fanged snakes and thorn-covered ladders on the other. His white collared shirt was open to display three heavy gold chains that glinted in the sunlight along with the five gold hoops that pierced his left earlobe. Menace dripped from his every pore.

"I was just looking for you," Chloe said. "Are you with the entertainment company? Or are you a guest?"

"Neither." The magician reached out and pulled a coin from behind my ear. He placed it in my hand. "We have a mutual friend who is concerned that Simi wasn't paying attention when he paid her a visit."

I felt the blood drain from my face, and I looked around to make sure no one could overhear us. Why had Angelini sent one of his men here? Did he have a gun? Were the guests at risk? Was he going to shoot me in cold blood? My insurance policy didn't cover massacre by magician.

"I was paying attention," I said. "I got the message."

"If you got the message, you wouldn't be running around trying to buy fake passports in West Englewood."

Oh God. We were followed. Bile rose in my throat as he pulled a second coin from my ear and added it to the first in my palm.

"He has to understand that from my point of view, the whole thing seems a bit crazy," I persisted. "I'm just an ordinary woman. I run an event-planning business. I don't get involved in this kind of stuff."

"Apparently you do." He pulled a third coin from behind my ear and dropped it in my palm. His voice dropped to a low growl. "He gave you four weeks. If I were you, I'd stop wasting time trying to run from your problems and get busy trying to solve them."

"It's gone," Chloe blurted out. "The necklace was in a museum in India, and someone stole it. We have no idea where it is."

"Our mutual acquaintance thought you'd come up with more

excuses, so he's provided another incentive." The magician held up his phone and showed me a picture that made my stomach heave. Cristian—I only knew it was him because he had on the same green *Save the Whales* T-shirt he'd worn on Friday when he walked out on us—was chained to a chair in a dimly lit room. His face was badly swollen and covered in blood. He had two black eyes and a bloody lip, and his shirt was torn, revealing deep gashes on his chest.

My breath left me in a rush. Chloe gasped out loud.

"Let him go," she whispered. "Please. He didn't participate in the heist. At least not the first part. He walked out when he found out about the—"

"Shh." I grabbed her arm, nodding at Simone, who was walking toward us, a furrow in her brow.

"You involve the police; he dies." The magician's face morphed into a mask of menace. "Find the necklace or our mutual friend will gut you all like fish." He tucked away his phone just as Simone joined us on the grass.

"Simi?" She looked from me to the magician and back to me. "Is everything okay?"

"Yes." I forced a smile and dabbed the moisture from my eyes. "We were just marveling at the magician's tricks."

With a flourish, the magician produced another coin and added it to my collection. "That makes four," he said. "It's a lucky number, or unlucky if you waste any more time."

Simone studied him for a long moment and then put her arm around my waist. "I'll have to tear you away. I want to introduce you and Chloe to my friend Moira. She's dying to meet you both."

"Of course." I shot one last pleading glance over my shoulder at the magician, who slowly drew a finger across his throat.

"He's a bad guy, isn't he?" Simone whispered. "I saw the tattoos, and of course your face looked like death. Should I get the security guards to escort him out?"

"He came to deliver a message from Tony Angelini. I don't think he's going to stick around. I just don't understand how he got in. Everyone was vetted and I have security at the door."

Simone introduced us to Moira. By the time we'd finished our conversation, the magician had disappeared.

"This situation just gets worse and worse." I swiped two glasses of champagne from the tray of a passing waiter after Simone had gone to see Moira out. I handed one to Chloe and downed my drink in two big gulps to the tinny sound of "Entry of the Gladiators" played by one of the clowns on a toy piano. "If someone did rat us out to the mob . . ."

"You're going to kill them," Chloe said firmly.

"No."

"You're going to beat them to a pulp?"

"Babe . . ." I stared at her, aghast. Chloe was a sunshine-and-flowers kind of person. She loved floral dresses, romance novels, and tall, dark, and handsome men with tortured souls. During our last heist, she'd discovered she also had a tough side, but she was still cottage-core inside.

Chloe gave my arm an affectionate squeeze. "Don't worry. Whatever you want to do—kidnapping, beating, torture, even murder—I'll be right there with a shovel."

NINE

◇ ◇ ◇

What do you mean, 'It's just Cristian'?" I stared at the crew in shock. Everyone had shown up for the emergency meeting at Rose's garage, but no one seemed to care that Cristian had been kidnapped and tortured by the mob.

"He walked out on us," Emma said from her perch on one of our heist-planning tables. "And that wasn't the first time. Whenever the chips are down, Cristian goes running."

"He came back during our last heist," I protested. "He helped Jack and me escape from Joseph Angelini's study."

"I say he got what was coming to him." Gage leaned back so far in his chair I thought it might tip over.

"No one deserves to be tortured by the mob." Chloe shot him a glare. "What if it was me they kidnapped?"

"Then they'd already be dead." He dropped his chair forward with a bang. "Their friends would be dead. Their families would be dead. Their houses would be burned to the ground, and every trace of their existence would be wiped off the earth."

"How about we put that kind of passion into saving Cristian," I suggested. "He may not have been the best of us, but he is still one of us. We can't leave him in the hands of the mob."

"Call the police," Emma said dismissively. "Saving kidnapped people is their literal job."

"They'll kill him if we get the police involved," Jack said quietly. "Or worse, they'll cut him up and send the pieces to us one by one until time runs out, and then they'll come for us."

"Oh my goodness, this is exciting." Simone fluttered a hand in front of her face. "It's like a real-life movie."

I'd finally invited Simone to join us after she'd followed me around listing reasons why she should be included, one of which was a promise of access to a particular pool of her society friends who required an inordinate number of funeral services because their family members were prone to fatal accidents. She'd instantly won over the crew when she arrived at the garage with an enormous curated gift basket filled with an assortment of luxury foods. Only Gage dared to try the caviar, which, to her horror, he poured over the pizza slice he'd brought with him and washed down with beer.

"I still like the running-away option," Emma said.

"We're playing the long game here," I protested. "Yes, it's easier to get fake passports and run away, but we stand to gain more by seeing this through. It's like chess. You give up the short-term benefit of taking that rook because there are greater rewards if you follow your plan and play through to the end."

"I didn't realize we had a plan," Anil said. "In that case, the long-game strategy makes sense—it's how I became a chess grand master when I was sixteen."

"Is he serious?" Simone gave Anil an appraising look. "There are less than two thousand chess grand masters in the world."

"He's in Mensa," Chloe said. "He's a super-genius. You never know what's going on in that immense brain of his."

"Our plan is . . ." I made up a plan on the spot before the conversation went off track as it almost always did when we were all together. "Find the necklace and get our hands on $9 million before our time runs out. We've already wasted half a week trying to pretend this wasn't real. And we do it together. No one walks away."

Anil raised his hand.

"Yes, Anil?"

"With all due respect, that plan sucks. I think we should try to find Cristian before they kill him."

"They'll keep him alive as leverage," Jack said. "Giving them what they want is our best option for saving him."

Anil lifted his hand again. "What about Rose? She's part of this, too."

"I tried to get in touch with her again, but apparently she left the ship at their stop in Turks and Caicos and didn't get on again."

"I heard that happens a lot on cruise ships," Anil said. "She was probably kidnapped as a sex slave."

"She's eighty-two years old," Chloe pointed out.

Anil shrugged. "It takes all types."

"How would you know?" Gage chuckled. "You've never even had a girlfriend."

"I read." Anil gave an affronted sniff. "I watch TV and movies. Some of them are even rated PG-13. I'm not an ignoramus when it comes to the ways of love."

"We're getting off topic," I said. "Our biggest problem right now is finding the necklace. Chloe hacked into the Delhi police database. The robbery was a professional job. They have no leads. She and Gage checked the dark web, but it isn't for sale on the black market. It's like it disappeared into thin air."

"What about the person who ratted us out in the first place?" Anil asked. "Maybe we could find them and convince them to go back to Angelini and say they made a mistake."

I glanced over at Jack, who had been curiously silent. His arms were still folded, and he was toeing the ground with one of his boots. A sliver of dread slid down my spine. "Jack?"

He looked up and caught my gaze. My heart sank to my stomach when I saw the guilt in his eyes.

"You know, don't you? Who was it?"

Before Jack could speak, the door crashed open, and Clare walked into the garage followed by a couple who looked like they'd stepped straight out of a gangster film. The man was tall and heavily built, with a thick neck and a shaved head. He had a silver ring in one ear, and a jagged scar ran across his cheek. The woman was strikingly beautiful, with long dark hair and a heart-shaped face. She wore a tight-fitting black lace top, black leather pants, and a pair of knee-high thick-soled black boots. They looked like they were ready to cause some serious trouble, but it was Clare who drew everyone's attention because she was holding the Wild Heart.

"I heard you were looking for this." She held up the necklace, turning it so everyone could see the giant diamond pendant glittering in the light.

Blood boiling, I turned on Jack. "You knew she was the rat. You must have known she stole the necklace, too, and you just sat there letting us worry." I was shouting, all the stress and fear finding an outlet in my rage. "We all thought we were going to die."

"You may still die," Clare said casually, tucking the necklace into her bag. "I didn't say I would give it to you."

"Then we'll take it." Gage reached for his gun, but before he could even pull it from its holster, a knife flew through air and sliced into his shoulder.

Chloe screamed and ran to help him. Jack moved like lightning, crossing the floor in two long strides to grab the woman who had thrown the knife and pin her to the wall. Emma made a run for Clare but came up against a wall of muscle when Clare's male companion blocked her way, a gun in his hand. Anil dropped into a fighting stance and turned in a circle, although there was no one for him to fight. Only Simone stayed calm, taking in the chaos with a look that was at once horror and delight.

"Stand down," I shouted. "No shooting, beating, strangling, or throwing any more knives!"

It took a few moments, but eventually everyone calmed down. Clare and her minions moved to one side of the garage, and my crew and I stood on the other, with only the folding metal chairs between us.

"This is Clare," I told them. "She used to be a personal shopper at Bloomingdale's. Jack sent me to see her last year when I needed a dress for the charity ball where I met Joseph Angelini and got hired to run his daughter's wedding. I didn't know they'd been in a relationship, but I found out when Chloe and I saw them kissing at Bloomingdale's last week."

"Jack." Anil's usually calm faced creased with a frown. "That wasn't very nice."

"Yeah, dude," Emma said. "That's Cristian-like behavior. And this is my girl you're dicking around." She slammed a fist into her palm. "I think we'd better step outside."

"If anyone is going to beat him up, it's me," Anil complained. "I've already got my green belt in Brazilian jujitsu. What's the point in training to be a fighter when I can't even defend the honor of my friend?"

"Green belt?" Emma snorted a laugh. "He'll wipe the floor with you. Jack's a street fighter. He's not going to follow the rules. Let me handle this."

"Actually, Simi promised that I could have the first crack at him," Chloe said, pushing up the sleeves of her white cotton peasant blouse.

"Jesus, woman." Gage stared at her in dismay. "You can't fight Jack."

"Why not? I've been taking Krav Maga."

Gage yanked the knife from his shoulder like it was nothing more than a splinter and tossed it on the ground. "If you want him beat, then I'll do it for you."

"Chivalrous as that was," Chloe said, "I can fight my own battles."

"But it's not your battle," Anil pointed out. "It's Simi's battle. Maybe she wants to beat him up herself. And if she doesn't, she needs to choose who gets to do it for her."

A sharp whistle cut through the chatter. Everyone stopped talking and looked over at Clare as she pulled her fingers from her mouth.

"Are you guys serious?" She looked over at her companions and shook her head incredulously. "I'm standing here with the necklace you need to save yourselves from a ruthless mob boss and you're arguing about who gets to beat on Jack?"

"When someone saw Moira's husband cheating on her in the Hamptons, everyone gossiped about it for weeks," Simone whispered, "but no one offered to avenge her through violence. I'm going to tell her we need better friends."

"If I were you, I would stop worrying about Jack and start worrying about myself," I said to Clare, "because now that they know you're the one who ratted us out to the mob, you'll be next on the list."

It was a guess, but I had a feeling the menacing duo standing behind Clare weren't there for window dressing, and Jack had pretty much given it away before she walked in the door. The dude looked like he could crush heads with his bare hands, and the woman had just shown us she was equally lethal. Clare had come for a reason, and she'd brought her own protection.

"Jesus fucking Christ." Gage kicked over the nearest chair. "Are you telling me we're in this mess because of some kind of fucking ex drama?"

"She's a very distant ex," Jack said. "It was long ago and we agreed it was a mistake."

"I have a picture of Jack handcuffed to my hotel bed." Clare held up her phone. "Anyone want to see? I've also got some vacay pics, including one of us on a romantic cruise down the Nile."

"Clare. Enough." Jack's voice held a ruthless edge that I'd never heard before, a harsh, low rumble of warning that reached deep into my beating, betrayed heart.

"It's not what you think," Jack said, turning to me. "She's trying to mess with you to get back at me, just like she did at the department store."

"Aw, Jackie." Clare blew him a kiss. "It is exactly what she thinks. And yes, I set you up. I'm pissed. You derailed my heist. You outed me and you tried to get me arrested. And then I find out you're seeing someone else? After everything we had together. You made me think you don't care anymore."

I saw red, a blinding rush of blood that changed the world around me with a sickening crackle and color. He hadn't just put me in danger with his stupid ex drama; he'd endangered my friends.

"No one is going to touch him," I muttered under my breath. "Because there will be nothing left of him when I'm done." I had always considered myself to be an even-tempered person. As a child, when my needs had been overlooked in favor of my loud, demanding brothers, I swallowed the pain and hurt. But for some reason, this was different. I had opened my heart up to someone for the first time, and I wasn't prepared for the pain of betrayal, or the anger that came with it.

"Take a breath," Simone murmured, placing a gentle hand on my shoulder. "There's more going on here than a jealous ex out for revenge. She must have gone to a lot of trouble to get that necklace, and I am not getting anything from Jack except animosity."

"What do you want, Clare?" Jack spat out.

"You cost me my anonymity and damaged my reputation with that little stunt you pulled the other week," she spat out. "That was my score and now I can't go on-site or hire the people I need to get it done. So, you owe me. I need your crew to do the job I was hired to do. When you hand over what I want, I'll give you the necklace and we'll call it even."

"It's my job," Jack said. "I'm not giving it up."

"The way I see it, you don't have a choice unless you're done with this two-bit crew and you want to see them dead."

"What is the job?" Chloe asked. "It has to be worth one hell of a lot more than the necklace for you to fly to India, steal the Wild Heart, smuggle it into the country, and then out us to the mob."

"The Florentine Diamond," she said. "It's one of the world's most valuable missing treasures. It's a 137-carat yellow diamond originally from India that made its way to Europe in the 1400s and then into the Habsburg crown jewels in the 1600s. It was stolen in 1918 and disappeared for over a century until last year, when a billionaire treasure hunter tracked it down and purchased it from a private collector for $200 million. I was hired to retrieve it for a very generous fee, and I'm willing to give you the necklace, the interest in cash, and a bonus $1 million in exchange for your assistance. That's the same pay I'm giving Milan and Vito."

"Which billionaire has the diamond?" Simone asked. "I know them all."

"Peter C. Hearst. He owns a mansion in—"

"The Gold Coast." Simone laughed lightly. "Actually, he and his wife, Vera, bought three houses and knocked them down to build one big mansion as their city place. Vera is very much into art but Peter is best known as a treasure hunter. He searches for lost antiquities and prides himself on owning the rarest and most unique pieces. I've heard that he's got no scruples when it comes to getting what he wants."

"I guess we have our replacement 'insider,'" Chloe whispered. "With the added bonus that it's unlikely she'll have slept with the target's husband, putting us all at risk."

"We need a minute to discuss this in private." I gestured to the door.

Clare shot a lingering glance at Jack before nodding to her minions to follow her outside.

"So, what do we think?" I asked after they were gone.

"I think she's right. We don't have a choice," Chloe said. "But it makes me so angry that she put us in this position. If she hadn't gone to Angelini in the first place, he wouldn't have known who took the necklace."

"It's Jack's fault." Emma shot him a glare. "He pissed her off and put a target on our backs. I think we should beat on him for Simi, and then make him do the heist alone since he was going to do it alone in the first place."

"It's too big a job for one person," Jack said. "I was planning to hire a crew."

"So, you are a thief." Anil folded his arms. "I thought you were a good bad guy, like Robin Hood."

"I was sent to retrieve the Florentine Diamond and repatriate it," Jack said. "I had no intention of keeping it for myself. It belongs to the Austrian monarchy. They have a rhinestone replica at the Natural History Museum in Vienna and would be thrilled to replace it with the original."

"Does anyone have any other ideas for getting us out of this mess?" I asked, looking over my crew.

"There are seven of us and three of them," Anil said. "Couldn't we just overpower them and take the necklace by force?"

"Not a chance." Gage shook his head. "Her bodyguards are highly trained assassins. They had at least a dozen weapons hidden under their clothes. Jack and I might be able to take them if we were prepared and fully armed, but the rest of you would be liabilities, and sixty seconds tops, you'd all be dead." He twined his fingers and cracked the knuckles on both hands. "Still, if you don't want to agree to the deal, I'm up for the challenge."

"I don't think the necklace she showed us is real," I said. "Who would walk around with something that valuable, even with two highly trained killers as backup? I don't think she's stupid."

"She's not stupid," Jack said. "And you're right. It's not real. I was watching the way the light shone through the pendant. She'll have the original stashed somewhere safe."

"In that case, I think our best option is to pull off the heist, give Clare the diamond in exchange for the necklace and the cash, and make things right with Angelini." I swallowed my fear and fixed my crew with what I thought was a hopeful expression. "Who's in?"

One by one, everyone raised a hand. Except Jack.

"I have a conflict of interest," he said in response to my silent query. "I've been hired to retrieve the diamond, too."

"And you will retrieve it, except that it will unfortunately find its way into Clare's hands before you can hand it over to whoever you have to give it to, who is someone I suspect Clare knows since she seems to know all about your past. Unlike me. Your former girlfriend."

That made Jack wince. "I was trying to protect you."

"I don't need your protection," I snapped. "What I do need is for you to raise your hand and agree to join this heist because if you don't, there are six people in this room who will make sure you do."

Jack raised his hand.

"Then it's settled," I said. "We're doing another heist."

TEN

◇ ◇ ◇

Putting together a heist crew is more art than science. Yes, you need people to do specific tasks, but you also need them to get along so they can work seamlessly together. It's like a well-oiled machine, each cog turning in perfect synchronization with the others.

At least, that's how it's supposed to work in theory. In reality, my crew was a mess. We were a group of misfits who had come together in a moment of desperation and pure financial need, and now we had three unwanted additions plus Simone, who didn't seem to appreciate the gravity of the situation. It was a recipe for disaster.

"Is there any way to ditch the deadweight?" Chloe asked, sipping her Long Island Iced Tea. We had decided to meet with Jack and Gage at the Black Dog bar in the basement of the Hobie Hotel to go over crew assignments. Chloe loved the red velvet banquettes and British decor. I loved the dim lighting and the unique seating configuration that gave every party a sense of privacy.

"There is no way Clare will let us run the heist without her," Jack said. "She has a vested interest in the outcome, and she doesn't trust me."

"Would you really double-cross us, run off with the diamond, and leave us to die by mob boss?" I was on my second Long Island Iced Tea, and suddenly no question was off the table.

"I would never let anything happen to you," Jack said firmly. "But I also don't want the diamond to fall into the wrong hands. It's one of the world's missing treasures. It should go back to Austria and be put on display so its beauty can be shared."

"So that's a yes. Another black mark on your scorecard." I drew an *X* in the air with my finger.

"You two are going to have to agree to disagree so we can get this heist done." Gage looked around for the waiter. He'd already polished off two tumblers full of whiskey and was ready for another.

"Fine." I sighed. "What about Clare's minions? Aside from weapons skills, which we don't need because this will be a no-weapons heist, can we put them to good use?"

"We can get them out of the picture, so they don't slit our throats the minute we lay eyes on the diamond." Gage patted the weapon discreetly holstered under his jacket.

"You said that before, but do you have any proof?" I challenged.

"I don't need proof. It's a gut feeling." He thudded a fist into his stomach.

Chloe grabbed his hand and brought it to her lips. "Don't hurt yourself."

"Made of steel, babe. Couldn't hurt me if you tried." His face softened as she pressed a kiss to his knuckles. It was painful to watch, especially because I once had a man to turn into mush, too.

I looked across the table and caught Jack watching me while Chloe and Gage whispered sweet nothings to each other. "What are you looking at?" I demanded.

"You."

My heart squeezed in my chest. "Well, don't look at me. I would say don't talk to me, either, but we need to get this thing done."

"Would it help if I apologized?" Sincerity oozed from every pore of his handsome face. It was incredibly irritating.

"Apologize for what? For ghosting me? For kissing Clare? For failing to tell me about your past or your psychotic bunny-boiling ex? For making her so angry that she ratted us out to a Mafia boss who has threatened to kill me and my friends?" I slammed my empty glass on the table. "I never thought I needed stability or commitment in my life. I liked your itinerant lifestyle and spontaneous ways. But when you went off the grid, I felt alone and abandoned. And when I saw you with her, I felt betrayed. I never want to feel that again."

"She admitted she set me up," Jack said. "I should at least get a pass for that."

Without responding, I headed for the bar to get another emotion-numbing beverage and spotted Milan and Vito at a nearby table. Even in a room full of eclectic people they stood out. Not because of the way they dressed but because of the air of chaos that surrounded them. It was as if they were one move away from turning the bar into a bloodbath. Vito caught me staring and lifted his glass in a mock salute.

"They're here," I said after I returned with a glass in each hand. "Tweedledum and Tweedledee."

"They're probably noting where everyone's jugular is," Gage said, his face grim. "I say we wait in the alley and deal with them now before they become a problem."

"Violence isn't always the answer." Chloe patted his hand. "Sometimes you just need to talk things through."

"Is Clare here, too?" Gage asked. "I could deal with them all at once."

Jack shook his head. "No sign of Clare. I checked the place out before you all arrived."

I sighed in exasperation. "So, you knew Milan and Vito were here and decided not to share with the class?"

"I wasn't going to let you walk into a bar without knowing if it was safe," he said without even a hint of irony. "And I didn't want you to worry because I have the situation in hand."

I didn't know how he had the situation in hand since the two people Gage suspected had been hired to kill us at the end of the heist had somehow found out where we were meeting and were spying on us a few banquettes away, but I let that one slide.

"Let's get down to business so we can get out of here," I said, tearing my gaze away. "Jack's been to the mansion. What are we looking at in terms of location and security?"

"The jewel is held in a private museum contained within a bunker with bank-level biometric security beneath the house," he said, keeping his voice low. "The bunker is basically a lavish underground ten-thousand-square-foot fallout shelter that's got a swimming pool, cinema, library, wine vault, games room, hydroponic garden, and multiple living areas. It can only be accessed through a secure panic room on the lower level. It's blast-proof and has its own self-contained energy, water, and air supply."

"Jack gave me the details of their security system," Gage said. "It's top-of-the-line. They have a twenty-four-hour command center and on-site guards. The bunker and the museum have their own heat sensors, cameras, motion detectors . . ." He trailed off when I held up my hand.

"Is this a joke?" I looked from Jack to Gage and back to Jack. "Not even a team of elite professional thieves could pull this off, and you're expecting us—a bunch of nobodies with one heist under our belts—to get this done, and in under four weeks?"

"Clare has almost as much experience as me," Jack pointed

out. "And I suspect her two associates are professionals, but it's not about numbers. It's about expertise."

"And what's my expertise? Organizing events?"

"You're a leader," he said. "You're good at managing people, coming up with a plan, and putting all the pieces together. You can stay calm in difficult situations and you think outside the box. The last heist wouldn't have happened without you. There was no obstacle that you couldn't overcome."

"You make it very difficult to stay mad at you when you say nice things," I muttered. "Okay, fine. I'm the leader. Chloe will handle anything that requires hacking into computers, which I assume will be security systems, cameras . . ." I shot her a quizzical look, hoping my genius bestie would be able to handle all the things.

"Biometrics aren't in my wheelhouse," she said, "but yes to everything else."

"Anil can deal with the mechanical and electrical stuff." I ticked the tasks off on my fingers. "Maybe he can handle the biometrics, too. Emma can be our driver and lift heavy things. Gage can be our muscle . . ."

"Just because I have a military background and stay in shape doesn't mean I always have to be the muscle," Gage said with a sniff. "I can do other things."

"Like what?"

"I know six different martial arts, hand-to-hand combat, MMA, boxing, and tai chi. I can bench 250 pounds. I can move quickly and silently, and no one will know I'm there. I can guard, threaten, menace, beat, or rough people up. Torture is also on the table. I can handle attack dogs, knock guards unconscious, and analyze security patterns. There isn't a weapon I can't use—guns, rifles, assault weapons, knives of all types, nunchucks, throwing stars—"

"So . . . things the muscle does during a heist," I said, interrupting.

Gage stared at me. I stared at him. Finally, he said, "Yeah. I guess I'm the muscle."

"Clare can be our grease woman," Jack offered. "If we have to deal with a pressure-sensitive floor or lasers in the bunker or the vault, she'll be invaluable. She's very flexible and can get through tight spaces. I've seen her bend——"

I choked and spat my drink in Jack's face. It wasn't intentional, but I was also not unhappy his face was in my way.

"Dude . . ." Gage shook his head.

"That's not what I meant." Jack dabbed at his face with a napkin. "She's a burglar. She's who people call if they need someone to scale a brick wall, descend from the ceiling via a series of cables, or maneuver around a laser hallway."

I had a strong feeling Clare wasn't the type of person to do her flexible twisting and bending in jogging pants and a baggy tee. She would probably put on her whitest Lycra and ask Jack to set up a pretend laser field made out of string so he could watch her practice.

"What about Simone?" Chloe asked. "She knows the owners of the house. Could she help us get in? Or should we leave her out of it?"

"I'll talk to her," I said. "Maybe the owners are having a party and need an event planner. She's very excited about getting involved with us common folk. Apparently, the life of the ultrarich is very dull. Too many shopping expeditions, vacays, yacht trips, balls, and dinners."

"I've already been in touch with my contact at the Department of Buildings, who is going to get me the most recent set of blueprints for the mansion." Jack dabbed a rogue droplet on his shirt. "The Hearsts had to file current documents for their zoning applications and building permits."

"We'll also need a place to meet and rehearse," I said. "With

Rose away, her neighbors might think it's suspicious if they see us coming and going all the time."

"I know a place," Jack said. "It doesn't have the comforts of Rose's garage, but it has got a roof and electricity."

"Does it have room for six coffins?" Far from feeling heartened by the conversation, I felt the weight of despair. Even with two experienced thieves on the crew, there didn't seem to be any way we were going to be able to pull this off. "Or, after we fail, will Angelini's Mafia buddies just dump us in the lake with matching cement shoes?"

"Your parents would be devastated if you just disappeared," Chloe said. "They would never give up looking for you."

"I think they'd be more upset that I died unmarried."

"Well, if that's everything, I think Simi and I should get going." Chloe squeezed my hand under the table, our signal that one of us had had too much to drink and needed to be taken home before she embarrassed herself even more than obsessing about her own death, and it wasn't her.

Jack offered to drive us home, but we opted for the train so we could talk.

"What am I supposed to do about Jack?" I said as we made our way down the street. "My head is spinning and it's not from all the cocktails. I loved him. I hated him. I missed him. I hated him again. Then Clare admitted she set him up . . ."

"So back to loving him?" Chloe asked, yanking me to the side to avoid a group of drunk college guys.

"No, because he never told me they were together, or that she was a psycho ex who would put us all in danger, and I'm still not buying all the crazy excuses he gave me for why he could barely stay in touch or come back home for a visit."

Chloe stopped in front of the train station. "I'm your girl. If you love him, I love him. If you hate him, I hate him. But even I'm getting confused. Are we back to hating him?"

"No, because he arranged for his 'people' to watch my house to keep me safe from Clare, and he did some fairly decent groveling in my apartment and some even better kissing at the Sawmill, and you heard him in the bar . . ."

Chloe smiled. "He did say some nice things."

I threw my hands up in the air. "What am I supposed to do with that?"

"I think you need to sort yourself out before you can decide what you want to do about Jack," she said. "You're still afraid of getting hurt, and I get it. I love your parents. They always treated me like I was part of your family, but they let you down. They made you feel like you weren't worthy of love. You weren't the priority in their lives, and this last year Jack made you feel the same way. You feel like you can't trust him anymore. But seeing him now, the way he looks at you—"

I gave her a sideways glance. "How does he look at me?"

"Like he adores you. I don't think if he has a choice, he'd leave you again." She shrugged. "Of course, if you want the safe option, there's always Garcia."

Garcia had always been there for me, but he didn't make my heart pound and my knees weak. He didn't make me laugh with his sarcastic comments or amuse me with his banter. He hadn't traveled the world and seen incredible things that he would share with me when we were cuddled together in the still of the night.

Garcia was great. My parents would love him. I would never have to worry that he'd hurt me or walk away.

But he wasn't Jack.

ELEVEN

◇ ◇ ◇

More hungover than I'd been in a long time, I walked into my office late the next morning to find Jack sprawled out on my cream leather couch.

"How did you get in here?"

"Window." He jerked a thumb behind him. "It wasn't secure. I fixed it, but you'll need to speak to the landlord about something more permanent."

"What do you have against doors?" I dropped my bag beside my desk and headed back out the door to the small kitchen I shared with the other tenants on the floor. I'd picked up a coffee from the deli down the street, but one cup wasn't going to be enough to get me through the day.

"They're usually locked and take a few seconds to open," he said, following me. "Windows are easier."

I heaved a loud sigh. "Why are you here, Jack?"

"I need a wife."

"You've come to the wrong office. Wives-R-Us is down the hall. This is an event-planning business."

"I need you to be my wife," he repeated. "My contact at the

building department had a heart attack, so I can't get the blue-prints. I know where another set is located, but—"

"You want to steal them."

"That word has such a negative ring," he said. "The only thing I'll be taking is a copy of digital files."

"You managed to get in here without a wife," I said, filling the coffeepot. "I'm sure you can manage to copy some files with-out one."

"It's a two-person job." He handed me two mugs from the cup-board. "I found the name of the architect who designed the Hearsts' new house and confirmed that his firm keeps a digital copy of all their designs on-site. I need to access their system to download the blueprints, and that means I need a distraction."

I added extra-strong coffee grounds to the filter for the caffeine boost. It was going to be a four-cup day. "I have every confidence you'll find a suitable distraction. You managed to do it with Clare."

"I need you, Simi," he pleaded. "We know each other well. Our fake marriage will be believable. I don't think anyone else would be able to pull it off." His voice dropped to a low, throaty rumble and he gently cupped my cheek. "We have chemistry. You can't deny that. Look what happened at the Sawmill."

A wave of heat surged through my veins, and I pulled away. "Stop trying to seduce me with your . . . your . . . seductive ways. What happened in the bar wasn't real. I was acting the part of your girlfriend. Clearly, I did an excellent job."

"This time I need you to act as my wife," he said. "We'll go in there as a newlywed couple who has just purchased a house and needs an architect to do an extensive renovation."

"Won't he need the address? Some proof of ownership?"

"I've taken care of all the details." He pulled out his phone and tapped the screen. "I've sent you a link to the property listing.

You'll need to look it over and imagine how you would update the rooms. I'll also send you some extra pictures. If you think you'll need to visit the house before we meet the architect, it can be arranged."

"I know this house," I said, studying the listing for the 1897 Tudor he'd sent me. "It's in Evanston near Chloe and my parents. Chloe and I used to ride past it on our bicycles on our way to the swimming pool in summer."

"I thought something in Evanston would work well because you know the area and it would make for a more believable story." He gave me a hopeful smile. "We can say we wanted to settle down near your best friend and your family—"

"Well, that part is true. If I ever had the money to buy a house, I'd stay in Evanston, and I would love a house like this. It's got so much character. Look at these pictures . . ." I flipped through the photos. "It's got a huge yard, just like my parents' house. We could have all my relatives over . . . and oh my God . . . look at that kitchen. Nani would just die to cook in a kitchen like that. There's so much light, but it needs a redo. I'd go with white walls, spotlights, dark cabinets, white marble counters . . ." I kept scrolling, caught up in the fantasy of owning a house that only millionaires could afford. "Look at the master bedroom! It's the size of my entire apartment . . ." I trailed off when I glanced up to see Jack watching me, a wistful expression on his face.

"Sorry. I got off track." I tucked my phone away. "It's kind of fun to imagine buying a $6 million house and fixing it up, especially when it's not in the cards for me. I couldn't even have paid the deposit for a house like that with the reward money from our last heist."

"You need to be able to keep him busy for at least thirty to forty-five minutes," Jack said, his voice curiously rough. "I'll ask Chloe to call me during our meeting with a fake business issue so I can have her on the line while I find an open terminal to access the server and download the plans. I've made the appointment for tomorrow afternoon before our heist meet."

"That was very presumptuous. What if I'd said 'no' to the fake-wife charade?"

His handsome face softened. "I knew you wouldn't say 'no' because lives are at risk and you're all about helping people even if it means putting your own needs last."

I put that one on the back burner to mull over after he'd gone and I wasn't seriously regretting my decision to put the brakes on our relationship because it had been ten months since I'd had sex and he was looking particularly delicious in his black Henley and low-slung jeans.

"Won't he be suspicious if I'm making all the decisions alone?" I poured two cups of coffee and added four sugars and two creams to his cup. I'd been pleasantly surprised to discover I wasn't the only person in the world who liked her coffee sweet and creamy, but today I needed the punishment of black coffee to remind myself never to drink alcohol again.

"I'll just do the 'whatever makes her happy' routine." He took his cup and lifted it to his lips.

"Such a good fake husband." I absently patted his hand. Big mistake. A zing of electricity shot straight to my core. Jack jerked his hand away like I'd burned him.

"I could be a good real husband, too," he said quietly.

Whoa. I didn't see that one coming. "Marriage requires trust and trust means not keeping secrets."

"There are some jobs where the work is highly sensitive and the person involved can't share any details with friends or family," he said. "And during dangerous and discreet assignments, they can't tell people where they are in the world, especially if they are in a compromised position." Jack was more serious than I'd ever seen him, and his words carried the ring of truth.

"Are you talking about the CI—?"

Jack cut me off with a finger to his lips and shook his head. "There are many organizations that do covert work."

"Is someone listening?" I whispered, looking around my office for hidden cameras or recording devices.

"I checked for bugs when I arrived, but if someone is listening from outside . . ."

"Are you serious?" My voice rose in disbelief. "Who would be listening to me? I lead an incredibly boring life. Are people that desperate to hear me negotiate the best deal for funeral flowers, fight with my cousins about who has to bring what dish to the next family dinner, or talk to Chloe about menstrual cramps?"

Jack shrugged. "People know we were together, and in my line of work, you can't be too careful."

I took a sip of my coffee, wincing as the bitter black liquid hit my tongue. "Are you saying that going off-grid and barely contacting me for eight months was a work requirement? It wasn't a choice?"

"Yes." He hesitated, holding the coffee cup just below his lips. "And no. It's complicated. I'm a consultant. I can choose my jobs, but sometimes one leads to another, or I'm unexpectedly detained, or people come looking for me and I have to stay under the radar. That means no contact and no calls."

I sipped my coffee again, trying to process Jack's admission, but I was lost in a storm of conflicting emotions. On one hand, I was relieved to know he hadn't intended to abandon me. On the other hand, I couldn't help feeling slightly betrayed. Even if he had signed some kind of NDA, why didn't he trust me enough to tell me the truth, or something close to it? Maybe our relationship wasn't as deep and meaningful as I thought it was. But worse was the fact that I'd been blaming myself, thinking I was the problem, and the reason he had stayed away.

"There's more. Isn't there?" I could tell from the way he fiddled with the bracelet I'd given him that he hadn't told me everything.

"I'm not good with relationships," he admitted. "I've never stayed in one place or with one person for more than a few months. To be honest, it may be that my commitment issues played a part in my decision to keep taking on new work."

My breath left me in a rush, like I'd been punched in the gut. "I can't handle this right now," I said. "It's too much on top of everything that's going on. I need some space."

"I understand." Jack gently took the coffee cup out of my hand and replaced it with his own.

"Hey. That's my punishment coffee. I make it after a night of heavy drinking. I'm trying to elicit a Pavlovian response that would stop me from ever wanting to drink again."

His lips curled in a smile. "Clearly it doesn't work, so you might as well drink coffee you enjoy. I don't like to see you suffer, even if it is just coffee that tastes like tar."

I felt a sliver of warmth run through me, and with it a glimmer of hope.

"I'll pick you up tomorrow morning at ten A.M.," he said. "You need to know the house inside out and have your dream reno list ready."

"Are you sure there's nothing you want me to add? It would seem odd if you didn't have a single request."

Jack turned from the door, considering. "I would want a big glass heated conservatory for wintering plants, enough space in the yard for a garden and for kids to play, and a workshop or potting shed. Maybe a movie room with a giant screen and big leather seats. Possibly a pool table if there's space. And a mirror over the bed . . ."

"You're not getting a mirror," I said, biting back a laugh. "What if it falls on us when we're having hypothetical sexy times?"

His shoulders shook with suppressed laughter. "I can't think of a better way to go."

"Mr. and Mrs. Jack Danger to see Mr. Williams," Jack said to the receptionist at the architect's office the next day, looking every inch the well-heeled corporate tycoon in a bespoke wool suit, blue shirt, and red-and-blue silk tie, all from my dad's store. I'd measured him for that suit, and I'd enjoyed every minute of it.

"Excuse me?" I poked him in the back.

To his credit, he didn't even flinch until we sat in the ultramodern white-and-black waiting area, and then he rubbed his back and groaned. "Was that really necessary?"

"*Mrs. Jack Danger?* Like I have no identity beyond being your wife?"

"Most women would dream of having no identity beyond being my wife," he said with a smug grin. "What else is there in life? You've secured the most desirable male on the planet. Hashtag goals."

"I can't even . . ." I threw up my hands. "Your ego is so big, I'm amazed there is room for me on the couch."

"I'm amazed you didn't have *Jack's wife* tattooed on your ass, or even stamped on a T-shirt."

"I would have been happy to wear a T-shirt, but you told me to wear a suit."

"That's because you look hot in a suit," he said. "It was solely for my benefit." He placed a warm hand on my thigh and gave it a squeeze. "I want to peel it right off you—everything but the heels."

"Hands off." I slapped his hand away, but it came back like a boomerang.

"We're newlyweds," he said. "He'll expect us to be overly affectionate. The thrill hasn't gone yet. The bloom is not off the rose.

To sell this relationship, we need to be desperately in love, unable to keep our hands off each other except for the half hour I'll disappear to take a call and download the files."

"I thought we were supposed to be a professional couple," I reminded him. "Professionals don't act like horny teenagers in public."

"They do if the woman is so sexy the man can barely control himself." Jack leaned closer and threaded his fingers through mine. "Did you know that after I first met you in the bushes behind the museum, I went to your father's tailor shop and pretended I needed a suit just so I could spend some time with you and enjoy the gratuitous thrill of having your hands on me while you did the measurements?"

"You dragged me into the bushes and restrained me," I huffed. "If you hadn't been so charming, I would have laid you flat with a few well-placed kicks and punches." I brushed a small piece of fluff off his shoulder. "I still might, although you'll have to take off the suit. It would be a waste of my excellent measuring job if it were covered in blood."

"So romantic," he murmured. "Nothing turns me on more than your violent streak. I would buy another ten suits if you'd touch me like that again. I especially enjoyed your inseam-measuring technique. That little brush of the knuckles . . ."

My face heated at the memory of kneeling down in front of Jack to take his measurements. "I asked you which side you dressed on so there would be no risk of knuckle brushing."

Jack chuckled. "I lied."

"I cannot believe you." I punched him in the shoulder. "That's so inappropriate."

"I like to think that's when you fell in love with me." He nuzzled my neck, one hand sliding around my waist to pull me close. "You copped a little feel and were so impressed you just had to have me."

"And there's that big ego again, filling the room."

"That's not the only big thing in this room, sweetheart." He slid his hand around my nape and pulled me in for a long, deep kiss.

I stiffened and instinctively pulled away, but Jack tightened his hold. "She's watching," he mumbled against my lips. "We need to sell the story."

To be honest, I didn't want to fight it. I'd missed Jack. I wanted him. I wanted this to be real. No matter how hard I tried, I couldn't keep myself from melting into him and drowning in that kiss.

"That's my girl." His lips swept down my neck, his hand curving under my ass. Before I knew what was happening, he'd lifted me to his lap.

"Put me down." I shot a frantic gaze in the direction of the nosy receptionist, who didn't seem to have anything else to do but watch us. "I'm not a child."

"But you are good at hiding things." He gave a pointed glance down at his lap. "Although if you don't sit still, you're going to make the problem worse, not better."

I could feel the *problem* hard against my thigh, so I did what any irritated fake newlywed would do: I wiggled.

Jack bit back a groan. "Are you sure you want to share what has been solely yours since the day we met with the staff at the office? Because I'm not embarrassed about what you do to me." He trailed his fingers up my leg and along my inner thigh beneath my skirt.

"Stop saying things like that." I pushed his hand away. "I don't need you to get that deep into the role."

This time he laughed out loud. "Do you really want to go there?"

"And don't talk like that. You're making me horny. This is a professional office."

"And you are looking fuckably professional," Jack said. "I think after this, we should go to your office, bend you over the desk, push that naughty skirt up to your waist, and . . ."

A man cleared his throat and gave a little laugh. "You must be our newlyweds."

"Yes, indeed. Fresh from our honeymoon." Jack helped me up and introduced me to the architect Trey Williams, a tall, slim man in his early fifties with dark hair graying at the temples, long, thin fingers, and thick glasses. He wore a black shirt open at the collar and he smelled of fresh mint.

"I remember those days," he said wistfully. "Enjoy them while you can."

"I'm enjoying every minute." Jack slid his hand under my hair and stroked my nape with his thumb, sending delicious shivers down my spine. My knees wobbled and I had to force myself to walk so I didn't melt into a puddle on the white marble tiles.

"This is supposed to be for show," I muttered under my breath. "You're turning me on. I can't think properly."

"If I keep going, will you be so turned on, you'll forget you hate me and drag me to your place and have your way with me?" he whispered in my ear.

"I'll go home alone and get my biggest vibrator and—"

"Here we are." Trey gestured us into his clinically white office. White carpet, white walls, white chairs, white desk. The only spot of color was the black table covered in blueprints.

"Excellent performance so far," Jack said, keeping his voice low. "Five out of five. Highly recommend."

But it wasn't a performance. It was hope and longing mixed with disappointment and desire. I glared. He laughed. It was almost like old times.

"Has the sale gone through?" Trey asked.

"Yes. It went through last week," Jack said. "Simi is so desperate to move in, I'm paying a premium to my contractor to do the renovations on a rush basis."

"It's a beautiful home," Trey said. "So much character. I'd say it's probably one of the nicest homes in the area, particularly with that huge backyard."

"Lots of room for kids to play." Jack put his arm around me and leaned over to kiss my cheek. "We'll have to get working on that when we move in."

I offered my cheek but nothing else because my lips were frozen in a smile. Kids? With Jack? How was that supposed to work when he was away for months at a time and could only communicate by burner phone, if at all. Then I remembered. It wasn't real.

"Jack sent me the floor plan and details for your new home." Trey gestured to a large table by the window. "It looks like a major renovation was done just last year, so all the electrical and plumbing is up to date, a few walls were removed to make it more open, and the floors, roof, and windows were redone. I've got a few suggestions for the kitchen and bathrooms and for bringing in more light to the hallway, but I'd like to hear your plans first."

"I've got a lot of ideas." I pulled out my phone and scrolled to the list I'd made after poring over the house plans and pictures. It had been fun imagining the house was mine and all the things I wanted to do with it. Updated modern showers, a huge soaker tub in the master bathroom, a dining room big enough to accommodate my entire family, and a special office in the unfinished loft where I could work from home and watch my imaginary kids play in the backyard on sunny days.

Jack's phone rang and he took the fake call from Chloe. "I've got to step out for a moment," he said. "Urgent business. Is there an empty room with a secure computer I could use to send out some documents?"

Trey called his receptionist to find Jack a workspace, and then we talked through my ideas for the fictitious remodel of someone else's home.

"That was quite the wedding gift," he said, looking up from his notes. "You must have been surprised."

"Very surprised," I said honestly. "I never saw it coming. I still can't believe it's real."

Jack had been gone almost forty minutes when I heard the door open. "So sorry, babe." He leaned down to give me a kiss. "There seems to be a crisis every time I leave the office."

"We've been busy going through my plans," I said. "Some of them won't work because of the structure of the house, but—"

"I want you to be happy," Jack said. "I want this to be your dream house, a place where we can raise a family and enjoy a long, fulfilling life together."

"Well, then we can't have both your greenhouse and your conservatory," I said. "The children will need somewhere to play."

Jack's brown creased ever so slightly. "No greenhouse?"

"We can squeeze a few more feet into the conservatory." Trey tapped the blueprint. "And you'll have your garden and your potting shed."

"He does love his garden." I smiled at Jack, and he gave me the briefest nod to let me know the job was done. "I'm more of a wilderness kind of person."

Jack barked a laugh. "You? In the wilderness?"

"Yes. Me in the wilderness." I gave an affronted sniff. "Why is that so hard to imagine?"

"You're a city girl. You wouldn't know what to do if you found yourself alone in the forest at night without your phone."

"Why would I be there?" I let out an exasperated sigh. "Who goes into a forest at night? And alone? And without a phone? This is a stupid game. You're wasting poor Trey's time."

"Actually, I'm just waiting for my changes to the plans to render so I can print out a copy for you before you leave," Trey said with a smile. "Please feel free to continue. I haven't enjoyed myself as much in years."

"Fine." I folded my arms. "It's night. I stupidly decided to go for a hike *alone* and without my phone in a thick forest for God knows what reason and I get lost." My voice dripped sarcasm. I wasn't sure if newlyweds were sarcastic to each other, but Jack deserved everything he had coming to him.

"And it's cold," Jack said.

"I'm hot-blooded. I don't get cold. And why are you making this more difficult than it has to be? When have you ever seen me leave my house without a jacket or a sweater? We live in Chicago, not Miami."

"Okay. You have your sweater. How are you going to get home?" He leaned toward me, his dark eyes intense.

"Chloe would find me. I would have told her where I was going and she'd know something was wrong if an hour went by and she couldn't contact me by phone."

Jack sighed. "Chloe thinks you're somewhere else because you changed your destination at the last minute and forgot to tell her."

"He thinks he knows me so well," I said to Trey, "but he's forgotten I spent my entire childhood being left behind. Once my family drove off and left me at a gas station and didn't come back for five hours. Another time, they left me in a field when we made a bathroom pitstop because my younger brothers—they're twins—drank six liters of pop in five minutes to see who could burp the loudest. He probably thinks I'm going to tell him I'll find north by looking at the moss on trees or orient myself by looking for the sun rising in the east, neither of which are reliable."

For the first time, Jack's smile wavered. "You're stalling."

"I'm savoring the moment."

"I can't help," Trey said, holding up his hands as if my hesitation came from indecision. "City boy. Right here. Give me concrete or give me death."

I liked Trey. He'd been very helpful with my fake renovations. And it turned out he had a quirky sense of humor. I felt bad that Jack had just hacked into his computer to copy the blueprints of the Hearsts' mansion, but at least he hadn't stolen them.

"I think you'd stay put and wait for me to rescue you," Jack said. "And that would be the best decision, because I would stop at nothing until you were safe in my arms."

I snorted a laugh. "Seriously? I wouldn't need to be rescued. I would find out which way was downhill and locate the nearest water source to follow or I'd climb high and look for gaps in tree lines due to roads, power cables, or train tracks. At night, I'd look for artificial light sources . . ." I paused when I noticed the smirk had been totally wiped off Jack's face. "Do you want me to tell you how I'd read the night sky? I can do that, too. Oh, and I also know how to make a fire out of sticks and build a rudimentary shelter. I joined an orienteering club when I was a kid to learn outdoor survival skills, and every Christmas I asked Santa for survival gear."

Silence.

"Boom." I opened my hand and closed it again, giving Jack my most satisfied smile. "Mic drop."

"I thought I knew you," Jack said. "Now I feel like I don't really know you at all."

"You two are hilarious. You make a great couple." Trey pulled the plans from his oversize printer and carefully rolled them into a tube.

"Did you hear that, honey?" Jack kissed my cheek. "Trey thinks we make a great couple."

"Have a look over these while you're walking around the house and see what you think." Trey popped the plans into a tube and handed them to me. "Let me know a good time to stop by to take pictures and make measurements. I'll check for load-bearing walls and all that stuff, if you are serious about moving ahead."

"I'm very serious," Jack said, staring at me. "When I find something I want, I'll do what it takes to get it."

We shook hands with Trey and said good-bye. Jack didn't talk until we were outside the building, and then only to say, "In here," when he grabbed my arm and pulled me into an alley.

"What are we . . . ?" I trailed off when he slammed me up against the brick wall, bracketed my hands over my head, pressed his hot, hard body against me, and kissed me like the world was coming down around us and we would never kiss again.

Then there was no talking for a very long time, although there were a lot of hands going where hands shouldn't go when you're in public with your fake husband / ex-boyfriend, and not wanting to get arrested for public indecency.

"Jack." I arched against him, wanting more but not wanting to go to jail and worried about making our relationship, such as it was, even more complicated. "Jack. We have to stop."

"You are so fucking hot," he murmured, pressing his lips against my neck. "I would never have imagined you had survival skills. I want to get lost on a mountain with you. It would be so hot watching you save us."

"I thought you'd be annoyed because I thwarted your attempt to show off your own survival skills by making me look bad."

"I have a thing for competence." His hand was under my shirt, his fingers warm on my skin.

"I have a thing for not getting my heart broken again even if I'm so wet my panties have become redundant."

"You can't say things like that and not expect me to do something about it." He hesitated. "Can I do something about it?"

It was too much. The gritty alley. The risk that someone would turn the corner and see us. The hour-long foreplay with all the touching and kissing and verbal sparring. The beautiful house and the fake renovations and the imaginary life I'd never have. And Jack. So hot. So sexy. Driving me into a frenzy of desire. Wanting me in a way I had never been wanted before.

"Yes," I breathed out the word in a sigh.

Jack slid his hand between my thighs, fingers stroking where once dry panties used to be.

"This doesn't change anything." I sucked in a sharp breath when his fingers breached the cotton barrier. "I'm still angry with you."

Jack froze, his fingers only inches from where I wanted them to go. "Are you sure you're good with this?"

"Yes, so long as you understand that it doesn't mean anything. After this, things go back to how they were."

Twenty minutes later, disheveled and breathless, we held each other in the shadows.

"Jack?"

"Yes, sweetheart?"

"You can have your greenhouse."

TWELVE

◇ ◇ ◇

Jack's practice "space" was a run-down two-story warehouse in Chicago's Near North Side. The windows were barred, but outside I could see the heavy walls of a factory rising from the ground like a fortress. The air was thick with the smell of grease and motor oil, and the concrete floor was cracked down the center. Crates were stacked in odd configurations along one wall, and in the far corner, ropes and pulleys hung from rusted pipes above a twenty-foot square of worn blue mats. I stared at the corrugated tin walls, the rust-coated beams, the caged freight elevator, and the collection of safes scattered in one corner, and wished for the comforts of Rose's garage.

"This used to be a machine shop." Jack walked me around the warehouse pointing out the large wooden table where big pieces of metal had been cut and various pieces of rusted equipment with names I was never going to remember. Chloe had passed on the tour in favor of setting up her computer in the back office and hacking into someone's Wi-Fi to give us Internet access.

"It's um . . . got a lot of character," I said. "Very apropos for a heist."

Jack beamed and puffed out his chest like he'd built it himself.

"I knew it would be perfect. After Chloe's done in the office, you may wish to show your gratitude in a more personal way."

My face flamed at the memory of our moment in the alley. "We agreed that encounter was a one-off."

"I could wear the suit again," he whispered. "You liked the suit."

Yes, I'd liked the suit. I'd liked it a little too much. Suits, however, were not a good plan when it came to Jack. I only had so much self-control.

"No suits and no sex," I said, turning away. "We have more important things to think about, like being whacked by the mob."

"We could die happy . . ." He brushed the hair from my nape and nuzzled my neck, sending a shiver of electricity down my spine.

"Are we selling these safes to fund the heist?" Emma's loud voice pulled me out of the moment. She'd been playing with one of the safes since she arrived, spinning the wheel and trying random combinations to open the door.

"Clare is fronting the money," Jack said, glancing over when Clare walked in with her minions behind her and, curiously, Anil by her side. "This is her heist, after all."

Clare dutifully tossed a duffel bag on the big table in the center of the room. "There's enough cash in there to cover the cost of supplies."

"It had better be in unmarked bills," Emma said. "I had a tenant once who paid me in cash that he'd stolen from a bank, and they traced it to me. Nothing ruins a hookup more than having the cops bust down your door at three A.M. and handcuff you naked on the floor when the poor dude you're with was literally in the moment. It had taken me so long to get him there, too. I had callouses on my callouses."

"Don't be unkind," Anil said. "Clare wants this to succeed as much as you do."

Emma's mouth dropped open, and she shot me a puzzled look. I shrugged my shoulders, unable to answer the unspoken question.

Milan and Vito made themselves comfortable tossing knives at a torn work schedule on the far wall, riding up and down in the freight elevator, and testing each other on their safe-opening skills. When Simone and Gage finally arrived, I gathered everyone together around the large worktable and spread out the blueprints while Jack briefed them on the information he had gathered during his recon mission.

"The bunker where the vault and museum are located is here," he said, pointing to a separate diagram on the blueprint. "It can be accessed from the panic room through this door . . ." He tapped a blue line. "The panic room is accessible from the games room through this door." He pointed to another line. "That one looks like it's covered, so I suspect it's hidden."

"The door to the panic room is behind a big mirror in the downstairs games room," Simone interjected. "It's got a biometric lock that works when either Vera or Peter presses it with a finger. It's very comfortable. They've got a big-screen TV, computer access, a small kitchen, bedroom, and sitting area, and all the usual panic room security and supplies for short-term problems—thieves, kidnappers, and the like. Personally, I thought the dark wood and tapestry motif was a little dated and didn't fit in with the light, airy feeling in the rest of the house, but Peter likes to pretend he comes from money. If there's an apocalypse or a similar serious event, then they make their way to the bunker."

"How do you know all this?" I asked the question that was clearly on everyone's mind, given that everyone's mouth was hanging open.

"I went to visit Vera," Simone said as she reapplied her lipstick. "I thought we should find out if they were going to be away anytime soon because wouldn't that make it easier to get inside to steal the diamond?"

"Simone, you can't go off and do things that we haven't discussed." My voice trembled in a combination of shock and fear. "What if you tipped them off? What if Vera says to the police, 'You know . . . Simone was here the other day asking about when we were going away,' and then the next thing you know, the police are showing up at your door?"

Simone gave a light laugh and waved a dismissive hand in the air. "Simi, darling, subterfuge isn't rocket science. I told Vera I'd stopped by to solicit her help with a charity event. We'd only met socially, and I always wanted to get to know her better. I'm glad I did. She had a black eye that she'd tried to cover with makeup, but you can't cover up the swelling, and there are only certain foundations that are dark enough and last long enough to give you more than a few hours of coverage. I gave her a few tips . . ."

"Simone . . ." I stared at her in horror. "I didn't—"

"I have years of practice. It's nothing I can't handle," she said. "And it felt good to help her out. I want to be the kind of friend that you have—friends who would fight over beating up your boyfriend when he cheats on you with a heartless, conniving snake like Clare."

"I'm standing right here," Clare said.

"I know you are, darling." Simone gave her the sweetest smile. "That's why I said it."

"So, what else did Vera tell you?" I loved Simone in that moment and hoped she would say other mean things to Clare that I, as the leader of our ragtag heist crew, couldn't say.

"I asked about her security system," Simone continued. "I told her my husband, Richard, and I were planning to upgrade after seeing a lot of ne'er-do-wells on the street, and she gave me the name of the company they use: SecureCom."

"Oh my God." I scrubbed my face with my hands. "Now they'll definitely suspect you were involved."

"Don't worry." Simone reached over and patted my shoulder. "No one would ever, in a million years, think it was me, and that made it even more exciting. My heart was pounding. Pounding. The day I met you and unwittingly introduced you to a mob boss has turned out to be the best day of my life. At least, I thought it was until I met Joseph's brother Tony in your office . . ."

"Tony?" I shared an incredulous glance with Chloe. "Since when are we calling the mob boss who wants to kill us by his first name?"

"I didn't know I could feel like that," Simone continued as if I hadn't spoken. "What a man! So handsome and confident. Such a presence. And a criminal. Imagine. I didn't know my breath could still be taken away. It was a thrill. An absolute thrill. And now I get to be part of an actual heist and help people in real ways."

Apathy in a crew was bad, but I hadn't considered that overexuberance might be worse. "What else did you do while you were there?"

"I asked her for a tour, of course. I said Richard wanted more space for our city place and I would love to see what they'd done with their new home. She was most obliging. Vera told me Peter insisted on having a museum in the bunker to display his collection of erotic art and treasures. It seems very likely that's where the diamond would be. Vera says he often entertains his friends down there and she thinks he also uses it as a secret sex dungeon because she's caught him bringing young ladies down there when he thought she was asleep upstairs."

"And she thought that was okay?" Chloe stared at her, aghast.

"That's the price we pay to live this life," she said with a shrug. "Peter and Richard and many of the other new tech billionaires have the money but not the social status. They don't know how to navigate high society. They don't know what art to buy, what clothes to wear, what charities to support, or how to tastefully decorate their homes. So, they find a spouse who does, and we have an understanding. We introduce them to society, put on the charity events, and try to make them presentable in a level of society they would never otherwise be able to reach. They bail out our usually bankrupt established-pedigree families so we can live the life to which we are accustomed."

"But what about love?" Chloe asked.

"Love is rarely part of it," Simone said. "It's more like a business arrangement. But sometimes the trade-offs . . ." She pressed her lips together and then sighed. "The biggest issue is that men—and it is mostly men, I'm afraid—with that much money can buy their way out of any problem. When there is no accountability, there are no rules. And when there are no rules . . ." She touched her eye. "We don't always make the best choices when we're young."

"I'm sorry, Simone," Chloe said gently.

"No need to be sorry," she said. "I made my choices. The only one I really regret is the prenup Richard made me sign. If I divorce him, my family loses their estate and goes into bankruptcy, and I get only a small monthly allowance to live on. That's why I'm so invested in your heist venture. It's exciting to think that I might get $1 million of my very own. I might actually consider leaving him. It's an incentive to do my part."

"You did great at Vera's place," I told her. "It's too bad you couldn't get an invitation to see the museum. Then we wouldn't need to break into the house, the panic room, or the bunker."

"I could ask Vera to host a charity event at her house," Simone offered. "I would insist you organize it, but we'd need to do it soon. They're planning an extended trip on their super-yacht in the next few weeks."

"I was on a yacht once," Emma said. "This guy, Jerry, stole a boat to impress me and took us out on the Columbia River during a massive storm. Thirty minutes later we had to call the coast guard. I had tied myself to the railing so I didn't get tossed overboard, and Jerry thought it was some kind of kinky sex game. He stripped off his clothes and left the helm, all ready for stormy sexy times. A huge wave hit us and over he went. When the rescue helicopter picked him up, I got a good preview of what wasn't on offer. He said it was shrinkage, but in my book that was vacuumpacked. It all worked out for the best. He wound up in jail, so there was no awkward 'Sorry, your dick is too small' the next day."

"I learn so much from Emma," Anil said. "I miss living with her." He shot Clare a longing glance. "There's a space in my life for an older experienced woman to teach me things."

Bile rose in my throat and I fought back the urge to retch. Beside me, Chloe choked back a gasp.

"Simone may not need to ask Vera to host an event," Jack said, giving us a moment to recover. "I think I've found another way in." He pointed to a faint line on the blueprints. "There's an escape tunnel leading from the bunker into a back alley. The only problem is that the door is completely sealed and can only be opened from the inside."

"Does anyone have explosives experience?" Anil asked. "I can handle all the mechanical and engineering stuff, possibly the biometrics, but often in my video games, the simplest solution is to blow things up."

"Vito is an explosives expert," Clare said. "He has a PhD in chemistry."

"No fucking way," Emma whispered in my ear. "I would have put my money on *Walking Dead*, not *Breaking Bad*."

"I study energetic materials." Vito had never spoken before, and his Italian accent was so rich and captivating that it pulled me in and closed off all my other senses. Smooth and warm, it brushed over my skin like a summer breeze . . .

"You may want to close your mouth," Jack murmured in my ear. "It's embarrassing. You're starting to drool."

Vito continued as if unaware that his voice had more than a few members of the crew shook. "That includes pyrotechnics, propellants, and explosives. I mainly work in demolitions."

"I'm interested to hear how you got into that field," Emma said. "Why don't you start from childhood and just tell us your life story. Take all the time you need."

Disappointingly, he shook his head. "Not today."

"I think we've got a good idea of the obstacles we're facing." I shook off the spell and walked over to my old heist-planning whiteboard, which I'd brought from Rose's garage. "I've written down your roles, and now we just need to figure out who is going to do what."

"Unless Jack wants to step in, I'm the most experienced person here," Clare said, frowning at the board. "I should be the leader."

"This is my crew," I said firmly. "We've worked together before. We know each other's strengths and weaknesses. There's no way they would work for you."

"I'd work for her," Anil said. "I'd do anything for such a beautiful woman."

"Anil!" Emma barked out his name so loudly even Milan and Vito froze. "What the fuck, dude? She's the enemy. Cristian is being tortured because of her. The boss of mob bosses is going to be giving us all Sicilian neckties because of her. We're here because of her."

"I believe in second chances." He smiled at Clare. An amused Clare smiled back. I remembered that smile from when she'd tried to upsell me at Bloomingdale's. It had been hard to resist.

"Vito can handle explosives, but what about her?" Gage lifted his chin in Milan's direction.

By way of answer, Milan threw ten knives in quick succession, forming a frame around Gage's head in the thick wooden pillar behind him.

"Yeah, I remember the knives." He absently touched his shoulder. "You got any other tricks?"

Milan shrugged off her jacket and posed beside the wall. She was wearing a pair of tight black shorts over fishnet tights and a midriff-baring tank cut deep to reveal her substantial cleavage. With a flip of her long, dark hair and a pout of her lips, she earned herself the role of our Distraction.

Gage coughed lightly after I explained that Milan's role would be to distract people from what we were doing and then use her knives if anyone got in the way. When I looked in his direction, he drew a line across his throat. I wasn't oblivious to the threat. Gage wasn't the kind of man who made statements like, "They're gonna slit our throats at the end," without good reason. But Clare needed us alive to do the heist, so I tucked that worry away for later.

I could see the crew getting antsy, so I decided to wrap things up. "We'll meet back here tomorrow. Emma, you drive around Vera's house and check out escape routes. Jack, you can take another look at those tunnel doors. Vito, you can start putting together an explosive to blast the tunnel door if Jack can't find a way to get it open from the outside. Chloe will work on cameras and hacking the security system. Simone is going to find out when they're leaving for their cruise and whether there is any chance Vera would be interested in hosting an event. Clare can buy the list of supplies I've posted on the server—"

"What about Anil?" Chloe asked.

"Anil . . ." I trailed off when I saw he'd moved to sit beside Clare and was now whispering in her ear. "Anil."

"Yes, ma'am."

"Don't call me that. It makes me feel old."

"You are old," he said. "Approximately four dog years."

"We'll need a fake Florentine Diamond," I said, ignoring his insult. "There are pictures online of the replica in the museum in Vienna and Chloe has pulled up some additional pictures from the Internet. Do you still have access to the 3D jewelry printers at your work?"

"I run the department now," Anil said proudly. "I can make whatever illicit jewels I want, when I want, how I want."

"I'll help Anil get the specs for the diamond," Clare said, "and if I have free time, I can help Jack."

I didn't want her to help Jack, but I could hardly play the jealous girlfriend when I'd broken things off. I also didn't want Clare to know I cared. It was better to let her think her ploy to destroy our relationship had worked, rather than to let her know that every time I looked at Jack, I wanted to believe every story he'd told me about being detained in submarines, thrown out windows, and left in ditches. I wanted to believe that he was indeed part of a secret covert organization and not just a professional thief with a conscience. I wanted to believe that maybe there was a chance for us to work through our issues, rebuild our trust, and find our way back to each other. But deep down, doubts still lingered. Deep down, I was still afraid.

THIRTEEN

◆ ◆ ◆

S imone called me at seven the next morning. She hadn't mastered the art of messaging, so I was jolted awake by the unfamiliar jangling of my phone.

"Good news," Simone said. "Someone died."

"Uh . . . okay . . . ?"

"It's Vera's husband's nephew. He was a bad sort. He got involved with a Mexican drug cartel and killed a few innocent people during an armed robbery. He'd been in Sing Sing prison for the last five years, and last night, someone shanked him in the shower. Isn't that wonderful? I already sent a message to Vera offering your event services to do a circus celebration of life at her house. She loves a good party."

I didn't know whether I was more surprised that Simone knew the word *shanked* or that she had quickly turned what was a suspiciously convenient death into a criminal opportunity. "Well . . . um . . . let us know what she says."

"She says yes."

"That was fast."

"They don't want the funeral to interfere with their upcoming cruise, so she was happy not to have to plan it all herself." She crowed in delight. "It's perfect. Peter's family will all be there for the first time since the new house was built, and no doubt he'll want to show off his new museum. Vera says most of them have never seen a piece of art. Can you meet us at her place at nine?"

I wasn't one to look a shanked-drug-dealer gift horse in the mouth, so I arrived at the Hearst mansion at nine A.M. on the dot. I immediately felt underdressed in my work-casual black pants and patterned shirt when a coiffed and heavily made-up Vera swanned into the vast marble foyer of her mansion in a swath of chiffon and beige cashmere with diamonds dripping from both wrists.

Vera was tall and thin, with long, sharp features and botoxed lips. Her hair was dyed platinum blond and she had a way of looking at me that didn't involve our eyes meeting as people's eyes usually did when they conversed.

Vera didn't just want a circus-themed celebration of life. She said, "It's been done, darling. It must be a circus on steroids, bigger and better than anything you've ever done before. Peter's brother Raoul is married to Caroline Wilmington of the Rhode Island Wilmingtons, so everybody who is anybody will be there. Raoul was also very successful in tech, although if I'd known about the criminal element in the family, I would never have introduced them. We're telling people Peter's nephew was mugged . . ." She gave me an expectant look and I nodded, happy not to have to share the sordid details of his demise.

"Does Thursday afternoon around four work?" she continued. "We've booked the funeral home for a private cremation earlier that afternoon. After that's over, we'll have the party."

I had a feeling she'd forgotten that the point of the event was to remember someone who had died, but she was the client, so I tried not to judge.

"It will be tight, but I can get it done," I said. "We could put a miniature circus ring here in the yard with different acts happening over the course of the afternoon." I'd never seen anything like Vera's house. Three Queen Anne Victorian mansions from the 1880s sitting on a triple lot in the Gold Coast had been renovated into one grand mansion with one lot used as an extensive, impeccably landscaped outdoor space, something almost unheard of in Chicago. Usually, city lots were twenty-five feet wide, but this one was fifty feet, giving it the estate-like feel you usually only find in the suburbs. Behind it, a large mudroom connected the house to the original rear stable / coach house, which had been turned into a five-car garage with a second-floor apartment for staff.

"I want an elephant," Vera said. "I heard you can get elephants."

"Unfortunately, since the only way to your yard is through your house, I don't think an elephant is feasible. I'll see what else I can come up with."

"I've always loved the circus." Vera smiled. "Tell the caterers I want popcorn and cotton candy and a flying trapeze."

"Will people be allowed indoors, or do you want to restrict the event to the garden?" I asked, wondering if my insurance would cover death by trapeze.

"I'm happy for people to come inside on the main floor. We have so much space and it doesn't get used with just the two of us. The upper level will be off-limits, but Peter will likely be taking his family and some friends downstairs to see his museum."

"We should probably check it out." I tried to sound casual, although my heart was thudding in my chest. "I have a security team for all my events, and I'll want to brief them about where people can and can't go."

"Of course." Vera led us down a carpeted flight of stairs to the lower level. We walked past a fitness room, theater, yoga studio, sauna, underground pool, and then into a large, fully outfitted games room. She pressed her finger to a biometric pad on the wall and a door slid open to reveal a small sitting room, ornately decorated with wood-paneled walls and striped wallpaper. Two luxurious full-length mirrors flanked a small minibar on one end, and a giant TV screen faced an opulent cream couch on the other.

"This is our panic room," she said. "It's entirely secure, with bulletproof walls and doors. And if someone does get through"— she pressed her finger on a small indentation beside one of the mirrors, and it swung open to reveal a wide passageway—"we can escape into the bunker. Peter is convinced an apocalypse is imminent. He designed this space so we could survive for years without having to go outside, although I don't think I'd last a week locked up with him in only ten thousand square feet of space."

"Is this the only way out?" I studied the thick metal security door with the biometric panel beside it. "What if it gets stuck? Or you lose electricity?"

"It has its own power source," she said. "But Peter also designed an escape tunnel that leads under the garden to a back alley. I bought a painting to cover the door because it was so hideous, but aside from that, I don't know much about it. To be honest, I was more interested in making the house comfortable than preparing for a doomsday that is never going to happen."

Vera led me through the door and gave me a tour of the bunker. It was bigger than my parents' entire home and included LED panels to simulate windows, a designer kitchen, den, wine room, four bedrooms, a plunge pool and sauna, gym, movie room, two lounges, a games room, a huge vault with a round steel door and spinning lock, and more.

"The museum is through there." She pointed to an ornate wooden double door. "I rarely go in because it's not really to my taste."

"Oh, let's see it, darling," Simone said. "You've made me curious."

With a sigh, Vera pressed her finger against the biometric panel and the ornate wooden double doors opened, revealing at their edges a core of steel.

Peter's museum was about one thousand square feet of rich wood paneling, sophisticated spotlights, plush red carpet, and velvet benches. Paintings of all shapes and styles hung on the walls in thick frames. Pillars with glass cases containing jewelry and statues were interspersed with large sculptures in the center of the room, and at one end there was a row of glass cases filled with an assortment of curious objects. It took me a moment to take it all in, and then it hit me.

"You can see why I never come in here and would never allow his art, if you can even call it that, upstairs," Vera said. "It just so . . . tasteless."

I didn't need to know anything about art to understand her concerns. Peter's collection included some of the most erotic artwork I'd ever seen—everything from paintings of couples in highly sexual poses to ancient stone fertility statues. I spotted a hardwood chest carved with scenes from the *Kama Sutra*, some Chinese pillow books, and the Marquis de Sade's *La Nouvelle Justine*, but more disturbing was the collection of ancient and not-so-ancient intimacy objects in a glass case.

"Erotic art is easier to get on the black market," Vera said. "If not for his fetish, I don't think he would have gotten involved with the kind of people who convinced him that he was some kind of Indiana Jones–type character and encouraged him to become a treasure hunter." She pointed to a worn yellow-and-white skull. "He thinks this is one of the Peking man skulls that disappeared from Beijing during the Japanese invasion of China, and that"— she pointed to a book in a glass case—"is supposedly a first-century surviving copy of the canonical Christian gospels." She gestured to an ornate green egg on an enameled stand. "He is convinced that this is one of the missing imperial Fabergé eggs, and over here"—she gave a bitter laugh as she pointed to another glass case—"are supposedly the lost crown jewels of Ireland."

"Do you think they're all fake?" The artifacts certainly looked genuine to my untrained eye, if old, cracked, and worn were any indicator.

"Of course they're fake," she said. "The people who organize these treasure hunts for him are dubious characters at best. They got him hooked on the thrill of the chase. I'm certain they make fake objects and arrange fake meetings with pretend princes so they can pocket the millions of dollars he pays for these supposedly lost treasures. He's got a trip planned after Christmas to go to France to find the legendary Scepter of Dagobert."

"An expert could easily determine their authenticity," Simone said. "Don't you have a curator for your collection? Surely they could give you a quick assessment. Or does Peter not get someone to look at them before he transfers the funds?"

"Peter won't let anyone except his closest friends near them," Vera said. "He's afraid that a foreign government might make a claim for repatriation, or that a descendant might claim ownership. He'll be upset that I was even in here, and I'm sure I'll pay a price. When he does bring people in to show off his collection, he won't even take the pieces out of the cases. Everything is alarmed and temperature controlled. He truly believes these are the real deal."

"At least they're down here," Simone said. "You don't have to look at them."

"They won't be here for much longer." Vera pointed to a stack of cardboard boxes and large wooden crates in the corner. For the first time since we'd entered the bunker, a smile tugged at Vera's lips. "Peter bought a private art island in the Mediterranean and we're taking his entire collection with us when we leave on the yacht next weekend. I insisted we also bring the artwork from the vault. We don't have enough space here to do it justice, and the pieces are truly priceless. I had him build a special wing in the new museum just to display it. The special art shippers came last week to assess everything, and they dropped off the packing materials yesterday afternoon. Peter even hired a special curator to travel with us and set up the new museum when we arrive on the island."

"Richard has been toying with the idea of buying an art island, too," Simone said. "We went to see a twenty-six-acre property off the Florida coast, but he thought it was too small. I told him we should just buy a super-yacht like yours, and then we're not tied to one place, but sales are currently so buoyant there's a three-year waiting list. We could just buy an island next month."

Just buy an island. It was an almost unbelievable conversation. Simone and Vera lived in an entirely different world.

"It sounds like a difficult decision," I said, nodding in feigned sympathy while Simone and Vera had a conversation about which pieces she wanted to keep in the city—the Picasso, definitely, but not the Gauguin, and heavens, she couldn't part with her Renoir—and which would go to the island.

I was about to turn away from the salubrious display of erotic toys when a sparkle of yellow caught my eye. There, nestled in a sea of blue velvet, was a sparkling yellow diamond with an elegant handwritten card beside it that read, *Florentine Diamond*. On a rough guess it was just over one inch long and less than an inch wide. I was surprised at how something so small could be worth so much, and it stood out because of its relative normalcy compared to everything else.

"That's his newest acquisition," Vera said, following my gaze. "He says it's the real Florentine Diamond. He 'found'"—she emphasized the word with finger quotes—"it in the private collection of an Ottoman prince whose family were exiled from Turkey in the early 1920s and came to America to live in Pensacola. They had fallen into bad times and he had his people broker a deal to buy it. Foreign princes in Pensacola. Can you imagine? He was so adamant it was real that I actually checked the history of the diamond with De Beers. They said it had to be a fake. They support the theory that the real diamond was last seen intact in 1918 and was subsequently recut into something much smaller. The whole thing is utterly ridiculous, and I told him so." She unconsciously touched her left eye. "But it's his money and if he wants to throw it all away . . ."

"Darling." Simone gave her hand a squeeze. "I know."

"Be careful of men who are too charming," Vera said. "Peter swept me off my feet and made me laugh. He won over my parents when he offered them a substantial interest-free loan to save them from bankruptcy. I thought he did it because he loved me, but I was just a means to an end. If someone had told me he had criminals in the family . . ." She shook her head. "He made me sign a prenup. I'll get next to nothing if I walk away, and the loan to my family will come due immediately. They'll be ruined. I just thank God that he was never interested in having children."

"I'll put one of my security guys on the stairwell and have him periodically check downstairs to make sure no one has slipped through," I assured her, putting her warning about charming men on the back burner. "Hopefully the guests will be happy to stay out in the garden."

Wary of the 24/7 cameras recording our every movement in the museum, I made notes on my phone with the details of the camera positions, access panels, size and placement of the display cases, and the possible trajectory of the floor lasers that I assumed were the purpose of the black outlets near the floor. As a recon mission it was a total success.

"It's a shame about the elephant," Vera said, leading me up the stairs. "Now, that would have been a celebration of life to die for."

FOURTEEN

◇ ◇ ◇

We reconvened the next day in the warehouse. Vito, embracing his demolitions role, demonstrated his newest explosive by blowing up one of Jack's practice safes. Emma was entranced.

Simone was the last to arrive, rushing in just after I'd spread the blueprints over the large wooden table, her silk scarf fluttering behind her.

"Am I missing something here?" Chloe whispered after Simone excitedly told everyone about the shanked nephew and her role in securing my event company for his celebration of life. "I mean, the dude is barely dead and they're organizing a party. And why? He was a murderer."

"He was also someone's son," I pointed out. "Maybe he was good before he turned bad."

"I'm more concerned about the convenient coincidence," Jack murmured under his breath. "I do this for a living and it's suspicious even to me."

"She's a socialite who doesn't even know how to message on her phone," I said. "How would she have arranged to have some random criminal shanked in the shower in a prison in New York?"

"People will surprise you," Jack said. "I never expected to

meet the woman of my dreams attempting to break into a museum in the rain."

My heart skipped a little beat at the memory. Jack had dragged me into the bushes to save me from the police and not once had I been afraid. Even then, there had been something about him—some connection that went straight to my heart.

Anil was almost bouncing up and down with excitement. "I'll do magic tricks. My parents give me a magic set every year at Christmas. Last year they gave me a box for sawing people in half and a real saw."

"Your parents scare me," Emma said to him. "They seemed nice when we met them, but the things they're prepared to do to make you happy . . ."

"Chloe, I need you to be in the box," Anil called out. "I'm going to saw you in half and—"

Gage cut him off with a growl. "She's not getting in any damn box."

"It's a trick," Anil protested.

"The only trick Chloe's doing with you is the one where she disappears before you show up."

"Although I appreciate the sentiment"—Chloe gave Gage a warning look—"I can make my own decisions about whether I get sawed in half."

"What if it goes wrong, babe?" Gage protested. "I don't want to have to put Anil in the box and saw off his body parts one by one while he screams in agony. And then I'll have to saw up those pieces and saw the pieces into pieces and then I'll keep sawing pieces until there's nothing left. Do you really want him to suffer? Think of his parents. All they'll have left to bury is the fucking box they gave him for Christmas. That's called irony."

"I used to have a side gig as a clown," Emma interjected. "I've got the costume, the juggling pins, and all the toys. I'm set."

"I hate clowns," Gage muttered. "Not showing up if there are clowns present."

"When did you become so high-maintenance?" I asked him. "No sawing your girlfriend in half. No clowns. What's next? Do you have a problem with trapeze artists, too?"

"Only if they're monkeys," he muttered. "Hate monkeys."

"There will be no monkeys at the celebration of life," I assured him. "It will be a somber, respectful, and dignified circus. Any more potential acts?"

"I can eat fire." Vito looked up from the safe he'd just exploded, dazzling me with his smooth velvet voice.

"Have you ever eaten fire before?"

By way of response, Vito pulled out his bus ticket and lit it on fire.

"Please don't eat that flaming bus ticket right now," I said. "This place is supposed to be secret, and it will be ruined if we have to call an ambulance." I looked over at Chloe. "Add that to my list of 'things I never thought I'd say in my lifetime.'"

"Is this for real?" Clare walked into the center of the room. "This is the crew that stole the Wild Heart from Joseph Angelini?" She shook her head at Jack. "Are you messing with me? How are they not all dead?"

"That's really offensive," I said. "We absolutely slayed that heist. In fact, we slayed two heists—"

"To be fair, the first one failed, which is why we had to do the second one," Anil said, cutting me off.

Emma glared at him. "Shut up, Anil."

"And we worked well together," I continued. "We were a well-oiled machine, each of us doing what we did best—"

"Until you all got kidnapped and Gage was knocked unconscious, and Rose and I had to come and save you." Anil looked over at Clare and shrugged. "I thought you should know the facts."

"Thanks, hon." She gave him a slow, sensual smile. "It's nice to know someone here understands what it means to be part of a serious team."

Anil dipped his head and looked up at her through the thicket of his dark brown eyelashes. I almost heaved.

Chloe gave me a nudge and whispered, "He likes her."

"More than likes her. I think he's trying to flirt in his awkward Anil way."

"I mean . . ." Chloe shrugged. "She is an attractive woman and she's really working that dress."

I turned on my bestie. "Whose side are you on?"

"Yours. Always. She's a total hag. Her hair is overbleached. She could benefit from some shape wear. Those four-inch heels are totally impractical for a heist, and I'll bet she found that dress in her grandmother's attic."

"Actually, the dress is Gucci Couture Spring 2022," Simone whispered. "And the shoes are Manolo, this season. Her only flaw is that she didn't read the room. I would never wear Gucci to a decrepit warehouse. Balenciaga, yes. I brought my Balenciaga trash pouch after I had my assistant look up the location of the warehouse. Moschino definitely. If you watched his show in Milan, it was garbage couture, and I don't mean that in the pejorative sense. His models were literally dressed in garbage bags. My skin doesn't do well in plastic, so I went for Prada couture casual with these lovely Dior J'Adior slingback flats in case we have to do some running away."

Chloe and I shared a look. Sometimes I suspected that Simone didn't realize how she sounded to ordinary people.

"How do you know your skin doesn't do well in plastic?" Chloe asked the question I wanted to ask but hadn't asked because I didn't really want to hear the answer.

"Oh, darling." Simone waved a hand in the air. "So innocent.

Get naked and wrap yourself in plastic kitchen wrap, then lie on the kitchen table when your man comes home from work. You'll never have to worry that he's going to stray, at least not until the novelty wears off."

I held up my hand when Chloe opened her mouth to ask Simone a question. "Don't," I said. "I can guarantee you won't be prepared for where this conversation is going to go."

I heard a *whoosh*, a gasp, a choked cry. Turning my attention to the back of the room, I spotted Vito with his lips pressed tight together, smoke pouring out his nose, and a guilty look on his face.

I folded my arms and glared. "Did you eat the burning bus ticket after I told you not to?"

Vito shook his head.

"Open your mouth."

He shook his head again.

"Open it or you're going to suffocate and I'm not calling an ambulance because then we'll need to find another decrepit warehouse for Simone to accessorize with her $2,000 garbage handbag." I was beyond irritated. No wonder Clare couldn't believe we could get the job done.

"To be precise, it's called the Trash Bag Large Pouch, darling."

"Sorry, Simone. I'm just feeling a bit overwhelmed by the fact that no one seems to be taking this seriously, and if the event doesn't go well, I'll be on the hook. Aside from the fact that we're trying to pull off a heist, my company's reputation is on the line."

Emma put her fingers in her mouth and blew an ear-piercing whistle. "Anyone else with skills that might be useful for a circus celebration of life?"

"How about a little knife throwing?" Gage gestured toward Milan.

Chloe shook her head. "Don't you think it would be in poor taste considering the dude was stabbed to death?"

"He was shanked," Simone said. "Apparently, it's not the same. They make shanks out of shaved-down items like plastic toothbrushes, strips of metal or wood."

I clapped my hands to get everybody's attention. "We need to focus on the heist and not the circus. I'll integrate you with my vendors—catering, decorating, performance, and serving staff, and I'll post your assignments on the secure server. You'll have an on-site job plus a heist mission. For example, Chloe and Gage will be our on-site security team, but really, they'll be dealing with the cameras and security system. We have to prepare for two possibilities. Either Peter will be bringing people downstairs to the museum, in which case we need to find a way to get at least two people down there with him, or Peter doesn't open the museum and we have three doors with biometric sensors to get through before we even get close to the diamond, not to mention the cameras outside, and the laser beams and the sensors inside."

"It's not possible to bypass the biometrics," Anil said. "I looked at the information you wrote down from your visit. If they'd been optical, capacitive, or mechanical scanners, we could possibly have fooled them, but they are thermal—very high-end. They detect the heat given off by your finger, stronger or weaker where the ridges touch. They are completely impossible to fool with paper or a lifted print on tape or even attached to a substrate. You need the actual finger. Maybe more experienced thieves have a way to bypass them, but not us."

"I'll ask Peter to take us for a tour," Simone said. "Don't you worry."

"I am worried," I said. "What if he says no? We'll need a plan C."

"I'll be plan C." Chloe pulled her hair out of its usual ponytail, letting it fall in a golden sheet across her shoulders. "Vera said he enjoys entertaining young ladies downstairs . . ."

"No fucking way." Gage's bark echoed in the room. "Not letting you go into a bunker alone with some middle-aged perverted treasure hunter who collects stone dildos." Gage folded his arms across his chest. "Simi can go."

"Simi's not going, either," Jack said firmly.

I'd never seen this side of Jack, and although I could make my own decisions about whether to indulge in a little erotic art appreciation in a bunker alone with the man who had hurt Vera, his protective tone made me feel warm inside—not because I needed protecting, but because it meant he cared.

"It's not up to either of you," Chloe said, her voice laced with irritation. "And if you recall, Gage, your overprotective bullshit got you friend-zoned. Keep pushing and you'll be in enemy territory."

I heard a *whoosh* and three knives thunked into the wood above Gage's head.

"For fuck's sake!" He leaped forward. "I can't work with freaking knives flying around."

I looked over and caught Milan's gaze. For the first time since I'd met her, I saw a smile. "She was helping Chloe make a point," I said, acting on a hunch. "Play nice or she'll knife you."

Gage scowled at Milan. She held his gaze and stared at him, unblinking, until he backed down. "Send her," he said. "Or Clare."

"Absolutely not." I shook my head. "I have no reason to think they'd do anything other than take the diamond and we'd never see them again. Plan C is Chloe. End of discussion."

Gage opened his mouth to protest, and another knife landed above his head.

"Thank you for that, Milan," I said politely. "Although the sentiment is greatly appreciated, perhaps you could hold back on throwing knives at the overprotective crew members for now."

We spent the rest of the day practicing everything from handing off the diamond to helping a Lycra-clad Clare twist through what we had roughly figured out to be the arrangement of the laser array while Anil cheered her on. Chloe worked on a plan to hack into the home security system to loop camera feeds and deactivate the museum sensors, and Emma used a driving program to test escape options in different types of traffic. Vito alternated between swallowing burning pieces of paper and blowing up random things in the warehouse. Jack showed us how to quickly change the real stone for the fake to fool the sensors if Chloe was not able to deactivate them, and Simone took detailed notes on everything we did.

"I'm a bit concerned about the cohesiveness of this crew," Chloe said when we stopped for a break. "The newbies are causing a lot of friction. Maybe we should do some team-bonding exercises."

"I don't think anyone wants to bond with Milan and Vito. I get a strange vibe from them. Maybe Gage is right and they are professional assassins just waiting to kill us when we get the diamond."

"I'm not sure about Milan." She dropped her voice to a low murmur. "I don't think she likes her brother, or Clare. You saw how she was when Gage got all in my face . . ."

"What was that all about? What did you mean you friend-zoned him?"

"I broke up with him," Chloe said quietly.

"What?!" I immediately forgot about the crew and the heist and grabbed her by the shoulders. "I thought you were solid—well, as solid as you can be with someone who flits in and out of town on mysterious jobs like Jack. Why didn't you talk to me? Why didn't you let me know when it happened and I could have come over?"

Chloe shrugged. "We were okay until the Mafia guy showed up at our circus celebration. Gage told me that was it for me and the heist. I was done. Out. It was too dangerous. He wouldn't let me be involved. I told him—"

"I can imagine what you told him." Chloe was all sweetness and light, but she had a core of steel.

"So, it's over." Her voice trembled. "After being bossed around by Kyle for all those years, there is no way I'm letting a man tell me how to live my life, even if it comes from a good place. Overprotective is nice. Too much is almost as bad as Kyle's abuse."

"I'm sorry, babe." I gave her a hug. "You have to do what's right for you."

I was about to get everybody back to work when Milan held a cautioning hand in the air. Everyone froze as she slipped through the shadows to the warehouse door. I heard a bang and then a thud and then a familiar voice said, "Ow."

"Olivia?" Chloe stared, aghast, as Milan shoved Olivia forward into the room.

"This your kid?"

"I'm not a kid. I'm fifteen." Olivia pulled herself up, towering over Chloe in her three-inch platform Demonia Goth boots. She'd dyed her hair green the previous week and was wearing ripped black stockings, a torn black skirt, and a green-and-black-striped shirt that made her look like a demented Waldo. She'd drawn odd squares on her cheeks and across the bridge of her nose. Even without the knives, I was more afraid of Olivia than the professional assassin behind her.

"Olivia Dawn." Chloe's hands found her hips. "What are you doing here?"

"I knew you and Simi were up to something," she said, her voice wavering. "You were always whispering and looking serious, and we didn't hang out last weekend. I thought maybe we needed more money and you were doing another heist, and this time I wanted to help."

"It wasn't a heist," Chloe corrected her. "We were just retrieving a stolen item and returning it to its rightful owner."

"Sure, Mom. I get it. But this time I want in. I have skills. I've been here for an hour, and no one knew. I can dress as a server at the circus funeral thing and listen to conversations for you. People won't notice me."

"You are absolutely not getting involved," Chloe said firmly. "This is a dangerous situation with dangerous people. I'm calling an Uber and sending you straight home."

"If it's dangerous, why are you doing it?" she demanded. "What if something happens to you? You need me, Mom. I'm not just good at blending in. I understand modern technology and social media in a way you Boomers never will. I can help you."

"Boomers?" I snorted my disdain. "We're barely even Millennials."

"She just says that to irritate us." Chloe patted my arm. "If I didn't know you, I'd guess you were Gen Z. You're just that cool. And you don't like avocados."

"I don't like toast, either," I muttered. "Or working on just one screen."

"I'm pretty sure that social media isn't going to help us get a diamond out of an underground museum," Chloe said, turning back to Olivia. "My old-school hacking skills will work just fine." She pointed to the door. "Let's go."

"Gage, tell her." Olivia shot Gage a plaintive look, all dewy eyes and downturned lips. If she hadn't been offering to put herself in danger, it would have worked. Gage was tough, but when it came to Olivia, he was a softie inside.

"Are you fucking kidding me?" He folded his arms. "Don't even try it with that face. If I had my way, you *and* your mom would be staying home."

"I think we're done here anyway." I rolled up the blueprints on the table. "I'll send out next steps on the server."

While everyone gathered up their stuff and made their way out, I made a quick check of the warehouse to ensure all Vito's fires were out before heading to the door.

"You don't need to stick around," I said to Jack when I saw him lurking outside. "Emma is taking me home with Olivia and Chloe."

"Just wanted to make sure you were okay," he said. "You seemed stressed."

"There are just too many unknowns. Last time we knew exactly what kind of system they used, and it was easy for Chloe to hack. We had the location of the necklace—"

"But it wasn't where we thought it was," he pointed out as he walked me to Emma's car. "We had to improvise."

"The stakes are much higher this time. The security is much tighter. And what if the jewel is a fake like the other items in the collection? We'll be taking a huge risk for no reward."

"Our deal was to get the jewel in that museum in exchange for the necklace," he assured me. "If it is a fake, that's Clare's problem."

"What if she won't give us the necklace?"

"She will," he said. "Her boss approved the deal. It's a matter of honor."

"How do you know him?"

"I'll trade you an answer for a kiss." He backed me up against Emma's car and trailed a warm finger along my jaw.

"Jack . . ."

"If you don't want to know, I'll get going." He moved to leave, and I grabbed his arm.

Jack leaned in and his lips brushed over mine, sending delicious shivers down my spine. "We worked for the same person for many years."

"Was it Mr. X?"

"Yes. That's two questions. Two kisses."

His kiss was soft and gentle at first, but quickly turned urgent and demanding, as if he had been waiting for this moment all afternoon.

Unable to resist, I wrapped my arms around his neck and deepened the kiss, our tongues tangling, stroking, tasting each other. Jack's hands moved down my back to my hips, pulling me closer to him. I could feel his hardness pressing against my thigh and a moan escaped my lips.

He pulled back for a moment, his eyes raking over my body, as if memorizing every curve. "So beautiful," he murmured, his hands gripping my hips tighter.

The loud blast of Emma's horn jolted us apart. "Get a room," she shouted through her open window.

"I have to go." With the greatest reluctance, I pulled away. "Emma is waiting to verbally eviscerate me as soon as I step into her car."

"I'm not going anywhere," Jack said. "Not this time. Not ever again."

"You say that like it's a threat."

His face softened. "It's a promise. I'm here for you until you send me away."

FIFTEEN

◆ ◆ ◆

Someone was sleeping in the hallway outside my apartment door Wednesday night when I finally got home, exhausted from four days of trying to juggle work, family, and heist preparations with the crew in the warehouse.

"Did it ever occur to you to wait until I'm home and then call and ask if you can come over like a normal person?" I stepped over Jack's prone body to unlock my door.

"I was worried you'd say no."

"That's exactly what I would have said." Sometimes Jack reminded me of my younger brothers when they were naughty but too cute to be punished.

"But now we're both here so we can talk." He gave me a hopeful smile. "Can I come in?"

"Are you a vampire? Will you be physically unable to come in unless I invite you?"

"No, but I won't come in if you don't want me."

"Honestly," I said. "I don't know what I want. I'm exhausted and starving. I was going to just order a pizza and chill."

"I already ordered a pizza from Skip. It should be here in a few minutes."

"Double mushroom and pepperoni?"

"Yes."

"Extra cheese?"

"Yes."

"Side of cheesy bread and a bottle of Sprite?"

"Yes and yes."

"What about dessert?"

"They're bringing a dozen donuts from your favorite place on Franklin Street."

How could I say no? I was weak. I was a total foodie. And I hadn't eaten since breakfast. I moved to the side. "You may come in. We need to debrief before tomorrow anyway."

Jack walked in and shrugged off his leather jacket. He was wearing a black T-shirt that hugged every hard ripple of his muscular body. So sexy. Sweat beaded on my forehead and trickled down my back. Had I left the heat on? Was the window closed? Why was I wearing so many clothes?

"What do you want to talk about?" I took off my jacket and tossed it beside my purse on the nearest table. It was just a jacket. People didn't wear jackets indoors. No other clothes were going to be removed.

"You've got a lot on your plate," he said. "Talk is the best therapy for stress."

"I'll deal with my stress in my usual way," I said. "It involves watching romantic comedies with Chloe while eating Chinese food and ice cream, but not at the same time. Any other topics you want to discuss?"

"Anil can't be trusted anymore." He followed me to the kitchen. "He's in Clare's thrall."

"Thrall? What is this? The eighteenth century?" I pulled two pops out of the fridge and handed one to him. My pinkie may have extended slightly to brush over his knuckles, or that zing of electricity that shot through my veins may have been caused by a faulty fridge wire. Either way, the resulting rush of heat was exacerbated by the excess-clothing situation.

"She seduced him," Jack said, flexing his hand. "She'll turn him against us. I think we should cut him loose."

"I think you're underestimating him. He surprised us once before. Maybe he'll do it again."

"Not when Clare is involved. She can be very persuasive." Jack made his way into my living room and settled on the couch, feet up on my coffee table. I lifted an eyebrow in warning. He put them down.

"You're not helping your cause if you came over here for more than talking." I settled beside him. "I don't want to hear again about how Clare handcuffed you to her bed during a romantic Nile cruise so she could have her way with you in some naughty sex game before stealing something out from under your nose or whatever."

Jack grinned. "The only fun part of that encounter was when I threw her overboard."

Now, that caught my interest. "Really?"

"I picked the lock on the handcuffs when she wasn't looking."

"Were you naked?"

Jack took a long sip of his pop. "She drugged my wine and broke into my room after I went to sleep."

"Why wasn't she looking at you while you were picking the lock? I've seen you naked and I had no desire to look away." Okay. Maybe I was flirting a bit. But it was his fault for showing up looking all gorgeous when I was at my weakest, having had very little sleep or food over the last few insanely busy days.

He gave me a slow, seductive smile. "She was looking for something I'd retrieved that she wanted."

"I still wouldn't have looked away," I said. "Even if it was a $200 million diamond."

Jack laughed, and for a moment it was like old times. "I escaped, grabbed her, and tossed her over the balcony. She almost drowned."

"An opportunity missed," I mused.

"Unfortunately, someone saw me, and I was arrested and put in prison."

"But you got out."

"Clearly."

"So, she was lying about that," I said. "Was she lying about you and her?"

"There is no me and her except for an ill-considered few months in the very, very distant past. There is only me and you." He pulled me into a straddle across his lap and put his arms around me. I could feel my tension ease. It felt right in Jack's arms. Like coming home.

"That feels nice," I whispered. "It's been a rough week so far. I haven't had a chance to catch my breath. We went from wondering how to get into the Hearst mansion to a shanked-nephew celebration of life falling in our laps twelve hours later, and I had to hit the ground running. I still can't believe it."

"It was an incredible coincidence." Jack nuzzled my neck. "Almost too incredible."

"I thought so, too, but how could Simone arrange for someone to be shanked in a prison in New York? She has no understanding of the real world of normal people. I don't think she understands that our lives are truly at risk. But something just feels off."

Jack pulled away, twisting his lips to the side, considering. I liked that little quirk of his lips when he was thinking hard. It let me know that he was serious about the conversation. "I know someone who used to be at Sing Sing," he said finally. "We could ask him about Peter's nephew's murder. He might still have contacts there who could tell us what happened. That kind of thing occurs all the time in prison, so it might just be a fortuitous turn of events, but in any event, it would put your mind at ease."

"You said 'we' . . . " I hesitated, not overly keen to meet Jack's criminal contact. "Is he . . . safe?"

"He was a guard," Jack said, laughing. "Not a prisoner. He's working at Cook County Jail now, but he should be getting off his shift in about an hour. I can offer to buy him a few drinks in exchange for some information."

"I don't know . . . maybe I'm just overthinking things. It's late. We have the heist slash celebration of life tomorrow. I need to be at my best."

"I brought my motorcycle and an extra helmet . . ."

A smile tugged at the corners of my lips. I loved riding on Jack's motorcycle. I loved the freedom, the speed, the wind in my face . . . "First we have pizza and donuts," I said. "Then we go and meet your friend."

An hour later we pulled up in front of the Iron Cell, a bar just off East Pershing Road in Bronzeville. Pressed tight against Jack's back, with my arms around his waist and nothing to think about but the world rushing by, I could have stayed on his bike forever.

The scents of old beer and fried food wafted through the door as we walked past the flickering neon sign and down the stairs. Inside, the bar was a symphony of sounds: the clink of glasses, the low hum of conversation, the occasional burst of laughter, and the catchy rhythm of "Sweet Home Alabama" playing over the tinny speakers.

We found Jack's contact, George Mendez, hunched over a half-empty pint in a dark corner near the dartboard. He was a mountain of a man, his broad shoulders a testament to years spent maintaining order in the jail.

Jack introduced me as a friend, and we chatted about George's work both as a corrections officer and as a former soldier until our drinks arrived. The conversation shifted to stories about the past punctuated by coded phrases and veiled references to their shared history. I sipped my drink, listening quietly as I tried to piece together their relationship. George was at least twenty years older than Jack, but they'd clearly worked together several times, although what a professional thief and a prison guard could have in common, I didn't know.

"Jack's had a lot of lady friends." George's eyes twinkled with mischief as he turned his attention back to me. "Never met one like you."

"What do you mean 'like me'?"

Jack's face remained impassive, but his eyes hardened slightly. "We're here on business, George."

George's smile faded, replaced by a stern, no-nonsense expression. "Cut the chatter, is that it? Well, let's get down to it, then."

Jack pushed an envelope across the table. "What did you find out?"

"I've still got a few contacts back in Sing Sing." George finished the last sip of his beer. "They said your boy was targeted. It was a mob hit."

"Mob?" I leaned forward. "Which mob? The New York five families or the Chicago Outfit?"

"New York," he said. "The other crime families—Chicago, Jersey, Pennsylvania, Ohio—don't usually operate in their territory."

I looked over at Jack. "I guess you were right. It was just a coincidence."

"Unless . . ." George tapped his empty glass and jerked his head in the direction of the bar.

Puzzled, I frowned. "Unless what?"

"I'll get us a fresh round of drinks." Jack grabbed the empty glasses and left the table.

"You drive a hard bargain," I said to George.

"Corrections doesn't pay very well." He leaned back in his chair and folded his arms behind his head. "I make most of my money on these side gigs."

"This is a side gig? Sharing information about what's going on in prison?"

"You'd better believe it." George tucked the envelope into his jacket. "Everyone wants to know what's going on inside. Friends, family, rival gangs, the DA, lawyers, cops . . . you name it."

"I never even imagined there was a business in prison information."

"And I never imagined I'd ever see Jack with a girl like you." He leaned forward, giving me a whiff of his beer breath. "What are you doing with him, honey? You're not his type."

For some reason his assertion rankled. "We're friends."

"You're not his friend," George said. "You're something else entirely, and I can't quite figure you out. You've made him go soft, and in the business he's in, soft isn't always a good thing."

"Are you trying to scare me?" I folded my arms. "Because it's not working."

"I'm saying that I've known Jack a long time and he's never been with a woman long enough to bring her to meet me. I'm saying you look like a nice girl from a nice suburban family, and you've probably got yourself a nice job and maybe a pretty apartment in a safe area of the city. You don't belong in Jack's world, and he doesn't belong in yours. My advice is to get out while you can."

I glared at him with a mixture of disbelief and annoyance. "You think you know everything about me, but I'm not a nice girl. I've done bad things. I've been arrested, handcuffed, and interrogated in the police station as an accessory to crime. I've broken laws. I've

been threatened, kidnapped, tied up, and I was an active partici-
pant in a high-speed car chase. I know who Jack is. I have a good
idea about what he does. And I can make my own decision about
whether we're good together or not, which, by the way, we are,
subject to smoothing out a few wrinkles."

George chuckled. "So, you're saying that what you see isn't what
you get. You're no lightweight."

"Damn right." I would have pounded the table with my fist for
effect, but Jack returned at that moment with two pints of beer and
a fancy cocktail with an umbrella and two cherries.

"What were you two talking about?"

George raised his glass in a toast. "Just getting to know the
Bonnie to your Clyde."

"You had something else to tell us," I reminded him. "You said
organized crime families wouldn't carry out a hit in another crime
family's territory unless . . ."

"Unless someone owed someone a favor, and even then, the hit
would have to be carried out by someone local—in this case, someone from the New York mob."

I scrubbed my hands over my face. "And no one would ever
know who was behind it? I mean, I guess the guards would know
who shanked him . . ."

"Not if they were paid to look the other way. The way the mob
operates, you never know who is pulling the strings."

George and Jack shared a few stories about a job they'd had in
Rio while I mulled over the new information. I couldn't see any
connection between Tony Angelini and Peter's nephew, and by the
time George had finished his drink and said his farewells, I'd decided we'd just been lucky.

"What were you and George talking about when I was getting
the drinks?" Jack asked as we put on our helmets outside.

"He said I wasn't your type. You would hurt me. A nice girl

like me shouldn't be with a bad boy like you. And that you hid many secrets."

"He's right."

"I'm not your type?"

"I didn't think I had a type," Jack said softly. "Now I know it's because I've been waiting for you."

My cheeks heated and I looked away. I didn't know how to react to his sweet but unexpected words. Jack was the type of man who kept his secrets close and his emotions even closer. But then so did I.

SIXTEEN

◇ ◇ ◇

Everything went smoothly at the celebration of life until Anil tried to saw Chloe in half.

We had great weather, and a good turnout of guests ranging from dubious to dramatic. My catering team outdid themselves, and the string quartet kept the vibe chill between circus performances. Emma made for a terrifying clown—more Pennywise than Bozo. Vito ate a range of flaming swords, set fire to his fingers, and lit cigarettes and vapes for all who asked. Clare did some mind-blowing acrobatics and walked a tightrope that she'd strung five feet off the ground. Milan threw knives at a delighted Simone against a plywood backdrop, making the crowd gasp with horrified pleasure.

Chloe, as Anil's assistant, had wandered around the party with him as he pulled coins from behind ears and doves from his sleeves, surreptitiously checking cameras and security until it was time for the big performance. An hour into the party, Chloe had found a way to loop the cameras and block the motion detectors, but Anil still hadn't solved the problem of the biometric panels. Vito was on standby to blast the tunnel door if everything went sideways, and

Milan had proved to be a very good "distraction" in her red leather outfit and thigh-high boots.

"You're supposed to be downstairs in case Peter takes anyone into the museum," I whispered to Gage when he suddenly appeared by my side for the "sawing Chloe in half" performance.

"You think I'm going to be anywhere except here when crazy Anil takes a saw to my girl?" he grumbled. "If she gets even one bruise, one cut, if she even loses a hair . . ."

"She'll be fine. He practiced it with his mom at home."

"Where is his mom? I haven't seen her," he grumbled. "She's probably buried in a shallow grave in the backyard."

"For some strange reason, she wasn't invited to a stranger's nephew's celebration of life," I retorted. "And Anil isn't the crazy one here. Get back downstairs. What if this is the time Peter decides to take his friends and family to see his collection of ancient dildos? What if someone else steals the diamond? I don't think my business insurance would cover something like that."

"Now who's the crazy one?" Gage muttered.

"You're here to do a job. I'll watch out for Chloe."

"With all due respect," he said. "And this is with full acknowledgment that you and Chloe have been best friends since you were kids, I'm not going anywhere. Jack can deal with the downstairs security. Where the fuck is he, anyway?"

"You know Jack. He's all over the place. He was following Peter around for a bit. So far, the dude hasn't invited a single person down to his chamber of erotic horrors. I think after Chloe is sawed in half, we'll have to put plan C into action."

Gage's faced tightened. "The plan where she goes down to a billionaire's sex dungeon alone? The plan I did not approve?"

"Yes, Gage. That plan, except she won't be alone. As soon as Chloe lets me know Peter is taking her down to the museum, I'll get Simone to intercept and join them. She can talk her way into anything. You should be happy. Plan C presumes she'll survive being sawed in half."

Gage growled his frustration. "If I don't die of a heart attack after today, it will be a miracle."

"You need to give her some space. She spent years dealing with Kyle's controlling behavior. The last thing she needs is more of the same."

"I lost people . . ." Gage stared out into the garden, where Anil was making a big production of getting Chloe into the box. "People I should have been able to save. I couldn't protect them. I can't let it happen again, especially not when it comes to someone I . . ." He trailed off, his eyes widening in horror. "For fuck's sake. Is that a real fucking saw?"

"Anil said he needed a real saw to make sawdust so the illusion would be realistic." I put a warning hand on his arm. "Don't ruin his trick. He knows what he's doing."

Gage shuddered, his big, hard body trembling as Anil sawed through the box. For a moment, I thought he wouldn't be able to hold himself back, but suddenly Olivia, dressed in a black server's uniform, was in front of him, wrapping her arms around his waist in a big hug.

"She'll be okay. I saw the trick on TikTok. There's no risk. None at all."

"What the hell?" He glared at Olivia. "What are you doing here, Liv? Your mother specifically forbade you from being involved."

"But isn't it a good thing?" she said. "You almost lost it, and I was here to save you."

"Your mom is going to be seriously pissed when she sees you." His face was stern, but his hand, as he ruffled her hair, was gentle. "This isn't a game, kid."

"I know, but I can't just sit home and do nothing when you're at risk of being whacked by the mob."

A reassembled Chloe stepped out of the box a few moments later to the applause and cheers of the crowd. Only seconds after her final bow, she spotted Olivia and rushed over to join us. Poor Olivia got an earful, although Chloe's tirade was delivered in a hushed whisper and behind a bush.

"You take that uniform off and go home this instant," she hissed, pulling Olivia to the side. "And don't think Gage will save you. If he wants any chance of being in our lives, he'll take you home himself."

"Chloe." I tugged on her arm with some urgency. "I know this is important, but we're running out of time and we need to move to plan C. Emma finished her clown gig and is waiting outside. I'll take Olivia to the car and Emma can look after her until we're done."

"But I know things," Olivia protested. "I've been here all afternoon listening to conversations, sneaking around, and taking pictures."

"Car." Chloe pulled out her ponytail and fluffed her hair. "I won't have you witness me destroying a hundred years of feminist progress."

"It's okay for feminists to flirt," Olivia said. "Seduction is also fine. Why shouldn't women be in charge of their own sexuality? The patriarchy wants to keep us weak and repressed. They want men to feel like hunters and women to feel like prey. If you want a man, go after him. Don't wait for him to make a move."

"Um . . . thank you for that fifteen-going-on-fifty." Shaking her head in exasperation, Chloe went to collect the replica diamond from Anil on her way to seduce Peter. While I waited for her to let me know she'd successfully convinced Peter to take her down to the museum, I walked Olivia out to the car, where Emma was waiting.

"The guests were thrilled at the idea that I would put them on social media," Olivia said. "It's like a novelty for their generation.

I have a gazillion pictures. They also don't think I'm fully human because you wouldn't believe the tea they spilled in front of me. I know all the secrets. Affairs. Conspiracies. Secret babies. Bankruptcies. Corporate takeovers. I'm the world's greatest spy."

"You're going to be the world's most grounded teenager when your mother gets home," I warned her. "What were you thinking?"

"I could start a gossip channel and hit one million followers in a week with what I know," she continued. She was clearly desperate to tell me something, so I decided to indulge her.

"Okay. Give me your top three, although I don't know most of these people."

"Ron Fitzgerald is sleeping with Cari Winnow."

"Okay . . . means nothing to me."

"He's the son of a tech billionaire and is engaged to the daughter of a world-famous soccer player. She's a princess from—"

"Yawn. Moving on."

"A woman named Martha was having an affair with someone's husband, but then she ate a peanut and died. She was deathly allergic to peanuts. It was ruled accidental, but some people think it might have been murder because they found her locked in the pantry without her phone or EpiPen."

Now, *that* was interesting. I made a mental note to ask Simone more about the friend who had inspired the whole "circus celebration of life" theme.

"Anything else?"

"Vera's husband is having an affair with his private secretary. Apparently, they were seen together in the Hamptons, and—"

"No more," I said. "It makes me think there is no such thing as love." We reached the car, and I explained the situation to Emma. "Don't let her out of your sight," I told her. "She's a slippery character."

Chloe messaged to say she had the replica, but she couldn't find

Peter and she was going to do another search of the house. I returned to the party and made my rounds, checking on the food and music, making sure glasses were filled and my people were where they were supposed to be. By the time I was done, about forty-five minutes had passed since Chloe had checked in and she still hadn't messaged an update. I was about to go looking for Simone to see if she would have more luck with Peter when Vera came barreling around the corner, her face sheet white.

"Simi! You have to come. It's Peter."

"What's wrong? Is he okay?"

"No, he's not okay." Her fingers dug into my arm. "There's so much blood . . . I think he's dead. I don't know . . . I don't know what to do."

"Where is he, Vera?"

"In the garage."

I sent a quick message to Gage and Jack as I raced behind Vera through the garden.

"I hadn't seen him for ages, so I went looking for him," Vera said. "It's not like him. Peter loves being the center of attention." Her words tumbled over one another as we made our way across the garden.

"I thought maybe he was showing people his new Bugatti . . ." She trailed off when we reached the side door to the garage and stopped so suddenly I almost ran into her. "I can't go in there again. I'm feeling faint. I need to go inside and lie down."

"Of course. When I see Simone, I'll ask her to sit with you. I don't want you to be alone."

I pushed open the door and walked into a garage the size of a small house, with five luxury vehicles gleaming on a highly polished floor beneath a grid of hexagonal LED lights. Sleek gray cabinets with track lighting above a marble counter took up one wall while pictures of race cars adorned the rest. A white-and-black

Bugatti was parked nearest the entrance with the door hanging open. But even before I saw Peter slumped over the steering wheel in the front seat, I knew from the spray of blood inside the front windshield and the pool of blood on the shiny gray floor that he was dead.

Bile rose in my throat and my knees weakened. I'd seen an almost-dead body during our last heist, but not a really dead one. I staggered forward, but Jack was suddenly behind me and yanked me back.

"It's a crime scene. You don't want to contaminate it. We need to call the police."

"I can't believe this," I stammered. "Vera went looking for him and . . ." My stomach heaved as the acrid scent of blood filled my nostrils.

"Look at his hand," Gage said. "He's missing his index finger."

Jack's body stiffened behind me. "Someone else must have been after the diamond."

"They might still be here." Gage pulled out his weapon and motioned us back. Keeping to the wall, he circled behind the car. That's when I heard a sound I never want to hear again—a gut-wrenching cross between horror and pained anguish.

"Gage?" Heedless of his warning about contaminating the crime scene, I ran over to the car, where he'd disappeared from view. "What's wrong?"

"It's Chloe." His voice cracked, broke, as he looked up from the floor, where he was kneeling with Chloe's head in his lap. "They got her, too."

SEVENTEEN

◇ ◇ ◇

With both Gage and me frozen in shock and unable to function, Jack ran over to check Chloe's vital signs.

"She's not dead," he said gently. "She has a big bump on her head and a bleeding cut on her temple." He looked up at me. "Breathe, Simi. She'll be okay. Someone hit her over the head and knocked her out. Look at her chest. It's rising and falling."

"I can't . . ." I looked away and my vision blurred. "I can't see her like that."

"You need to see her breathing, so you know for yourself." He grabbed Gage's shoulder. "C'mon, bud. She's okay, but we need to call an ambulance."

I forced myself to look back and saw Chloe's chest rise and fall, although her face was so white and her body so still, it took me a few long moments to shake the sense of panic.

Gage, on the other hand, was not okay. Let's just say even the strongest man can be overcome with emotion.

I stroked my bestie's cheek as I called 911. Jack was at the door to ensure no one else came inside.

"Someone needs to check the museum," I said. "Although I'm

pretty sure by now they've gotten away. Who kills someone at a celebration of life? It seems unnecessarily cruel."

Jack looked back over his shoulder. "I don't think someone who slits a dude's throat, chops off his finger, and ruins a multimillion-dollar car cares about people's feelings."

"I need to let Olivia know. And the rest of the crew. I have a feeling the police won't want anyone to leave, so I also need to talk to Vera's security team." Although it was the last thing I wanted to do, I forced myself to stand, leaving Chloe with Gage. Olivia was my goddaughter. This was my event. I had responsibilities. Someone had to take control and it had to be me.

"Gage . . ." He still had Chloe's head in his lap, his big hand wrapped around her limp one.

"I'm not going anywhere," Gage said. "Fuck the heist. Fuck the mob. Fuck Cristian. Fuck rich people and Bugattis and diamonds and missing treasures."

"You don't have to convince me," I said. "I don't want her to be alone."

Jack came with me as I did the rounds. I stopped by Emma's car to let Olivia know there had been an accident and the ambulance was coming for her mom. I let Vera know that Peter was, indeed, gone, and I asked her security team to keep people on-site until the police arrived and took charge of the scene. One of them checked the security system and confirmed that all the cameras and sensors had been turned off. I messaged the rest of the crew to tell them what had happened and asked them to circulate and keep their eyes open for suspicious behavior.

"We should check out the bunker," Jack said quietly. "If something is missing, it will become part of the crime scene and we'll lose access."

"I'll let the crew know where we are so they can warn us when the police arrive."

We quickly made our way downstairs. Of course, the panic room was open, and the mirror door to the bunker was ajar, with a bloody fingerprint on the biometric panel on the wall.

We ran through the bunker toward the museum, stopping briefly in front of the closed vault door.

"Why didn't they break into the vault?" I studied the large metal door and the untouched biometric panel beside it. "Vera told us that the paintings she had in there were priceless."

"It's got extra layers of security," Jack said. "That's a bank-level vault with both retinal and biometric scanners as well as a ten-digit lock code. It would take a professional hours to crack that safe and they would need some high-tech, specialized equipment, a finger, and an eyeball."

We made our way to the museum. As I'd feared, the double doors were wide open, and everything was gone save for the empty display cases, the marble pillars, and the bare hooks on the walls.

"They took everything." I stared in stunned disbelief. "Even the boxes and packing crates that were going to be used for shipping. Why would they take everything if they just wanted the diamond? Except for the erotic art, Vera said it was all fake."

"The bigger question is how did they get it all out?"

"They would have had to use the escape tunnel," I said. "There is no way they could have carried everything up the stairs and through the house without someone seeing them. But how did they get downstairs in the first place? Between you, Gage, and Vera's security team, the entire area was being watched."

"Gage and I were distracted for around ten minutes when someone knocked over one of the flaming desserts and started a kitchen fire," Jack said. "It spread everywhere. We managed to put it out, but that would have given them a window to get down the stairs."

We walked through the bunker, searching for a painting large enough to conceal the tunnel door.

"This must be it." I stopped in front of a six-foot painting of a woman standing in front of a cauldron with a stick in her hand, all grays and browns save for the fire under the pot. "It's pretty gloomy."

"It's *The Magic Circle* by John William Waterhouse," Jack said. "It was painted in 1886. It's worth close to half a million dollars, which isn't gloomy at all."

"Sometimes I forget you're an art expert and not just an ordinary thief." I pulled on the frame and the painting swung to the side. Behind it, a steel door opened into a tunnel and there was another bloody print on the biometric panel beside it.

Although hewn out of rock, the tunnel had been carefully crafted with smooth surfaces and carved edges. Motion-activated lights flickered on as we walked, filling the eight-foot-high space with an orange glow. Despite the fact the door had been open, a musty smell filled my nostrils. "I don't think this tunnel was ever used until today."

"And yet, there isn't any dust." Jack bent down to inspect the polished wood floor.

"There had to be at least two people involved," I said as he squatted and pulled out his phone. "There wouldn't have been enough time for just one person to pull this off."

"They dragged the boxes." Jack pointed to the long scuffs and scrapes leading down the tunnel, clearly visible under his phone light.

"That makes sense. Some of those fertility statues were made of stone. They would have been very heavy. Maybe the nephew wasn't the only criminal in the family."

"This was definitely a professional job," Jack said. "They de-activated the entire security system, evaded two security teams, and they knew they would need Peter's finger to open the biometric locks."

"You're missing the part where they were prepared to kill Peter to get his finger." I unlocked the steel exit door at the end of the tunnel and pushed it open. I had expected something fancy, but it looked like an ordinary door save for the fact that it was at least ten inches thick. "Do professional thieves slit people's throats?" I paused on the threshold. "Have you killed anyone, Jack?"

"This isn't the time," he said brusquely.

"Is that a 'yes'?" I stared at him, aghast. "You killed someone?"

"It's not that simple."

It seemed simple to me, and I added it to my list of things I didn't know about Jack that he was going to have to explain.

I stepped into the alley, blinking while my eyes acclimated to the bright light. "Where are we?"

"West edge of the property. They got special permission to build the tunnel to the alley." He bent down and studied the dirt. "There are tire tracks here from a large vehicle—likely some kind of moving van or truck. If this is how they transported the goods, they have a big head start. We'll need to ask around the neighborhood. Maybe someone saw something."

"I'll get the rest of the team on it." I pulled out my phone, hesitating. "I could also call Garcia. Serious thefts are his thing. Once the police find out the contents of the museum have been stolen, he'll be looped in anyway. He'll be able to track them faster than us."

"He'll also confiscate the contents of the truck if he finds it first," Jack warned. "It will be almost impossible to get to the diamond if it's in police custody."

"At least we'll know where it is." I sent the messages and made the call to Garcia. Judging by the tone of his voice, he wasn't happy to hear that I was at another crime scene.

Simone met us at the top of the stairs. Her hair was uncharacteristically disheveled, and she appeared flustered. "I went straight to see Vera after I got your message. I can't believe it. Poor Peter."

I gave her a quick update about what we'd found, including the more gruesome details about Peter's death, and assured her Chloe was going to be okay.

"Oh my." Simone waved a hand in front of her face. "I feel like I'm in a game of Clue. Mystery person in the garage with a knife . . ."

"Simone . . ."

"I'm sorry. I'm sorry," she said. "I don't know what to say. It's just so terrible."

"Do you mean the part where Peter was murdered in his Bugatti? The part where someone cut off his finger? Or the part where the diamond we were supposed to steal was stolen by someone who had not only the finger, but also the skills to override the rest of the security system and clear out the museum while we were all standing right here?"

"All the parts." She smoothed down her hair, patting it into place. "What are we going to do?"

I had no idea what we were going to do. My mind was racing with a hundred things at once. I still had to deal with all my contractors, who were waiting to go home. I had to make sure that my crew didn't give anything away during police questioning. I had to make sure Chloe was okay. I had to find the truck with the stolen treasures. And we were running out of time.

"You look surprised," I said to Garcia when he walked into Vera's kitchen, where I was impatiently waiting for my turn to talk to the homicide detective in charge of the case. Gage and Olivia had gone to the hospital in the ambulance with Chloe. Jack, Clare, and her team had disappeared as soon as the police arrived. Apparently, they didn't "do" police. I'd sent Anil and Emma back to the warehouse with our heist supplies after the police had taken their statements. Simone had insisted on staying at the house in case Vera needed her and so I wouldn't be alone.

"I am but I'm not," he said. "You seem to be attracted to crime scenes like a bee to honey. I hoped we'd stop meeting like this, but it seems you just can't stay out of trouble."

"I'm an event coordinator. I'm in a lot of places at a lot of times. Vera hired me for her nephew's celebration of life. That's why I'm here."

"Trust you to organize a funeral where someone gets murdered," he said dryly.

"I didn't plan it," I said. "Murder doesn't fit in with my circus theme."

Garcia shook his head. "I talked to Detective Johnson. He briefed me about the death in the Bugatti and the theft of some artwork. Did you have a chance to speak to Vera? By the time he arrived, she'd already taken a sedative and her assistant said she won't be available to talk to anyone until tomorrow morning."

"I was with her," Simone said. "She was in shock. She didn't say anything about who could have murdered poor Peter, but he was not well liked in our circle. He was very charming, but a bit of a rogue, with a fondness for younger women and utterly no discretion. He was obsessed with his treasure-hunting hobby. When he did join her at social events, it was to solicit donations to fund his travels or offer dubious business opportunities connected with his archeological digs."

"That's very helpful." Garcia pulled out his notebook and made a few notes. "You're a friend?"

"Yes, indeed," Simone said. "When her nephew got shanked in Sing Sing, she called me up, desperate for Simi's number. She and

Peter were about to set sail for their private island, and she needed someone to organize the funeral and celebration of life right away. I'd told her about Simi and how she organized a delightful circus-themed celebration of life for my dear friend Martha, so she wanted to hire her."

I was worried Simone would get carried away, so I tried to divert the conversation with my theory about the case. "It looks like whoever killed Peter used his finger to get into the bunker and steal everything from the museum. Theft was clearly the motive for the murder."

"Maybe." Garcia looked up over his notebook. "Maybe not. Sometimes the obvious explanation isn't always the right one. Where is the museum?"

"We can take you to it." Simone and I led Garcia downstairs, stopping at the door to the panic room. "The finger would have been used three times," I said. "First on the biometric lock to open the panic room, then the bunker, and a third time to access the museum."

"How do you know everything wasn't already open?"

"I had a security guy keeping watch downstairs and he said everything was locked. Also, there's blood below all the biometric sensor panels." I pointed to a smear on the wall. "I can't imagine why else it would be there."

"Hmmm."

I didn't like the way Garcia said, "Hmmm," as if there were other possible explanations for the reason the thieves had cut off Peter's finger. Time was ticking and the thieves were driving, and I needed him to come to the right conclusion so he would check any CCTV cameras in the area and tell me whether our theory about the thieves loading the stolen artwork onto a truck in the back alley was right, and if so, where that truck might be.

We stopped at the entrance to the bunker and then the museum. Garcia made some notes and called for a forensics team and police officers to secure the area as part of the crime scene.

"Our DNA will be in the museum because Vera took Simone and me to see it when we were planning the event," I said. "She thought her husband might bring his friends or family down to see his collection of erotic art and treasures and I was concerned about security."

"Is that what was in here?"

"Yes." I waved vaguely at the bare walls. "There were lots of paintings of people going at it from back in the day. Over there was a glass case filled with sex toys dating from ancient times up to now. I didn't even know what some of them were for and I have an excellent imagination."

"I'm curious why you're so invested in this robbery." Garcia seemed as disinterested in the details of Peter's erotic art collection as he was in my vivid imagination.

I stared at him, trying not to give any of the telltale signs of lying I'd seen in a psychology TikTok. "I feel responsible. This was my event. I had security people circulating and they didn't see anything."

"Didn't Vera have her own security?"

"Yes. Two guards, plus twenty-four-hour camera surveillance, heat and motion detectors throughout the museum, plus the biometric access panels. The thieves must have found a way to bypass everything."

"I'll talk to the head of Vera's security," he said, moving to leave.

"Aren't you wondering how they got everything out?" I tried to hide the desperation in my tone. "Vera and Peter have an escape tunnel in case they have to leave the bunker during an apocalypse. It leads to the alley on the west side of the property. That's got to be how they got everything out without being seen."

Garcia lifted a bushy eyebrow. "And you know about this tunnel . . . how?"

"Vera told us about it when she showed us the museum," Simone blurted out when I went "deer in the headlights," scrambling to think of a reason why I would know about a secret exit. "She mentioned it was behind a painting."

"That's right," I said. "It's over here." I led Garcia through the bunker to the painting.

"Kinda gloomy," he said.

"It's *The Magic Circle* by John William Waterhouse. He painted it in 1886." I silently thanked Jack for making me sound like I knew what I was talking about.

"I didn't know you knew art," Simone said, frowning.

"I have many special skills. Art appreciation is just one of them."

Garcia shot me a look that could or could not have been disbelief, but he was curiously silent as I led him through the tunnel and out to the alley.

"Oh look!" I bent down where Jack had seen the tire tracks and pretended to study the sand and gravel at the edge of the paved road. "It looks like a large vehicle was parked here. Maybe they loaded the stolen art into a vehicle that they parked in this alley."

Garcia walked up and down and checked the tire tracks before calling for uniformed officers to canvass the street. "We'll get to the bottom of this," he said when he was done. "I know where to find you if I have any more questions."

"But I want to help," I protested. "I have some free time now that the event was cut short. Why don't you let me know if anyone spotted a vehicle in the alley and I can go after it and save you some time?"

"You don't have a car," he pointed out.

"My friend drives for Uber. She always gives me a discount."

"This is police business. You do your job, and I'll do mine."

"We would make a great team," I insisted. "We could be like all the police shows where the police officer gets help from a quirky consultant: *Bones*, *Lucifer*, *Castle*, *The Mentalist*, *Monk*, *Elementary*, *Carter* . . ."

"You watch too much television," he said, but his lips finally quirked in a smile. "What skills do you bring to the mix? You're not a criminal psychologist, mystery writer, retired detective / CIA operative, or devil, as far as I know. And you don't have any special psychic gifts."

"I have a team of people with special skills," I said. "You know Chloe is good with computers. My magician is a great with mechanical things and he's in Mensa. And my fire eater has a PhD in chemistry. My tightrope walker is . . . um . . . very flexible and can get into tight spaces. I saw my security guy get stabbed in the shoulder and it didn't even slow him down. We have a knife thrower who is good at distracting people, and my clown drives an Uber but she's training for Formula One. She can get us places super-fast. It's like the traffic doesn't even exist."

"Speeding?" His eyes narrowed.

"Of course not," I said, backtracking quickly. "She is just very efficient."

"Anyone else on your team I should know about? Maybe somebody who always seems to get you into trouble?" He stared at me intently and my skin prickled in warning. Did he know about Jack's shadowy past? Somehow I didn't think he would appreciate Jack's thieving and lock-picking expertise, his knowledge of the criminal underground, or his association with nefarious individuals.

"Nobody with relevant skills."

"Hmm." Garcia gave me a lingering look and then shook his head. "I could never put you at risk, Simi."

"Please." I put a hand on his chest and gave him my best pleading expression. "My business is at risk. I could be ruined if Vera sues me. I feel crushed by guilt and the burden of responsibility. I failed her."

"If anyone failed, it was her own security team." Garcia's eyes softened, and he gently moved my hand away. "If I have some information I can share, I'll give you a call, but I won't put you in any dangerous situations."

"Thank you." Relief flooded through me, and I smiled. "You don't have to worry. I am totally averse to dangerous situations. When I see a dangerous situation, I turn and run."

"You didn't run last time," he pointed out.

"That was an exception."

He gave me a look of disbelief. "I certainly hope so, Simi. For your sake and mine."

EIGHTEEN

◇ ◇ ◇

I was totally unprepared to find my entire crew in Chloe's room when I finally arrived at the hospital later that evening. Olivia and Gage were sitting on either side of her bed. Emma and Anil were squeezed into one corner, and Jack was in another. On my way in, I'd spotted Milan in the hallway, hovering near the door, but when I tried to speak to her, she ran away.

Even more surprising was the fact that everyone was quiet. There were no fights. Emma wasn't sharing crazy stories about her past. Gage wasn't giving Anil a hard time about being a mama's boy. No one was making snarky comments about Clare, and Jack wasn't preparing to run out the door on some mysterious errand that he couldn't share.

"I thought I sent everyone home." I tried to put on a brave face, but seeing my bestie lying there so pale and still with a bandage wrapped around her head made my throat thicken. On my way to the hospital, I'd been thinking over what Garcia had said about dangerous situations. Chloe had almost lost her life. We were in over our heads. It was time to run, just like I'd promised.

"Chloe was here," Anil said. "We wanted to be here, too. Like you always say, we're a team."

I didn't point out that they rarely acted like a team because their gesture of solidarity made my heart squeeze in my chest.

"What about Milan?"

"I think she likes our team better than her team," Anil said, keeping his voice low. "Chloe was kind to her even though she's here to slit our throats."

"Was?" Chloe's voice wavered. "I'm not dead yet."

"She has a concussion," Gage said, looking up. "They did a brain scan and everything else is clear. No bleeding or swelling in the brain. She just needs to rest." Gage uncurled his hand from the railing on Chloe's bed. "The doctor said someone must have hit her hard from behind, causing her brain to bounce around in her skull. She was in the wrong place at the wrong time."

"And now the person who did this to her will pay." Anil slammed a fist into his hand. "We've been waiting for you to show up and make a plan for revenge."

"Me?"

"You're the leader," Anil said. "Lead us into vengeance. This isn't just a simple heist anymore. Someone hurt one of our own and their suffering will start with Chicago's next featherweight MMA champ pounding the dude's ass into dust."

I looked over at Olivia, who was busy scrolling through her phone. "Liv, could you give us a minute? We need to talk about grown-up stuff. Take my purse and grab yourself a pop."

Olivia sighed and unfolded herself from the seat. "As if I don't know everything that is going on. But fine. I'll humor you."

I waited until I was sure Olivia was out of earshot and said, "This heist ends now. We're in way over our heads. We should have called the police on day one." Hands shaking, I pulled out my phone. "I've decided to call Garcia and tell him everything. We can't do this alone. We need police protection. We need them to find Cristian and save us from the mob."

"That's not how the mob works," Gage said. "Cristian will be dead before the police even get their paperwork in order."

"Then Clare needs to fix this. It's all her fault. I'm going to find her and make her go to Angelini and give him the necklace." I held out my hand. "I need your gun."

Gage shook his head. "Not giving you my gun, Simi. You're not thinking straight."

I turned to my bestie. "Where's your gun?" Gage had given Chloe a gun to protect herself from her ex and trained her how to use it. She was now a certified badass with mad shooting skills.

"Not giving you my gun, either," she said. "You said this is a 'no guns' heist. Don't you remember?"

"That was before someone almost killed you. Now it is a 'yes guns' heist, at least until Clare agrees to fix this."

"What are you going to do?" Gage asked. "You're not going to kill her. That's not who you are, and she knows it. And even if you did have it in you, Milan and Vito won't let you close enough to do any damage."

"Is this you giving up?" Emma gave me an incredulous look. "We're all here because we believe in you. We're here because we thought you'd have a plan. You always have a plan."

"That is my plan. Lean on Clare until she breaks."

"It won't work." Jack came up behind me and wrapped his arms around my waist. I allowed myself a moment to sink against him and soak in his warmth. "She's been doing this for a long time. You can't break her."

"I can't let anyone else get hurt."

"It's not your fault," Jack said. "Clare set something in motion that can't be stopped. We can't go back, Simi, and we can't go to the police. We have no proof Angelini is involved or that he took Cristian. We make any move against him, and Cristian will die."

I closed my eyes and took several deep breaths to clear my

head. A few weeks ago, we were living our ordinary lives, worrying about ordinary things, and now someone was dead, Cristian had been kidnapped, a diamond had been stolen, and the only way of saving our friend and freeing ourselves from the Mafia noose was to find a truck that we knew nothing about and could be headed in any direction.

"We have faith in you, babe," Chloe said when I opened my eyes to find the entire crew staring at me. "That's why we're all here."

"You're here because someone hit you over the head," I said dryly.

Chloe laughed, and it was that sound, the best sound, the sound that told me she was going to be okay, that gave me the strength to keep going.

"Okay," I said finally after taking a moment to gather my thoughts. "Our best option is to figure out who got there before us and track them down."

"Clare got a lead on the vehicle from a guy walking his dog," Milan said from the doorway. "He saw a white ten-foot container truck with a purple and orange J & J Trucking logo parked in the alley around five thirty P.M. Clare drove over to their local office with Vito to see what she could find out. They had closed for the day, but she got in through the back door. She's there now trying different passwords to get into the system."

"Trying different passwords? Seriously?" Chloe pushed herself to sit. "We don't have the time for that. Who has my laptop? Milan, get over here with your phone and put her on video chat."

"You're injured," Gage protested.

"I'm fine."

He opened his mouth again and I shook my head in warning. "She says she's fine, so she's fine. Maybe you and Jack should go and watch the door, so no nurses or doctors walk in while she's engaged in nefarious deeds."

Olivia returned with Chloe's bag and set the laptop up on her mom's lap. Milan got Clare on the phone. Chloe talked Clare through the information she needed to hack into the system and guided her screen by screen. Her fingers flew over the keyboard and her laptop screen lit up with lines of white code.

"I'm in," Chloe said after five stressful minutes. "It wasn't that secure at all."

"I'm looking at the screen, but I don't see anything," Clare said over the video chat. "Where are the files?"

"I didn't give *you* access. I gave *me* access." Chloe shot me a sly grin. "You and Vito can meet us here and Simi can share what we find."

Clare's lips pressed into a thin line. "I didn't think subterfuge was your style."

"You never made an effort to get to know me," Chloe said. "Never trust a hacker."

"My mom is the *bomb*." Olivia pumped her fist. "I'm going to be a hacker just like her."

"You can be a white-hat hacker and help people," Chloe replied. "If I ever catch you doing black-hat hacking like this, I'll take your phone away forever."

After Clare ended the chat, Chloe pulled up the details of the truck that been parked in the alley outside Vera's house. "This is it. The address is right and a contactless pickup was requested for five thirty P.M. in the alley. The notes say the shipment will be prepacked in boxes and left just inside the door, which will be unlocked when they arrive."

"They left the door open?" Anil's eyes widened. "Anyone could have just walked in and taken those boxes. They could have even entered the house and wandered around."

"The alley is pretty much hidden by the bushes along the wall and the trees leaning over the edge of the wall of the property across from it," Jack said. "The door is also painted to blend in. You'd really have to be looking to see it."

I perched on the edge of Chloe's bed to look over her shoulder. "What's the customer's name?"

"William H. Hunt." Chloe opened another window and did a few searches. "The booking was placed over the phone, but the billing address is false, the phone number is out of service, and there is no e-mail address. Payment was made in cash and the documents were signed in person."

"Someone really wanted to cover their tracks," I said. "The name is probably fake, too."

"The booking was made last Friday afternoon just before closing," Chloe said, reading off the screen. "He paid extra for a rush delivery. The shipment is headed to a freight forwarder's warehouse in Barkeyville, Pennsylvania, where it will be consolidated with other shippers' goods into a single container that will be transported to the Port of New York, specifically, the container terminal in Newark. From there, it will be shipped to Belize."

"Belize?" Anil asked. "What's in Belize?"

"The Florentine Diamond if we don't intercept that truck." I pulled up a map on my phone. Barkeyville was a seven-hour drive, but with breaks and traffic, we were looking at a minimum of eight hours, and the delivery truck already had a head start. "We need two vehicles to maximize our chances of catching up to them."

"My truck is in the shop, but I can borrow a truck from my cousin Lou," Jack said. "Clare can bring her car and we'll meet back in the parking lot in one hour."

"We'll see what else we can find out about the warehouse in Barkeyville," I said. "Everyone get ready for a road trip. If we don't catch them there, we'll have to follow them to New York."

Anil cleared his throat, drawing everyone's attention.

"What is it, Anil?"

He gave me a smug smile. "I knew you'd have a plan."

Jack showed up at the hospital parking lot an hour later in a beat-up pickup truck with a truck-bed camper in the box, a canoe on top, and two mountain bikes attached to the back. Emma took one look as he parked under a light in the dimly lit lot, and she snorted in disgust.

"I'm not driving that piece of crap. I have a rep to protect."

"What kind of reputation do you have left after driving around in a bright blue Chevy Bolt EV?" Jack retorted. "We're lucky to get something this spacious and so well-equipped. Lou and his wife just got back from a camping trip. We'll be ready for anything."

"Pretty sure the thieves aren't going to escape down a river or through the mountains," Emma said with a snide expression. "We'll be carrying excess baggage. It's going to slow us down."

"It's better to be prepared." Jack folded his arms across his chest. "We can't afford to take any chances when we're on the road."

"What are you? Some kind of Boy Scout?"

"I was a Boy Scout," Jack said. "For a few years."

My heart gave a little squeeze when pain flickered across Jack's face. His parents had died when he was young, and he'd spent a few happy years living with his grandmother, an avid gardener. His life had taken a dramatic turn when Joseph Angelini's men pushed his grandmother down a flight of stairs after she refused to vacate her house to make way for the real estate development he'd planned for her street. After her death, Jack had been left to fend for himself. He'd avenged her death by framing Joseph Angelini for the theft of Simone's necklace after the last heist, something he had failed to share with the crew, along with the rest of his mysterious past.

"You're our driver," I pointed out to Emma. "It is literally your job to do the driving. Also, you told me there was no vehicle you couldn't drive."

"I *can* drive it," she said. "But I won't. Anyone getting behind the wheel of that monstrosity needs to be wearing plaid Bermuda shorts, a T-shirt with some lame barbecue saying, thick glasses, a ball cap, and Sperry Top-Siders. Do I look like someone's dad? I think not."

"We've got everything we need in here." Jack pulled open the door to the truck-bed camper. "Stove, fishing poles, sleeping bags, mini-fridge full of beer . . . He even gave us his tablet loaded up with horror films."

"My mom doesn't let me watch horror movies," Anil said. "I wet myself when I saw the barracuda scene in *Finding Nemo*, and since then horror movies aren't allowed."

"How old were you?" I asked.

"Fourteen."

"Jesus." Emma shook her head. "I had hopes for you when I got you outta that house for a bit, but come on, dude. Man up. The worst part of that movie was the goddamn jellyfish."

"Since Emma won't do her job"—I gave Emma my best disapproving look—"she can drive her Bolt with Clare, Milan, and Vito. The rest of us will ride in the truck."

"So now it's punishment time?" Emma shot me a glare. "We are no longer friends. Don't expect any more free Uber rides."

"You never gave me free Uber rides. All I got was your friends-and-family discount."

"I might have considered it, but now it's totally off the tab—" She cut herself off with a gagging sound.

"What's wrong?"

"Don't look over at Clare's Elantra."

Of course, we all looked. Barely visible in the darkness, Milan and Vito were wrapped around each other, hands under clothes, tongues down each other's throats in a very non-PG way.

Emma gagged again.

"Calm down." I patted her back. "So, they're together. Big deal. Who else is going to want to date an assassin except for another assassin?"

"They could just be very close," Anil said, joining us in our huddle. "My mom kisses me every night when she puts me to bed."

"Dude . . ." Emma shook her head. "Please don't tell me she kisses you like that, because I had burritos for lunch and I'm pretty sure you don't want them all over your fancy shoes."

"She kisses my cheek."

"Thank God."

"A few weeks ago, it was on the lips, but that was because I turned my head to ask her to turn on my Captain America nightlight. I didn't like it."

"Here they come . . ." Emma doubled over, putting her hands on her knees just as Simone's black Bentley pulled up under the light beside us.

"Wait for me!" Simone flew out of the Bentley dressed head to toe in black. "I want to come."

"There's no room, Simone. And we need you here to support Vera and stay on top of what's going on."

"Please." She wrung her hands. "I won't take up much room. I don't want to miss out on the fun."

"It's not a game," I said. "If our lives weren't on the line, we wouldn't even be here. You shouldn't have been involved in the first place, and if we get caught or someone sees you—"

"No one will see me." She tugged a balaclava over her head, and everyone stopped talking and stared.

"What the actual fuck?" Emma gave voice to the question everyone was thinking. "Is that for real?"

I also wanted to know if the knit wool balaclava in a black, off-white, and beige colorway with jacquard mirror GG logos throughout was for real. The mask featured cutouts for the eyes and mouth, a ribbed-knit hem at the collar, and tonal stitching.

"It's Gucci from their 2018 Fall/Winter collection, but I couldn't find anything else." Simone's voice was slightly muffled because the mouth cutout was a tad too small.

"I think we should let her come if she promises never to put that on again," Jack said. "She can squeeze in the back."

"You've filled the back seat with junk. We're one seat down."

"It's not junk," Jack protested. "I like to be prepared for both road trips and truck hijackings . . ."

"Hijacking?" Anil's face lit up. "I have lots of ideas if we get hijacked. I've played every *Grand Theft Auto* game plus the expansion packs."

"Those games are dope," Emma said. "I spent an entire winter playing *GTA* after a bad breakup involving a trucker with a furry fetish. I mean, on a cold winter night, sure, I'd put on the suit, but in summer I'd be sweating buckets and the last thing you want to do when you're trapped in four inches of foam and fur and wearing a giant bear head is build more heat. I was slipping around in that thing like a greased-up sausage. Like, dude, why not ears and a tail, maybe some paws, and do the bear bare."

Anil's eyes glazed over. "I have questions."

"I'm sure you do," I said. "Talk to Emma about it later."

"I'm all ready," Simone called out from inside the truck. I hadn't even seen her climb inside. "I have more than enough room."

"Simone . . ."

"It's cozy," she insisted. "And I can keep the stack of things from falling." She pulled her seat belt on, struggling to clip it under the pile of supplies. "All ready to go."

"Heads up," Clare called out. "Simi's cop friend is headed in this direction."

There was a scramble of movement. Jack dove into the truck camper and slammed the door. Clare and her minions scattered.

"Garcia." I gave him a wave as he approached. "What are you doing here?"

"Chloe's the only witness to the murder so far," he said. "I told Detective Johnson I'd check in on her, but there was a pit bull standing outside her door with Olivia."

"That's her boyfriend, Gage," I said. "He's very protective. She says they broke up, but I think she's just trying to teach him a lesson. He's also the head of my security team." I introduced Anil and Emma. Everyone else had disappeared. Thankfully, Simone stayed quiet inside the truck.

Garcia's gaze slid to the vehicle. "Are you going camping?"

"It's been a stressful week," I said. "I thought it would be a good idea to treat my staff to a weekend away."

"At night?"

"We're going to the Allegheny National Forest," I said. "It's always crazy in July, so we thought we'd hit the road tonight so we could be first in line for the first-come, first-served campsites."

"Didn't really take you for a camper." Garcia frowned. "When was the last time—"

Desperate to steer the conversation away from my nonexistent camping skills, I blurted out, "Do you have any information about the murder you can share yet?"

"I do, but I need you all to sign an NDA first." Garcia pulled a piece of paper from inside his jacket pocket and laid it on the hood of Jack's truck. "We can use the same one for everyone. Just print your name and sign underneath." He held his phone light up so

Emma, Anil, and I could sign the document, and then he folded the paper and tucked it away.

"Other than Chloe and Gage in the hospital, is there anyone else around who might need to sign?" he asked.

I thought about Simone in her Gucci 2018 ski mask and decided not to involve her more than necessary. "We're still waiting for the others to arrive."

Garcia opened his little black book. "The final autopsy results are still pending, but I got the preliminary report from the coroner. A deep, obliquely placed, long, incised injury was found on the front side of the neck—"

I cut him off with a warning hand. "I don't need the graphic details. I was there. You can just say he died from a slit throat."

Garcia chuckled. "I guess that means you don't want me to go into detail about the finger."

"Probably a good idea."

"We haven't found the murder weapon yet," he said. "I suspect the same weapon was used for both injuries. Homicide is looking into the victim to see if he had any enemies."

"The celebration of life was for his nephew, who was shanked in Sing Sing," I offered. "Maybe some of his unsavory ex-con friends came to pay their respects and decided to steal some art while they were there. Or maybe there are more criminals on Peter's side of the family, and since they were at the house for the funeral anyway, they decided to kill Peter and steal his collection. It makes total sense."

"You have a good imagination and no facts," Garcia said.

"Who needs facts when the pieces fit together? Criminals in the family. Murder. Theft. Boom. The butler didn't do it."

"Simi watched a lot of mystery and crime shows when she was living with her former landlady, Rose," Emma interjected in what I assumed was an attempt to steer Garcia in the direction of Peter's criminal family. "*Murder, She Wrote, CSI, NCIS, Criminal Minds, The Wire*—"

"*Bones*," I interrupted to make sure she didn't miss any. "*Brooklyn Nine-Nine*—Garcia reminds me of Detective Peralta, by the way."

"He's not a Peralta," Emma said. "I'd go more with Horatio Caine from *CSI: Miami* but without the red hair."

"I'm not that old," Garcia protested. "But I am a better detective. I'll need a copy of the guest list to show Vera when I speak to her tomorrow. I want to go over the security tapes with her to see if there were any unwanted guests."

"I can e-mail a copy to you," I said. "Don't forget about the nephew's prison connection. He may have told someone inside who told someone outside who showed up at the house as a guest all ready for thieving."

Garcia tucked his book away and gestured for me to follow him around the other side of the truck camper. "What's really going on?" he asked in a hushed tone.

The truck camper creaked and shifted to the side where we were standing. My breath hitched and I prayed Jack wouldn't cough or sneeze.

"I'm not sure I know what you mean. My staff are traumatized after what happened at Vera's house, so I wanted to take them camping to decompress."

"There's no way you would ever leave Chloe in the hospital to go on a camping trip," he said. "You were prepared to go to jail to save her. I've never met friends so close."

"Maybe we're not so close anymore," I said with a shrug. "She's got a new boyfriend. You know how it goes."

"Is that why Olivia said she would be staying with you tonight?" He brushed my hair back over my shoulder, a soft, tender, and utterly unexpected gesture that made me shiver. "I'm worried about you."

"Garcia . . ." My stomach turned backflips when his fingers moved from my shoulder to brush along my jaw. "Jack and I . . ."

"I know you're still hung up on Jack." His voice took on an earnest tone. "But he's involved in this, and not in a good way. I can feel it and I'm concerned for your safety."

The truck camper creaked again. For a second, I thought I saw the top of Jack's head in the window.

"He's not good for you." Garcia's gaze softened. "I think in your heart you know that. I would never hurt you. I would never abandon you or betray you. I would never drag you into something that would put your life or your freedom at risk."

Creak. Crack. Thump. The truck camper was most definitely weighted toward us—about 180 pounds at a guess, maybe 185 if you counted Jack's jeans and shoes. I could almost hear him huffing his indignation through the aluminum wall.

Garcia leaned closer, and for the briefest of seconds there was only a whisper of air between us. But there was only one person I wanted to kiss, even though I still hadn't completely forgiven him.

"I appreciate that." I stepped back to put some distance between us. "But I can look after myself."

Seemingly unfazed by the rejection, Garcia nodded. "If there's anything you want to tell me, I promise I will be here for you, and I'll do everything I can to protect you."

And there it was. Only half an hour ago I had seriously been thinking of telling Garcia everything and letting him handle this mess. I might even have taken him up on his offer.

But I didn't need to be saved. I had a new plan. My crew was ready to go. Jack was . . . well . . . Jack. The diamond was out there just waiting for us to grab it, and I wasn't ready to give up yet.

"Thanks, Garcia. If anything changes, I'll let you know."

NINETEEN

◇ ◇ ◇

We had just sorted out who was sitting where and in which vehicle when a fully dressed Chloe came shuffling out of the hospital with an agitated Gage holding her up on one side and Olivia hovering by the other.

"Babe," Gage pleaded when she reached the truck. "Please. Go back inside. They weren't ready to discharge you."

"I'm not letting Simi go on a car-chase heist without me," she grumbled. "Deal with it."

"Simi . . ." Gage tried to cut her off, moving in front of the passenger door. "Do something."

Even I didn't want Chloe coming with us. She was still pale, with dark circles under her eyes and a bandage around her head, but I knew my bestie, and when she had that fierce determination on her face, nothing was going to get in her way.

"Where would you like to sit?" I asked her.

"In the back beside the window so I can rest my head." She skirted around Gage, climbed into the truck, and screamed.

"It's okay," I called out. "It's Simone. She's wearing a ski mask."

Emma leaned into the truck. "I screamed, too, but because it was Gucci 2018 and not the new collection."

"Simone, I'm afraid you'll have to sit this one out," I said gently. "I need Chloe and her hacking skills, and we've only got six seats."

A dejected Simone pulled off her ski mask and climbed out of the truck. "I have to miss out on all the fun."

"It's not going to be fun," I said. "It's going to be dangerous and stressful, and we may not even recover the diamond, in which case, we're going to need to disappear for a bit. We also need a point person here in the city in case something comes up. And Vera needs you. This must be an incredibly difficult time for her."

"She did ask me to stay with her tonight." Simone sighed. "She wants to watch *Thelma & Louise*. It's her favorite movie. She said she's seen it sixteen times."

"It's a wonderful film." Rose had made me watch the 1990s film about two best friends who set out on an adventure that becomes a flight from the law when one of them kills the man who tried to assault her friend.

"Do you want my mask?" She offered me the neatly folded bundle.

"No, you should keep it. Who knows when you might need it again."

"We need to split up between the two vehicles," Jack said. "I don't trust Clare and her team, so one of us should go with them and one of them should go with us."

"That hurts," Clare said. "I've been nothing but honest since this started."

"You stole the Wild Heart and ratted us out to the mob and then blackmailed us into doing a heist," I said. "'Honest' is not a word I'd use to describe you."

"Is this going to be like middle school where each side picks the people they want on their team?" Anil asked. "I was always picked last, so this time I'll volunteer to go with Clare. She has a good side. You just haven't given her a chance."

"That's sweet, hon." She gave him a smile that made my toes curl, and not in a good way.

"Three pizza dogs coming back to Earth." Emma bent over. "I'm gonna hurl."

"Vito can go with you," Clare said.

"I was going to pick Milan," I said, thinking of how she'd come to the hospital to check on Chloe and how she'd tipped us off about the trucking company.

Clare shook her head. "I need her with me."

We decided to put all Jack's stuff in the truck camper so Chloe, Gage, and Vito could ride in the back of the cab and Jack, Emma, and I could ride up front. Simone offered to take Olivia to her grandparents' house to spend the night, soothing Olivia's ruffled feathers by promising to take her to a fast-food drive-through in her Bentley.

After we'd seen them off, we hit the road. Clare raced ahead of us through the city, weaving in and out of traffic until she disappeared in a blur of gray. Milan sent us mocking texts for the next few hours that did nothing to settle the already fraught atmosphere in the back of the truck.

"Can't this bag of bolts go any faster?" Emma thumped the dashboard as we approached Toledo. "How are we supposed to catch up when we're weighed down by one thousand tons of gear?"

"We watched your show last time," Chloe said when Vito pulled up *The Towering Inferno* on the tablet Lou had left for us. "How about a rom-com? Something light and fun to bring up the mood."

Vito snorted. "I can't believe you watch that mindless crap."

Without warning, Gage ripped the tablet out of Vito's hand. "Chloe likes rom-coms, so you don't say shit about them."

"Gage took the tablet," Vito called out. "I was about to watch a show."

"The kids are fighting again," I said to Jack. "Maybe traveling together wasn't such a good idea."

We made good time, stopping only twice for gas and a restroom break. Emma and Gage, who both had experience driving large vehicles, offered to take over driving, but Jack insisted he wasn't tired even though I caught him yawning on more than one occasion. We finally met up with Clare's vehicle outside the warehouse in Barkeyville, arriving just as the sun began to rise.

"We've already been inside," she said. "Security wasn't very tight. There was no cell receiver, so Anil was able to cut the telephone line and deactivate the cameras and sensors and we walked right in. We couldn't find the truck, so we decided to open the shipping containers to see if the boxes had already been loaded. So far, no luck."

"If you'd just waited, I could have hacked into their system and told you where the goods are," Chloe snapped. "Now they'll know there was a break-in. You'd better hope you didn't miss a single camera. You also took a terrible risk because some companies put security sensors inside the containers. They send out a silent alarm when the door has been opened. The police might just be on their way."

"Since when did you become an expert on shipping containers?" Jack asked.

"I had to do something during that long drive. I couldn't sleep with Vito and Emma fighting. I'll go inside and check it out."

Chloe returned from the office twenty minutes later with bad news. "The truck had some mechanical problems outside Youngstown, Ohio. They made their way to the nearest freight-forwarding trucking company, which took the goods and consolidated them with one of their own shipments. The Youngstown company sent an e-mail confirming the container number and advising that their truck was scheduled to leave this morning at six A.M. They should be arriving in New York midafternoon."

"We just missed them," Anil said. "Maybe we could catch up and break into the truck when they're at a rest stop."

"It's going to be pretty hard to find them on the interstate when all we've got to go by is a number stamped on the back of a shipping container," I said. "Do you know how many trucks are on the road?" I slumped in my seat, exhausted and utterly dejected. Why couldn't we catch a break?

"We can find it. Don't give up. It will be like the games my parents played with me on long road trips," Anil said, smiling. "Five points for the first one to spot a semitrailer truck and twenty points for taking a picture of the container number. Winner gets a candy bar."

"A candy bar?" Emma sniffed. "That's what you got as a prize when you were a kid? In my family, you'd get a pack of cigarettes or a bottle of rum, and if you were under twenty-one, you'd have to hand them over to the folks."

"It wasn't just when I was a kid," Anil said. "But now that I'm an adult, the candy bars are giant-size."

"I'll play for a giant-size bottle of rum." Emma raised her hand for a round of high fives. "Come on, guys. Get your game on. It's not over yet."

We'd been on the road no more than three hours before we got a message from Milan in Clare's Elantra. They were about thirty miles ahead of us and the police had closed the 80 East due to a crash involving a propane tanker, a water tanker, and a box truck. There would be at least a three-hour wait until the road was cleared for traffic.

"They'll almost be in New York by then," Chloe said as we neared a bridge. "We'll lose our chance to intercept them."

"No, we won't." Jack yanked the wheel and turned off the highway onto a dirt service road leading down a steep hill into the forest.

"Stop. What are you doing?" I braced myself as the truck skidded on the gravel while we drove under the bridge.

"I know a shortcut."

"What shortcut? How would you know about a shortcut in the middle of the woods in Pennsylvania? Go back up to the road or we'll get lost."

"I can't." Jack grinned. "It's one-way."

"There are no other cars down here and it's a dirt service road. No one is going to give you a ticket if you turn around."

"The shortcut will give us a better chance of catching up with them," Jack insisted. "I was traveling with some guys a while back and I'm pretty sure there was a logging road that bypasses the I-80 and takes us all the way to Bloomsburg. There's a map in the glove compartment."

"We have phones. Why do we need a map? I didn't even know they made them anymore." I pulled out the worn map, unfolded it, and was immediately engulfed in paper. "I don't know how to use this thing."

"There might not be any service in the backcountry, so you need to figure it out," he said. "I'll need a navigator. My entire focus has to be on the road. It's a challenging drive."

"I don't like that word, Jack."

"What word? Challenging?"

"Backcountry. We're not backcountry folk. We're front country. City people. I don't want to wind up in a *Deliverance* situation."

Vito leaned forward. "What's *Deliverance*?"

"It's a 1972 American thriller film about a bunch of city guys who get lost in the backcountry and fall afoul of the locals," Emma said. "If Anil cried at *Finding Nemo*, he would shit himself at *Deliverance*."

"Could we keep our language clean, please?" Chloe asked. "Just because we're off-roading, there's no need to be crude."

"How about defecate?" Emma asked. "Or poo? Vito needs to understand what we're about to face, and his likely physical response."

"We're not going to encounter any inbred mountain men in the Appalachians," Jack said. "No one uses these roads anymore. There's nothing out here. No cabins or service boxes or houses. No highway markers, electricity poles, or cell towers. Nothing. Just flora, fauna, and the logging trail."

"Now it's a *trail*?" My voice rose in pitch. "I didn't sign up for off-roading on a trail in the middle of the wilderness. It's not me."

"I thought you were a survivalist," Jack retorted. "Or was all that stuff you told our architect a lie?"

"Why do you two have an architect?" Emma asked. "Did someone get married and buy a house and forget to tell the rest of us? Is Simi pregnant?" She covered her mouth and gasped. "Was it a shotgun wedding?"

"No one is married or pregnant," I snapped. "And I didn't lie about my survival skills, but I didn't expect to have to use them for real."

"Pull over so I can get my bag of guns." Gage leaned over the seat. "Three or four ought to do it."

I turned and glared. "I told you this is a 'no guns' heist."

"Actually, you changed your mind and said it was a 'yes guns' heist so you could shoot Clare," Jack pointed out.

Vito scowled. "You'll have to go through me if you're planning to shoot Clare, and FYI, you won't survive no matter how good your skills."

"Relax. I retracted that statement when I came up with a plan."

"You didn't say it was a 'no guns' car chase, or a 'no guns' trip into the backcountry," Gage said. "This is definitely a 'yes guns' scenario. Who knows what we'll encounter up there? Bears, wolves, cougars, serial killers . . . I promise not to say 'I told you so' when it turns out we needed them after all."

Jack pulled to a stop beside a battered pickup truck parked in a small clearing half in and half out of the bush. He checked his GPS while Gage retrieved his bag of guns from the truck camper.

"Jack . . ." I poked him in the side. "There's a guy watching us from the bushes. I don't think we're supposed to be here. Let's go back to the interstate."

Instead of doing the sensible thing and listening to me, Jack rolled down his window and called out a greeting. Moments later a man dressed in full camouflage with a bag slung across his front and a rifle across his back was walking toward us. Gage stiffened, his hand reaching under his jacket.

"Why did we get your bag of guns when you've already got one with you?" I asked.

"Been working with Jack for a while now," Gage said. "I've learned from my mistakes."

"Are you looking for mushrooms?" The man's forehead creased in a frown. "This is my patch."

"Oh God. He's a drug dealer." I slumped down in my seat. "We're all going to die."

"We're trying to bypass the roadblock," Jack said. "I was pretty sure there was a logging road around here that leads to Blooms-burg."

"Yeah, it's that way." Camo Man pointed to a roughly hewn trail barely wide enough for a vehicle that led into the forest. "I thought you were after the chanterelles. Best season ever." He opened the bag slung across his body to show us his fungi. "I've been picking here for two days now."

Jack tipped his chin. "We won't get in your way."

"The logging road is pretty rough going," Camo Man said. "Pretty isolated, too, if you get into trouble. No cell service after the first mile. You sure you want to take that truck through the woods?"

"This baby can handle anything." Jack patted the steering wheel. "It was made for this kind of off-roading. It'll be a blast."

I sent my parents a text to tell them I loved them and to give Nani a kiss for me, and to tell Nikhil that I was the one who broke the drone he got for his sixteenth birthday, and to tell the twins there was some part of me that loved them even though they'd made my life a living hell.

Then I prayed.

TWENTY

◇ ◇ ◇

At first, the road wasn't too bad. We drove through a dense forested area and then across a field of wildflowers. Chloe and Emma were on the right side of the vehicle and got the best view. However, when we started to climb up the mountain, the road narrowed and the trees became taller and thicker. We lost the sunshine and then cell service. Our road turned into a narrow, bumpy, single-lane path. When I looked out the window, all I could see was a sheer drop so far, I couldn't see the ground.

"Oh God." I sucked in a sharp breath and stared straight ahead. "There's nothing there, Jack. No guard rails. No logs. No stones. No barrier. And it's barely wide enough for the truck. If even one of your tires goes off the road, we'll fall over the edge."

"That's the beauty of off-roading." Jack grinned. "Pure adrenaline."

"What if someone is coming from the other direction?" I asked. "There's no room to pass."

"One of us will have to back up until there's room."

My breath left me in a rush. "Back up down a winding, twisty, narrow, bumpy, sharply inclined gravel trail full of potholes and cut into the side of the mountain with what looks like a one-thousand-foot drop on the other side? Are you freaking kidding me?"

"It'll definitely be a challenge." Jack was still smiling. He'd been smiling since we'd started on this insane off-road adventure. I'd been busy drafting a will on my phone to ensure my collection of plants would find a good home.

"I think I'm going to be sick," Chloe moaned.

"I wouldn't suggest opening your window," Vito said. "You might fall to your death."

"You might survive if your fall is broken by some of the many trees in the valley below," Jack said cheerfully. "*Pinus pungens, Pinus rigida, Pinus virginiana . . .*"

Chloe sucked in a sharp breath when the truck tilted precariously as we rounded a sharp corner. "You can take your *Pinus* and shove it up your—"

"There are over sixty-three hundred plant species in the region," Jack said, cutting her off. "The Appalachian Forest is one of the great floral provinces on earth. It's very exciting to see such incredible biodiversity. It's hard not to get distracted."

"Try and make an effort." I couldn't hide the sarcasm in my tone. "I don't want to die because you saw a rare giant *Pinus* in the bush."

"I'd drive over a cliff for a giant *Pinus*." Emma snorted a laugh. She'd been loving the thrill ride, even daring Jack to drive faster, but I wasn't in the mood for jokes.

"I'm not interested in going over the cliff. No one knows where we are. There are no signs of human life. No telephone poles or electrical boxes. No cell signal. We would be lost in the wilderness and they'd never find us."

"We've got everything we need to survive," Jack assured me. "Tent, camp stove, sleeping bags, canoe, and you and your survival skills. We've even got a fishing rod, so we won't starve."

"That's not as reassuring as I'm sure you think it is."

"I can't eat fish," Vito said. "I'm allergic. I'll have to eat one of you."

Gage slammed his fist into his palm. "You freaking try to eat me and you'll get a fist sandwich that goes all the way through."

"Food won't be a problem," Jack assured them. "There are many edible plants and fungi: blackberries, chicory, dandelions, thistles, chanterelles, of course, and a wonderful fungus called chicken of the woods, but that one you have to get fresh, or you find maggots."

Chloe retched. Gage growled. He'd been doing a lot of growling and clutching his bag of guns. I'd planned to make him put them away, but Emma had whispered that they were his "support guns" and we should let him keep them close. An overprotective alpha male trapped with the woman he loved in a dangerous situation where he had no control was a recipe for disaster, she said, unless he had something to soothe him, and since we didn't have any blankies or binkies, a bag of guns it had to be.

One sweaty, heart-pounding hour later, the road widened slightly, turning inward and away from the cliff. Jack tried to keep up our spirits by attempting to identify as many of the sixty-three hundred plants as he could. He was so focused on the flora, he didn't see the cloud of dust ahead of us until we were completely engulfed.

"What the hell?" He didn't slow down, of course, because that would have made sense.

"There are two cars ahead," I said. "A beat-up red sedan followed by a blue pickup truck. They're driving very slowly."

"Jesus," Gage said. "Who would drive a sedan on this road?"

Jack shook his head. "Probably an ignorant city dude who thought he'd be cool and avoid the roadblock without learning anything about the road."

Gage leaned over the seat, peering into the cloud of dust. "I'm amazed he's made it this far in that piece of junk."

"He's slowing everyone down," Jack muttered. "That truck

must have been following him for a long time. He needs to get off the road and let the off-road vehicles pass. It's good etiquette."

"Where could he go?" Chloe asked. "There's barely enough room to drive."

"He could drive into the bush. We'd be able to squeeze past." Jack pushed the accelerator as we went up a hill, and the engine roared. He waited a few moments and did it again, bringing us closer and closer to the blue truck.

"What are you doing?" I shouted over the roar of the engine.

"Letting the sedan know we want to pass."

"That's pretty aggressive," I said. "You're just going to make him angry by menacing him."

"If he's going to off-road in a sedan, he should at the very least learn the rules." Jack revved the engine again. "He's not just slowing us down. The blue truck must be getting impatient, too. I'm surprised he isn't honking his horn or tailgating that moron."

We followed the vehicles for another five miles before the sedan finally pulled off to the right side of the road in a small clearing beside the forest. The blue truck pulled up behind him. For a moment I thought the driver of the blue truck was going to get out and say something to the driver of the sedan, but as we got closer and no one got out, I got a bad feeling in the pit of my stomach.

"I think they know each other," I said. "They were traveling together, and you menaced them both. Just pass them and keep going."

"I want to check out the guy in the sedan," Jack said. "What's he doing on this road in a car like that?"

"It's none of our business. Just drive."

Of course, Jack didn't drive. Instead, he pulled up beside the sedan and opened the passenger window beside Emma. Only then did I notice that the sedan's windows were tinted. I couldn't see anything until the driver's window lowered slowly and a thick, muscled arm emerged to rest on the door.

If the full sleeve of ink—mostly skulls, snakes, swords, and daggers—didn't raise the alarm bells, the spiked iron bracelet and the missing baby finger certainly did. Behind me, I heard a soft click as Gage unholstered his gun. Sweat beaded on my forehead and I sank down in my seat between Emma and Jack, willing the ground to swallow us up.

"Hey, bud. How's it going?" Jack shouted over me and Emma. "Never imagined I'd see a sedan on this road."

A scarred and heavyset face emerged from the window. The dude was bald with tattoos on his head, spacers in his ears, and four piercings through his left eyebrow. Despite the morbid accessories, he was handsome in a sinister and menacing way, with piercing blue eyes, a chiseled jaw, and the kind of full lips I would have died for—or maybe I would.

"*Deliverance* or drug dealers?" Chloe whispered to Gage. "What do you think?"

"I think we need to get outta here before they start shooting up our car," he muttered. "They're clearly locals and they won't want us here in their territory, especially if we're asking questions. Guys like that don't like questions. Makes them suspicious."

"You doing some touring?" The dude's voice was rough and gravelly, as if the knife that had left the scar across this throat had done some deeper damage.

"Just taking a detour to Bloomsburg and enjoying some off-roading."

The dude said something to the people in his car, and I heard laughter. He flicked something in his hand that looked suspiciously like a knife. "Nice truck. Maybe we should check it out. See what you've got under the hood."

"Please just go," I whispered under my breath. "Please just go. Please just go."

"Don't worry." Emma patted my knee. "I got this."

"No . . ." I trailed off when Emma leaned out the window and I realized she wasn't scared.

"Nice ink," Emma called out. "It looks like Kirk Styles's work."

"He did the skull." The dude gave her an appraising look. "You know him?"

"Kirk did my ass, and yes, I mean that in all ways an ass can be done."

A grin tugged at the corners of his mouth. "What you got on your ass, babe?"

"What I've got in the back is nothing compared to what I've got up front." Emma leaned farther out the window. "Have you heard of Tex? He inked Rihanna, Bieber, Drake, a couple of Jenners . . ."

The dude nodded. "I know Tex. Tried to get on his list, but it was a three-year wait."

"Not for me. He saw my tits and he wanted them right then and there. You should see his work. They are a goddamn master-piece. I'm donating them to the Louvre when I die."

"What are you doing with that bunch of city slickers?" He thumped his door with his four-fingered hand. "Come ride with me."

"Looks kinda cozy," Emma said, peering into the passenger window. "But we've got somewhere we need to be. Another time."

"You got a name?"

"I put it on my tramp stamp. You get the privilege of the stamp, you get the privilege of the name."

His grin spread wider. "Damn, woman. You want to find me, look up Nick's Autobody. Ask for Axel."

"Will do." Emma looked over her shoulder at a stunned Jack and lowered her voice to a whisper. "Drive. Now."

"Nice meeting you." Jack raised the window and hit the gas.

I waited three whole seconds before I shouted at Jack, releasing all my tension in one burst. "What the hell were you thinking?"

"I was curious."

"There's a saying about curiosity and cats," Emma said. "And I can tell you from experience, it might not get you killed, but it may land you in the hospital with your life force coming out both ends."

Jack floored the accelerator and the truck bounced and skidded down the trail at twice the speed we'd been going before.

"You're driving pretty fast," I pointed out. "Are you worried they're going to come after us?"

"Just want to make sure we catch up to the semitrailer truck," he said as we careened wildly around a corner.

"I still don't understand why you stopped to talk to them. They were very clearly up to no good. Why else would they be in the middle of the wilderness looking the way they looked in vehicles that had likely just been pulled out of the junk pile? Did you notice they had no license plates? Or that the windows were tinted? Or that the dude was missing a pinkie and had what looked like gang tattoos on his remaining fingers? I think they were hiding out from the law."

Jack looked over at me and shrugged. "I'm a friendly guy. There's nothing wrong with being friendly. You need to trust me on things like this."

"I'm trying," I said. "I was very impressed with your mad driving skills, and I trusted you to keep us safe, but when you stopped to chat with the terrifying mountain men in the middle of nowhere, it was a challenge to keep the faith."

We didn't talk for the rest of the way down the mountain. We didn't talk when Jack took the wrong fork in the road and the trail led to a pond in the middle of a dark forest. We didn't talk when we finally emerged onto a paved road, and we drove in silence all the way to a gas station in Bloomsburg, where our cell phones suddenly came back to life.

That's when things really went wrong.

"I've got five missed calls from Garcia," I said, frowning as we walked around the parking lot to stretch our legs. "Maybe he's got some information for us."

"Maybe you're a suspect," Emma said. "He likes to accuse you of things."

"Or maybe he talked to the same witness Clare talked to and he's already tracked down the truck and we can all go home." Chloe leaned against the truck, her eyes half-closed while Gage suffered in silence beside her.

"The witness won't talk," Vito said.

I didn't want to know, but I did. "What do you mean 'he won't talk'? Please tell me you didn't kill him, threaten him, or tie him up somewhere."

Vito shrugged. "Okay, I won't."

I took a deep breath and then another, but my attempt to find some calm in the storm was shattered by another text.

"Milan says they cleared the roadblock in twenty minutes and now they are way ahead of us." I glared at Jack, who was busy pumping gas. "We didn't have to take the long, windy, dangerous road up a mountain pass with the *Deliverance*-style drug dealers on it. All we needed was a little patience."

My phone buzzed again, and I answered when I saw Garcia's name on my screen.

As it turned out, Emma was right. He wasn't calling about a break in the case. He was calling to accuse me of murder.

"Where are you?" he demanded without so much as a hello.

"Bloomsburg."

"You need to get back here, Simi. Detective Johnson wants to talk to you again. A witness said he saw Peter talking to a woman in the garage before he died. She had dark hair—"

"Lots of women at the party had dark hair. Vera said he just got his fifth Bugatti. I'm sure he showed it to lots of people."

"You've just run away in the middle of a murder investigation. It's not a good look."

"We didn't run away." I tried to keep my voice steady while my heart drummed in my chest. "I told you. We're on a camping trip, and for your information, Chloe is with us. Like you said, I would never leave her behind."

"You need to come back," he said quietly. "Right away. I shouldn't even be talking to you because you might be a murder suspect—"

"Do you seriously think I would take a job and then slit the host's throat in the middle of the event and run off with an entire museum full of erotic sex toys?" I was beyond irritated. "What kind of business would that be? I'd run out of clients."

"I don't understand how you keep getting mixed up in these things." His voice tightened. "It's him, isn't it? I was right this afternoon."

"Who?"

"Jack. Is he there with you? You need to stay away from him. If he's got something on you, I can protect you."

I'd spent my whole childhood wanting to hear those words, to feel that cared for, that seen, that cherished. My parents had done their best, but they'd been utterly overwhelmed by my rambunctious brothers, struggling to manage them and their sports while working full-time and trying to make ends meet. I'd faded into the background, trying not to make waves and burden them further, but it just meant I'd been forgotten and often unseen.

"I don't need protecting from Jack. He's never put me in danger." I glanced over at the dust-covered truck, the window Jack had lowered to talk to the men on the mountain, which he was now squeegeeing clean. "I'm perfectly safe and FYI not a murderer or a thief."

"Come back, Simi." Garcia's voice took on a pleading tone. "Please don't make me put out a warrant for your arrest."

Our detour had cost us precious time. Not only that, but Clare's engine had overheated, and she was stuck in a small town ahead of us trying to get it fixed.

"Did you turn off the air conditioner and turn on the heat?" I asked over the phone. "If there is steam coming from under the hood, don't open it for at least thirty minutes. When did you last have the radiator coolant checked and the belts and hoses swapped out?"

"Nothing sexier than a woman who knows her car engines," Jack whispered as he drove past a U-Haul truck. "Maybe we should make a quick stop in a densely forested area, and I can show you how much it turns me on."

"I'm still trying to recover from our last *Pinus* experience," I whispered, my cheeks heating, and not just from the compliment.

"Now we definitely have to pull over."

"No one is pulling over when we have a lost diamond to find, no matter how badly you need some," Emma said, interrupting our quiet moment. "Although I still don't understand why the thieves would want the entire collection if most of them are fake."

Annoyed at being interrupted from a deliciously flirtatious conversation, I sighed. "The erotic artwork is real."

"But it doesn't add up," she insisted. "If they're sophisticated enough to override all the security and clear out the museum in the middle of a party, how do they not know which pieces are fake?"

"How do we know which pieces are real?" Chloe lifted her head from Gage's shoulder. "Maybe Peter really did find some lost treasures. Both you and Clare believe he found the real diamond. And if the diamond is real, who is to say some of the other pieces aren't, too?"

"Vera checked with De Beers," I said. "They told her the diamond had been cut down in 1918. The stone I saw in the case hadn't been cut. It was an exact replica of the one in the museum in Vienna."

"I would have heard about lost treasures being found," Jack said. "Just like Clare and I heard about the diamond."

"He had more than enough money to keep it secret," I pointed out. "Maybe someone just slipped up. De Beers would have known about the diamond and so did the art shippers who had to assess the collection for transport. And probably some insurance broker as well. Or maybe he was betrayed by a friend."

"I think we should be focused on planning what to do once we retrieve the diamond." Gage caught my gaze in the rearview mirror, glanced over at Vito beside him, and drew his finger across his neck.

"We're a long way from that moment," I said. "We have to assume the semitrailer truck will get there before us, so we're going to have two problems: first, getting past security and into the shipyard, and second, finding the container."

"We've got the container number so we should be able to get an exact location if I can get into their system," Chloe said. "But we'll still have to deal with CCTV and whatever security they have on-site."

Anil called on video chat to let us know they'd fixed the car and were only about thirty miles ahead of us. He'd done some research on the shipyard and confirmed that in addition to CCTV, they had security guards patrolling the premises 24/7.

"We can just take out the guards," Clare said over the chat. "That's the easiest solution. Then we'll have unfettered access to the shipyard and the control center."

"We're not 'taking out' anyone," I said firmly. "This is a 'no deaths' heist. If we need access to the command center, then Vito can create some kind of distraction."

"When I got my PhD in chemistry, I never imagined I'd be paid to use my skills to blow up a shipyard," Vito said. "I couldn't find a job when I graduated and was working a side gig with a demolition company when Clare found me. She said I could do so much better."

I wasn't sure if working as a paid assassin slash demolitions expert counted as "better," but I knew what it was like to be overeducated and unemployed. I gave Vito the briefest nod in solidarity and turned to Jack, only to find him leaning out the window.

"Something wrong? Do you need some air? Emma can take over if you want a break."

"Not driving this piece of crap," Emma said. "I have a rep to protect. Who does a getaway with a camper in the box, a canoe rolling around on the roof, and bikes rattling in the back? They'll spot us a mile away."

"It's all we've got unless you want to drive with Clare in the Elantra." I was getting tired of Emma's excuses. She was the driver. Her job was to drive regardless of the state of the vehicle on offer.

"Fuck that piece of tin."

"I heard that," Clare said over the phone.

Emma grabbed the phone from my hand and brought the screen up to her face. "Good. I was worried I would have to repeat it."

"Think of it as hiding in plain sight," I assured her. "If we do have to run, they'll be looking for a speeding sports car and not a lumbering camper truck. I'm sure it will all be fine."

Looking back, I wonder if I'd jinxed us with that statement, because no more than two minutes after the words had dropped from my lips, Jack said, "I think we're being followed."

TWENTY-ONE

◇ ◇ ◇

Everyone buckle up." Jack's voice was cool, calm, and authoritative, with none of the lightness I'd come to associate with Jack and all the steel of the man who'd delivered a beating to two bodyguards outside the Sawmill without breaking a sweat.

"Who are you and what have you done with Jack?" With the truck camper in back, I couldn't see anything in the rearview mirror, but I caught a glimpse of not one but two cars in the sideview.

"I've always been here. You just weren't looking."

Maybe he was right. I'd spent so much time trying to uncover Jack's secrets, I hadn't been looking at what was right in front of me. It was easy to keep lighthearted, easygoing Jack at a distance, but this man, dark and dangerous, confident and commanding, could do some serious damage to my heart.

"Everyone take a gun." Gage grabbed the bag from the floor as Jack hit the gas.

"Not everyone knows how to use a gun," I protested. "I've never fired a weapon, and Chloe . . ." I trailed off when I remembered that my bestie did indeed know how to use a gun, thanks to Gage and the lessons he'd given her so she could defend herself from Kyle. "What about you, Emma?"

"I learned to shoot when I was three," Emma said. "I lived in a rough neighborhood."

Jack made a sharp turn onto a dirt road that led into the forest. As soon as we were well hidden in the trees, he and Gage jumped out of the truck and ran back toward the highway. A few moments later I heard the sound of cars zooming past, the roar of engines echoing through the air. "I think they passed us." I took a deep breath to calm my racing heart.

Gage returned to the vehicle, his face grim. "It was the fucking dudes from the mountain," he said, holstering his weapon. "I don't know if we saw something we shouldn't have seen or they're after the truck, but they're looking for us. They slowed down up ahead. Pretty sure they've figured out we turned off and they'll be heading back this way."

"Where's Jack?" I had a few words for "friendly" and "curious" Jack who had brought the wrath of the mountain men down on our heads.

"He climbed the hill to get a better view of the lay of the land."

"I'll get us turned around," Emma said, opening her door. "If they do come back, we'll need to move quickly."

Emma turned the truck around and drove back to the main road, where Jack was waiting. He climbed into the truck beside me and we resumed our journey.

"There's another turnout in a few miles," he said. "We can exit if they come back."

I looked over at him and glared. "I have things to say."

"I'm sure you do, sweetheart." His focus stayed on the side mirror.

"Don't sweetheart me," I said. "Your curiosity might do more than kill the cat."

"Damn." Jack gritted his teeth. "They knew we turned off and they've played the same trick. They're behind us again. Hit the gas."

"I can't go any faster without risking a tip over," Emma said. "There's too much wind resistance up top. We need to lose the canoe. Someone needs to get up there and cut it loose."

"This isn't the movies," I said. "People don't climb on moving vehicles in real life."

"People also don't get chased by sexy sedan-driving drug dealers in real life," Emma shot back. "And if we don't lose the canoe, you won't have a life to lose."

Gage pulled a knife from his boot. "I'll go."

"No." Chloe grabbed his arm. "You can't. It's too dangerous."

"Those guys aren't messing around."

I heard the swish of a window, the thud of boots on metal. Seconds later, only Jack's feet were in view.

"Jack. No." I leaned out the window and looked up. Jack had a knife in his teeth and was clinging to the top edge of the truck camper, legs dangling over the side.

"Emma, slow down," I shouted. "He's going to get killed."

"They're gaining on us. If I slow down, they'll catch up."

"Someone's going to call the police if they see him," Chloe said. "Turn onto a back road."

"Not at this speed and not with Jack hanging from the roof." Emma shook her head. "He'll get thrown if I even switch lanes."

With an incredible show of strength, Jack managed to haul himself onto the roof of the truck camper. "Tell Emma to keep it steady," he called out. "I'm going to drop the canoe when they get close and slow them down." I heard the sound of sawing, the squeak of the roof. The truck swayed and something cracked overhead.

"Jack? Everything okay?" I leaned out the window again and heard the scrape of metal.

"Hold on," Jack yelled. "Here it goes."

An ear-splitting groan echoed in the cab as the canoe slid off the roof. I heard the screech of tires, the sound of breaking glass, and the unmistakable crunch of metal hitting metal.

Gage leaned out his window and whooped in delight. "We got them both. The canoe hit the front of the sedan and the blue truck hit it from behind. Two for the price of one."

Chloe grabbed his sleeve. "Was anyone hurt?"

"Doesn't look like it," he said. "They both veered onto the shoulder. Four dudes got out. Fender bender for the truck. They might still be mobile."

"Stop the truck so Jack can get in."

Emma slowed and pulled over to the side. Jack climbed down the back access ladder and detached the bikes. I jumped out and helped him load them into the truck camper. When we were finally back in the cab and on the road, I threw my arms around him and held on tight. "That was awesome."

Jack gave a contented growl and pressed a kiss to the top of my head. "If I knew I just had to climb on a moving truck camper to get some affection, I would have done it long ago."

"Don't do anything like that again," I warned him. "You scared me to death."

"Scared means you care."

"Of course I care. I don't want you to be dead." In those terrifying moments, my feelings about Jack had become crystal clear. I couldn't lose him. I wanted him in my life, even if he couldn't be there every day.

We finally reached the container terminal around midafternoon. A vast industrial peninsula reaching into the Harbor Estuary with channels on either side, the shipyard seemed to be a world of its own. Huge warehouses surrounded by wire fences flanked mountains of tires, gravel, lumber, and empty shipping containers. Except for the constant stream of semitrailer trucks going back and forth, the area seemed deserted. The sea breeze carried the sound of the waves lapping at the dock, and in the distance, we could hear the crash and bang of the giant cranes as they loaded and unloaded the endless sea of metal containers.

"I counted four truck campers so far," Emma said as we pulled up beside Clare's Elantra in a discreet corner of yet another vast concrete parking lot. "We fit right in."

Anil came to greet us with the bad news that Clare and Milan had gone ahead to scout out the shipyard. "She says security is very tight during the day. We need to wait until after dark."

"Why didn't you go with her?" I couldn't believe he would let Clare go off without someone watching her. "You had one job."

Anil shrugged. "She said it's easier to get in with just two people."

"I'm sure it is. Now they're free to find the diamond and disappear. We'll never see her, the diamond, or the necklace ever again."

"She'll have Vito take care of us if she does find it," Gage said, reaching for his weapon. "That's why she told him to stay with us. She's probably texting him right now. I say we shoot him before he shoots us."

"Do you always have to be so negative?" I asked him. "Maybe it really is easier to get in with two people. Maybe she thought Anil was a liability."

"Maybe Angelini is going to call you up and say it was all a big joke and invite us all to his birthday party, where we'll be served a cake full of lead," Gage said. "The world is full of possibilities."

I decided to be optimistic and operate on the assumption that Clare would come back. Gage, Anil, Emma, and Vito squeezed into the Elantra and went to buy supplies. Chloe stretched out in the back seat of the truck to have a rest. Jack and I decided to stay with her in case Clare showed up with the diamond and tried to steal our vehicle. Trust, once broken, is very difficult to repair.

After everyone had gone, Jack and I inspected the truck for damage and then pulled out the bicycles to check the interior of the camper.

"You're not an ordinary thief," I said after the door swung closed behind us. "You've got some mad skills." I wanted to tell him how I felt. I wanted to tell him that I believed him about Clare. I wanted to tell him that I wanted this to work even if we couldn't always be together. Something had changed inside me when he'd climbed on the roof of the moving truck to keep us safe. My fear of losing him forever had overridden everything else. If he could risk his life, how could I be any less brave? How could I continue to hide behind the wall that I'd built to keep my heart safe?

"What skills?" Jack picked up some fallen dishes and put them back into one of the cabinets.

"Fight skills. Gun skills. Off-roading skills. Take-command-of-a-dangerous-situation skills. Climb-on-top-of-a-moving-truck-camper skills . . ." I sucked in my lips and leaned against the camper door. "Which one is the real you? The charming rogue slash professional thief or the highly trained secret undercover agent?"

Jack walked over and leaned his forearm against the door above my head, his gaze never leaving mine. "Which one do you want?"

My pulse kicked up a notch and a white-hot heat shot through my veins. "I want the real you."

Jack cupped my jaw, tilting my face back as his lips came down on mine. "You have the real me."

I melted against him, drowning in his kiss. I wanted to go back to the time when there was trust between us and life hadn't gotten in the way.

He lifted my hand and brushed his lips softly over my knuckles.

"I never saw a more beautiful sight than you hanging out the window of a speeding truck, screaming my name."

"You didn't answer."

Slowly, carefully, he kissed my hand, claiming every inch of bare skin with a gentleness I didn't know he possessed. "I had a knife between my teeth."

"I suppose that's a good excuse." I tipped my head back for another kiss. Alone for the first time since the chase, knowing he was safe, I felt overwhelmed with the need to have him close, to feel his body against mine. His smell, his taste, his heat, his desire—I wanted them all.

His lips met mine and I explored the depths of his mouth, tangling my tongue with his as I slid one hand under his shirt to feel his warmth and the firm, steady beat of his heart beneath my palm. When we broke apart to take a breath, I pressed a kiss to his throat, licking the saltiness from his skin.

He backed away, one step, then two, leaving me bereft.

"What's wrong?"

"Chloe is in the truck."

"She's a very heavy sleeper." I trailed my fingers over every hard ripple of his abdomen, following the soft trail that disappeared beneath his belt. I reached for the buckle, but Jack caught my wrist, holding me still.

"Do you want this?"

"I need this," I said. "I need you. I thought I'd lost you today."

He caught me around the waist and lifted me to his hips. With my legs wrapped around him, he walked me to the camper bunk that jutted over the top of the cab.

"Up you go." He hoisted me onto the bed and then climbed up beside me. The bed was wide but there was no more than three feet between us and the ceiling overhead.

Jack put a finger to my lips. "You'll have to be very quiet."

"So will you," I teased.

With quick, efficient movements, he stripped off my T-shirt and bra, releasing my breasts for the sensual slide of his tongue. Shivers ran down my spine as he sucked my right nipple. I wanted his lips, his hands, his mouth on every part of my body. His gaze never left mine as he took in my responses. When I moaned, he turned his attention to my other breast, and when I closed my eyes, his mouth moved slowly downward, trailing little kisses over my belly.

"Jack . . ." I urged him lower, my hands reaching to undo my jeans. He stopped me with a gentle touch.

"What do you want? Tell me."

"I want you," I said.

He hooked his fingers into my jeans and panties and slid them down over my hips. "How do you want me?"

"Your mouth," I whispered. "I want your mouth on my clit."

"I want that, too." He tossed my clothes aside and settled between my spread legs. "Maybe you should give me more details . . ." His face was pure innocence when he looked up at me, but his gaze was teasing.

"Jack." I threaded my hands through his soft hair and pulled him down where I needed him to go.

With a satisfied growl, he sucked my clit into his mouth, swirling his tongue until I was almost boneless with pleasure. My hands dug into his hair, pulling him down for more. Then suddenly he stopped.

"Do you trust me?"

I would have said anything to have his mouth back on me, but I didn't have to lie. Not after he'd shown me through his actions more than he'd been able to say in words. "Yes, Jack. I trust you."

His eyes warmed and his mouth returned, along with two fingers that he pumped inside me. My body tightened and trembled, my fingers tugging his hair, my back arching off the bed. It took almost no time to reach the peak, my heels digging into the soft blanket, my skin hot, his name a moan on my lips. Jack held me down with one firm hand and tipped me over the edge with a coordinated thrust of his fingers and a swirl of his tongue.

And then I was falling, soaring, breathless, as I was swept up in a tidal wave of ecstasy. So good. So beautiful. My legs went limp, and I closed my eyes and succumbed to sensation.

I was vaguely aware of the clink of a belt, the rustle of clothing, the crinkle of a condom. I opened my eyes as Jack climbed over me, his body hot and hard and so, so ready. Taking my hands in his, he wove our fingers together and pulled them over my head, pinning them to the bed. Then his mouth found mine, and he kissed me slowly and gently, like he had all the time in the world.

"Look at me," I whispered. Our gazes met, locked, and then he pushed deep inside me.

"Fuck, you feel so good," he muttered, and his eyes briefly closed before he began to move in and out, slowly at first, and then faster, harder. Everything faded away except the rasp of our breaths, the heat of our bodies, and the intensity of his gaze.

I climbed quickly, matching his rhythm with my own. His hand tightened around my wrists, and I moaned.

"Simi. Fuck. You're killing me." He quickened his pace, and I climaxed with an intensity that grabbed me and pulled me under.

With his eyes still on mine, Jack followed me, burying himself deep as he groaned his release.

Shuddering, he dropped down on top of me, holding his weight on his forearms as he pressed a soft kiss to my forehead.

"What happened to quiet?" He nuzzled my nose with his own.

Languid, I curled my arms around him, pressing his heavy body against my own. "I couldn't hold back."

"This is how I want you," he murmured. "I want all of you.

204 ❖ SARA DESAI

I never want you to feel like you have to hold anything back
with me."

◇ ◇ ◇

Clare didn't return until early evening. By then, I'd almost resigned myself to the possibility that she had found the diamond and taken
off, leaving us at the mercy of Vito and his supposed mandate to
slit our throats.

"You're pretty visible out here." Clare walked out of the shadows like the wraith she was. "If you weren't all so badly dressed
and the truck wasn't so run-down, people might get suspicious."

"Is that your way of apologizing for disappearing for hours?"
My hands found my hips. "You had a phone."

"Give her a break. She's doing her best to help," Anil said,
throwing a simpering look at Clare.

Emma and I shared an incredulous glance. "She's helping herself," I said. "She's the one who wants the diamond. She's the reason we're standing in a vacant shipyard parking lot at sunset. We
were just happy living our lives until she came along."

"To be fair, you'd all run out of money." Anil gave an apologetic shrug. "Emma was back to driving for Uber. You were planning funerals. Jack and Gage were heisting. Cristian had spent all
his money on unwanted TV pilots, and Chloe unwisely put all her
money in a savings account. If you'd all just listened to me about
how to invest your money, you'd realize that sometimes you have
to make short-term sacrifices for long-term gains."

"Is there a point to this friend-bashing exercise?" Emma asked.
"If you're trying to tell us you're switching sides, we got that message long ago."

"You never take me seriously." Anil shuffled over to Clare.
"You always make fun of me. Clare listens. She thinks I have good
ideas. She sees me for who I really am."

Emma made a show of doubling over and retching. "Here come the chili dogs. I knew I should have stopped at three."

Clare gave Anil a warm smile before turning back to me. "I stole some gear and went in dressed as a longshoreman. They have an advanced security system with at least a dozen CCTV monitors in the control room, which are watched by two guards. Their foot patrol varies between two and four guards plus two dogs." She turned to show us a nasty rip on her jeans. "There is no way we can go in until it gets dark, and even then, if Chloe can't locate the container, we're going to have a tough job finding it with a manual search. There are hundreds of containers, and we won't be able to use our flashlights without attracting attention."

"Do we even know if the container is here?" Gage leaned against the camper, thick arms crossed. "Could be the driver stopped for a break."

"It's here." Chloe looked up from her laptop. "I still have access to the consolidator's system, and they were notified when the container was delivered to the terminal. You just need to lure the guards away from the control room so I can loop the CCTV cameras and hack the computer." She shot a look at Clare. "Lure, not kill."

"I've got something that will do the trick." Vito held up a metal jar. "It's sexy and spicy with a lot of heat. I call it 'the Vito.'"

"Of course you do." Emma patted his arm. "Every good narcissist needs something named after him."

When the sun finally set, we made the long trek to the dock, keeping to the shadows of steel warehouses, towering rock piles, and abandoned heavy equipment. Clare had cut a hole through the wire fence in a camera blind spot, and we slipped inside one by one. Vito stayed near the entrance, where he planned to set off a series of small explosions to draw the guards away so we could get into the control room.

"There's no way . . ." Emma surveyed the endless rows of shipping containers. Between them, twenty-foot gantry cranes on rubber wheels stood motionless, waiting for daybreak, when they would start lifting the containers onto terminal tractors, which would take them to the massive cranes that would then load them onto the cargo ships berthed at the dock. "If Chloe can't find a location, we're screwed."

"How do we know we're safe here?" Chloe asked, looking around.

"I went into the control room pretending I was new and had lost my way," Clare said. "I got a quick picture of the screens and then checked out the cameras until I identified a blind spot."

"I hope this is a blind spot for the dogs, too." Anil fiddled with the drone he'd bought during the supply run. He'd been disappointed we'd left his bulk pack of ski masks in the camper, but there had been no takers when he offered them around. "I've got to sit still to operate the drone, and dogs don't like me. I told you once about the bad experience I had as a child."

"I remember you wet your pants," Emma said. "Or was that some other childhood trauma?"

"Emma . . ." I shot her a warning look.

"What?" She shrugged. "Clare needs to know what she's getting herself into."

Anil opened his mouth to respond, but his words were cut off by a series of explosions near the front gate. Vito had worked his magic. Moments later the door to the control room opened and two guards ran into the yard. Chloe and I quickly slipped inside, and within minutes she had looped the camera feed so we could move around the shipyard undetected.

"Can you find the container?" I asked after she'd uploaded her hacking software into their system.

Chloe's fingers flew over her keyboard. "It's a lot more complicated than I expected. I'll need more time. I also think you should get people started on a manual search in case I can't get in."

I sent a quick message to Vito asking for more explosions and then returned to the group to explain the situation. "We need to split up and start a manual search. You all have the number. The container is twenty feet long, so you can eliminate any forty-foot containers. Jack and I will have the bolt cutters, so when you find it, let me know. Communicate on the server and set your notifications to vibrate. Jack and I will take the northeast quadrant. Emma and Vito, when he's done, can search the northwest. Clare and Milan, you've got the southwest, and Gage and Anil—"

"Not leaving Chloe unprotected," Gage said. "Someone needs to run interference when the guards come back. If she can't crack the system by that time, we'll take the southeast corner."

"I need to stay here and operate the stealth drone," Anil said. "I'll be able to track the security guards and send out warnings if they are in your area. I can also try to search the southeast quadrant by drone until Chloe and Gage are done."

"We've got six hours until daylight," I said. "On your mark. Get set. Go."

TWENTY-TWO

◇ ◇ ◇

Here's the thing with heists: They only work if everybody does their part. If even one person slips up, the entire operation collapses like a house of cards.

I would never have imagined Anil would be the one to bring us down.

My first inkling that things were about to go awry was Anil's frantic video message forty minutes after we'd separated echoing from my phone in the stillness of the night. "I think the dogs found me. I was eating a burger and—"

"Get off the video," I snapped. "The guards will hear you. And why would you eat burgers when there are dogs around?"

"My mom made me promise to eat every few hours, so I don't have a blood sugar crash. I picked up a bag of cheeseburgers when we went for supplies and . . . HELLLLLLLP." He screamed and the camera showed flashes of the ground, a paper bag, a worn sneaker, and the corner of a container. I could hear dogs barking. A man shouted, "He went that way!" and then the screen went dark.

I moved to run in his direction, but Jack grabbed my arm. "We have to keep going. Now that they know someone is here, they'll start looking for accomplices."

"We can't just abandon him. He's got a dog phobia."

"Pretty sure he'd rather deal with the dogs than the Mafia, which is who we'll be facing if we don't find that jewel."

My heart squeezed in my chest, and I forced myself to check the next container as Anil's screams faded into the distance. I told myself he'd be fine. He'd spent a year training to be an MMA star. He was smart and resourceful. So, he had a tendency to panic, and he was still very naive about the world and an awkward runner . . .

"Simi." Jack's voice broke my train of thought. "You need to focus. This is—"

"Focus?" My fear turned to anger, and Jack became my outlet. "Anil is in trouble. How can you be so calm? Don't you care?"

"I do care, but . . ." He trailed off when my phone buzzed again. This time the message was from Chloe.

"Oh God." I held up the phone. "Chloe sent Gage to help Anil, but before she could get out of the control room, one of the guards came back. She's hiding in a closet. Even worse, the guard knows there is a problem with the cameras. I don't know if he has the skills to figure out how to remove her hacking software program, but we have to go and help her because if he calls the police—"

"Simi." Jack's voice rose to an impatient shout. "This is it."

"The end. I know." My shoulders sagged. "But we can't just leave them to fend for themselves."

"This is the container." He said each word slowly and emphatically until he had my full attention.

"This is the container?" I stared at the red door in front of me, trying to get my brain to process any information besides the fact that my bestie needed me. "The one we're looking for?"

Jack nodded. "You've been standing in front of it for over a minute."

I double-checked the white painted numbers with what I had on my screen. Finally, the information sank in, and I stared at him, incredulous. "We found it."

"Yes." He pulled the bolt cutters from the pack on his back. "Help me break the lock."

"But Chloe . . ."

A loud BOOM rocked the night and the sky glowed with an eerie green light. I heard shouts, a whistle, and the fading barking of dogs.

"Vito's on the case," Jack said. "Trust the crew to do what they do best. You know Chloe can take care of herself, and you know she would tell you to get the damn diamond so we can be free of this mess. You also know that once Gage finds out that she's trapped, he'll drop everything to help her, and nothing will stand in his way."

He was so confident, utterly unshakable in his faith in the crew. I wanted to believe him, trust him, trust them, but something felt wrong, like the tide was shifting, and any moment we were going to be swept away by forces beyond our control.

"Jack . . . I have to go." I turned in the direction of the control room and Chloe.

"I've got it." Jack broke the lock on the container and pulled open the door. Gritting my teeth against the urge to run to Chloe, I turned on my flashlight and stepped inside.

"What's that smell?" My noise wrinkled at the acrid chemical smell coming from the tightly packed rolls of carpet in front of us.

"Volatile organic compounds," Jack said. "They're chemicals used in the manufacturing of household products like paint, wallpaper, and some floor finishes. It's why I prefer natural hardwood floors." Jack moved aside roll after roll of carpet, clearing a trail to the boxes stacked at the back of the container. "This must be the shipment that was consolidated with ours."

"I hope you told our architect about your love of hardwood," I teased. "I would hate to move into our fake new home only to have to move out again because you're unhappy with the flooring."

"I told him there should only be carpet in the bedrooms." Jack looked back over his shoulder and gave me a naughty smile that made my stomach tighten. "To dampen the sound."

"This isn't the time," I warned him.

Jack chuckled. "It's always time when we're alone in the dark."

"I think those are paintings." I pushed past him when I spotted a stack of thin boxes leaning against the wall. "Hand me the knife."

Jack passed over a box cutter and I sliced open the top of the nearest box and shone my flashlight inside. I recognized the erotic painting of the woman and the octopus right away. Even on my second viewing, it made my stomach churn.

"This is it! Jack! We found the collection."

We set up our flashlights on one of the wooden crates and started slicing open the boxes one by one. Everything was there, from the fertility statues to the Chinese pillow books and from the suggestive paintings to the gruesome skull. We worked quickly and steadily for another ten minutes until, finally, I found the diamond wrapped in its blue velvet cloth, tossed in with the rest of Peter's fake treasures like a worthless piece of trash.

"I got it!" I ran over to Jack and threw myself into his arms. "We did it. We'll get the necklace, hand it over to Angelini, he'll free Cristian, and we'll all be safe."

"I like this happy, excited you." Jack wrapped his arms around me, pulling me against his solid strength, and to the place I wanted to be. Taking me by surprise, he leaned down and kissed me. "I want to keep you right here and never let you go."

"Your wish is about to come true," Clare said from the doorway. "Give me the diamond."

I froze as Jack whirled to face her, blocking me with his body.

He was fast, but not fast enough. I caught a glimpse of Milan with a knife in each hand and Vito with a gun pointed in our direction. I wished I'd listened to Gage and let everyone take a gun from his bag. I wished I hadn't declared this a "no guns" heist.

"We'll hand it over when you give us the necklace." Jack's voice was deceptively calm, but his arm pinning me against his back was as solid as steel. "As we agreed."

Clare's laughter echoed through the container, and her lips curled into a sneer, turning her features into a twisted grin of malice and triumph. "I'm taking it now, and I'm keeping the necklace. Did you really think I was going to hand over something worth $30 million?"

"No," he said. "But I thought Xavier would make you do it as a matter of honor."

"There is no honor among thieves. You taught me that." She stepped to the side and Anil walked into the container behind her.

"Anil!" My heart soared. "Show her your MMA moves. Call Gage. She's trying to steal the diamond."

"That was always the plan." He stared at the floor and toed the rough metal surface with a worn sneaker.

Nothing in my life had ever shocked me more. Not Clare double-crossing us. Not the appearance of Tony Angelini in my office. Not the sight of Rose doing a *Mission Impossible* drop from the ceiling of a warehouse to save us during the last heist. Not even the twist of events that had led us here in the first place. I opened my mouth, and no words came out. Not even a sound. Instead, I felt the punch of betrayal hitting my gut, knocking the breath from my lungs.

At a gesture from Clare, Vito walked toward us. Jack took a step back, keeping me behind him with one arm twisted behind his back.

"Phones." Vito held out his free hand. "And the diamond."

"Vito . . ." I swallowed hard. "I thought we were a team. You ate fire for us. You blew things up. You made that special Vito blend that lit up the sky. You have a PhD in chemistry. Surely, you realize Clare is going to double-cross you, too."

"It's a job," he said. "Nothing personal."

"What are you going to have him do if we don't hand it over, Clare? Shoot us?" Jack's voice was tinged with exasperation. "Do you really think Xavier wants me dead?"

Xavier had to be the real name of Jack's nemesis, the mysterious Mr. X. He had plucked Jack from the streets on the pretense of giving him a better life, only to force him into a life of crime instead.

"He wouldn't complain." Clare's throat tightened as she swallowed. "Not after what you did."

My blood ran cold, and I reached behind me for something to throw. Seconds later, I was pinned to the crate, a knife through the sleeve of my hoodie holding me in place. The sudden impact and the sheer precision of the throw took my breath away. Behind Clare, Milan gave an apologetic shrug.

"Jesus Christ." Seemingly oblivious to the threat, Jack turned his back and yanked the knife out of the crate. "Show me your arm. Did she hurt you? If you've even got a scrape . . ."

I wasn't sure what Jack would do in the face of Vito's gun and Milan's knives, but I appreciated the sentiment beneath his protective fury.

"I'm okay." My voice wavered despite my best efforts to remain calm.

"Phones." Milan gestured with her knife, and Jack and I reluctantly gave Vito our only means of communicating with the rest of the crew.

Vito tucked the phones in his jacket and then pointed his gun at Jack. "You first or her?"

Jack stepped in front of me again, shielding me with his body. "Clare . . . you don't want to do this."

"It's been fun, but I'm getting tired of you interfering with my work." She waved a dismissive hand that belied the pain and anger on her face. "You should have stayed with Xavier. With me. We were good together. We were a good team."

Jack stared at her for a long moment, and his voice softened. "We weren't a good couple, Clare. You know that. We're too much alike. We didn't trust each other. You can't have a relationship without trust."

"I thought we had something more than trust." Her bitter voice echoed in the container. "We had a bond. We were forged in the same fire. No one else could understand what we had to do to survive on the streets—to survive Xavier."

"It made us hard," Jack said. "It made us cold. And Xavier took us and turned us into ice. That's why it didn't work. We each needed someone warm, someone who could undo what Xavier did. If I hadn't left, I would have wound up just like him."

"You were supposed to take me with you," Clare spat out. She plucked one of the knives from Milan's hand and threw it hard and fast. Jack jerked to the side, pulling me with him, and it narrowly missed his shoulder.

"You're out of practice," he said, all cool and calm like his ex-girlfriend hadn't just thrown a knife at him with almost Milan-like precision.

"You can't win this one," Clare said. "Give me the diamond."

"Fuck you."

Another swish. Another knife. This one from Milan, and this time it grazed Jack's ear before clattering onto the floor behind us. Jack grunted but he didn't move, a protective shield of muscle in front of me.

"You missed." He had me pinned between his body and a

packing crate. I could feel his heart pounding inside his chest, hear his rapid breaths. Fear soured in my mouth, bitter and acidic, as I watched Clare's eyes narrow. I didn't understand why he was taunting her. We both knew Milan could turn him into a pincushion in seconds if she was serious about killing him.

Clare sighed. "This is getting tedious. You have nowhere to go. You have no weapons. You could knock out the flashlights and try to escape, but you won't last three seconds once Vito starts shooting. If you manage to get past him, you still have to deal with Milan. And me. And even Anil. Apparently, he's got some serious MMA skills."

I couldn't look at Anil. His betrayal made me feel sick inside. I thought we were friends, but it turned out I didn't know him at all.

"Vito . . ." Clare gestured behind her. "Get the diamond. Now. Do what it takes."

"Xavier will never forgive you." Jack's muscles tightened as Vito stepped forward, his body going rigid. Clearly, he didn't think we'd leave here alive.

"No. Stop." I stepped out from behind Jack. "I'll give you the diamond on the condition that you take it and walk away. No knives. No bullets. No killing."

"You aren't really in a position to make demands," Clare said.

"And you're not in a position to have to deal with the rest of the crew coming after you if you kill us, because they will. We're family and there is nothing we won't do for each other, even if it is to avenge the death of one of our own. There is nowhere you can run. Nowhere you can hide. No corner of the earth too remote. Nowhere you will ever be safe—"

Clare laughed, the sound cutting into my heart like shards of broken glass. "You forget I've seen your crew in action. Trying to get them to do anything is like herding cats. They are easily distracted. They bicker and fight. They're never serious. Without you, they can't even agree on what to order for dinner. I'll just tell them you and Jack ran off with the diamond."

"Chloe will never believe you." I had absolute faith in my best friend. No one knew me better.

"I can be very convincing, and I have two . . . no, three witnesses, including one of your own." Clare waved vaguely behind her. "People have done crazier things for love."

"Except for Jack, you've never had a friend," I said, finally understanding. Milan and Vito were mercenaries, not friends. Clare was alone. She had always been alone. This heist wasn't just about the diamond. It was about Jack. He'd hurt her and she wanted to hurt him back.

"I'll take my chances with your ragtag crew." She nodded at Vito and Milan. "Take care of them. I'll pry the diamond out of her cold, dead hand."

"If you shoot them, the sound will echo in the container and carry around the shipyard," Anil said, his voice curiously flat. "It would immediately draw the attention of the rest of the crew and the security guards. A better option would be to lock them in the container."

"Anil!" I looked at him in horror. "You can't—"

"That way you won't get in trouble with this Xavier person," he continued, cutting me off. "Or Chloe, because I could tell her in all honesty that you didn't kill them. We can lock the container and paint over the number. Its location in the shipyard is already in the database so it will be picked up by the crane and put on the ship to Belize, but after that it can't be traced."

"That doesn't help if they're still alive when they get to port," Clare said. "They'll just come back and cause trouble."

"They'll be dead well before then." Anil still wouldn't meet my gaze. "I calculate that they'll have roughly 48.7 hours of oxygen if they breathe an average of fifteen times per minute and the shipping container is tightly sealed. However, the carbon dioxide buildup will kill them well before that. And even if my calculations are off, they won't survive ten days without water, which is how long the trip will likely take. You still achieve your goal of ending their lives without getting your hands dirty or taking any risks. If their bodies are discovered at their destination, they'll have no ID and people will probably think they were stowaways."

"You really are brilliant." Clare gave him an appreciative look. "You were undervalued in your crew. I won't make the same mistake. It's a good plan, although I'm still tempted to just get it over and done with because the idea of the merry band of misfits coming after me is the most amusing thing I've ever heard."

"We're wasting time," Vito said. "One of the guards saw Anil before Gage knocked him out. They know someone messed with the cameras. They'll be looking for us."

Clare nodded. "Get the diamond."

Vito gestured to me with his gun, and I put the diamond in his outstretched palm. A chance at living was better than resisting and dying an instant and painful death. Maybe Clare would let us go once she had the diamond in her hand.

Vito passed the diamond to Clare and she tucked it in her pocket before murmuring a few words in his ear. She gestured to Anil and Milan, and they followed her out of the container. I took a step forward and Vito raised his gun.

"Don't move." He walked backward, his weapon pointed in our direction. The hair on the back of my neck prickled and my blood ran cold.

"You've got the diamond," Jack called out. "Let us go, or at the very least let Simi go. This is between you and me, Clare."

"Are you going to . . . ?" My mouth went dry. Had Clare decided to kill us instead of locking us up? Was this it? Was my life really going to end with a gunshot to the heart in a dusty shipping container in Newark? What about my family? Chloe? Olivia? I hadn't had a chance to say good-bye. I hadn't told Jack that I loved him and forgave him and wanted to be with him forever.

"Clare . . ." Jack grabbed my hand and yanked me forward as soon as Vito stepped out of the container. "Don't do this . . ."

"Do what?" I stumbled behind him, my arm almost leaving its socket with the force of his tug. At first, I thought he was going to use me as a human shield, and I mentally took back the loving thoughts I'd had only a moment before. Only when I heard the creak of hinges did I understand what was happening. But by then, it was too late.

The door slammed, the vibration knocking our flashlights to the floor. Barely able to see in the flickering light, we hit the door at full speed, forearms slamming against the plywood-enforced steel.

"No," I shouted. "Let us out. You don't need to do this. You have everything you want." I pressed my ear to the door, but there was no response, only an eerie silence that seemed to devour our voices.

"Clare!" Jack was livid with rage, his voice raw and ragged and filled with fury.

"We'll die in here." My heart pounded in my chest as panic set in. I could feel the darkness closing in on us, suffocating and relentless. "There's no water. No food. No oxygen . . ." My lungs seized and I bent over, gasping for breath.

"Don't panic." Jack pulled me into his arms. "You heard Anil. No more than fifteen breaths per minute."

"I am panicking. This is exactly the kind of situation panic was made for." My words came out in a terrified rush. "Why else would humans be born with the capacity for panic if not to use it when they've been locked in a shipping container by an evil psychopath, her hench people, and a betraying friend? The bigger question is . . . why are you so calm?"

"I've been in worse situations," Jack said.

"Worse?" My voice rose in pitch. "What could be worse than being shipped off to Belize? My parents won't even have a body to bury. They'll probably think I ran off with you, and they'll spend the rest of their days telling everyone that they knew white boys were trouble and they should have married me off to a nice South Asian boy as soon as I turned eighteen."

"I am trouble." Jack brushed his lips over my hair. "You're here because of me."

"We're here because of Clare. She's the villain of this story." I leaned against his chest, soaking up his warmth until my tension eased. "I feel better now. It's time for screaming and shouting and pounding our fists against the door. Whoever makes the most noise wins."

TWENTY-THREE

◇ ◇ ◇

I screamed myself hoarse, pounded on the walls until my hands bled, and kicked and stomped until I'd torn a hole in my shoe. Jack participated in the noise fest for the first half hour, but after that he left me to it and searched through the crates and boxes for something we could use to escape.

"How can you want to do anything except break down this door?" I shouted at him between poundings. "We might die in here."

"I don't believe in suffering until it's time to suffer." He held up a stone dildo and a circular ring made of jade. "And if we do get to that point, at least we'll die happy."

"I can't believe you can think of sex at a time like this." Exhausted, I slumped against the door, resting my head on the cold steel in the semidarkness. We'd turned off one of the flashlights to conserve the batteries, and Jack was using the other to search the boxes. Without even a glimmer of outside light to let us know if dawn was approaching, I had no idea how long we'd been trapped.

"I think about sex all the time when I'm with you," he said. "You're a very sexy woman. I'm often amazed I can even function when you walk into a room. All I want to do is drag you to my bed and—"

"Stop." I held up my hand. "We are not having sexy times while there is still work to be done. When we've run out of options and there is no hope and we are in the depths of despair, then we can have sex. All the sex. As much sex as you can handle with only fifteen breaths per minute. We can die having sex. In fact, I'd like to die in the middle of an orgasm so when they find our bodies, I'll have a smile on my face and my mother will know that even though I ran off with a white boy, I was happy."

"Are you happy?" He dove into one of the crates and pulled out a fertility statue.

"I was happy until Angelini walked into my office and said he was going to kill us if we didn't bring him the necklace." I leaned against the door, dropping my hands between my legs. "Well, sort of happy. My business wasn't doing so well. There is a lot of competition in the event-planning world, and I didn't have the kind of connections I needed to make it big. I had to move into funerals, and honestly, except for the circus-themed celebrations of life, they were really getting me down. Who wants to be reminded of their mortality every week when they haven't even figured out their life?"

"It's not easy starting your own business," he said. "I was impressed how you jumped right in without any hesitation. You wanted it, and you went for it. Not a lot of people have that kind of courage."

"Not a lot of people get an $833,333.33 reward so they have a cushion when they start out."

Jack looked up and frowned. "I thought you used most of the money to pay off your parents' mortgage."

"Yes, I did. And my student loans. And then there was the down payment for my condo and the rental for the office. There wasn't much left after that. I never realized my parents had taken out a second mortgage to put us all through college, and that was after we'd all maxed out on loans. And then there was Nikhil's wedding, and they'd put aside money for the twins' weddings, and my wedding, which I guess isn't going to happen since I'll be dead in 48.7 hours. Just as well. I used to want to have kids, but they're too damn expensive."

"If I had kids, I'd want one who wouldn't think twice about using her money to pay off my mortgage even if I'd treated her unfairly all her life." He pulled out the skull I'd seen when Vera had first taken me downstairs to view the collection.

"They were doing their best in a difficult situation. They love me and that's what's important. I've worked through the rest and moved on." I hesitated. "Well, I thought I had until you ghosted me, and then it all came back." I pushed to stand and walked over to help search the boxes. "What about you? Did you get some closure after you put Joseph Angelini in jail? What he did to your grandmother was beyond awful."

"It felt good, but it didn't bring her back." He held the flashlight closer to the skull. "If this is a fake, it's a very good one. I could swear it's real."

"If it can't help us get out of here, it doesn't matter if it's real or fake." I picked up the fertility statue. "Do you think this is heavy enough to bash our way through the wall?"

"Not a chance."

"There has to be something in here that we can use to pry the doors apart." I pulled out a four-inch diamond star that consisted of a sea of shining jewels surrounding a cross of rubies and a trefoil of diamonds around a sky-blue enamel circle. "What about this? Vera said Peter thought it was one of the missing Irish crown jewels. Diamonds are supposed to be the hardest substance on Earth. Maybe we could use it to cut our way out."

"Too small," Jack said, picking up the second piece of the set, a matching diamond badge with a similar pattern of emeralds, rubies, and rose diamonds, the whole thing surmounted by a crowned harp. They'd been haphazardly tossed in the box, wrapped only in an orange silk scarf. "They're probably glass and if we apply any pressure, they'll shatter." He held the flashlight over the badge and frowned. "Although . . ."

"What?"

"Do you see the shimmer? A real diamond reflects light easily and provides a disco-ball or rainbow effect. Fake diamonds don't reflect spectral rays, but a real diamond's refractive index is high; it makes the white light entering the diamond split into multiple colors before it exits on the other side of the stone."

I studied the light pattern on the badge. "I see a rainbow. Does that mean they're real?"

Jack held the light to the badge at different angles. "Possibly. It's hard to tell for certain without proper light or equipment."

"I forgot you were a jewel thief." I put the pieces back in the box. "Sometimes I think you're just a regular guy."

"I thought you wanted a regular guy." He leaned against the boxes, his face half-hidden in the shadows.

"I did, too. I complained incessantly to Chloe about the fact you were never around when I would go home for Sunday dinner and a slew of eligible bachelors would be paraded through the door. Or when I'd had a bad day and needed a hug. Or when I needed to get out of the city and my friends only wanted to do tame things like go for a hike or drive along the coast . . ."

"I would have thought of something interesting," Jack said. "Bungee jumping or cliff diving, maybe kayaking over a waterfall—"

"Or taking me to the worst bar in Chicago to meet a man who makes fake passports, or to an architect to talk about a fake renovation while you break into his computer, or into a dark alley for illegal sexy times."

Jack grimaced. "I put you in danger."

"The things we did made me feel alive." I pulled out a marble plaque with a hideous face on it—half animal, half man. "I think I got addicted to the adrenaline rush of being left behind as a kid. I'd be alone in a gas station or at a sports hall or in a shopping center, and I'd have a few heart-pounding moments of terror before I could think clearly enough to make a plan."

"You do like your plans," he said, smiling.

"They keep me calm." I tipped my head to the side. "What makes you calm?"

"Being in control."

I flipped through a few paintings securely crated in boxes. "I guess you would need that after losing all the people you loved when you were a kid."

"And when I was older and found myself tethered to someone who took me down a dark path." His voice hitched and I froze, afraid even to breathe. Jack had told me about his life before his grandmother died and a bit about the foster homes he'd stayed in after that. But he'd never shared anything about his life with Mr. X.

"Do you . . . work for Mr. X now?"

"No." He used his penknife to open another box. "But Clare does."

I tried to play it cool, like he shared secrets about his past with me every day. "Clare said you betrayed him."

"I did." He hesitated. "I betrayed her, too, when I left. We'd known each other a long time. We'd been close . . ." He sucked in his lips. "I don't want to make you feel uncomfortable."

"I know you have a past," I said. "I do, too. I don't have a problem hearing about yours."

"He took us both off the streets around the same time," Jack continued. "He offered us food, a home, and the opportunity to go to school if we worked for him in return. At first it was just simple errands, but then he wanted me to steal something, and then he set me up so that if I refused to do as asked, he could go to the police with proof of my crimes."

"He blackmailed you."

"He blackmailed all of us. That's how he put together his crew."

"But that was a long time ago," I said. "Why does he want to kill you now?"

"He wants me to suffer now." Jack pulled a rolled blanket out of a box. "He wants to kill me later. You saw how his minions beat me almost to death during our last heist, but that wasn't the first time. He'll keep sending them after me until he gets bored, and then he'll end me for betraying him. No one leaves Xavier's crew."

My throat closed at the thought of Jack gone forever. "You seem pretty nonchalant about the whole thing."

"I was, but not now. I get an immense amount of satisfaction from repatriating stolen historical artifacts, especially because I'm often working against Xavier's interests, but I never had anything to look forward to, except the next assignment. I never had a real home after my grandmother died. I never had someone who made me want to survive the next beating or shooting. And then I met you."

Despite our dire predicament, a smile spread across my face. "You kidnapped me and dragged me into the bushes. That's not the traditional meet-cute of romance."

"You were cute," he said. "You made me laugh. You were brave and so fiercely loyal that you refused to leave Chloe even when you knew you'd be arrested. And now you are determined to save Cristian even though it would be much easier just to flee the country." Jack unrolled the blanket and gasped out loud.

"What is it?" I studied the long, gleaming, curved sword in his hands.

"If it's real, it's a legendary samurai sword that was passed from generals to shoguns throughout the centuries. It was supposedly created by Gorō Nyūdō Masamune, who lived from 1264 to 1343 and is considered by many to be the greatest sword maker in Japanese history." He swung the blade in an arc, the fine edge cutting through the air with a terrifying *whoosh*. "The sword was a Japanese national treasure, lost after the Second World War when Japan was forced to hand it over to American soldiers."

"It's very shiny," I said. "Too shiny for something that's almost eight hundred years old."

"Someone might have taken very good care of it." Jack laid it over the box and inspected it with his flashlight.

"Come on." I gave him a nudge. "Do you really think an amateur billionaire fortune hunter really found so many of the world's missing treasures and not one of his finds hit the news or your underground black market jewel thief network? What did he have that hundreds of years' worth of treasure hunters didn't? I met him briefly at the party and he seemed spectacularly unremarkable to me."

"He had billions of dollars," Jack said. "There is nothing he couldn't buy. No one he couldn't hire. He'd be able to trawl the bottom of the sea for Atlantis or blow up a mountain and still have money left over to buy an art island or two."

"This whole thing doesn't make sense." I walked through the piles of boxes. "Someone killed Peter to get his finger to open the museum. If they thought all these treasures were real, why would they just haphazardly toss them in boxes? Wouldn't they take more care than to wrap an eight-hundred-year-old sword in a blanket or bundle the Irish national jewels in a scarf?"

"They likely didn't have enough time," Jack said. "They had to get Peter alone, kill him, cut off his finger, knock Chloe out, get through three security doors, shut down the system, load up the boxes, and carry them through the bunker and down the tunnel before their truck arrived."

"They had to have been invited to the party." I studied the boxes, considering. "There is no other way they could have been inside. I had security at every entrance checking invitations. I also think they knew the art was about to be moved and the boxes had been delivered, because otherwise how were they going to transport everything?"

We searched all the boxes but didn't find anything that would help us escape. Eventually exhaustion overcame me, and I slumped to the floor, leaning against a thick roll of carpet. Jack covered me with the blanket that had been wrapped around the sword and sat beside me, pulling me into his arms. The blanket was exquisitely soft and thick, and the cozy warmth eased my tension. After twenty-four hours without sleep, it didn't take long before my eyes closed, and I fell asleep nestled in the crook of Jack's arm.

I don't know how long we slept, but I awoke to the sounds of grating gears, rubber on asphalt, and a hydraulic whine. A low rumble like an idling C-130 shook the container. Above us, the ceiling shuddered.

"What's happening?"

"It's a gantry crane taking the container on top of us." For the first time since we'd been locked in the container, Jack's brow furrowed the tiniest bit. "We'll be next."

"We can't be loaded onto a ship, Jack." I pounded on the container wall. "I don't want to die at sea. I don't even like fish. When my dad makes Malabar matthi curry, I run for the hills." I thudded again. "Make some noise."

"There's no operator," Jack said. "The cranes are fully automated.

A computer sends them to pick up containers based on their serial numbers."

A tidal wave of despair crashed over me. "Chloe will come," I said, to reassure myself more than Jack, who didn't seem very concerned about the imminent danger.

"If anyone can find us, it's her," he agreed. "She's incredibly resourceful, and in my business, I've worked with the best."

"Your current business or your past business when you worked for Mr. X?"

"Both."

"And you can't tell me what you do or who you work for?" I looked up at him. "Even if we're going to die in here?"

Jack sat beside me and pressed a soft kiss to my temple. "If it gets to that point, I'll tell you with my next-to-last dying breath."

Frowning, I said, "Next to last? What are you going to say with your dying breath?"

"I love you."

Silence hung in the air between us. Jack had told me he loved me before, but this felt different. We'd hurt each other—him with his secrets and his absence, and me with my lack of trust—but clearly, for him it hadn't changed the way he felt.

"I suppose that's not a bad thing to say with your last dying breath." I leaned against him, my cheek against his chest, listening to the steady beat of his heart.

"It's not a bad thing to say with any breath. The question is whether you believe it."

"It was hard when you ghosted me. It made me feel like I wasn't important, just as I did when I was a child. Seeing you kiss Clare was triggering, to be honest. Even now, knowing she set you up, I can't move past the fear that I'm an afterthought. I can't go through that again."

"You have never been an afterthought to me." He tightened his arm around me. "But I've never been a commitment kind of guy. I think I subconsciously stacked my jobs so that there was no opportunity to come back to Chicago. Part of me knew I still needed to sort myself out. I needed time to figure out what I really wanted, and as soon as I realized it was you, I came home to tell you. And then you dumped me."

"You waited too long."

"Yes." His jaw tightened. "And Garcia was waiting to pounce."

Laughter bubbled up in my chest. "You make him sound like a wild animal. He's a very even-tempered kind of guy. Very kind, straitlaced, by the book—"

"Boring." Jack puffed out his chest. "You need someone who can give you adventure and excitement."

"Like getting locked up in a shipping container that's about to be sent to Belize?"

Jack sighed and rested his cheek against my head. "This was supposed to be my last heist. After it was done, I had planned to stay in Chicago and find a new job so I could be with you."

"You were going to quit?" I sat upright. "For me?"

"For both of us." He pulled me in a straddle across his lap and took my face between his warm palms. "I didn't have anything, Simi. I lost everyone I loved, and the people I thought were my family turned out to be thieves and criminals. It wasn't a life I wanted to lead, so I broke those ties. And then I had no one. You changed that for me. You and your beautiful smile."

He kissed me ever so softly, and I wound my arms around his neck. I was tired of keeping secrets. I had been keeping Angelini's final demand from him even though I'd long moved past the fear that he would abandon us. Instead, I was afraid he would offer himself up to save us. I'd needed time to figure out a way to save him, to protect him from himself. But our time had almost run out and I wanted to come clean.

"I need to tell you something, Jack. I've been keeping something from you and . . ." I hesitated, not sure how to explain.

Jack's brow creased in consternation. "What is it? You can tell me anything."

"At first it made sense not to tell you because of what happened between us and the thing with Clare . . ." My words ran over one another as I tried to get everything out at once. "And then it was just easier not to tell you because part of me was still afraid to trust you. But now . . . I was wrong, and you need to know—"

"Simi!" Chloe's voice outside the container was muffled, but I would know my bestie anywhere. A wave of emotion swept over me so fierce and hard it knocked the breath out of me. Relief flooded my veins, pushing back the suffocating darkness.

"Chloe! We're in here."

"I found them," she shouted. "Quickly. Bring the bolt cutters."

"Give us a minute," she said. "They've chained and padlocked the door."

I heard the scrape of metal on metal. A grunt. The walls trembled. Beneath my feet I could feel a familiar rumble. "Hurry. The gantry crane is coming. It already took the container above us. I think we're next."

"Gage, get the fucking door open or your life won't be worth living," Chloe screamed. "They're about to be snatched up by the crane." I heard a series of loud thuds followed by a string of curse words I'd never heard from Chloe before.

I heard a snap, the rattle of chains, a creak of rusty hinges. The doors opened and cool ocean air rushed in, carrying the scent of freedom with it. A frantic Chloe ran into the container, grabbed my hand, and dragged me outside with Jack following close behind us. Gage slammed the door closed, slipping the remnants of the chain through the lock before he joined us in a narrow passage between container stacks. Moments later, a giant yellow gantry crane stopped above our container, its three-foot wheels resting where we'd stood only seconds before. The crane lowered and lifted the container, then whisked it away toward the dock.

"Oh my God," I whispered. "That was close. How did you find us?"

Chloe threw herself at me and wrapped me in a hug. "When you stopped responding to my messages, I knew something was wrong, so I messaged Emma and Gage while I checked for your signal on my finding friends app." She drew in a ragged breath. "It showed your phone was at the bottom of the Harbor Estuary, and I would have lost it if Emma hadn't run back to the parking lot and discovered the Elantra was gone. That's when I knew you must have found the diamond and they got to you first, but I didn't know . . ." Her voice cracked, broke, and she shuddered in my arms.

"Don't let those tears fool you," Gage said. "My girl was fucking *pissed*. We searched that quadrant for over an hour, but we couldn't find the container. Chloe decided not to waste any more time and marched straight into the control room. She told them she was from the Port Authority and had been alerted to a system breach." Gage's eyes shone with pride. "When they wanted to call a supervisor, she shouted at them and told them they were incompetent. She made them cower like dogs."

"I didn't shout," Chloe muttered under her breath. "I might have raised my voice."

"She sent them outside to check the system box, and as soon as they were gone, she hacked that computer like there was no tomorrow."

Chloe's voice thickened and she shrugged. "Failure wasn't an option."

"She got the last known location of the container and removed her software so no one would know about the hack." Gage beamed as he shared the story, and it warmed my heart that my best friend had found someone who utterly adored her. "Then because she knew we'd show up on the cameras, she told them she was going to check a container location at random to make sure everything was operational because she no longer had faith in their abilities."

A smile tugged at Chloe's lips. "I made them grovel. But really, they should have caught me the first time. I was doing them a favor."

"I knew you'd come," I whispered to Chloe.

"I would have shut down the entire New York City power grid if I had to." She squeezed me so tight I could barely breathe. "But there were moments . . ." Her voice wavered. "There were so many containers, and we'd been searching for so long, and their system was tough to crack, and the app showed your phone at the bottom of the estuary, and I started to think . . ." Her eyes welled with tears. "That I'd never find you."

"But you did." I squeezed her tight. "You found me just in time."

TWENTY-FOUR

◇ ◇ ◇

Despondent and unable to function after very little sleep, we crashed in a hotel for a few hours before starting the long drive home. No one spoke once we hit the road. What was there to say? Clare had the diamond. Our time was almost up. I'd messaged the number on the card Angelini had given me to see if negotiation was an option and received no response.

"We'll have to leave the country after all." Emma finally said the words we'd all been thinking after Jack pulled over at a rest stop to step out and make a quick call on Gage's phone.

"If we run, Cristian dies," I reminded her.

"If we don't run, we all die."

Gage had his arm around Chloe in the back seat of Jack's truck. "We have to find Clare. We'll make her give us the necklace." He cracked his knuckles in front of Chloe's face, and she pushed him away.

"Knuckle cracking isn't going to stop Milan from giving you a chest full of knives."

Gage gave an indignant huff. "You have that little faith in my skills?"

"I've seen her in action, and if she doesn't get you, Vito will."

"Amateurs."

"She threw a knife into your shoulder." Chloe's lips grazed his shirt over the injury.

He stroked her cheek, his gaze softening. "Barely a scratch."

"Clare is back in Chicago." Jack climbed into the driver's seat. "She's meeting Mr. X to hand over the diamond. I'll pay him a visit when we get back to see if we can work something out."

I didn't like the sound of that. What could he possibly work out with a man who wanted to torture and kill him and a woman who had just locked him in a container to die? What deal could be made that didn't involve a cost that I could feel in my bones would be too high?

"I'd like to meet Mr. X," Emma said. "After what he did to you in that meat freezer, it's payback time. I'd start off by kneeing him in the nuts and then I'd go full throttle on his ass."

"That's only if I didn't get to him first," Gage said, his voice rough. "And if I did, there would be nothing left for you."

"That's very selfish." Chloe folded her arms and shifted away from Gage. "Maybe other people would like to have a go at him. After what he did to Jack, I'd like to hear him scream."

"He was . . . is my boyfriend." I shot Jack a sideways glance. We hadn't talked about our relationship since leaving the container, but he'd shown me through his actions what I hadn't believed in words. "If Jack goes after Mr. X, I'm going with him."

"If you're going, I'm going," Chloe said.

Gage growled in frustration. "If Chloe's going, I'm going, too."

"I'm not missing out on the fun. Count me in." Emma lifted her hand, but no one slapped her palm. "Where's Anil when you need him?" she grumbled. "He was always up for a high five."

"Where do we meet this former boss of yours?" I stretched out in my seat, already stiff from our drive. "Your friends and contacts all seem to like to drink in seedy bars. I'm hoping he has some class, and we can meet him in a fancy restaurant or some swanky hotel lobby bar with expensive cocktails."

Jack didn't even crack a smile. "I'm going alone."

"Have you got backup from your secret government organization friends?" Emma laughed when a startled Jack caught her gaze in the rearview mirror. "Do you think we don't all know you work for the CIA or the FBI or some off-the-books institution? We're not idiots."

"I didn't know." It hadn't even occurred to me that Jack might be totally legit. I'd always assumed he'd just left one criminal organization and joined another with a more Robin Hood–like ethos. "Are you a government employee?"

"No." Jack's hands tightened on the steering wheel. "Let's just drop the subject."

"He has to say that." Emma mocked a whisper. "If we knew the truth, he'd have to kill us."

"Maybe he's in organized crime," Chloe mused. "He knew all about how the Mafia torture people and cut off their toes and fingers."

"Speaking of missing fingers," Emma said. "Who here thinks the dude we met in the mountains was hot?" She raised her hand. "Now, that was a real man."

"He was the kind of man who eats people like us for breakfast," Chloe said. "Have you forgotten he followed us and tried to run us off the road?"

Emma licked her lips. "He could eat me anytime."

There was an awkward silence and then Chloe said, "I miss Anil. He wouldn't have understood Emma's joke and then she would have had fun explaining to him, and Gage would have told him he had to get out of his parents' basement." She sighed. "He said Clare made him feel valued in a way we didn't. Maybe he didn't like to be teased."

"Clare identified him as our weakest link and used him to drive a wedge between us," Jack said. "It's all a game for her. She'll ditch him as soon as he outlives his usefulness."

"I still can't believe he'd betray us that way," Chloe continued. "He's not as naive as he was when we first met, and he's got a genius IQ. He has to know she doesn't really care about him."

"Intelligence IQ isn't the same as emotional IQ," I pointed out. "Even a genius can be blinded by love."

Chloe shook her head. "I still can't believe he would have left us to die."

"Hey, we're coming up to Bloomsburg," Emma said. "Maybe we should find a certain autobody shop and make sure the truck's running the way it should. I've been hearing a suspicious rattle . . ."

"If you wanted to see the mountain man again, you should have given him your number." Gage made a derisive grunt. "Also, you shouldn't have let us send a canoe through his windshield. That ship has sailed, my friend. You let him get away."

"Probably just as well," she said. "We'll probably be dead by the end of the week or hiding out in some faraway place."

I swallowed past the lump in my throat. I'd been trying not to think of what lay ahead when we reached Chicago. "We should probably say good-bye to our friends and families when we get home. I'm surprised my parents haven't sent the police out looking for me. I haven't contacted them in three days."

"I don't have anyone to say good-bye to," Gage said. "The only people I care about are right here."

"Same." Emma caught Jack's gaze in the mirror, and he nodded in agreement.

I'd never thought about the fact that except for Chloe, no one else in the truck had people waiting for them at home. No one to talk to about relationship troubles or problems at work. No cozy kitchen chai time. No big Sunday dinners. No meddlesome aunties and marriage-obsessed parents. I had a sea of love waiting for me in Chicago, but for everyone else, the crew was family.

"I haven't called Simone," I said abruptly, realizing we'd left someone out of our impromptu love-in. "Someone give me a phone. I have to tell her the bad news."

"Simsim!" Simone's cheerful voice lifted my spirits despite our dire predicament. "I've been trying to get in touch. I must have left a dozen voice messages for you."

"We're on our way home. Clare has the diamond." I quickly updated her on our situation and Jack's plan to talk to Mr. X.

"I'll help, of course, in any way I can," she said. "But something terrible happened while you were away that I have to deal with first. It's Richard. He was utterly distraught after we were interviewed by the police at Vera's place. I told him the police were talking to all the guests, but just the idea that we would have had anything to do with a murder . . . it was too much for him. I suggested we take the helicopter to New York and go out on the yacht to get away and I invited Vera to join us. Poor thing is a wreck and it wasn't good for her to be in that house with the police running around with their yellow tape and rubber gloves. They still haven't cleaned Peter's blood off the garage floor—"

"Simone, what about Richard?"

"Oh, Richard." She sighed. "We flew out to the yacht and had a lovely time on the water. Richard got very drunk as he often does when he's stressed, and on our way home . . ." Her breath hitched. "Oh, Simi, he went overboard."

"Oh my God. Is he okay?"

"No, darling. He was eaten by sharks. I need you to organize his funeral."

We pulled over at a truck stop for gas and snacks midway through our journey. Jack motioned me around to the back of the brick building where the grimy exterior, filled with garbage cans and empty oil containers, gave way to a dark forest of trees. The air was cool and damp, and the smell of diesel hung heavy in the air, mingling with the scent of burned coffee. As soon as we were alone, he pulled me into his arms. I could feel his heart beating strong and steady in his chest, his breath warm against my ear. I leaned closer and his lips brushed over mine.

"Are we going to have some secret sexy times while everyone is grabbing something to eat?" I nuzzled his neck. "I was kind of disappointed we didn't get to do it in the container. Did you see all those ancient erotic toys? It would have been fun figuring out how to use them."

"I'm leaving you here." Jack squeezed me tight. "I don't know when . . . or if I'll see you again."

My good mood faded faster than the pounding of my heart. "What are you talking about? You can't leave. We still have to find Clare and get the necklace. We have to rescue Cristian. We have to save Anil. We can't do it without you."

"Simi . . ." His voice cracked. "You are a great leader. You'll be able to handle it without me."

My bottom lip trembled. "You are not doing this again," I said. "You are not leaving me. And you are certainly not going to throw yourself on your sword. You are not alone, Jack. Were you not listening in the car? We are a team. A family. Don't you understand what that means?"

After a long, heavy pause, he said, "No, it's been too long."

I took a step back, studying him closely. "When we get back to Chicago, the first thing I'll do in the morning is go and see my parents because I know they will be frantic with worry. Nani will already have been on the phone with the family gossip network asking if anyone has seen me. There is nowhere I can go in Chicago without a cousin or an uncle or an auntie or a family friend spotting me—and I have been spotted in some very compromising situations."

Jack gave a half-hearted chuckle, but his smile didn't reach his eyes.

"I wouldn't have been surprised if they'd found us in the container," I continued. "Certainly, they would never have stopped looking. They are always there for me no matter what. I hold that in my heart every day. It makes the hard times easier. It gives me strength. That's family, Jack. That's what we have with the crew. It's a bond that means we care what happens to you. It means you never have to be alone."

Jack's eyes flickered with pain and something else I couldn't quite identify. "I don't want to leave, but it's the only option. I won't put anyone else in danger." He pressed his lips to my forehead. "Especially you."

I studied his face, saw the resolve in his eyes. "I don't want to go back to where we were when you left me in the dark. If you are going to leave again, then respect me enough to tell me why."

For a moment, I thought he would just walk away, but finally he said, "Mr. X . . . His real name is Xavier Braithwaite III. I'm going to offer to return to his crew in exchange for the necklace."

My heart sank into my stomach, but I wasn't surprised. Despite his past, he was an honorable man. Without any leverage, he had only one thing to offer to get us out of this mess—himself. It was why I hadn't told him that Angelini had made Jack part of the deal.

"Why won't he just keep the necklace and kill you?" I didn't see any point in beating around the bush.

"He wants me back. He thinks I still owe him a life debt. That's why his men haven't ended me already. He'll torture and humiliate me until he gets bored, and then he'll kill me at his leisure."

A shiver ran down my spine. Between Angelini and Mr. X, it was an impossible situation. All I could do was keep my secret and hope I could figure out a way to save him. "All the more reason not to go alone."

Jack cupped my jaw, his thumb brushing over my cheek as he tilted my head back for a searing kiss. I breathed in the smell of him, the scent of soap mixed with coffee and something that was purely him. It was different, that kiss. Soft and gentle but filled with love and longing. And regret.

Finally, Jack pulled me into a tight hug. We stayed like that for what felt like an eternity, our bodies entwined, until finally we broke apart.

"Simi. Jack. Let's hit the road." Emma's voice rang out over the hum of the traffic, the blare of air horns, and the rumble of semitrailer trucks pulling on and off the highway. "I bought out their entire supply of beef jerky, so make sure you roll all the windows down when you get into the truck."

"We'd better get going." I took a few steps, and a soft breeze made the hair on the back of my neck stand on end.

I turned and Jack was gone.

TWENTY-FIVE

◇ ◇ ◇

went straight to my parents' house the morning after we returned to Chicago, expecting hugs and kisses, maybe even a few tears. Instead, I got sarcasm and tightly leashed anger.

"She's not dead," Nani shouted when I walked in the door. "She's just selfish and inconsiderate."

"I was on a road trip to New York." I reached for a fluffy pav from the basket on the kitchen table, and Nani slapped my hand away.

"No food for you until your parents have decided your punishment."

"I'm thirty years old, Nani. Too old to be punished."

"You're never too old to be punished when you almost give your Nani a heart attack. Your mother was crying for three days."

"I've only been out of touch for three days. Did she start crying the minute she hung up after our last call?"

"Three days," she shouted, wagging her finger at me as Mom walked into the kitchen. "We couldn't console her. The floor was wet with her tears." Nani just loved her drama.

"Mom, did you flood the house crying for me because I didn't message you?"

"I may have wondered why you hadn't called . . ." She shook her head in exasperation. "Is Nani telling stories again?"

"The stories tell themselves," Nani said. "I'm just the vessel."

"Beta, nice to see you're still alive." My dad wrapped me in a hug. "Your mother cried for three days."

"So I heard." Part of me wished my mother had cried inconsolably for three days because I hadn't been in touch, but my mother wasn't an emotional person. It was my dad who was the emotional center of the family, with the occasional assist from Nani.

"I went to New York with some friends for a few days," I said. "Work has been very stressful. I'm sorry I didn't let you know. My phone got stolen and—"

"Of course it was stolen," Nani said. "They're all thieves in New York. I'm amazed you weren't stolen, too."

"What friends did you go with?" Mom asked, leaning against the counter. "Was Chloe there?"

"Yes. And Anil."

My dad's face brightened. "Anil? The drone boy? Are you seeing him now? I told you that your parents know best. He's a little immature but he'll grow up once he has the responsibility of children and a family."

"Whoa." I held up my hand. "No. I'm not seeing Anil. He's just a friend. I was there with other friends, too, including Jack."

"Jack, the man who broke your heart?" Dad's smile faded. "Why were you with that loser?"

"He's not a loser, Dad. We just had some things to work out."

"You said he kissed a woman in front of you just to hurt you. That spells loser in my book. Where is he? I want a word with him. I'll pull out his ears."

"I'll take a piece of him when you're done," Nani said. "We'll make sure he never hurts our Simi again."

My heart ached at the thought I might have to leave the country and never see my family again. Yes, I'd had a rough childhood, and sometimes my family could be annoying—okay, they could be especially annoying when it came to the idea of marriage—but they loved me in a way no one else would ever love me. I couldn't imagine a life where I didn't drop by at least once a week to share my news, ask for advice, or just drink a cup of chai and listen to them talk about work and family and how our next-door neighbor refused to cut the strip of grass beside our front lawn.

"She set him up," I tried to explain. "She was trying to hurt him by hurting me. I didn't believe him at first because part of me had never really believed what we had was real. But I trust him now. Not just because of things he's done and said to ease my mind, but because I think I finally believe in myself. I'm worth loving."

"Of course you are, but he's still a loser." Dad wasn't impressed by my epiphany. "He must have hurt her to make her want to hurt him by hurting you. What kind of man hurts a woman so badly she would want to hurt a stranger?"

Mom laughed. "That's a lot of hurts."

"It's the kind of thing Cristian used to do when he worked for me," Dad said. "Always, the girlfriends coming in to see him when he was supposed to be selling suits, and there he was in the back room kissing a different girl, and then the crying and shouting and drama. Next day they'd be back to throw a drink in his face, or squirt ketchup on his shirt. One of them brought her brother, a big man with thick arms, to beat Cristian up, but he escaped out the back door. I think there was goodness in him, but I wasn't sad when he decided to leave. When he rear-messaged last week, I didn't respond in case he was thinking of coming back." Dad shrugged. "He was good with the ladies. Not so good with the men."

"Wait." My heart skipped a beat. "What do you mean he rear-messaged last week?"

"He sent a text message that didn't make sense," Dad said. "Your brother said that happens if the phone is in the back pocket."

"Butt dial?" I burst out laughing. "He butt-dialed you, Dad."

"Simi, please." Mom shook her head. "No bad language in front of Nani."

"Nani could give us all lessons in inappropriate language." I lifted an eyebrow at Nani, who waved me off with a sniff.

"You said it was last week? Can I see the message?" Cristian had been taken just over two weeks ago. Had they let him go and he forgot to tell us?

Dad pulled out his phone and showed me Cristian's message: 9114401wmonroewgp. "Maybe he was meaning to call or text you," he said. "We are both Chopra. He might still have me in his contacts."

"That does look like a butt dial." I tried to make sense of the seemingly random letters and numbers. "But the timing is odd. He's been away somewhere without cell service for the last two and a half weeks." I forwarded the message to Chloe to post on the server to see if anyone could figure it out. She answered right away and said she would send Gage to check out Cristian's apartment and studio to ask if he'd been around.

"Let me see the butt dial." Mom held out her hand and I passed her the phone.

"I might have to go away for a while, too," I told them, bringing the conversation around to the topic I'd been trying to avoid. "I won't be able to contact you, so I just wanted to say while I'm here that I love you and I forgive you and—"

"What's going on?" Nani looked up from her recipe book. "Are you eloping with the loser? You'd better not elope. Your parents have saved money for your wedding and your mother will be devastated if she doesn't get to be with you for the big day. She'll cry rivers of tears."

"I might shed a tear or two," Mom said. "But if you want to marry him—"

"I'm not getting married."

"Are you pregnant?" Dad stood so quickly, his chair toppled over. "Are we going to have another grandchild?"

"No, Dad. It's work related. There's something I need to sort out and it would be better if I do it from another location."

"She's in trouble with the Mafia," Nani said. "That's the only reason people skip town. They'll come after the family and Simi is trying to keep us safe."

Damn Nani, her sixth sense, and her razor-sharp intellect. "There are other reasons people leave town," I said evenly. "I could just want a change of scenery. I could have a new job. I could want to make a fresh start. I could be running from debt collectors, bounty hunters, assassins, the police, or one of many other different types of organized crime gangs—Russian, Irish, Mexican drug cartels, triads, outlaw bikers . . ."

"Look at her eye twitch," Dad said. "She's hiding something."

"It's the mob." Nani sighed. "I told you so."

Dad leaned across the table. "Is it the Angelini brothers? Did you take a loan from them and you owe them money?"

I startled, sitting upright in my chair. "How do you know the Angelini brothers?"

"I'm the top custom tailor in the city," Dad said. "I dress everybody." He pulled out his wallet. "How much do you need?"

"Dad." I covered his hand with mine. "I don't need your money."

"We can't have you going on the run," Mom said. "You aren't even married yet. We only have two grandchildren. Look at the size of this yard. We need at least six grandchildren, and I have little hope for the twins."

"You want me to have four kids?" I fiddled with the edge of

the faded red tablecloth that had been a kitchen staple for as long as I could remember. "You're making me want to run away."

"I suppose we'll just have to go with her." Dad put down his men's fashion magazine. He liked to stay up-to-date on the current trends the old-school way. "We'll all go on the run. I'd better pack a bag."

"In my day, we didn't run from our problems," Nani said. "But if that's all she can come up with, then it would be better to hide her. There are enough people in the family that she could stay with everyone for two or three days and then we would move her. We could circle her through the family for years and no one would ever know. Everyone has a basement or an attic. Even a closet would do."

I stared at her, aghast. "I'm not spending the rest of my life hiding in closets or attics, and I'm not putting anyone at risk . . . I mean, I wouldn't put them at risk if I were running from the mob, which isn't true." *Yet*.

She lifted an eyebrow. "So why the good-bye speech?"

"It was . . ." I shrugged. "Just in case. I might have to leave suddenly, and I wanted to be prepared."

"I'll call the Angelinis and sort this out." Dad gestured to my mom. "Hand me my phone."

"Dad . . . you can't . . . please. Don't get involved."

"This looks like an address," Mom said, studying Cristian's message. "'Wmonroe' could be West Monroe. Is there a West Monroe Street in the city?" She handed me her phone and I looked up the street name.

"There's one in West Garfield Park." I looked over at the string of letters and numbers, 9114401wmonroewgp. "That's the 'wgp.' He was giving an address: 9114401." I did a map search but couldn't find anything with that number.

Someone rang the doorbell and Dad left to answer the door.

"I think the address is 4401," Mom said. "And the 911 . . ."

Emergency services. Cristian had been calling for help.

"Someone is at the door for you," Dad called out. "Her name is Emma. She says it's urgent. Something about Jack. Simone knows his boss? She was talking very quickly. Is this the good-bye time?"

"No." I jumped up from the table. "This is the 'save the friends' time. I might not have to leave after all."

TWENTY-SIX

◇ ◇ ◇

JACK

Let's say life has finally taught you that you are not an ordinary guy. Your evil ex sliced up your brand-new truck. Your girlfriend broke up with you for something you didn't do. You couldn't quit your job after what was supposed to be one last assignment. You almost died in a shipping container. And your friends are pissed because your ex ratted you out to the mob, and now she's run off with the only thing that can keep the Mafia from fitting you and your friends with cement shoes.

Maybe you haven't been an ordinary guy since you were plucked off the streets by Mr. X at the tender age of thirteen and trained to be a professional thief. Yes, he gave you clothes and food, and a place to stay. But nothing was free. You incurred a debt and the only way to pay it off was to join his crew. The heists got bigger. The risks higher. Weapons were needed. And then innocent people died. You didn't know you had a line, but that was it. You told him you were out. It was over. So long, farewell. Auf Wiedersehen, adieu, and all that.

Of course, it wasn't that simple. Mr. X didn't like good-byes. The debt was unpaid. No one had ever left his crew before, and he wanted to ensure it would never happen again. So it was beating after beating along with the odd stabbing, shooting, and locking you in a meat freezer. There was also that weekend in the Sahara desert with the honey and the ants, and the time he tried to bury you alive, but that's another story.

You got it. Mr. X felt betrayed, and he hadn't processed his childhood trauma, so he projected it onto you along with some of his own trauma to ensure you were properly screwed up, because losing both parents and your grandmother when you were young wasn't enough. But it had been years. You'd moved on and it was time for him to do the same. You'd even offered him the name of your therapist. She'd done wonders for your self-esteem. But Mr. X wasn't ready to unpack his emotional baggage. Instead, all you got for your efforts were bullets.

And yet here you are, walking into the lion's den, aka a private members' club called the Albert House, to meet the man, the mentor, the nemesis, the bane of your existence, and the villain of your story . . . Mr. X.

"Jack Danger to see Xavier Braithwaite III." You fully expect the tuxedoed concierge to toss you out onto the street even though you're wearing the bespoke suit you purchased from Chopra Custom Tailors. Membership fees to the Albert House, one of the most exclusive private members' clubs in Chicago, are $50,000 per year, and that's just to start.

"Mr. Braithwaite is expecting you in the Red Room."

Your blood chills and you pat your chest to ensure you didn't forget to put on your bulletproof vest when you got dressed this morning. Sometimes you just don't want the added bulk.

Mr. X is sitting on an enormous red leather chair edged in gold, across from an elderly man in an expensive black suit. He is stroking his chin and studying a chess board intently, as if he were an amateur pretending to be a pro. His opponent is watching Mr. X with a smug expression. Little does he know, it's all a scam. Mr. X is a world-class chess player, but chess doesn't pay the bills.

"What's the bet?" you whisper to the tuxedoed concierge.

"Mr. Braithwaite has lost the last two games with a bet of $50,000 per game. Now it's double or nothing."

Two hundred grand for an hour of work is nothing to sneeze at, and there is nothing Mr. X loves more than chess. You take a seat. You've always enjoyed watching Mr. X play with his food.

Ten minutes later, Mr. X has a credit note for $200,000 in one hand and a fine bourbon in the other. You both retire to the smoking room, and he orders two Cuban cigars while you settle in leather armchairs in front of a roaring fire. The room is decorated to look like an old English castle with red velvet curtains, tapestries, and suits of armor scattered throughout. You are the youngest person in the club by about thirty years.

"I don't smoke," you say when the waiter offers you a cigar on a gold-embossed plate. "It causes cancer."

"Considering your life expectancy is about ten minutes, I suggest you enjoy it while you can." Mr. X pushes his jacket aside just enough to show you the weapon holstered beneath the vintage red-and-black velvet smoking jacket that he's wearing sans shirt to reveal a smattering of graying hair. Mr. X has never been a paragon of style.

Smoke the cigar and die of lung cancer in ten years, or don't smoke and die in ten minutes. Mr. X has always been a fan of Hobson's choice—a choice that is really no choice at all.

You take the cigar and puff away in the uncomfortable silence, trying not to inhale on the slim chance you might leave the club alive. "You should get a smoking jacket," Mr. X says, as if he hadn't just threatened to kill you. "It stops the smoke from sticking to your clothes."

"I didn't realize you were wearing any." You give a nod toward his bare chest flex. "I prefer the more modern look of my weed-smoking hoodie. It has the added bonus of hiding my face in case the police break down the door."

"Always the joker." Mr. X doesn't laugh. He has never laughed at your jokes. He laughs only when he has revealed an evil plan or has done something particularly heinous, and then it's the "Whoo-hoo ha-ha-ha" maniac cackle straight out of the *Villain Handbook*, chapter 1.

"I'm Batman." You try to lower and roughen your voice to emulate Michael Keaton's badass delivery of the iconic line from the 1989 movie of the same name, but without the drums.

"Is this really how you want to spend your last few minutes on this earth?" He puffs away, blowing smoke rings in your face, but his aim is off and with the smallest shift to the side, your head manages to go through the center.

You puff on your own cigar. Mr. X taught you how to smoke when you were fourteen. You didn't realize he was trying to kill you even then.

"I'm here because of Clare." You're getting nauseous from the cigar and it's time to get the show on the road. You've already got an exit strategy, and it involves going through the window and using the red velvet curtains to break your fall before the waiter returns with another tray of cancer-causing treats. "We had a deal."

Puff. Puff. Puff. Mr. X is smoking like a freight train. "Clare's decision to retrieve the Wild Heart from the museum in Delhi was entirely her own."

"She would have needed funding, assistance, contacts, and pay-offs to get the necklace out of India and into the US. She couldn't have done it alone. It may have been her decision, but you backed her up."

"You got me." His thin lips twitch at the corners. "So now you want me to give it to you as a matter of what . . . honor?" He snorts in derision. "I'd rather have the $30 million than a clean conscience."

"I thought there was some decency left in you," I said. "A man's life is at risk."

"So is yours." Mr. X lifts an eyebrow, and you instantly realize your mistake. You learned a long time ago never to show Mr. X you care. About anything. He is a man who preys on weakness. Although you didn't lie when you told Simi you'd stayed away all year partly to figure yourself out, you neglected to mention that you were afraid to come home to her in case Mr. X was watching. Only when you were 100 percent certain his goons were looking the other way did you dare return.

"Why do you care so much about this stranger?" He sips his bourbon, licking his lips the way a predator does before it's about to feast.

"I'm curious to know how far Clare has fallen." You scramble to cover. "Is she totally corrupted, or is there any decency left in her?"

His dark eyes meet yours and his jaw twitches. "Do you mean is she a failure like you?"

Your pulse kicks up a notch and you try to regulate your breathing. If anything, Mr. X knows how to wind you up. "I used to admire you." You put down the disgusting cigar and wash down the taste with the even worse bite of bourbon. "You were cruel and brutal, but you saved me from the streets, and I still use the skills you taught me. But when you crossed that line and innocent people died, you stopped being a professional jewel thief and became an ordinary thug."

Mr. X bristles. Above all else, he is most concerned about his image and his reputation. He himself started as an ordinary pickpocket and rose to become one of the most renowned jewel thieves in the world, known for his daring and stealth and his elite crew.

"This is Clare's gig," he says. "If anyone's life is at risk, it's on her head."

Clare joined Mr. X's merry band of thieves shortly after you. Two years younger, but streetwise, she learned fast and the two of you quickly became a team, rising in the ranks to join Mr. X's "best of the best" and developing a deep and solid friendship. When he left small-town thieving and moved into high-end burglary, Mr. X brought his elite team with him to Europe, and you and Clare spent more time together, often posing as a couple to pull the cons. One thing led to another led to a few heated nights in Paris and a relationship that was doomed from the start. You ended it. Badly. And then you quit Mr. X and the whole sorry business. Clare went from being a close friend and lover to becoming a deadly enemy, as disenchanted with love as you had then become with the world of crime. You don't know what she's doing with Anil, but the Clare of now does not have the limits of the Clare who was your friend.

"She's going to kill an innocent man." You don't particularly like Cristian. His repeated betrayals and lack of loyalty are indicative of a lack of character, but he doesn't deserve to die.

His faces twists in a grimace. "You might have been my best student, the closest I've ever had to a son, but you care too much about people. What have you gained by throwing your lot in with a bunch of amateur misfits?"

Family. Love. Not things Mr. X has ever had or will ever understand.

"It's a weakness Clare doesn't have," he continues. "She can put the job above everything else. You've lost your edge and I have no regrets about what I'm about to do. You still owe me a life debt and it's time for me to collect."

You hear a rustle of cloth and two of Mr. X's henchmen step out from the balcony behind the red velvet curtains you had planned to use in your escape. They are armed, of course. Virgil, with his thick mustache, has a Colt .45 pointed at your head, and redheaded Rusty has a Beretta. They are both smirking because they think you have been outplayed—at least you think Virgil is smirking. It's hard to see what's going on beneath all that hair.

"Only two?" Usually, Mr. X sends a handful of hench.

You hear movement behind you. Moments later the waiter—who is clearly not a waiter, and you should have known that because he served the cigars with the tray in his left hand—walks into the room. He lifts the cloth on his tray to show you a .44 Magnum before closing the door.

Now you know why everything in the room is red. What is a private members' club if there isn't a special room for killing, and a concierge willing to take a hefty payment to look the other way?

You quickly assess the situation. There are two armed henches at the only window and a waiter slash hench at the door. There is a blazing fire in the fireplace and no other way out of the room. Mr. X is also armed, but he likes to leave the killing to others so he doesn't dirty his hands. Nothing says "innocent" like a lack of gun residue on the fingers.

"What about a little beating first?" you suggest. "We could take a trip back to the meat freezer where I almost died of hypothermia, internal injuries, and blood loss. That was fun. Or how about another game of shoot Jack and leave him in an airport bathroom to bleed out all over the unsanitary floor?"

"We've come to the end," Mr. X says. "I'm tired of the games."

"That's just age. If you go back on your supplements, get a good sleep every night, and walk every day, you'll feel twenty years younger."

A scowl creases Mr. X's overly large forehead. "I don't understand you. I don't think I ever have. You have no way out of this situation, and yet you're still cracking jokes."

"That's because I came with an offer." This is the ace up your sleeve that you hoped you wouldn't have to play. "You want my life; you can have it. Tell Clare to return the necklace to my crew and I'll come back and work for—"

My words are cut off by a disturbance at the door.

"What do you mean I can't go in?" A woman's voice—oh so familiar—rings out in the hallway. "My late husband was a member of this club for over thirty years . . . and . . . oh, poor Richard." A sob. A murmur of voices. "I simply must see Jack. He was Richard's very best friend, and he doesn't know . . ." Another sob. A wail. "He doesn't know what happened."

"Tell him you'll call the police if he doesn't let us in." Another voice. A beautiful, rich, melodic voice that makes your heart sing and your blood quicken.

"The police?" Simone's voice rises with incredulity. "Darling, we don't call the police. It would be crass. We're already causing a scene. Look how many people are watching. I am going to die of embarrassment. Die. Dead. Remind me to tell the accountant to cancel Richard's annual donation to the club. If they can't even honor his memory . . ."

"Jesus fucking Christ." A third voice, this one lower, rougher, and decidedly male. "This is taking too long."

A thud. A moan. An urgent murmur. The rattle of a door handle. The click of a lock.

In an instant, the henches disappear behind the red curtain. The waiter covers his gun. Mr. X tightens the silk belt on his smoking jacket and puffs on his cigar.

The cavalry arrive.

Simi, Chloe, Gage, and Emma burst into the room, followed by a billow of orange chiffon and a sparkle of diamonds. Simone takes one look at Mr. X, seated beside the fire, and her laughter rings out around the room.

"Oh heavens! A smoking jacket. How utterly déclassé."

TWENTY-SEVEN

◇ ◇ ◇

SIMI

West Garfield Park. Population: eighteen thousand. Rated as the most dangerous neighborhood in Chicago. The violent crime rate is 943 percent higher than the national average. If you are involved in organized crime and need a place to hide someone you've kidnapped, West Garfield is the place to be.

Still riding the high of saving Jack from the clutches of Mr. X and his henchmen, we drove straight to West Garfield to rescue Cristian. We'd left Mr. X with his cigars and brandy and the shame of his smoking jacket. Gage had been all in for delivering the kind of beating Mr. X had given Jack after the last heist, but we didn't want to attract police attention, and as for getting him arrested, there was no evidence he had done anything wrong, his unfortunate sartorial choices aside.

I was too angry to speak to Jack, although I had given him a quick pat-down to make sure he hadn't been harmed. If Simone hadn't recognized the name Jack had given me at the truck stop, if she hadn't had her extensive social network track him down, if we hadn't shown up when we did . . . I couldn't even finish the train of thought.

Emma pulled Jack's truck up outside an abandoned building

boasting all the features a Mafia kidnapper could want—boarded-up doors, broken windows, iron bars, crumbling brick, and an overgrown yard with grass so high it could have hidden multiple dead bodies.

"I hate to say it, but this truck fits right in." Emma turned off the engine. "No one's gonna want to carjack us while we're waiting for you."

"It's got wheels and an engine that works," Jack said. "I give it thirty minutes. Slightly more if this is Mafia territory. Less if this is gang turf."

"This must be the bad end of town." Simone pressed her face against the window. "There isn't even a doorman out front."

"We just need to establish if Cristian is inside," I said. "Then we can call the police. It's one thing to steal from the mob; it's another thing entirely to break into a house guarded by armed Mafia enforcers."

"Um . . ." Emma raised her hand. She'd definitely been spending too much time with Anil. "The house we broke into during the last heist was guarded by armed Mafia enforcers."

"Yes, but their sole purpose for being there wasn't to guard someone they'd just kidnapped."

"Except they were supposed to make sure the bride didn't do a runner, which effectively made her a kidnap victim, thereby giving us experience with this exact situation." Gage pulled out his weapon and checked the clip. "I've done more hostage retrievals than I can count. I'll be in and out of there in five minutes. Don't need to wait for some city beat cop."

Chloe pulled her handgun out of her purse. "I'll come, too."

"Babe." Gage shook his head. "There is no fucking way I am going to let you near that place. I don't care if you never speak to me again. I don't care if you cut me out of your life. I would rather live without you, knowing you were alive, than take the chance of losing you." His voice caught, broke. "I can't live in a world where you aren't there."

"I hate it when you say sweet things at inopportune moments," Chloe grumbled. "But I'm not letting you go alone."

"Babe . . . this is what I do."

"Not anymore. You don't want me to put myself in a dangerous situation? Well, I feel the same about you. I don't want to lose you. I can't lose you. You take backup or you don't go at all."

"You don't want to lose me?" A maelstrom of emotions flickered across Gage's face, softening his steely blue eyes.

"No, you idiot."

"She doesn't want to lose me," Gage said softly. He reached for Chloe and pulled her in for a kiss. "Never leaving you, babe. Not unless you tell me you never want to see me again."

Chloe sniffed in derision. "As if that's ever going to happen."

"I'll go," Jack said. "I've got hostage retrieval experience, too, although usually I'm the hostage."

"What the hell is wrong with you?" The words I'd been holding back since we'd walked into the club finally came tumbling out in a fury. "Is this another case of you trying to stupidly sacrifice yourself when you've got people who care about you and would be devastated if you got yourself killed?"

"Uh-oh." Emma grimaced. "I'd say everyone should take a walk, but in this neighborhood, we'll be safer in the truck even though the sparks are about to fly."

"I did what I had to do," Jack said. "And I would do it again."

"You didn't trust us. You didn't think about what it would do to us if you got yourself killed. That's not how this works. That's not how family works." My fear and anger bubbled over as I yelled at Jack, and my vision blurred. "I went to say good-bye to my parents, and they guessed . . . GUESSED . . . that I was in trouble with the mob. Dad threatened to speak to Angelini. My Nani was planning to hide me in my aunties' closets. My mom was going to pack a bag so they could run away with me. THAT is family, Jack. There was no question of me running off alone. The way they saw it, we were in it TOGETHER."

"This is better than a soap opera," Simone whispered to Emma, even though we were all sitting right there. "Richard and I never had that type of relationship. I could have run naked down the interstate and his only concern would have been for his reputation."

"Here's what we're going to do," I said. "Emma and Simone will stay here and the rest of us will go and do some recon. If we can confirm he's in there, we'll assess the situation and decide whether we can rescue him safely or whether we need to call the police."

"What about me?" Simone was still dressed in her flowing orange tunic, matching palazzo pants, and gold stilettos. "I want to come. I brought my mask."

"Do not put that thing on." Emma held up her hand. "I still have nightmares from the last time. And look at you. You walk out there glowing orange in your diamonds and pearls and all they'll see is fresh meat."

"She's right," I said gently. "You saved the day at the club, and we need you in the car with Emma as backup in case you need to save the day again."

Simone beamed. "I'll do the getaway drive if she gets shot. I took lessons from our chauffeur when I was a teenager."

I had only just processed that Gage was no longer in the vehicle when the back passenger door opened and he slipped back inside.

"I found him," he said. "They're keeping him in a room at the back of the house. The windows are barred. He's on a bed and his wrist is handcuffed to the metal frame. His legs aren't broken so we won't have to carry him. There are three guards inside, all armed: two in the kitchen and one near the front door."

"What part of 'we'll all go together' did you not understand?" I glared at him. "You missed the entire plan."

"Must have been the part after I'd already left the vehicle because there was too much talking and not enough action."

I drew in a deep breath and allowed myself a moment of relief that Cristian was still alive. "I'll call 911 right now. I'll need someone's phone."

"I thought Tony's man said he'd gut us like fish if we contacted the police." Simone's hand fluttered to her chest. "Or am I misremembering?"

"I think we should just go in and get him," Gage said. "Fish gutting aside, if you call the cops, Cristian will have to answer questions, and we don't know whether he'll tell them about the necklace and the diamond and our involvement in the last heist. I don't trust him anymore. Cristian will look after Cristian, and he'll throw us under the bus without a second thought. Look how easy it was for him to just walk away. He didn't give a damn about the repercussions, or what might happen to anyone except himself."

Gage's words rang true, but the thought of taking on three armed Mafia dudes set all my alarm bells ringing. "It's too risky," I said. "Emma needs to be here to drive the truck. Chloe only just learned to shoot. I've never even held a gun, and even though you and Jack have experience, the guys in there probably shoot two people before breakfast and three after lunch. Killing is their job."

"Jack and I can take them," he said without hesitation. "You just have to walk in and set Cristian free." Gage pulled his bag of weapons from under the seat. "We've got the element of surprise. Jack can take out the one in front, and I'll deal with the two in the back."

"Can't you just wound them?" I asked. "Like maybe just shoot a leg or an arm so they can't chase us or shoot a gun?"

"They're bad guys," Jack said. "They kidnapped Cristian and

beat him up. They're probably the same guys who will come to kill us if we don't bring Angelini the necklace. It's kill or be killed."

"But it was supposed to be a 'no guns' heist . . ." I protested.

Jack shook his head. "It was never really a 'no guns' heist. Not since the moment Angelini threatened to kill you."

I heard the roar of engines, faint at first, then louder, followed by the squeal of tires. A blinding sea of headlights illuminated the street, coming from both directions. I heard the slam of doors and the thump of feet on pavement.

"Get down," Gage shouted. "I'll hold them off."

Too late. We were surrounded.

TWENTY-EIGHT

◆ ◆ ◆

Was this supposed to be my rescue?" Cristian pushed himself to sit on the worn mattress, the handcuff on his wrist clanging on the iron frame.

"You should be grateful we didn't abandon you the way you abandoned us," Emma spat out, pulling and twisting the ropes around her wrists. "For the record, I wasn't in favor of rescuing you. My vote was on the 'let him rot' side."

Two carloads of Mafia guys had dragged us out of the truck at gunpoint and tied us up in the bedroom with Cristian. Gage and Jack, who had caused some serious damage before they were forced into compliance with multiple guns, were chained to the bed frame.

"Why did you take so long?" he snapped. "I sent that message ten days ago when they brought in someone's sister to take over for one of the guards who had some concrete to pour."

"You seduced her?" I said, incredulous. "You seduced a mobster's sister while beaten, kidnapped, and chained to a mattress with two armed mobsters in the other room?"

"It's what I do." Cristian rolled his eyes and sighed. "Her husband was having an affair. He didn't notice her anymore. He didn't appreciate everything she did to look after the kids and the house. I figured they were going to kill me anyway, so why not bring some joy into someone's life before it was all over. I was already on a bed, and she was into the handcuffs. I told her to lock the door and I'd show her how a woman should be treated."

"Fuck me," Gage muttered, shaking his head.

Cristian shrugged. "It was an opportunity, so I took it. Afterward, I asked her to bring me my phone, but by the time she found it, her brother was pulling up outside and I didn't have much time. I had to text with one finger while she held it for me. It was damn close."

"You sent your message to the wrong Chopra," I said. "It went to my dad, and my brother told him it was a butt dial. I only just found out about it, and when I figured it out, we came straight here after rescuing Jack."

"I didn't need to be rescued." Jack shifted against the bed, his chains rattling as he tried to work his way free.

"Really?" I lifted an eyebrow. "What was your plan to escape from four armed men in a locked room? Do tell."

His mouth turned down in a pout. "I would have thought of something."

"I'm going to ask to talk to their leader," I said. "They probably don't know who we are. It's counterproductive to have us here. We have one more day to get the necklace. Angelini will want us out there trying to find it."

"Is that really what you're going in with?" Cristian rolled to his side and propped his head on his elbow. "*Do you know who I am?* They'll probably think you're some low-level influencer with ten thousand followers, or a D-list celebrity who is only known for her appearances on panel game shows and reality TV."

"I'm not just going to say, 'Do you know who I am?' without

context." Why was he being so annoying when we were in this predicament because of his betrayal? "I'm going to explain our relationship with Angelini and then they can call him to confirm, and he'll tell them to give us our day to find Clare and the necklace."

"Or he'll realize we don't have it and off us now because if they let us go, there is a high chance we'll run away." Cristian shrugged. "Just saying."

"Then he still doesn't get the necklace and he has six dead bodies to deal with," I shouted, all my stress and anxiety finding an outlet in Cristian's defeatist attitude. "He's not an idiot."

"But you were, coming here without the police and no backup."

"We were discussing what to do." My anger and frustration finally tipped me over the edge, and I called out in the direction of the door. "Hey, out there. We don't want to rescue him anymore. You can let us go. We take it back."

"Shut the hell up." The door slammed open and one of the Mafia goons, a heavyset dude with thick dark hair and a bushy mustache, pointed a gun at me. "One more word and I'll gag you."

"Do you know who we are?"

"Oh God." Cristian groaned. "Here we go."

"Tell Tony Angelini that you've got Simi and her crew tied up, so we can't do the job he asked us to do."

The man smirked. "He knows you're here. We checked your ID and told him who'd come to visit."

"Surely, if Tony knows I'm here, he wouldn't expect me to stay in this kind of situation." Simone gave him a withering look. "We had an arrangement. I thought you Mafia types were honorable men beneath your crude and brutal criminal exteriors."

"Mr. Angelini says you're even."

"I would beg to differ," Simone said coldly. "Considering the night he had and my considerable efforts to help him through his 'problem'"—she emphasized the word with air quotes, holding her bound hands in front of her—"he more than owes me. Perhaps you could convey that message and my intention of sharing that 'problem'"—again with the air quotes—"with all and sundry should I be forced to remain in these abhorrent circumstances."

Silence.

Without another word, the dude closed the door.

"Is there anything you want to share with the class?" I asked Simone when I was finally able to peel my tongue off the roof of my mouth.

"Oh, darling. Really. Can you not figure it out for yourself?"

"I can figure out what you did." My stomach churned. "The question is why?"

"We needed a reason to hold an event at Vera's house to get access to the diamond." She spoke slowly, enunciating each word as if she thought I couldn't follow. "Vera had confided in me that Peter's family were not good people. She told me about his nephew in Sing Sing. The family let people think he was there on drug-related crimes, but in fact he'd been imprisoned for sexually assaulting a young girl. She wanted my advice about how to distance herself from the whole sordid affair. I wanted to help her, and it occurred to me that I could use the situation to help us, so I went to see Tony . . ."

I held up a hand to stop her mid-sentence. "You went to see Tony? As in Tony Angelini? How did you find him?"

"Darling, he's a businessman above all else. Just like Jack's Mr. Braithwaite. Businessmen have places of business, and places to talk business—golf clubs, social clubs, and the like. It wasn't hard to find him, and when I went to his office and gave his people Richard's name, they waved me through. One thing led to another, and we wound up at his place . . ."

"But you are . . . were married," Chloe said. "To Richard."

"Richard and I had an arrangement," she said with a dismissive wave of her bound hands. "We were free to sleep with other people so long as they were not in our social circle. He broke that agreement when he had an affair with Martha."

Olivia had mentioned at the celebration of life that Martha had been having an affair, but I hadn't paid attention. What else had she overheard?

"The same Martha whose funeral I arranged?" My voice rose in pitch. "The Martha who you thought would appreciate a circus? If she cheated with your husband, why on earth would you arrange her celebration of life?"

"Everyone knew about the affair, darling, even her husband. And they knew I knew. It was humiliating, but I had to let them think I didn't care and that I still thought of her as my friend, especially after her tragic accident. But the theme . . ." She laughed. "It was inspired. Nothing says 'tawdry whore' like a circus."

I'd never equated circuses with "tawdry whores," but I made a mental note to take that theme off my list for future celebrations of life.

"What was Tony's 'problem'?" Emma asked the question that was on everyone's lips with her own version of bound-hand air quotes.

"He was a lot of work, as men that age often are." Simone sighed. "My hands were so sore afterward I used up my entire pot of La Crème, but I gave him a night to remember. After he woke up, I mentioned my own little problem and how it would be so much easier for us to get the necklace if we were able to hold an event at Vera's house, and how Peter had a nephew in Sing Sing who had done terrible things, and the next morning, bingo. We had our way in."

"Oh my God, Simone!" I couldn't disguise my horror. "You had him killed so I could plan his funeral?"

"I did no such thing," she said. "I mentioned my problem. It was solved by the next morning. What happened to him in prison had nothing to do with me."

I tried to take a breath, but the air didn't seem to be getting into my lungs. I heard the rattle of chains. Jack was trying to reach me, but he couldn't move more than a few feet from the bed.

"Put your head between your legs," he said. "Take deep breaths."

"A man is dead because of me." I wheezed out the words, staring down at the scratched wooden floor.

"To be fair, it sounds like he was a piece of shit, and they would have killed him in prison anyway," Gage offered. "Dudes who hurt young girls don't last long. The world is a better place."

"Bad," I wheezed. "Killing is bad."

"It's a gray area," Gage said. "I wouldn't waste time or energy mourning a guy like that."

"Okay. I'm done with this." I toed off my right sneaker, dragged it near my hands with my foot, and dug out the razor blade I had hidden under the insole.

"Am I the only one wondering why Simi has a razor blade in her shoe?" Emma asked. "Or why it took her this long to take it out?"

"I thought they'd let us go after they talked to Angelini," I shot back. "And why don't you have a razor blade in your shoe? After what happened to us last time, I resolved to always be prepared in case I was kidnapped and tied up again. I've practiced escaping from ropes and I put a razor blade in every pair of shoes. It's a basic survival tactic."

"After being tied up during our last heist by a Mafia daughter's fly boys as she tries to pawn her daddy's necklace so she can escape an arranged marriage to his rival's son, I never imagined I'd be tied up by Mafia goons again, so the answer is no on that count." Emma grimaced. "My bad."

"I have a lower tolerance for risk." I gestured to Chloe's foot.

"I put razor blades in Chloe's shoes, too. Olivia needs her mom during her vulnerable teen years."

"Please don't secretly put razor blades in my shoes," Emma said as Chloe toed off her sneaker. "I love you like a sister, but sometimes you're just too weird and dangerous for me. I'd be worried I'd lose a couple of toes."

Using the razor blades, Chloe and I managed to saw through the ropes and then free Emma. We were just trying to figure out how to free Jack, Gage, and Cristian when we heard the low growl of engines outside.

"Did they call for reinforcements or is that the concrete for our new shoes?" I peered out the barred window, but I couldn't see the street.

"Either way, we need to get out of here right now." Jack's voice was tight with urgency. "You'll have to pick the lock on the handcuffs. Do you have something long and thin to make a shim? A paperclip, bobby pin, or piece of wire?"

"They took everything." I searched the room, poking into every corner on my hands and knees. Outside, the roar of engines grew louder, and the building began to vibrate with the sound.

"I know." I reached under my shirt. "The wire from my bra. I can use that."

"Jesus." Emma shook her head. "Who wears underwire anymore? Talk about pain."

While Chloe pulled out her wire, Jack talked me through how to bend it into a Z shape, and how to twist it in different directions to lift the locking device inside the cuffs.

"What about me?" Cristian whined as I worked on Jack's handcuffs while Chloe used hers on the cuffs around Gage's wrists.

"You lose out because my girls like to be free." Emma looked out the window again. "That sounds like motorcycles, not trucks. And a lot of them."

"There are a lot of gangs in this area," Gage said. "We might wind up in the middle of a turf war."

"One step at a time." Jack kissed me lightly on the forehead when the cuffs opened before taking the makeshift key over to Cristian. Five minutes later, we were all free, the sound of our movements swallowed by the bone-jarring rumble that was growing louder by the minute.

"We don't know who is going to come through the door or what weapons they're going to have." Jack flipped the bed on edge. "Gage and I will stand on either side of the door. Everyone else get behind the bed."

I heard a thud, a crash, and then a loud voice shouting what sounded like Emma's name. The sound of gunfire echoed through the house, and we hit the ground behind the bed, staying close to the wall in the hopes of dodging any stray bullets. As the metallic taste of fear coated my tongue, I shared a glance with Chloe, our eyes reflecting the shared terror that coursed through our veins. Time seemed to slow as I clung to her hand, our bodies pressed against the cold wooden floor.

"Emma!" The door slammed open and the man from the red sedan burst into the room. He was wearing a black leather biker vest, and he held an enormous pistol in his four-fingered hand.

"Axel!?" Emma pushed to her feet and smoothed her hair, something I'd never seen her do. Then she gave a casual shrug. "What's up?"

"'What's up?'" Chloe whispered beside me. "'What's up?' And how does she know his name?"

"I think the bigger question is how does he know her name? She said she would only tell him if he got the privilege of her tramp stamp."

Chloe swallowed hard. "He's a biker."

"Not just a biker." I studied the *Hell's Fury Motorcycle Club* patch, along with the *President* rocker on his vest. "He's the president of an outlaw motorcycle club. I learned the meaning of that one-percenter badge on his arm from *Sons of Anarchy*."

"Jack decided to get friendly with outlaw bikers?" Chloe sucked in a sharp breath. "And then we dropped a canoe on their car? Between them and the Mafia, I'll be shocked if we get out of here alive."

"You okay, babe?" Axel took Emma's hands and inspected her wrists while three of his biker buddies blocked the door. "Did they hurt you?"

"Just some scratches on my wrists from trying to get out of the ropes. Maybe a bruise or two from trying to fight my way free when they grabbed us. No big deal."

"Fucking bastards." He turned and made a curt gesture for his buddies to follow him out the door. Moments later, I heard multiple shots, and we dove for the floor again. Born and raised in Chicago, we all knew how to deal with gunfire.

He returned with his face and vest splattered with blood, and gently kissed each of her wrists. "They're not gonna bother you anymore."

"Excuse me . . . Axel?" I raised my hands as I emerged from my bed shield. "Um . . . are they all . . . dead?"

His gaze slid to me, narrowed. "As doornails. Shot 'em all a second time for hurting my girl."

"When did you become 'his girl'?" I asked Emma.

For the first time since I'd met Emma, she actually blushed. "He gave me the name of his garage when we were on the mountain. I looked it up and got in touch with him while we were on the road. We chatted and I told him we were heading back to Chicago. He got here before us, and we hooked up last night."

I shot a frantic look at Jack and then back to Axel. "We're sorry about your vehicles . . ."

Axel shrugged. "No big deal. They were stolen. And we got a free canoe."

He said "free canoe" in a way that made it clear the canoe wouldn't be returned. I called that a win.

Still, I felt the need to explain. "We thought you were after us for not good reasons."

"I'd just found my woman," he said. "I wasn't about to let her go that easy, and after I watched her drive the hell out of that piece of shit truck—"

"You should see me on a bike." Emma grinned. "I didn't get my tramp stamp for sitting pretty."

"Fuck me." Axel pulled her against his blood-splattered chest and kissed her hard.

I took a peek out into the hallway and counted five dead Mafia guys and about six bikers going through their pockets.

"I'm a bit concerned that Angelini might take offense when he finds out five of his guys got whacked." I glanced over at Jack to see if he was also concerned about the mass murder in the hallway, but he was busy staring at his phone.

Axel looked over at me like I'd said something nonsensical. "They kidnapped my woman."

"Right. Okay. But she wasn't hurt, so the quintuple homicide seems disproportionate to the crime. Not to me, of course. But if I were a Mafia boss . . ."

Axel's face darkened, and his fierce expression made my blood run cold. "They. Kidnapped. My. Woman."

I swallowed hard and took an involuntary step back. "Are you saying that in the organized crime apex predator hierarchy, one per-centers are higher than the Mafia?"

Axel grunted. "Mob's gone soft."

"Angelini's henchman threatened to gut us like fish."

"Fucking waste of time," Axel said. "I could blow off fifteen faces in the time it would take them to turn you into sushi."

"That's an interesting image I never wanted in my head." I stepped over the first two bodies. "Could you leave a calling card or something to let Angelini know that this was your work?"

"Don't worry about it," he assured me. "He'll know."

I wasn't sure what Angelini would think when he found out his leverage was gone, but with only two days left to find the necklace, I had a feeling he wouldn't care.

TWENTY-NINE

◇ ◇ ◇

We reconvened later that afternoon at our warehouse, with twenty bikers standing guard outside the door.

"I like this place." Axel gave the crumbling warehouse a nod of approval. "Cozy."

"What the fuck?" Gage muttered quietly to Emma. "How are we supposed to keep a low profile with the Sons of fucking Anarchy parked outside?"

Emma hadn't stopped smiling since Axel had killed five mafiosos and stormed the house to save us. "He's the president," she said. "Where he goes, they go."

"And where you go, he goes." My heart squeezed when Axel slung his arm around Emma's shoulders. I'd never seen her so happy.

"Em got me up to speed," Axel said. "Some bitch stole from you. Let's get busy hunting her down and pumping her full of lead."

"It's not that simple," I said. "First, we need her to give us a necklace she stole from a museum in India. Then we need her to give us the money to pay the interest. Then we have to take them both to Tony Angelini to pay off our debt. After that——"

"About the 'pumping her full of lead' part . . ." Chloe said, cutting me off. "I thought this was a 'no guns' heist."

"I think we're way past that. Guns, knives, handcuffs, explosives . . . anything goes."

"I don't understand why we're still in the city," Cristian whined. "We lost the diamond and the necklace. Angelini will be coming for us. We should already be on a plane and heading to a remote island where he'll never find us."

Tension curled in the air. We'd gone through a lot without Cristian, and after his betrayal, he no longer fit in with our tight-knit crew.

"We rescued you even though you abandoned us. We're not leaving Anil just because he fell for the wrong woman," I snapped. "Yes, he went over to the dark side, but he's still on Angelini's list and I have no faith that Clare will protect him. 'No person gets left behind.' That's our new crew motto."

"It's a bit overused, darling. We're not a platoon of soldiers facing enemy combatants in a made-for-the-Oscars movie. How about something fresh and new?" Simone pulled her ski mask over her head. "'No job too big. No danger too great.' 'Together we're stronger.' 'Teamwork is dreamwork.' I could get everyone a ski mask, so we feel more cohesive."

"Jesus fucking Christ. What the hell is that?" Axel recoiled in horror when Simone turned in his direction.

"Gucci 2018," Emma said. "It's almost vintage."

Gage shook his head. "I'd rather be tortured by the mob than wear that piece of sh—"

"Thanks, Simone." I cut Gage off with a glare. "Anil actually bought us black ski masks, so I think we're good. I'll consider those mottos—all great ideas—when this is all sorted out."

Simone gave Gage a smug look. "She liked my ideas."

"She doesn't like that travesty of a hat," he retorted. "Or did you not pick that up?"

"It's not a hat; it's a ski mask. Not that you would know given you seem to only have two items of clothing in your wardrobe. Was there a sale on jeans and black T-shirts at Target or are you really that lacking in style?"

"Simone . . ." Emma whistled in admiration. "I didn't know you had it in you."

"That's not all I've got," she said smugly. "I know this is terrible to say, but I suddenly feel free. Richard . . . his death was a tragedy, of course, but he wasn't a good man." She lifted her right arm and pulled back her sleeve to show us several long, jagged scars. "One time he threw me down the stairs and broke my arm and hand so badly, the bones had to be replaced with steel rods and pins. I lost my fine motor control and had to learn how to write with my left. Other than that, my right hand is mostly functional. There are just a few things I still can't do."

"Simone . . ." My throat tightened. "I didn't know. I'm so sorry."

"Are you sure he's dead?" Axel said. "I can send my boys over . . ."

"He's dead." Simone pulled down her sleeve. "They found his body—well, parts of it. He'd been eaten by sharks. It's unfortunate because it means we can't have an open casket at the funeral."

Cristian's hand went to his mouth. "Jesus. What a terrible way to die."

"I don't know," Emma said. "Sounds kind of fitting to me."

"We need to have his funeral as soon as possible," Simone continued. "Vera and I need to get away. There's been too much tragedy. Too many deaths. My entire world has been turned upside down."

"One thing at a time," I said. "First, we need to find Clare and

Anil and get the necklace. We know they're in the city . . ." I looked to Jack for confirmation, and he nodded. "But the question is how to find them. Any ideas?"

"We like to flush our prey out," Axel said. "Set fire to the building, shoot out all the windows . . ."

Chloe shook her head. "We're not going to—"

I cut Chloe off abruptly. "Actually, he's right. Why are we hunting for Clare? Why don't we make her come to us?"

"You mean lure her," Gage said. "What do we have that she would want? She's got the jewels. She's got the money . . ."

I looked around the circle of expectant faces, and the answer came to me in a heartbeat. "Jack."

"You're going to offer her Jack?" Chloe's brow creased in a frown. "What's she going to do with him?"

"I know you're pissed at the way he left us on the road," Emma said, "but don't you think that's taking it too far?"

"Before you came to the club to 'save' me"—Jack emphasized the word "save" with a sarcastic tone—"I was going to offer myself to Mr. X in exchange for the necklace and your freedom. Clare would be more than happy to bring me in."

"Not happening," I said. "We're a team and we'll stick together. This is now a 'no self-sacrifices' heist. I have a better idea. You're going to be dead." I'd come up with the idea when we'd passed a billboard on the way home from West Garfield advertising a community theater production of *Romeo and Juliet*. My romance-loving bestie had made me watch countless versions of the play over the years. She saw it as a love story. I thought it was a tragedy, especially at the end when everyone wound up dead.

"You're going to kill me rather than let me offer myself up in exchange for the necklace?" Jack scratched his head. "I'm kinda liking the other plan."

"You're going to be fake dead," I said. "Like in *Romeo and Juliet*.

Clare still has feelings for you. If we kill you, she will come. We just need to make sure she knows. You'd better get your affairs in order while I plan your funeral. You've got one day left to live."

◆ ◆ ◆

Since our only connection with Clare was through Mr. X, I sent Simone back to the private members' club the next morning to hand deliver a funeral announcement that would hopefully find its way into Mr. X's hands.

"I don't want my funeral to be in a church," Jack said, sitting across my desk as I scrambled to put the event together. I'd done rush jobs before, but I'd never planned a funeral in one day. "I'm not religious."

"We can have a short ceremony in the funeral home," I assured him.

"No lilies. They're a symbol of death. I want the room to be filled with exotic flowers: *Passiflora caerulea*—it's a blue passionflower representing that I'm a passionate man. If you can arrange for a bowl of water or mud, I'd also like a few lotus flowers, and a bird-of-paradise flower. Amaryllis will brighten things up—I'm thinking a mix of salmon and orange. Maybe some hyacinths, calathea, and lilacs for the scent. Throw in some irises, dahlias . . . oh, and peonies, but not from Leo's greenhouse because they're suffering from a blight, azaleas, hydrangeas . . ." He trailed off when he noticed I wasn't taking any notes. "Why aren't you writing this down?"

"You're supposed to be dead. I'm not decorating with brightly colored flowers. And most of the flowers you mentioned are either out of season, difficult to get, or very expensive."

"Are you saying I'm not worth it?" He folded his arms with a huff. "I want to go out the way I came in: in a blaze of glory."

"What blaze of glory brought you in?" I tapped on the computer screen, sending out emails to my usual contractors to see if they could help out on short notice.

"I was born in the back seat of my father's 1968 Chevy Chevelle."

"'Blaze of glory' is not the phrase I would use to describe having a baby in the back seat of a car."

"It was the way my mom told it." His face softened. "She was a good storyteller."

It was hard to stay angry with Jack when he was sharing memories of his mother. "Do you have any mementos of her?"

"Just one," he said. "I've been keeping it for a special day."

My new bargain-basement burner phone rang with a call from the funeral home. I turned my screen around so Jack could pick his funeral flowers while I made the necessary arrangements. *Keep the cost down*, I mouthed at him. Jack sniffed, and for the rest of the call, all I heard were clicks.

"I've got the funeral home sorted," I said after I was done. "I found one that doesn't require embalming and has a chapel on-site for the service. I told them we want to keep your body at home until just before the service. They'll pick you up and put you in a casket—"

"I want something nice," Jack said. "Not a plywood box."

"I'm not paying for an expensive casket when you're not really dead."

"Then it won't be believable. You supposedly love me. Wouldn't you want the best for me when I die?" He pointed to the screen, where he'd been searching for caskets and not flowers as I'd instructed. "I like this one. It's oak. Polished. Very sturdy and finished with high-end details including a satin lining, tufted velvet interior, and lots of thoughtful design elements, including carved flowers."

"Are you crazy? It's $3,000." I flipped through the screen.

"The Eco Pine Box is only $1,000 and better for the environment. Cristian would approve."

"Or we could go for stainless steel," he said, flipping back. "I would last forever."

"That one is $3,500. Absolutely not."

"I'm beginning to feel unloved," Jack said, sulking. "I might just come back to haunt you from my grave."

I looked up, suddenly hit with the magnitude of what we were doing and the enormous risk of Jack taking a cocktail of medication that would make him look dead. "You'd better come back, or you'll be sorry."

A smile tipped his lips. "Does that mean you forgive me for trying to sacrifice myself to save your life, only to demand that I do it all again, but this time it's okay because it was your idea?"

"You're twisting the facts," I muttered as he walked around the desk. "You abandoned me again. You left me at a truck stop. It was the one thing I told you is triggering for me. It's the one thing that makes me feel . . ."

Unworthy. Unwanted. Unloved.

But I hadn't felt that way. I'd been angry—angry that he would put himself at risk. Far from feeling like I wasn't worthy of being loved, I felt his love like a warm, solid presence deep in my heart. He'd shown it to me again and again in the lengths he had gone to protect me, the small things he'd done to make me happy, and his faith in my ability to lead the crew out of this nightmare. Far from feeling unwanted, I could see his desire in the way he looked at me whenever we were together. Far from feeling unloved, I felt both loved and truly seen. And, I had my crew. They believed in me, supported me, and made me feel that even if Jack did walk away again, I wouldn't lose what I'd finally found—validation, and a love I'd never had for myself.

"What do you feel?" His voice dropped to a sensual rumble as he pulled me out of my chair.

"I feel . . ." My breath caught as he reached out and ran a finger along my jaw, down my neck, and into my cleavage.

"Do you have any clients scheduled for the next hour?" The deep rasp of his voice and his simple touch undid me. I needed Jack in that moment like I needed air to breathe.

"No."

His gaze followed his fingers as he unbuttoned my blouse. "What about Garcia? Do you think he might come by for a visit? Maybe a cup of coffee? Or a pair of handcuffs?"

"Garcia's a good friend, but he's not you," I said. "You get me in a way he doesn't. You understand the secret part of me that craves adventure. You push me to be better. You have faith in me. When you listen, you really listen. When you look at me, you really see me."

"I'm the best." He gave a satisfied growl and unbuttoned the rest of my shirt.

"Very best," I agreed as he lifted me and propped me on the desk, facing the chair with my skirt bunched around my waist.

"You love me."

"I do."

He sat in the chair facing me and slowly slid my panties over my hips.

"What are you doing?" I could barely hear my own words for the pounding of my pulse in my ears as he eased me back on the desk.

"We're going to play show-and-tell." His hands found my thighs and he spread me wide. "It's my dying wish."

"Don't say things like that." I was trembling, suddenly overcome by the risk he was going to take. What if his friend mixed up the wrong cocktail? What if he didn't wake up? I needed him in my arms. I needed to feel his body on mine. I needed his voice in my ear telling me it was all going to be okay. "There's only one game I want to play right now, and it involves you taking off your clothes."

Jack pulled his chair closer. "I love you, Simi."

And then he showed me just how much.

THIRTY

◇ ◇ ◇

As far as deaths went, it was perfect.

Jack obtained a puffer fish toxin called tetrodotoxin from a chemist friend. The chemist had calculated a dose that would put Jack in a suspended state for several hours but allow him to revive naturally without supportive care.

"Who is this guy?" I stretched out beside Jack on my couch, studying the tiny vial in his hand. "Do you trust him?"

"He's a friend of Lou's, and Lou says he's a good man."

"Lou? Lou can't even keep his peonies alive." My voice rose so high, Gage and Chloe came running out of the kitchen. They'd come in case there were any problems when Jack went under. "They've been suffering from botrytis blight for over a year."

"That's because he didn't prune off and destroy the infected parts," he said. "I hope you bought the funeral peonies from someone else."

"I didn't get peonies. I got lilies. I didn't want you to have such a good funeral that you wouldn't want to come back. If you want a real funeral with all the expensive exotic flowers you ticked on the list, you'll have to die properly, preferably when you're over ninety and I've already passed away."

"That's very romantic." Jack slid his hand around my neck and pulled me down to his lips. "Give me a kiss before I die."

I kissed him and kissed him and couldn't let go.

"I'll be okay, sweetheart." Jack gently eased away. "I'm coming back. I've got something to give you." He put the vial to his lips. "I love you."

"I love you, too." I buried my forehead in his neck, breathing in his scent, tasting the salt on his skin with a flurry of last frantic kisses.

He swallowed the contents and closed his eyes while I listened to his heart slow to a barely discernible rhythm. And then he "died" in my arms.

"Jack?" I shook his shoulder. "Jack?"

No response. Bile rose in my throat and a surge of panic rushed through me as I clung desperately to Jack's lifeless body. I gasped for air, squeezing my eyes shut so I couldn't see him lying there so still and silent. "I can't do this. There has to be another way. Where's the antidote?"

"There is no antidote." Gage gently pulled me away. "It has to work its way out of his system. When people get puffer fish poisoning in Japan, unless they're having symptoms, they are often just monitored until they recover."

"What if he doesn't recover?" The weight of his sacrifice bore down on me, crushing my spirit. I thought I'd be able to stay strong, but it was too real. What if I lost Jack when we'd only just found each other again? "What if he took too much? What if he misread the instructions? What if the chemist is as clueless about puffer fish poison as Lou is about peonies? I didn't get the fancy coffin Jack wanted." My breath came out in a sob. "I didn't even get his flowers. He's going to die with lilies. He hates lilies."

Chloe knelt beside me and wrapped her arms around my shoulders. "Take a breath, babe. It's going to be fine. You need to call the funeral home and let them come and get him. He's taken this risk for us; we owe it to him to play it out to the end."

I don't know how I managed to get through the next few hours. I made the call and sat with Jack until they came to take him away. Chloe and Gage stayed with me to help wrap up the final details of the plan and then we made our way to the funeral home where Emma, Axel, Simone, and Cristian were waiting. I had turned down the offer to have the twenty bikers as funeral guests and hired ten actors instead, including an elderly woman who wouldn't stop crying.

"He's in the viewing room," the funeral director said, shaking my hand. "A relative called last night to upgrade his casket and he's now in our premium oak Bellmont with an adjustable bed and mattress for optimum viewing. It's a beautiful choice."

"Did this relative also change the flowers?" I shot an irritated glance at Chloe, who had to cover her mouth to hide her laughter. Jack had obviously been busy last night.

"Yes, indeed. We received a delivery of exotic flowers," he said. "The driver came with instructions to donate the lilies to other bereaved families, so we've placed them in the cooler until the next service."

"I cannot believe him," I grumbled as we made our way to the viewing room. "I specifically told him we needed to keep the costs down."

"You were just sobbing in your apartment about the pine box and lilies," Chloe reminded me.

"I take it back. We should bury him in cardboard with only dandelions at his service."

Axel's men had been instructed to keep a lookout for Clare and to alert us as soon as she showed up. We had arranged a short—one-hour—viewing window before the service, after which Jack was to be cremated since we hadn't arranged for a burial plot. The

plan was for him to wake up in the funeral home before the cremation but after we'd caught Clare, and then we'd all rejoice and go
home to torture her for information about the necklace. My biggest
worry, aside from Jack never waking up, was that he might wake
up too late. The funeral home had a legal obligation to deal with
the body, and since I'd ticked "cremation" on the "burial choices"
form, they would likely be keen to wrap things up after the service.

"Where is she?" I paced up and down the aisle in front of the
casket. "Why isn't she showing up? She cares about him. I know
she does."

"We've got a bigger problem than Clare not showing up." Emma
held up her phone. "Axel is outside. He says Jack's got an influx of
unexpected visitors. Dozens of them."

Chloe and I shared a horrified look. "What visitors? Who are
they? Who else knows that Jack is dead?"

"Beta." My dad walked into the room, his face creased with
worry. "We just heard about Jack. Why didn't you tell us?"

Stunned, I could only stare as my mom, aunties, uncles, and
cousins followed him into the room and gathered around Jack's
coffin.

"What's going on?" I dragged my father out into the hallway.
"How did you find out?"

"Anil heard from a friend that Jack had passed. He mentioned
it to his father, and his father called me to offer his condolences.
He remembered Jack from when he visited them last year and then
ran out of their house without saying good-bye. Anil had told him
that you and Jack were together."

"Anil passed on the message?" I was at once happy because the
message had clearly gotten through to Clare, and sad that Anil
was still with her. Part of me had hoped that he would come to his
senses after she tried to kill us.

"Is he not here yet?" Dad asked. "He told his father not to

prepare his usual bagged lunch because he was taking the day off work to attend the funeral."

"I haven't seen him." I asked Chloe to tell the rest of the crew that Anil might show up and when he did, to make sure no one touched him because if anyone was going to hurt him for what he'd done, it was me.

"You didn't answer your phone when I called," Dad continued, "but I realized you'd probably turned it off when you came here out of respect. Your mom called the funeral home to get the details of the service. Nani called your aunties, and they got everyone together, and thank goodness we made it here in time to be with you for your final good-bye."

I felt a prickle of awareness and a shiver ran down my spine. Out of the corner of my eye, I caught a glimpse of blond hair, but before I could check to see if it was Clare, Anil was by my side.

After sharing a greeting and a few words with my father, he pulled me away. "I need to talk to you."

"We have nothing to say to each other," I spat out. "Jack and I almost died in that container, and you did nothing to save us. I thought you were my friend."

"I convinced her to leave you in the container instead of having Vito kill you right then and there," he protested. "After they locked you in, I landed my drone on the roof so I could track you." He gave me a pleading look. "It was the best I could do."

"Your best wasn't good enough. Chloe found us only seconds before the container was picked up by the gantry crane, and since Clare had painted over the number, once the ship left port, there would have been no way to find us. Drone batteries don't last forever."

A maelstrom of emotions flickered across Anil's face. "I had a plan. I just thought I'd have more time."

"Your plan sucked." I folded my arms so I wouldn't be tempted to throttle him.

"What happened to Jack?" His eyes watered. "Was it Clare? Did she kill him? Or was it Mr. X? I didn't have anything to do with this. You have to believe me."

"No, she didn't do it." I couldn't trust him, so I gave the lie that we'd prepared in case anyone asked. "He was shot by the Mafia when we went to rescue Cristian. He refused to go to a hospital because gunshots have to be reported and he didn't want to put us all at risk. Gage did his best to patch him up, but . . ." My voice caught as I added a few more details to the story we'd come up with the previous night, knowing Clare would have found out Cristian was free.

"Simi . . ." Anil crumpled to the floor, one knee down, an arm across his face as his voice cracked, broke. "He died thinking I was a bad guy, that I betrayed you . . ."

He was so utterly distraught, I knelt beside him. "What were you thinking? She doesn't care about you, Anil. She's going to use you and throw you away. Was it really worth losing all your friends?"

Anil let out a loud, ragged sob. "You were all so unkind to me. You looked down on me, teased me, laughed at me, made me feel unworthy. Clare didn't do that. She thinks I'm brilliant. She makes me feel like a real man. She loves me for who I am." He grabbed my shoulder as if trying to give me a hug and whispered in my ear, "How am I doing?"

"What?" Puzzled, I frowned. "How are you doing what?"

"Is it too much? I decided to give up MMA and get into method acting. I've immersed myself in this role." He clutched my sleeve and wailed in a loud voice. "I can't bear it. Jack might still be alive if I'd been there to help you. Forgive me. Please."

"Never." I raised my voice, because I was, in fact, beginning to realize that we might not have lost him after all. "You made your decision."

"I'm sorry. I'm so sorry." Anil grabbed my hand and pushed something into my palm. "If you can't forgive me, I'll go. You'll never have to see me again. At least, Clare needs me."

I helped Anil to his feet and glanced over my shoulder. Clare was watching us, a thoughtful expression on her face.

"It was the long game, like you said," Anil whispered in a broken voice before he walked away. "I just wish Jack could have been alive to know that I was always on your side."

I slipped away to the restroom and locked myself in a stall before I opened my hand. There, in my palm, lay the Florentine Diamond.

By the time I'd processed what had happened and shared the news with Chloe, the viewing and ended, and we were late for the service.

"There are too many people for our small chapel," the funeral director said, running a hand through his graying hair in agitation. "You may wish to reschedule and hold it in a larger facility."

I looked over at the hired actors, dutifully crying in the hallway.

"It's fine. I'll send some of them home."

"I beg your pardon?"

"Um . . ." I shot a frantic look at Chloe.

"They just came for the viewing," she said quickly. "They don't like services. Too emotional. I'll look after them. Tell the minister we'll be ready in five minutes. Anyone who can't fit can stand in the hall."

"What's the plan here?" Emma whispered after Chloe had gone. "Milan and Vito are in the chapel with Anil and a whole pile of sobbing aunties who don't even know who Jack is. I haven't seen

Clare, but I'm just itching to get my hands on her. Gage brought his bag of torture tools and Axel knows a place nearby with good soundproofing."

"We need to keep her away from Milan and Vito," I said. "Tell Axel to get a couple of guys to drag them out to the van. When we have Clare, we'll take them all to the warehouse like we planned. I don't think we'll need any violence. We have something to trade." I opened my hand and showed her the diamond. "Anil just gave it to me. He said he was playing the long game."

Far from being excited, Emma shrugged. "And you believe him?"

"Why would I not?"

"Because he works at a place that makes fake jewelry." Her voice was ice-cold. "Because he made a replica of the Wild Heart so good it fooled everybody. Because he betrayed us, and he's probably betraying us again."

Anil had been closer to Emma than anyone else in the crew. She'd taken him under her wing and made it her mission to turn him from a naive mama's boy into a respectable man. Of anyone, she must have been hurt most by his betrayal.

"But we'll have Clare," I said. "Either it's real and she trades us for the necklace, or it's fake and we let Axel and Gage torture her until she tells us where she's put the Wild Heart."

"You've become a hard woman," Emma said. "I like it."

"We only have six hours until midnight," I reminded her. "I'm prepared to do what needs to be done to keep us all safe." I returned to the viewing room to do one last check for visitors, and found Clare standing beside his coffin.

"What happened?" she said, studying his face.

"He was shot by the Mafia when we went to rescue Cristian. He wouldn't go the hospital, so Gage patched him up. He said he was fine. One minute he was cracking jokes on the couch. The next he was . . ." I didn't have to feign the emotion. The sight of Jack lying so still was still hard to shake. "Gone."

"He was the only person who was ever kind to me." Her voice wavered. "He would take the blame when I screwed up, so Xavier would beat him instead of me. Sometimes the beatings went on so long he would pass out."

"I didn't know it was that bad." No wonder Jack had been reluctant to share that part of his life.

"He was the only real friend I ever had." She turned to me, and for a moment I saw the woman and not the monster. "I loved him."

"I know."

"He didn't love me back, so then I hated him," she continued. "It got out of hand."

"I was thinking that when you locked us in a container to die." Clare shrugged. "It's the job."

It occurred to me in that moment that this was the perfect opportunity to incapacitate Clare. Unfortunately, I didn't have a weapon, and the only thing in the room, aside from the coffin, was a wreath made of exotic flowers on a wire stand beside me.

"Jack loved his flowers." I bent over as if to smell the flowers, grabbed the wreath, spun, and smashed it over Clare's head. Flowers scattered across the carpet and the wreath came apart in my hands.

Stunned, Clare just stared, her hair adorned with a sea of pretty pink plumeria.

"Simi, what are you doing?" Dad stood in the doorway, his face a mask of horror.

"This is the woman who kissed Jack with a gun to his chest. She also tried to kill me. She tried to make it so I would never see you again. I still might have to leave you because of her." My hands tightened around the wire frame so hard my knuckles turned white.

Dad's brow creased in a frown. "Use your fist like you did when you were playfighting with your brothers."

"Pathetic." Clare grabbed the remains of the flower wreath out of my hands and threw it on the floor. "If you really wanted to hurt me, you'd pick something more substantial."

I threw a hard right, grazing her cheekbone when she ducked to the side.

"That's it," Dad called out. "A little higher."

"What's going on?" Mom walked into the room with Nani. "Why is Simi hitting that woman beside Jack's coffin? We're at a funeral. It's disrespectful."

"This is the woman who tried to break them up," Dad said. "She's the reason for all that talk of leaving us. She tried to kill our Simi."

"Hit her harder." Mom held her fists in the air. "Give her a one-two punch."

"Mom? Seriously?" My mother picked up spiders and carried them out of the house. She shooed flies out the window and even checked the grass for insects before she mowed the lawn. She so abhorred violence that she couldn't even watch my brothers wrestle in the backyard.

Clare still hadn't raised her hands to retaliate, and I was contemplating just what kind of person I really was when Axel and Gage burst through a side door, grabbed Clare, and dragged her away.

"Simi, who were those men?" Dad took a step forward. "You didn't even have a chance to break her nose."

It was then that Nani screamed. "He's alive! It's a miracle!"

I turned to see Jack sitting up in his coffin, a confused expression on his face.

"Are you okay?" I rushed over to check on him, running my hands over his face, his chest, feeling his wrist for the steady beat of his pulse.

"I thought I was supposed to wake up in the chapel." His voice was hoarse, rough, and his breathing was fast and shallow as he took in the mess of flowers and my family standing openmouthed behind me.

"We had some unexpected guests." I waved vaguely at the people crowding in the door to see the dead man come to life. "It caused a bit of a delay." I dragged myself away from his side to quickly explain to my family that Jack had never really been dead, and we'd staged the funeral to get back at his ex-girlfriend for all the mean things she'd done. Nani wouldn't accept my apology that they'd been dragged into the charade. She wanted the miracle. It made for a better story.

After they'd gone, I returned to the coffin and filled Jack in on what had happened while he'd been dead. "Axel and Gage have Clare." I wrapped my arms around him. "We may have the diamond, too, thanks to Anil. If it's real, we should be able to make a trade."

"The bikers have Milan and Vito," Chloe said, joining us. "They're bringing everyone to the warehouse. Can Jack walk?"

"I might just lie here for another minute," Jack said. "This extra cushioning is very comfortable, but for my next funeral, I think I'll go with the super-deluxe."

THIRTY-ONE

◇ ◇ ◇

What the fuck took you so long?" Gage greeted us at the warehouse with an impatient growl. "Jack came back from the dead over three hours ago. We made it here in record time, tied up Clare, Milan, and Vito, handcuffed Anil to a post because Emma still doesn't trust him, and Simone had her chauffeur bring us food from some five-star restaurant that serves burgers the size of walnuts. We've got less than three hours. We're on the clock."

"We had to fill in the 'corpse revival' paperwork to get back our deposit. Apparently, this wasn't their first corpse awakening."

"She also took the time to punch Clare in the face." Chloe laughed. "I don't think she's anti-violence anymore."

"Being locked in a shipping container and left to die does that to a girl." I walked over to Clare, who had been expertly tied to a metal chair. "I need that necklace and I'm prepared to do what it takes to get it."

Clare didn't respond to my threat. Instead, her gaze was fixed on Jack as he made his way toward her. Relief flickered across her face so quickly I wondered if I'd seen it. "I thought you were dead."

"I was. Almost." He forced a laugh. "Remind me to take puffer fish off the list of exotic foods I want to try."

"We don't have much time, so I'll put this in simple terms." I held out my hand to Jack and he gave me the diamond Anil had returned to us. He'd studied it for the entire Uber ride to the warehouse, at one point using the flashlights on both our phones and the Uber driver's emergency flashlight. "You need this, and we need the necklace. We trade and everyone goes home in one piece."

"Do you really think I'd fall for that?" Clare's voice was curiously flat. "It's a fake. I have the real diamond."

"You have a piece of glass," Anil called out. "I didn't have time to make a second replica, so I ground down a piece of glass that was a similar size and weight and swapped it out for the diamond when you were otherwise occupied. You were keeping it in your bra if you don't believe me."

"Anil, you dog." Cristian gave a low whistle.

"Enough." I held up a warning hand. "We're not here to socialize. Anil was working as a double agent, so someone free him from the cuffs."

"Someone needs to search Clare," Chloe pointed out. "We need to make sure she doesn't still have the real diamond in her bra."

"Let her do it."

Gage released one of Clare's hands and she fumbled around in her shirt. Finally, she pulled out a piece of glass about one inch around. "Dammit." She flung the glass on the ground.

"Where's the necklace?" I held up the real diamond. "And the money?"

"If I wait it out until midnight, Angelini will hunt you down and kill you," she said with a shrug. "Then I get to keep them both."

Axel put one hand on each arm of Clare's chair and leaned in until he was so close their noses were almost touching. "Emma is my woman. She is under my protection. That means her friends are Hell's Fury friends. The fucking Chicago Outfit is not going to touch them. They've seen what happens when they mess with us."

"He had one of his men draw the Hell's Fury logo on the wall of the house where they kidnapped Cristian using the blood of one of the mob guys they'd just pumped full of lead," Emma explained. "He did a great job, even though he usually paints with watercolors."

"I take back all the mean things I said about being friendly to strangers," I whispered to Jack. "You should go ahead and menace as many strangers on as many isolated mountain roads as you like."

"I'll require more than a quick apology," Jack said, cupping my neck gently with his hand. "When this is all over, get ready to grovel."

"Xavier isn't going to stop," Clare said to Jack. "He'll keep coming after you."

"Not if he thinks I'm dead."

She studied him for a long moment and said, "Why would he think that?"

"Because you'll tell him you went to my funeral. I've paid off the funeral director so he's not going to talk. I'm getting out of the business, Clare. I'm done. You won't have any more competition. You won't have to keep looking over your shoulder. I won't get in your way. This was always going to be my last heist. I want to live a normal life. Just like we talked about when we were kids."

I didn't know Clare very well, but I could see in her face the unspoken part of Jack's dream. It wasn't just something they'd talked about when they were kids. It was something they had planned to do together. "What's in it for me?"

"You'll get all Xavier's attention. He'll put you on the big jobs instead of wasting your talent chasing after me."

Her mouth twisted. "It won't be as much fun."

"It stopped being fun when you decided that winning was more important than friendship."

Clare let out a long sigh. "It's in the biggest safe in the corner. I had Vito put it in there on the first day we got together, but he changed the combination from the one stuck to the side."

"Oh my God." Chloe shook her head. "I can't believe it's been here all along."

Jack got the new combination from Vito and retrieved the necklace, holding it up for all of us to see.

"My goodness." Simone gasped. "I've seen some beautiful pieces, but that is really something."

"You'd better check it to make sure it's real," I said to Jack. "We've been fooled before."

Jack took the necklace and held it up to the light, then examined it with his phone. "Without the proper equipment, I'm not 100 percent sure, but—"

"I had it checked," Clare said. "It's genuine."

"What about the cash?" We were running short of time. We still had to call the number on Angelini's card to get the delivery location before midnight. "We have to pay the interest, and you promised us each a little bonus."

"Freight elevator." She lifted her chin in that direction. "There is a loose board under the operating panel. Milan put it under the floor."

"The money, too?" Emma tipped her head back and groaned. "We could have saved ourselves weeks of pain and heartache, murders, funerals, road trips, heists and hospitals, kidnappings, shoot-outs, fake deaths and resurrections."

"But then you wouldn't have met me." Axel grabbed her by the neck and pulled her in for a long, hard kiss.

"Damn," Emma said, coming up for a breather. "It was worth it. Every single second."

Jack and Gage pried up the elevator floor and pulled out a duffel bag. I vaguely remembered Clare bringing it with her the first time we got together, but I hadn't paid attention to what had happened to it when she left.

"It's all here," Jack said after a quick check. "Text Angelini."

"You've got what you wanted from us," Clare said as we waited for Angelini to respond. "Give me the diamond and cut us loose. Our business is done."

Gage and Axel cut their ropes and I handed over the diamond before Emma escorted them to the door. Clare paused on the threshold and looked over her shoulder at Jack.

"I hope it all works out," she said. "It would be good if one of us got to live the dream."

After the door closed, Jack grabbed the duffel bag and slung it over his shoulder. "Give me the necklace. As soon as Angelini sends the address, I'll hit the road. Alone."

Nausea roiled in my belly. I'd been dreading this moment since Angelini had come into my office. He didn't just want the necklace and the money. He wanted Jack. My Jack. And I wasn't prepared to lose him.

"I can't let you go."

Jack's mouth opened and closed. I saw the moment understanding dawned. "He wants me."

"The way he sees it, you have to pay for setting up his brother and sending him to jail."

"His brother put himself in jail by being corrupt, stealing people's homes, and sending his thugs to push old ladies down the stairs." A pained expression crossed his face. "How long have you known I was part of the deal?"

"From the beginning."

Anger, so rare in easygoing Jack, kindled in his voice, making me feel sick inside. "Why didn't you tell me? What about yesterday or the day before? How about when we were locked in the container? Or do you still not trust me?"

"I didn't trust you at the start," I said honestly. "After you ghosted me and then I saw you with Clare, I was worried you'd just run away if you knew your life was on the line."

"Is that the kind of man you think I am?" His voice hitched. "After everything we've been through together, did you really think I'd leave you to face this alone?"

"I didn't know what to think. You were there and then you weren't and then you showed up with Clare. I was afraid, Jack. Afraid I'd made a mistake. Afraid to trust myself and my feelings. Afraid of getting hurt all over again."

"And you wanted me to stay, why?" he asked in a frigid voice. "So, you could give me up and meet the terms to save yourself?"

"No. Of course not."

"What else do I have to do, Simi?" He was shouting, his voice echoing in the warehouse, where the rest of the crew watched in stunned silence. "Why can't you believe I'm a good man? I would never hurt you, never leave you, never make you feel the way your parents made you feel."

"I do believe you." I drew in a shuddering breath. "I think I even knew in my heart that what I saw with Clare wasn't real. But I needed time with you, time we didn't get when you were away, time to see the kind of man you were through your actions and not just your words."

Still his expression didn't change. I'd hurt him as much as he'd hurt me. "When I got over that fear and saw you for who you really are," I continued, "I knew in my heart that you would give yourself over to Angelini. I couldn't let that happen. I wanted to protect you. I wanted to find a way to save you before you ever had to make that choice. I did come close to telling you twice, but both times we were interrupted and I'm glad we were because you would never have let us do this . . ." I nodded and the entire crew moved to block the door. I'd sent a message to them from the Uber, letting them know about Angelini's demand and my plan to save Jack.

"We're in this together," I said. "I would rather go on the run from the mob than lose you, and I think everyone feels the same. We didn't abandon Cristian or Anil, and we won't abandon you. No one gets left behind."

Anil took the bag from Jack's shoulder, and Emma took the necklace from his hand.

"Sorry, bud." Gage yanked Jack's arms behind his back and snapped a pair of handcuffs on him. "I don't always agree with Simi, but this time she's right. He'll shoot you where you stand."

"He'll kill you all if you show up without me." Jack yanked on the cuffs as we made our way to the door. "Simi. Don't do this."

"I'll stay with him," Cristian called out. "I know you've got bikers outside, but someone should be here to free him in case you don't come back."

"Gage, you bastard," Jack hollered as we walked away. "Simi . . . come back. Chloe, you know it's dangerous. Think about Olivia. Emma . . . take these cuffs off me and let me go. Simone . . . it's not the adventure you think it is."

He was still shouting after I closed the door.

THIRTY-TWO

◆ ◆ ◆

Gage parked his SUV in front of a sprawling Arts and Crafts–style home in the heart of Oak Park. With a vast manicured front lawn and surrounded by mature trees, it seemed both inviting and foreboding in the moonlight.

"Crime definitely pays." Emma checked the rearview mirror for Axel, who had insisted on following us with five of his men. He'd left the rest at the warehouse to watch over Jack. "I wonder where Axel lives. I don't know that much about him."

"Most bikers live in a clubhouse," Simone said. "I've been watching *Sons of Anarchy* to understand the world of crime. If Axel decides he likes you enough to keep you as his personal property, you'll become an 'Ol' Lady' and get your own vest with a property patch that says 'Property of Axel,' and he'll probably want you to tattoo his name on your rear. 'Ol' Lady' is wife status, and because he's the president, you'll be accorded the most respect of all the bitches in the club. If he isn't that serious, then you'll be a 'Mama' or a 'Sweet Butt.' In that case, your job will be to sleep with the other bikers, keep the clubhouse and motorcycles clean, and try to convince Axel to take you as an 'Ol' Lady' through underhanded techniques and political and sexual manipulation. If you don't want to be part of the club, then he could take you as a 'Citizen Wife,' but he'll likely have an 'Ol' Lady' on the side."

"Fuck that," Emma said. "I want the whole damn package."

"So, what do we do here?" I asked. "Do we just go up to the door of a Mafia boss at night, ring the bell, and hand over the goods?"

"We've got five minutes left and it's not going to get to the door itself," Gage pointed out. "Let's get going."

We walked up the long driveway together—Gage, Chloe, Simone, Anil, Emma, and I. My heart pounded as I thought through all the things I could say to convince Angelini to change his mind about Jack. I could appeal to his sense of honor. His brother had brought it on himself. Jack had a right to vengeance and now they were even. Oh, and by the way, Axel's woman was our friend, which meant that if they touched Jack, they would face the wrath of Hell's Fury.

Hands shaking, I rang the doorbell. I could see a TV flickering in the darkened living room, but no shadows in the brightly lit windows upstairs. After a few minutes of waiting, I rang the doorbell again, acutely aware that the clock was ticking.

"Look at the door," Gage whispered. "It's open."

"We can't just walk into a mobster's house," I said quietly. "He'll shoot us on sight."

Axel took a slow walk across the front lawn and returned with his brow furrowed. "He's got cameras set up around the yard, but it doesn't look like they're on. I didn't see any guards and his sensor lights didn't activate." He waved over the nearest biker and asked him to send men to check out the backyard and the rest of the street. "I don't like this. Something's not right."

"He knew we were coming," Chloe said. "He responded to the text. Maybe he turned off his security system."

"Or maybe someone got here before us." Gage pushed open the door and stepped inside.

I closed my eyes and counted to five before I followed him. "Mr. Angelini," I called out. "We're here with . . ." I pulled up short when Gage made a frantic gesture with his hand, waving us back.

"Fuck." His harsh whisper froze me in place. "Fuck. Fuck. Fuck."

"What is it?"

"He's dead. Sitting in his chair in front of the TV. He's got a bullet hole in his forehead and a big fucking knife through his heart."

"Ohmygodohmygodohmygod." Chloe sucked in a deep breath. "The Mafia is going to think we did it."

"We need to get outta here and fast," Gage said. "I'll get his phone. It will have Simi's number on it, and we don't want anyone to know she was the last person he talked to."

"I'll wipe down the doorbell and the door," I offered. "But what about security cameras on the street? And our license plate?"

"The police aren't going to waste resources hunting down the killer of a Mafia boss," Axel assured us. "The house across the street is vacant, probably owned by him, and the nearest neighbors aren't close enough to get a good look at the plate. He picked this house for a reason. People can come and go and they won't be easily traced."

Axel talked to his men while we piled into the SUV. "There were three guards outside," he said. "Someone took them all out in the backyard. One with bullets. Two with knives."

It was a quiet ride back to the warehouse. For the first time ever, Simone had nothing to say.

Jack took one look at us when we walked back into the warehouse and his face paled. "What happened?"

"He's dead." I tossed the duffel bag on the floor.

Cristian recoiled in horror. "You killed him and brought his head back in a bag?"

"No, idiot." Emma shook her head. "Someone got there first."

"They took out three guards, disabled the security system, put a bullet in Angelini's head and knife in his heart," Gage added. "I found this on the table beside his phone." He held up a piece of paper. "Does it mean anything to you?"

Jack studied the paper and then slumped against the pole where he'd been cuffed. "Yes."

"You have to give us more than that," I said. "What does it mean? Who killed Angelini?"

"It's the date Clare and I promised each other that one day we'd be free to live our dreams." He sucked in his lips and studied the floor. "It was the combination to the safe where she hid the necklace."

Once he'd said it, the whole scene made sense. Milan's knives. Vito's guns. Clare stabbing Angelini right in the heart.

"She did it for you," I said softly as I undid his handcuffs. "To set you free."

"Yes." He shook out his wrists. "It makes it just that little bit harder to hate her."

"What do we do now?" Anil asked. "We've got the necklace, the interest money, and our bonus cash. Should we buy an island? Live in paradise? You still haven't thanked me for playing the long game. I fooled Clare, a master thief. I fooled all of you with my incredible acting skills, and I made the ultimate sacrifice. Now, my future wife won't be my first. But it's the emotional trauma that was the worst. It hurt my heart when you all hated me. Maybe I should have a little extra for my trouble."

"Thank you, Anil." I gave him a hug. "For everything."

"There won't be money to give out any extra," Jack said. "I'm going to take the necklace back to the museum in Delhi, where it belongs. We can keep the bonus money Clare gave us, but the nine million in interest should go back to her."

"Are you kidding?" Cristian spluttered. "She's the reason I was kidnapped by the mob. You don't know what it was like. We had to eat out of non-compostable fast-food containers and throw our trash in plastic shopping bags. There was no recycle bin. They left taps running and the toilet didn't have a short flush to conserve water. They didn't give a damn about the environment. And there were no vegan options where they got our food. No fruit. No vegetables. It was all meat and carbs all the time. I lived on fries and the buns from their burgers. I must have gained twenty pounds in captivity."

"What about the part where you were beaten and tortured?" Anil asked. "Wasn't that worse?"

"I could survive the pain, but the earth will not," Cristian spat out. "Do you know how much damage they did to the ozone layer with their cigarettes? Once they even put wood in the fireplace and had a fire. If I'd been able to look out the window, I'm sure I would have seen the actual climate change."

"Clare's going to need the money because the diamond she has is a fake," Jack said. "I didn't get a good look at it in the shipping container, but on the way here after I died—"

"You didn't die," I interrupted. "It was a fake death."

"If I had died, you would have been sorry you didn't trust me, and even more sorry that you went cheap with the pine box and lilies," he grumbled. "So much groveling is going to have to happen when this is done. I can hardly wait. "

"What if I preorder you a nice super-deluxe oak coffin for when I strangle you in your sleep?"

"Someone hose these two down," Gage barked. "I want to hear about the fake diamond."

"There isn't much to say." Jack shrugged. "It's a replica—a very good one."

"How many fake diamonds did you make?" I asked Anil.

"Just one. I gave it to Chloe just before she was hit over the head. She was supposed to switch it for the real one once she got Peter to take her down to the museum."

"We never made it to the museum, so it should still be in the pocket of my jeans," Chloe said. "Vera was right about the entire art collection being fake."

I scrubbed my hands through my hair. It had been one hell of a day. "Poor Peter thought he was Indiana Jones, and it turns out he was the victim of an elaborate scam instead."

"He died for nothing," Chloe said quietly. "That's what's really sad. Whoever robbed the museum killed him for a collection of replicas and a worthless piece of glass, and now they are out there walking free. The only bright light is that the container can't be tracked, and they'll waste time and resources trying to find a collection that has no value anyway."

"I don't think we should tell Vera she was right." Simone folded her Gucci mask and tucked it into her purse. "I think it would just make her feel worse."

"Clare is going to be in a difficult position when she gets the diamond appraised," Jack said. "I almost feel bad for her. Xavier won't be kind."

"Everyone in favor of returning the interest money to Clare because she saved Jack's life and freed us from the Mafia raise your hand." I looked around the room and frowned. "Cristian, raise your hand."

"It's a lot of money."

"Hand. Up." I glared at Cristian. "Or you don't get your $1 million in bonus money, which some of us are on the fence about giving to you after what you did."

"Without Cristian, we would each get $1,166,666," Anil said. "I say we cut him out."

Cristian raised his hand.

"Excellent." I opened the duffel bag and smiled. "Now, who wants $1 million?"

"Actually, count me out," Simone said. "You can have my share as payment for the best adventure I've ever had."

THIRTY-THREE

◇ ◇ ◇

Simone chose an ocean theme for Richard's celebration of life, and I was able to get a last-minute booking at Shedd Aquarium, where the guests would be able to view over thirty-two thousand marine animals while dining in the conservation-conscious venue. Cristian was in his absolute element and insisted on being my right-hand man, not only helping with the planning and organizing, but also taking the guests around to talk about the exhibits.

"Don't you think it's in poor taste to have an ocean-themed memorial for someone who was eaten by a shark?" Chloe picked up one of the shark cookies on the buffet platter and bit off its head.

"I did gently try to convince her to celebrate one of Richard's other passions—golf, wine, whiskey, treasure hunting, and collecting taxidermied animal heads . . ."

Chloe gagged and grabbed a glass of water to wash down the shark head lodged in her throat. "I know it's terrible to say at a time like this," she said between gulps, "but when I saw those scars on Simone's arm, I thought she was better off without him."

We made the rounds, checking that everything was going smoothly, and returned to the buffet to find Detective Garcia munching on a shark.

"I was just about to go looking for you," he said. "This is some party."

"It's a memorial," I corrected him. "Richard's celebration of life."

"The dude who got eaten by sharks." He picked up another shark cookie and ate it in one bite. "I came here to ask Simone a few questions and to talk to Vera Hearst. I went to both their houses. Vera's assistant said they were here. Could you point me in the right direction? Either one would do."

I couldn't believe Garcia had come to interrogate Simone during her husband's celebration of life. It wasn't like him to be so insensitive, especially when a loved one had died. "Can you come back another time? We just had Richard's funeral this morning and now we're remembering the deceased. Poor Simone is in mourning."

I grimaced when I heard laughter and cheering from the guests enjoying the beluga encounter. Simone had wanted the event to be fun above all else. She had even insisted that we rent a photo booth with a live aquarium backdrop, and it was a big hit.

Garcia took yet another cookie. "It can't wait. I still have a few questions for them about Peter Hearst's death."

"I thought you were investigating the burglary." I moved the cookies away in case other guests wanted to remember Richard by eating a wheat-and-sugar-based replica of the animal that had eaten him.

"I'm still on the burglary, but I've been promoted." Garcia pulled out his wallet and flipped it open to show me a shiny new badge. "Homicide. There has been an increase in murders lately and they wanted to expand the team. I've been assigned to both cases."

"Congratulations." I was genuinely happy for Garcia. He was a smart guy, hardworking and ambitious. He deserved the promotion. "How is the Hearst case going?"

Garcia's smile faded. "We got an anonymous tip about a truck that was seen leaving the vicinity of Vera's house around the time of the murder. We tracked the shipment all the way to a container terminal in Newark and spoke to the drivers involved. They were hired to collect forty boxes from an exit in the alley beside Vera's house during Peter's celebration of life. The shipment was pre-packed and left inside the unlocked door."

"Wait . . . everything was already there, packed and sealed? How is that even possible? Not more than forty-five minutes passed between the time Chloe left me to talk to Peter, and Vera came to tell me he was dead." Although I already knew the shipment was packed and waiting, I still hadn't figured out how the thieves had managed to get the job done so quickly.

Garcia nodded and stroked his chin. "There are a lot of unanswered questions. I was hoping Vera or Simone might help me shed some light on them."

"Maybe the thieves accessed Peter's museum the night before," Chloe offered. "Could they have packed it all up and moved it into the tunnel ready to go? The boxes were already there because the collection was going to be shipped to their yacht that weekend."

"But how did they overcome all that security?" I'd been so focused on trying to save Jack, I hadn't given much thought to how the art had been stolen in the first place. "And why kill Peter and cut off his finger if they had already bypassed the biometrics?"

"Maybe they were at the party and overheard him offering to take me downstairs after showing me his new car," Chloe suggested. "They were worried he'd find out he'd been robbed before the truck arrived, so they knocked me out, killed him, and then cut off his finger so it looked like the theft had just happened."

"That's not a bad theory," Garcia said. "But then why did they need to knock out the security on the day? Why go to the trouble of killing Peter and cutting off his finger? If it was just a matter of ensuring he didn't go down to the museum before the truck arrived, why not just knock you both out? And why did they not take the goods the night before? Why pull off the heist in broad daylight when there was a high chance of being caught? Why hire a commercial truck that could be easily traced? And why, if they were professionals, did they not steal the paintings in the vault, which Vera says are worth over $100 million?"

"That's a lot of questions." I picked up a shark cookie, suddenly finding myself in need of a sugar hit.

"I need a lot of answers."

"Were you able to trace the missing items?" Chloe asked.

"They were loaded onto a shipping container headed for Belize, but a few days into the voyage, there was an explosion on the ship, and a number of containers went overboard. When we radioed the captain, he said the container we were looking for didn't show up on the manifest. He thought it must have been one of over a dozen containers that they were unable to recover."

My stomach twisted and I snapped the shark cookie in two. If not for Chloe, Jack and I would have been in that container, lost at sea.

"Poor Vera," Chloe said. "First her husband and then all his precious possessions."

"Vera didn't seem too concerned about the contents of the museum." Garcia picked up a shark-tooth puff-pastry canapé filled with caviar. "I stopped by a few days ago to give her the bad news, and she didn't even want a copy of my report to file an insurance claim. She said the entire collection was fake and her husband had been taken advantage of by unscrupulous black market art and antiquity dealers."

I sucked in a sharp breath, feigning surprise. "Are you saying Peter was killed for nothing?"

"We don't know," Garcia said, "but we are interested in talking to the woman who booked the truck. The receptionist at the trucking company told us that a woman made the booking over the phone, but because she wanted to pay in cash and it was a substantial sum, the manager insisted she come in person and sign the paperwork. Apparently, she was oddly dressed in overly large clothes and she wore a hat and sunglasses even though it was raining."

"Do you think she was the killer?" I wrapped a napkin around my shattered shark and discreetly dropped it in the nearby bin.

"Right now, she's our prime suspect," Garcia said. "The signature on the shipping documents is consistent with someone who writes with their left hand. The autopsy report also concluded that we were dealing with a left-handed killer, and one who didn't have the strength to make a clean cut. Given the short time frame between when Peter was last seen alive and Vera found him, I'm still working on the theory that the suspect was at the party. I've been collecting signatures to compare, but it's been one hell of a job to track everyone down."

"Is that why you got us to sign the NDA?" I said, suddenly understanding.

Garcia chuckled. "Yes, but I also didn't want any of you sharing information about the investigation, so it served two purposes."

Something niggled at the back of my mind, but I was too focused on what Garcia had just told us to figure it out. "What about Chloe? Why didn't they kill her? She would have been a witness."

"Chloe said she was standing on the opposite side of the garage checking things out. Peter was sitting in the driver's seat when she was struck from behind with a length of pipe that we found at the scene. It is very unlikely that either of them would have stayed where they were if the other was being attacked, so we believe that the killer was already in the vehicle when they arrived in the garage and there was a second person involved who hit Chloe." He grabbed a handful of shark cookies and stuffed them in his pocket. "If Chloe hadn't been injured, I would have suspected you."

"Me?" I stared at him in shock. "Why would I kill Peter? He was my client. And what would I do with his art collection? Vera told me it was fake the first time we met." I didn't like where the conversation was going, or Garcia's slightly hostile tone, so unlike his usual gentle teasing.

"I don't have any facts," he said. "That means I have to consider all possibilities and coincidences, including the fact that a few short weeks ago Tony Angelini, the head of a known criminal organization, was sitting in your office, and now a collection of art has been stolen and three people all connected to you are dead."

"Three?" I shared a puzzled glance with Chloe. "Peter, Richard, and who else?"

"Tony Angelini was killed in his living room last Thursday night. He was stabbed in the heart and shot through the head."

"Tony Angelini is dead?" I faked a gasp. "I guess I won't get that event booking after all."

"That's a pretty tenuous connection to Simi." Chloe gave a light, forced laugh. "I almost feel like we're back to the days where you thought we were thieves."

"I feel like we're back there, too." His blue eyes hardened and there was no trace of the warmth I was used to seeing on his face.

My mouth went dry, and my heart pounded so hard I thought it might break a rib. "Are you going to arrest me?" I shot a frantic look at Chloe. "Should I call my cousin Riswan? He's a partner now at his law firm and his rates have doubled . . ."

Garcia studied me for a long time, and then he sighed. "No, I'm not going to arrest you. We have witnesses who saw you in Vera's garden almost every minute of the afternoon. In fact, I managed to track the movements of all your staff, and none of them left the party except for Emma, who was spotted in her car, and Chloe, who I'm pretty sure didn't knock herself out."

"That's a relief." With my knees shaking and my pulse pounding, it was everything I could do not to collapse in the nearest chair.

"But I do want to talk to Simone," he said. "I don't think her husband's death was accidental. We got the toxicology report on the parts of his body that were found and there was no alcohol in his system."

"She should be here somewhere," I said, frowning. "Although . . . now that you mention it, I haven't seen her since the funeral . . ." A shiver ran down my spine. "Usually, she's the life of the party."

THIRTY-FOUR

◆ ◆ ◆

imone video called a few weeks later during our farewell party. I had sent her a message letting her know the crew was getting together in the warehouse one last time before it was knocked down to make way for swanky condos. She'd sent her regrets but promised to call during our get-together so she could see the crew and catch up.

"Simsim! How are you?" She moved the camera around to show a deep blue ocean and a sky without clouds. "We're on Vera's super-yacht. It's been so good to get away."

"We missed you at Richard's celebration of life," I said. "You were supposed to give a speech."

"Oh, those things are such a bore," she said. "And really, what was there to say about Richard? He was dull, dull, dull. The only exciting thing he did in his life was get eaten by a shark."

"How long will you be away?" I moved the camera around so everyone could wave hello. We'd brought drinks and snacks, and Anil had set up the whiteboard to teach us all how to invest our money so we didn't lose it all again.

"I expect we'll have to stay in international waters for some time," Simone said. "How long do you think, Vera?" she shouted over the wind before turning back to the camera. "Vera doesn't know. We're enjoying our freedom. We're pretending we're Thelma and Louise from the movie, but instead of driving over a cliff, we're sailing the great blue sea."

"Detective Garcia was looking for you," I said. "He thinks Richard's death wasn't an accident. They've determined he hadn't been drinking."

"Oh dear." Simone shook her head. "It's a shame the shark didn't eat the rest of him. It would have been so much easier if it had. I told Vera to give him a few drinks, but she got nervous and just wanted to get it done."

"Simone?" My blood chilled. "Did you . . ."

"Oh, Simi. Always so innocent." Simone laughed. "You probably thought Peter's death was an accident, too."

The warehouse had fallen silent, everyone listening in horrified fascination to Simone as she flitted around the yacht, pointing the camera in different directions to show us the view.

"Well, no," I said. "Someone slit his throat. Garcia said the killer was left-handed."

Chloe raised her right arm and ran her fingers up and down her forearm, reminding me of Simone's scars. And her words. *I had to learn to write with my left hand.*

Bile rose in my throat, and I doubled over. "Was that you?"

"Do I have to spell it out for you, darling?" Simone settled in an overstuffed deck chair, finally holding the camera still as she adjusted her enormous sunglasses. "Peter was a bad man. He hurt Vera. When I went to see her that first time and saw her bruises, it made me so angry. Why did we both have to suffer? I resolved then and there to help her, and your celebration of life gave me the most wonderful idea. We would kill Peter and pretend it was a robbery, and since you wanted to rob him anyway, it was the perfect crime. Since Peter had been planning to move their collection to their art island, we thought our pretend thieves would do the same thing and ship the goods away. The boxes were already there, and they'd even marked where to put everything. We looked up a trucking company on the Internet, Simi! You would have been so proud. We decided to send it all to Belize because Vera spun her globe and closed her eyes and that's where her finger landed. Peter kept cash in his vault, so Vera took some and gave it to me, and I went to the trucking company office in disguise to pay them. It was so exciting. I think our only mistake was when they asked for a name for the shipping documents. I almost gave us away."

"Christ." Jack groaned. "William H. Hunt. He was a young Pre-Raphaelite artist who was known as a rebel without a cause."

"That's us," Simone said. "Vera and I are rebels, although we did have a good cause. And now we're free and very, very well off."

I heard Vera's voice and Simone moved out of the frame only to return a moment later. "Vera wants to know if you found an orange scarf when you were locked up in the container? She lost it when we were packing things up."

"Yes, it was wrapped around some jewelry, but that container was lost at sea."

"No matter." She waved a perfectly manicured hand. "Vera has more than enough money to buy dozens of scarves, don't you, darling?"

Vera appeared on the screen looking brighter and happier and more radiant than I'd ever seen her. "Hi, Simi and friends!"

"Hi, Vera." I forced a smile as I turned the camera in a circle to catch the shook faces of everyone in the room, still trying to process that our dear friend Simone was a serial killer.

"When did you pack it all?" Jack asked her. "There wasn't enough time during the party."

"Oh, we did it the night before," she said. "Vera put a few of her sleeping pills in Peter's nightcap so he wouldn't wake up, and then we spent all night packing and dragging boxes into the escape tunnel. Some of them were so heavy, we didn't think we'd be able to move them, especially with my bad arm. There was a risk Peter might want to take people down to the museum during the party before the truck came, but between us, we managed to keep his attention focused on all the pretty girls running around."

"Why didn't you just ship them out that night?" I continued.

"It wasn't about the collection," Simone said. "It was about Peter. He had to die, darling, and the theft gave us the perfect cover. We wanted people to think he was killed as part of the robbery. He put up quite a struggle when I slit his throat. I thought it would be easy, but his skin was quite thick. Vera had a worse time trying to get his finger off."

"I had to saw and saw and saw." Vera made a sawing motion with the little pink umbrella from her drink. "The blood was everywhere, but Simone had the good idea to wear rubber gloves, so we didn't leave fingerprints."

"I saw it on TV," Simone said. "I didn't know where one would buy rubber gloves, but Vera saw some when she was visiting her doctor and she got a pair for each of us when he was out of the room."

"I stole them," Vera said, laughing. "I broke the law."

I considered pointing out that murder was also breaking the law, but I didn't want her to get overexcited. She was already unhinged.

"Why did you hit Chloe?" I asked her. "You gave her a concussion."

"Vera had asked Peter to meet her in the garage," Simone said. "I was waiting in the Bugatti. But then Chloe walked in with him, and we had to do something because the truck was coming, and we had to get downstairs to turn off the security system, make the finger markings, and open the door so they could take the boxes."

"I saw a metal bar on the floor, so I hit her." Vera made a swinging motion with her pink cocktail umbrella. "One hit and she went down. I was surprised at how little effort it took. She must have a soft head."

"You could have killed her," I said, fighting back the nausea.

"I am sorry." Simone sighed. "We just had to be free. We just couldn't take it anymore. I hope there were no lasting injuries. How is she doing?"

"She's fine. No lasting damage. She and Gage are back together." I panned the phone over Olivia, Chloe, and Gage. "Olivia is here, too. We thought we'd invite her so she didn't have to sneak in, although I'm regretting it now that you had so much to share."

"No one is sneaking in here again," Emma said. "Axel's guys are all outside."

"Are you an 'Ol' Lady' now or a 'Sweet Butt'?" Simone said. "The biker life sounds so exciting."

I turned the camera so Emma could show off her new outlaw biker leather vest with the Hell's Fury patch in the center, surrounded by the words "Property of Axel."

"I'm an 'Ol' Lady,'" she said proudly. "I bought a Harley-Davidson Nightster with my money, and I've been showing Axel's boys how to eat my dust."

Axel chuckled and ruffled her hair. "She's a devil on wheels."

"I told her to invest the money," Anil said, "but she didn't listen. No one listens to me. I made a 20 percent profit on my investment from the last heist, but this time I've put most of my money in dividend stock. I need regular cash payments to fund my dream of becoming an actor. I quit my engineering job and I don't want to waste time waiting tables like all the other struggling actors. There's a high demand right now for funny South Asian sidekicks, and I want to get in while I can."

"We always need extras at the studio, where I'm back to film-ing my animal show," Cristian offered. "If you're happy to stir cooking pots, pretend to have seen alien life blobs, or stand still while I cover you in snakes to show kids that they're not danger-ous, you should stop by. I'm finishing up episode three next week, but in case it doesn't work out, I've already started planning my new business manufacturing biodegradable single-use plastic bags out of manure."

"What about your escort business?" Anil asked. "I have expe-rience now with older women. I took one for the team."

"He slept with Clare," I reminded Simone.

"I said 'older,' not 'ancient.'" Anil sniffed. "I took one for the team with Milan, not Clare. Milan is twenty-eight. She broke up with Vito to be with me, and she's the one who told me where Clare hid the diamond. She's been teaching me how to throw knives and I've been teaching her magic. I didn't invite her because I thought you might hold a grudge."

"A wise decision." I turned the phone back to look at Simone. "Did you hear all that?"

"I'm delighted to know everyone is doing so well," she said. "Vera is still having nightmares after our escapade, but it's nothing a little sedative can't handle. It worked well for her when she had a breakdown after Peter's death, and I had to keep her sedated so she wouldn't tell Detective Garcia where we'd stashed the finger."

Anil leaned forward, his face twisted in horrified fascination. "You kept it?"

Simone held up an ice bucket. "It's a souvenir. Once we reach the middle of international waters, we'll toss it overboard for the sharks."

Behind me I heard Emma retch.

"Emma really needs to toughen up," Simone said. "You can't

have any weak links in your crew, especially if your handsome Garcia comes knocking on your door asking questions about us, although I know you won't talk."

Chloe's eyes widened at the implicit threat. "We won't?"

"No, darling, because I left you a present." Simone pulled off her sunglasses and smiled. "When we were packing Peter's collection, I took the diamond so you could give it to Clare, but I noticed something odd about the way it sparkled. I know my diamonds, and that one was real. I was going to talk to you about it, but in all the excitement I forgot until I saw Chloe lying on the floor in the garage. I knew Anil had given Chloe the fake diamond to switch once she got downstairs, so I had Vera take the real diamond out of my pocket and switch it for the fake one in Chloe's pocket. I couldn't do it because I was covered in blood, and Vera did it before she cut off Peter's finger, so that worked out nicely. Then Vera turned off the security system and we took the fake diamond downstairs and put it in one of the boxes just in case Clare went chasing after it without you. I didn't trust her at all."

"So, at the warehouse you knew we were giving Clare a fake diamond?"

"And didn't I hide it well?" She beamed. "If Jack hadn't figured it out and been such a gentleman, you might have been able to keep your $9 million. But now you have a diamond worth more than ten times that amount. You should buy a super-yacht and come and join us."

"You've become a regular black widow," I said. "Peter's nephew, Peter, Richard . . . maybe even Clare when Mr. X finds out—"

"And Martha," she interjected. "Don't forget about her. But really, that was her fault. She shouldn't have broken the rules and slept with Richard, especially when she was so vulnerable. It's so easy when they have food allergies. One little peanut and they're done. No fuss. No mess. No drama. The world is full of bad people. I've just made it a better place."

I took another look around the room. Everyone was in shock. Even Gage, who I was sure had seen his share of death, had no expression on his face. It wasn't just what she had done; it was that she seemed to have no remorse. She was just as happy and cheerful as she had been the day we met.

"I don't know what to say, Simone."

"Say you'll have fun, darling. Enjoy your money. Enjoy your life. I've sent everyone a Gucci mask souvenir and a roll of Saran wrap. But if Jack doesn't treat you right, just give me a call."

THIRTY-FIVE

◇ ◇ ◇

Some people have trouble with boundaries. They say "no" but find themselves allowing guns in a "no guns" heist. They set rules about sacrificing yourself to save others and allow people to break them when the only way out of a situation is to take puffer fish poison and pretend that you're dead. They have a moral code but will throw it out the window when their serial killer high-society billionaire friend goes on the run in a super-yacht with her unhinged billionaire fly girl in international waters, where no one can touch them. They say they want a relationship but then they agree to let their boyfriend go away for several months to repatriate one of the world's lost treasures.

"Mom, could you and Simi please slow down? I don't want people to think we're together. It's not cool to go dress shopping with your fam." Olivia took three big steps, trying to distance herself from us on the first floor of Bloomingdale's.

"Do you remember just a few months ago when she was excited to go dress shopping with us?" Chloe's eyes watered. "It feels like it was yesterday."

"They grow up so fast," I said. "I remember her in Demonia

boots, ripped tights, and black dresses held together with pins. Now her tights have no rips in them."

"I hardly recognize her after her glow-up."

"I can hear you." Olivia turned and glared over her shoulder. "Take several seats."

"Do you have any heavy books with you in case I see Jack kissing another woman?" I peered into Chloe's tote bag. "I'm still traumatized by our last visit to Bloomingdale's, and I want to be prepared."

"I thought he was still away."

"He was supposed to be away last time," I said, "and then he snuck back to cause trouble and pull us into another heist."

"He won't get into trouble working at his cousin's greenhouse when he gets back. That's a pretty low-key kind of job."

I had doubts about how long Jack was going to last running the greenhouse. Yes, he loved his plants. And yes, he wanted to help Lou out after Lou had been arrested and thrown in jail when he confused two Mr. Browns and offered an undercover police officer a variety of stolen weapons instead of three cedar trees and some tulip bulbs. He also owed Lou a canoe.

Jack's life had been all about action and adventure. How did someone like that settle down? How was it going to be enough to spend his days recommending coral bells, dead nettle, and foamflower for shady gardens? How was he going to be fulfilled sending me lilies instead of tropical flowers for the funerals that now made up most of my event-planning business thanks to word-of-mouth advertising from the high-society types who had loved *loved* LOVED my circus- and shark-themed celebrations? Who would have thought so many rich people died every day? Or that they were all so clumsy?

Where was Jack going to stay when he came back? We hadn't

even talked about living arrangements during our nightly calls over regular and not burner phones. How was our relationship going to work as he settled into civilian life now that there was no longer a price on his head? Like Garcia had said, there were so many questions.

Olivia stopped so suddenly in front of us, I almost ran into her. "Is that Jack?"

In an instant, I was pulled into a terrible flashback: Jack, Clare, the kiss, the book, and then the walk with Garcia, who had stopped coming by for pizza nights after I told him Jack and I were back together. My stomach sank and I braced myself for the worst.

"Oh no. It's just someone who looks like him." Olivia looked over her shoulder with a smirk. "My bad."

"I think Olivia spends too much time on her phone," I said loudly. "I read that parents in Silicon Valley who work in the tech industry don't allow their children to have phones at all. It rots their brains."

"I'm going to tell Gage what you said," she snapped. "He lets me do whatever I want."

"He lets you do only what your mother tells him he can let you do," I reminded her. "She keeps him on a tight leash."

"We're going up to the personal shopper floor," Chloe said, heading for the escalator. "We followed Anil's investing advice about saving for the future, but Olivia has picked out a very special dress."

We emerged a few minutes later on the floor where the dresses were all chained to racks, and no one was wearing jeans, and made our way to the front desk.

"Pickup for Simi Chopra," Chloe said.

"I didn't buy anything here." I looked around at the five-thousand-dollar dresses. "What's going on?"

"Here you go." The personal shopper—not Clare, thank goodness—handed me a black dress bag.

"This isn't mine," I protested.

"Put it on." Chloe pushed me toward the changing room. "We're running late."

Still confused, I did as she asked. The dress she'd given me was a stunning burgundy sleeveless A-line chiffon midi dress with a high neck and a flowing skirt. It was quite simply the most beautiful piece of clothing I'd ever seen.

"The shoes are already in there," Chloe called out.

I slipped on the elegant black stilettos and stared at my stunned self in the mirror for a long moment before joining Olivia and Chloe outside.

"Now, will you tell me what's going on?"

"You look gorgeous." Chloe smoothed back my hair and slipped a beaded black clutch into my hand. "I wanted to take you for hair and makeup, but we've run out of time. The car is waiting for you downstairs."

"What car? Where are we going? What about Olivia's dress?"

"Did you seriously think I'd cater to internalized patriarchal beauty standards and wear something designed for the male gaze that would restrict my ability to run from predators?" Olivia huffed. "You don't know me at all."

"Do you trust me?" Chloe's smile was so wide it made her eyes crinkle at the corners.

"Always."

"Then for the next hour or so, just go with the flow. It's all going to be okay."

I followed her downstairs and she helped me into a big black Bentley that was waiting outside.

"Love you, babe." She and Olivia waved from the street as the driver raised the window.

"Love you, too."

Half an hour later, the Bentley pulled up in front of a large Tudor house set back in a sea of trees in the heart of Evanston. I was still trying to remember where I'd seen it when architect Trey Williams opened the car door.

"Simi!" He smiled and helped me out. "It's so nice to see you again. The renovations are all done on your new home, and I'm excited to show you around."

"I think there's been a mistake," I said as he ushered me up the walkway. "This isn't my house. I mean, I planned the renos, but—"

"I couldn't have started the renovations if the title wasn't in order." Trey laughed and opened the front door. "I know it will look very different now that the work is done, but it is indeed yours." He waved me inside. "Come. Let me show you around. Most of it was cosmetic, but with the amount of money you had allocated for the renos, the contractor was able to hire three separate building teams to get even the most substantial work completed in time."

I took a deep breath and put my misgivings aside. I trusted Chloe. She'd told me everything was going to be okay.

Trey had worked wonders with the renovations. Everything we had talked about had been done—the sparkling white kitchen, the open-plan living room, the greenhouse and the potting shed out back. Even the rooms we hadn't discussed—bathrooms, basement, and bedrooms—had been updated in a style I loved.

"It's amazing," I said to Trey after we'd finished touring the second floor. "You did a fantastic job, but I think there was a misunderstanding."

Trey handed me a set of keys and pointed to the door leading to the master suite. "I think if you go in there, it might all get sorted out. Congratulations. On everything."

After Trey had gone, I opened the door.

At first my attention was drawn to the incredible transformation. Two bedrooms had become one to create a master suite the size of my parents' living room, with big, airy windows; bright, bold colors; a marble en suite; and a giant walk-in closet. A king-size bed overflowing with pillows dominated the space in the center of the room. Above it, a sea of mirrors glistened. And on it, lounging back on the pillows with a self-satisfied smile, was Jack.

"What's going on?" I couldn't move, couldn't breathe, my brain still trying to process everything I was seeing. "Trey thinks this is my house."

"It is yours," he said. "I bought it. For you."

I staggered back and collapsed in the nearest chair. "You can't buy me a house."

"I did."

"But . . . the cost, Jack. It was six million dollars."

"I've pulled off a lot of heists over the years," he said. "I had no one to share the money with. Nothing to buy except my trucks. I lived a low-key lifestyle so no one would know how much I really had. And then I met a girl who made me want to be a better man. I fell in love, and when I saw this house . . ." He climbed off the bed and knelt in front of me. "Simi Chopra, will you marry me?" He opened the blue velvet box in his hand and showed me a beautiful sapphire ring surrounded by diamonds.

My mouth opened, but all that spilled out was, "My brain . . ."

A frown creased Jack's brow. "Not really the answer I was expecting."

"I can't . . ." I shook my head. "You organized all this? Chloe? The dress? The car? Trey and all the renovations were real? When did you buy this house? It had to be after I told you I wanted to take a break."

"Yes, it was."

"But how did you know we'd get back together?"

"Because if we weren't meant to be together, I would never have been in the bushes the night you tried to save Chloe in the museum. I wouldn't have held you in my arms and known deep in

my bones that I'd met the woman I'd been waiting for all my life—
a woman who is intelligent and beautiful and brave and loyal, who
has a secret love of adventure and a wicked sense of humor, a woman
who lights up every room she walks into and can take a group of
misfits and turn them into a family. A woman I want to call my
wife." He took the ring out of the box and slid it on my finger.
"This was my mother's ring. It is the only thing I have left to remember her by, and there is no one else I have ever wanted to give
it to but you."

I looked at the ring and then at the man who had stolen my
heart. "Yes, Jack, I'll marry you."

An hour later, after we'd christened the bed, we lay side by side staring
up at our naked selves. "Jack?"

"Yes, sweetheart?"

"The mirror has to go."

"I like it."

"Do you like what we just did?"

Jack gave a satisfied rumble. "Very much."

"Would you like to do it again? Ever?"

Jack froze as understanding dawned. "I've changed my mind
about the mirror."

"I thought you might."

"Is there anything else you don't like?"

I wrapped my arms around him and pulled him down for a kiss.
"Everything is perfect."

THIRTY-SIX

◇ ◇ ◇

JACK

Let's say you're dead. Your old boss thinks you died from a gun-shot wound and now you are free to live a normal life. You have a beautiful fiancée, a new group of friends, a kick-ass dream house, and a greenhouse full of plants. You have repatriated a stolen necklace and a missing diamond, and you are keeping busy running Lou's greenhouse while he's doing time.

Everything is perfect.

Until one day, you get a call. The brooch you slipped into your pocket while you were locked away to die is real.

You know what that means.

Somewhere, lost in the Caribbean Sea, there is a shipping con-tainer holding almost all of the world's missing treasures . . .

ACKNOWLEDGMENTS

◆ ◆ ◆

By the time I was twelve years old, I had read almost every book in the children's section of our well-stocked small-town public library but was not allowed access to the adult section, which was restricted to "mature" people over the age of fourteen. As a result, my mother, a voracious reader herself, took out what she considered to be "age-appropriate" books for me, and it was then that I first fell in love with daring detectives, clever criminals, murder and mayhem, capers and heists. I am deeply grateful for her love of crime fiction and her view that murder plots were okay for twelve-year-old girls so long as there was a mystery to solve.

So many people have contributed their talents to the success of my books. Hugs to my longtime agent, Laura Bradford, who encouraged me to jump into something new. Your steadiness and positivity have kept me from more than one anxious meltdown over the years. Huge thanks to Kristine Swartz for your patience and humor and for taking a chance on this wild ride of a story. Thanks also to the entire wonderful Berkley team, including Mary Baker, Anika Bates, Stephanie Felty, and the fabulous Lila Selle for her wonderful cover design and illustration. Working with you all has been a real honor.

Wholehearted thanks to my friends Alice Tseng and Sarah Buyers, who buy all my books, like all my posts, and cheer me up with their uplifting comments and unending enthusiasm. You were some of the very first readers of my stories, and I can't believe I still haven't chased you away.

My deepest gratitude as always goes to my family: Jamie, Sapphira, Alysha, Sharon, Rana, Adele, and Tarick. Without your love and support, I couldn't have gone on this crazy adventure. John, you are my rock and my inspiration for living a life of adventure. I couldn't do this without you. Dad, your pride humbles me and your words inspire me. I unashamedly admit that I may have slipped one or two of your sayings into my book. Mum, thank you for the mysteries, the gift of stories, and your unmatched love of reading.

Finally, hugs to all my readers. Never say no to a grand adventure!

Turn the page
for a preview of Sara Desai's

THE
MARRIAGE
GAME

Available now!

◇ ◇ ◇

When Layla walked into The Spice Mill Restaurant after yet another disastrous relationship, she expected hugs and kisses, maybe a murmur of sympathy, or even a cheerful *Welcome home.*

Instead, she got a plate of samosas and a pitcher of water for table twelve.

"There are fresh poppadums in the kitchen," her mother said. "Don't forget to offer them to all the guests." Not even a glimmer of emotion showed on her mother's gently lined face. Layla could have been any one of the half-dozen servers who worked at her parents' restaurant instead of the prodigal daughter who had returned to San Francisco, albeit with a broken heart.

She should have known better than to show up during opening hours expecting to pour out her heart. The middle child in a strict, academic, reserved family, her mother wasn't given to outward displays of affection. But after the emotional devastation of walking in on her social media star boyfriend, Jonas Jameson, as he snorted the last of her savings off of two naked models, Layla had hoped for something more than being put to work.

It was her childhood all over again.

"Yes, Mom." She dutifully carried the plate and pitcher to the table and chatted briefly with the guests about the restaurant's unique decor. Decorated in exotic tones of saffron, gold, ruby, and cinnamon with accent walls representing the natural movement of wind and fire, and a cascading waterfall layered with beautiful landscaped artificial rocks and tiny plastic animals, the restaurant was the embodiment of her late brother's dream to re-create "India" in the heart of San Francisco.

The familiar scents—cinnamon, pungent turmeric, and smoky cumin—brought back memories of evenings spent stirring dal, chopping onions, and rolling roti in the bustling kitchen of her parents' first restaurant in Sunnyvale under the watchful army of chefs who followed the recipes developed by her parents. What had seemed fun as a child, and an imposition as a teenager, now filled her with a warm sense of nostalgia, although she would have liked just one moment of her mother's time.

On her way to the kitchen for the poppadums, she spotted her nieces coloring in a booth and went over to greet them. Her parents looked after them in the evenings when their mom, Rhea, was busy at work.

"Layla Auntie!" Five-year-old Anika and six-year-old Zaina, their long dark hair in pigtails, ran to give her a hug.

"Did you bring us anything from New York?" Zaina asked.

Layla dropped to her knees and put her arms around her nieces. "I might have brought a few presents with me, but I left them at the house. I didn't think I'd see you here."

"Can we go with you and get them?" They planted sticky kisses on her cheeks, making her laugh.

"I'll bring them tomorrow. What have you been eating?"

"*Jalebis.*" Anika held up a bright orange, pretzel-shaped sweet similar to a funnel cake.

"Yesterday we helped Dadi make chocolate *peda*," Zaina informed her, using the Urdu term for "paternal grandmother."

"And the day before that we made *burfi*, and before that we made—"

"Peanut brittle." Anika grinned.

Layla bit back a laugh. Her mother had a sweet tooth, so it wasn't surprising that she'd made treats with her granddaughters in the kitchen.

Zaina's smile faded. "She said peanut brittle was Pappa's favorite."

Layla's heart squeezed in her chest. Her brother, Dev, had died in a car accident five years ago and the pain of losing him had never faded. He'd been seven years older, and the symbol of the family's social and economic strength; expectations had weighed heavy on Dev's shoulders and he didn't disappoint. With a degree in engineering, a successful arranged marriage, and a real estate portfolio that he managed with a group of friends, he was every Indian parent's dream.

Layla . . . not so much.

"It's my favorite, too," she said. "I hope you left some for me."

"You can have Anika's," Zaina offered. "I'll get it for you."

"No! You can't take mine!" Anika chased Zaina into the kitchen, shouting over the *Slumdog Millionaire* DJ mix playing in the background.

"They remind me of you and Dev." Her mother joined her beside the booth and lifted a lock of Layla's hair, studying the bright streaks. "What is this blue?"

Of course her mother was surprised. She had given up trying to turn her daughter into a femme fatale years ago. Layla had never been interested in trendy hairstyles, and the only time she painted her nails or wore makeup was when her friends dragged her out.

Dressing up was reserved for work or evenings out. Jeans, pony-tails, and sneakers were more her style.

"This is courtesy of Jonas's special hair dye. His stylist left it behind for touch-ups. Blue hair is his signature look. Apparently, it shows up well on-screen. I didn't want it to go to waste after we broke up, so I used it all on my hair. I had the true Jonas look."

Unlike most of her friends, who dated behind their parents' backs, Layla had always been honest about her desire to find true love. She'd introduced her boyfriends to her parents and told them about her breakups and relationship woes. Of course, there were limits to what she could share. Her parents didn't know she'd been living with Jonas, and they most certainly would never find out that she'd lost her job, her apartment, and her pride after the "Blue Fury" YouTube video of her tossing Jonas's stuff over their bal-cony in a fit of rage had gone viral.

"You are so much like your father—passionate and impulsive." Her mother smiled. "When we got our first bad review, he tore up the magazine, cooked it in a pot of dal, and delivered it to the reviewer in person. I had to stop him from flying to New York when you called to tell us you and Jonas split up. After he heard the pain in your voice, he wanted to go there and teach that boy a lesson."

If the sanitized, parent-friendly version of her breakup had dis-tressed her father, she couldn't imagine how he would react if she told him the full story. "I'm glad you stopped him. Jonas is a big social media star. People would start asking questions if he posted videos with his face covered in bruises."

"Social media star." Her mother waved a dismissive hand. "What job is that? Talking shows on the Internet? How could he support a family?"

Aside from her family's disdain for careers in the arts, it was a good question. Jonas hadn't even been able to support himself. When the bill collectors came calling, he'd moved into the prewar walk-up Layla shared with three college students in the East Village and lived off their generosity as he pursued fame and fortune as a social media lifestyle influencer.

"That boy was no good," her mother said firmly. "He wasn't brought up right. You're better off without him."

It was the closest to sympathy Layla was going to get. Sometimes it was easier to discuss painful issues with her mother because Layla had to keep her emotions in check. "I always seem to pick the bad ones. I think I must have some kind of dud dude radar." Emotion welled up in her throat, and she turned away. Her mother gave the lectures. Her father handled the tears.

"That's why in our tradition marriage is not about love." Her mother never passed up an opportunity to extol the benefits of an arranged marriage, especially when Layla had suffered yet another heartbreak. "It's about devotion to another person; caring, duty, and sacrifice. An arranged marriage is based on permanence. It is a contract between two like-minded people who share the same values and desire for companionship and family. There is no heartache, no betrayal, no boys pretending they care, or using you and throwing you away, no promises unkept—"

"No love."

Her mother's face softened. "If you're lucky, like your dad and me, love shows up along the way."

"Where is Dad?" Layla wasn't interested in hearing about marriage, arranged or otherwise, when it was clear she didn't have what it took to sustain a relationship. No wonder guys always thought of her as a pal. She was everybody's wingwoman and nobody's prize.

She looked around for her father. He was her rock, her shoulder to cry on when everything went wrong. Usually he was at the front door greeting guests or winding his way through the linen-covered tables and plush saffron-colored chairs, chatting with customers about the artwork and statues displayed in the mirrored alcoves along the walls, talking up the menu, or sharing stories with foodies about his latest culinary finds. He was a born entertainer, and there was nothing she loved more than watching him work a room.

"Your father has been locked in his office every free minute since you called about that boy. He doesn't eat; he hardly sleeps . . . I don't know if it's work or something else. He never rests." Layla's mother fisted her red apron, her trademark sign of anxiety. Pari Auntie had given the apron to her to celebrate the opening of the Spice Mill Restaurant, and she still wore it every day although the embroidered elephants around the bottom were now all faded and frayed.

"That's not unusual." Layla's father never rested. From the moment his feet hit the floor in the morning, he embraced the day with an enthusiasm and joyful energy Layla simply couldn't muster before nine A.M. and two cups of coffee. Her father accomplished more in a day than most people did in a week. He lived large and loud and was unashamed to let his emotions spill over, whether it was happiness or grief or even sympathy for his only daughter's many heartbreaks.

"He'll be so happy that you are home to visit." Her mother gave her a hug, the warm gesture equally as unexpected as their brief talk. Usually she was full on when the restaurant was open, focused and intense. "We both are."

Layla swallowed past the lump in her throat. It was moments like these, the love in two sticky kisses from her nieces and a few powerful words from her mom, that assured her she was making the right decision to move home. She had hit rock bottom in New York. If there was any chance of getting her life back on track, it would be with the support of her family.

"*Beta!*" Her father's loud voice boomed through the restaurant, turning the heads of the customers.

"Dad!" She turned and flung herself into his arms, heedless of the spectacle. Except for his traditional views about women (he didn't have the same academic or professional expectations of her as he'd had for Dev), her father was the best man she knew— reliable, solid, dependable, kind, and funny. An engineer before he immigrated to America, he was practical enough to handle most electrical or mechanical issues at the restaurant, and smart enough to know how to run a business, talk politics, and spark a conversation with anyone. His love was limitless. His kindness boundless. When he hired a member of staff, he never let them go.

All the emotion Layla had been holding in since witnessing Jonas's betrayal came pouring out in her father's arms as he murmured all the things he wanted to do to Jonas if he ever met him.

"I just bought a set of Kamikoto Senshi knives. They go through meat like butter. The bastard hippie wouldn't even know he'd been stabbed until he was dead. Or even better, I'd invite him for a meal and seat him at table seventeen near the back entrance where no one could see him. I'd serve him a mushroom masala made with death cap mushrooms. He would suffer first. Nausea, stomach cramps, vomiting, and diarrhea. Then liver failure and death."

Laughter bubbled up in her chest. No one could cheer her up like her father. "Mom has made you watch too many crime shows. How about just shaking your fist or saying a few angry words?"

He pressed a kiss to her forehead. "If I have to defend your honor, I want to do it in a way that will be talked about for years, something worthy of the criminal version of a Michelin star. Do you think there is such a thing?"

"Don't be ridiculous, Nasir." Layla's mother sighed. "There will be no murdering of itinerant Internet celebrities when we have a restaurant to run. Things are hard enough with the downturn in the market. I can't do this on my own."

Frowning, Layla pulled away from her father. "Is that why the restaurant is almost empty? Is everything okay?"

Her father's gaze flicked to her mother and then back to Layla. "Everything is fine, beta."

Layla's heart squeezed at the term of endearment. She would always be his sweetheart, even when she was fifty years old.

"Not that fine." Her mother gestured to the brigade of aunties filing through the door, some wearing saris, a few in business attire, and others in *salwar kameez*, their brightly colored tunics and long pants elegantly embroidered. Uncles and cousins took up the rear. "It seems you bumped into Lakshmi Auntie's nephew at Newark Airport and told him you'd broken up with your boyfriend."

Within moments, Layla was enveloped in warm arms, soft bosoms, and the thick scent of jasmine perfume. News spread faster than wildfire in the auntie underground or, in this case, faster than a Boeing 767.

"Look who is home!"

While Layla was being smothered with hugs and kisses, her father ushered everyone to the bar and quickly relocated the nearest customers before roping off the area with a PRIVATE PARTY sign. The only thing her family loved better than a homecoming was a wedding.

"Who was that boy? No respect in his bones. No shame in his body. Who does he think he is?" Pari Auntie squeezed Layla so hard she couldn't breathe.

"Let her go, Pari. She's turning blue." Charu Auntie edged her big sister out of the way and gave Layla a hug. Her mother's socially awkward younger sister had a Ph.D. in neuroscience and always tried to contribute to conversations by dispensing unsolicited psychological advice.

"How did you come here? Where are you staying? Are you

going back to school? Do you have a job?" Deepa Auntie, her mother's cousin and a failed interior designer, tossed the end of her *dupatta* over her shoulder, the long, sheer, hot pink scarf embellished with small crystal beads inadvertently slapping her father's youngest sister, Lakshmi, on the cheek.

"Something bad is going to happen," superstitious Lakshmi Auntie moaned. "I can feel it in my face."

Mehar Auntie snorted as she adjusted her sari, the long folds of bright green material draping over her generous hips. "You thought something bad was going to happen when the milk boiled over last week."

"Don't make fun, Mehar," Lakshmi Auntie said with a scowl. "I told you Layla's relationship wasn't going to work when I found out she left on a full-moon night."

"No one thought it would work out," Mehar Auntie scoffed. "The boy didn't even go to university. Layla needs a professional, someone easy on the eyes like Salman Khan. Remember the scene in *Dabangg*? I went wild in the theater when he ripped off his shirt."

Layla's aunties groaned. Mehar Auntie knew the moves to every Bollywood dance and the words to every song. She was Layla's favorite aunt, not just because she wasn't shy to bust out her moves at every wedding, but also because she shared Layla's love of movies from Hollywood to Bollywood to indie.

"Mehar Auntie!" Layla gasped mockingly. "What about Hrithik Roshan? He's the number one actor in Bollywood. No one can dance like him. He's so perfect he hardly seems human."

"Too skinny." Mehar Auntie waved a dismissive hand. "He looks like he was shrink-wrapped. I like a man with meat on his bones."

"Mehar. Really." Nira Auntie shook a finger in disapproval, the glass bindi bracelets on her arm jingling softly. She owned a successful clothing store in Sunnyvale and her exquisitely embroidered mustard yellow and olive green salwar kameez had a fashion-forward open back. "My children are here."

"Your children are men in their twenties. They're hardly going to be shocked by my appreciation of a well-muscled man."

"If you spent less time dreaming and dancing, you could have had one for yourself."

Layla winced at the burn. Mehar Auntie was well past what was considered marriageable age, but seemed content with her single life and her work as a dance teacher in Cupertino.

"Layla needs stability in her life, not some singing, dancing actor with no brains in his head." Salena Auntie pinched Layla's cheeks. She'd been trying to get Layla married off since her third birthday. "What will you do now? What are your intentions?"

"I'm done with men, Auntie-ji," she said affectionately.

"Don't call me Auntie." She tucked her gray hair under her embroidered headscarf. "I am not so old."

"You are old." Taara Auntie pushed her aside and handed Layla a Tupperware container. "And you're too thin. Eat. I made it just for you."

"What's this?"

Taara Auntie smiled and patted Layla's hand. "I've been taking cooking classes at the YMCA. I'm learning to make Western food, but I've added an Indian twist. This is Indian American fusion lasagna. I used roti instead of pasta, added a little halloumi cheese, and flavored the tomato sauce with mango chutney and a bit of cayenne. Try it." She watched eagerly as Layla lifted the lid.

"It looks . . . delicious." Her stomach lurched as she stared at the congealed mass of soggy bread, melted cheese, and bright orange chutney.

"You're going to put me out of business." Layla's father snatched the container out of her hand and studied the contents. "What an interesting combination of flavors. We'll enjoy it together this evening when we have time to appreciate the nuance of your creation."

Layla shot him a look of gratitude, and he put an arm around her shoulders.

"Don't eat it," he whispered. "Your sister-in-law tried her chicken nugget vindaloo surprise last week and she was sick for two days. If you're planning to travel in the next week—"

"I'm not. I'm staying here. I'm moving back home. My stuff is arriving in the next few days."

"Jana, did you hear that?" His face lit up with delight. "She's not going back to New York."

"What about your job?" her mother asked, her dark eyes narrowing.

"I thought it was time for a change, and I wanted to be here so I could help you . . ." Her voice trailed off when her mother frowned.

"She wants to be with us, Jana," her father said. "Why are you looking at her like that?"

"We aren't old. We don't need help. She had a good job. Every week I time her on the Face and she doesn't say anything is bad at work."

"It's called FaceTime, Mom, and it's not as good as being with the people you love."

"She loves her family. Such a good girl." Layla's father wrapped her in a hug even as her mother waggled a warning finger in her direction. Emotional manipulation didn't work on her mother. Neither did lies.

"Tell me the truth," her mother warned. "When I die, you will feel the guilt and realize . . ."

"Mom . . ."

"No. I will die."

"Fine." Layla pulled away from the warmth of her father's arms. It was almost impossible to lie to her mother when she started talking about her own death. "I was fired."

Silence.

Layla braced herself for the storm. Even though her mother was emotionally reserved, there were times when she let loose, and from the set of her jaw, it was clear this was going to be one of those times.

"Because of the boy?"

"Indirectly, yes."

"Oh, beta." Her father held out his arms, his voice warm with sympathy, but when Layla moved toward him, her mother blocked her with a hand.

"No hugs for her." She glared at Layla. "I told you so. I told you not to leave. New York is a bad place. Too big. Too many people. No sense of family. No values. You had boyfriend after boyfriend and all of them were bad, all of them hurt you. And this one makes you lose your job . . ." She continued her rant, mercifully keeping her voice low so the aunties wouldn't hear.

All her life, Layla had wanted to make her parents as proud as they had been of Dev, but the traditional roads of success weren't open to her. With only average marks and no interest in the "acceptable" careers—doctor, engineer, accountant, and *lawyer is okay*—she'd forged her own path. Yes, they'd supported her through business school, although they hadn't really understood her decision to specialize in human resource management. Her father had even wept with pride at her graduation. But underneath it all she could feel their disappointment. And now she'd disgraced herself and the family. No wonder her mother was so upset.

"Go back to New York." Her mother waved her toward the door. "Say you're sorry. Tell them it was a mistake."

"I can't." Her mother couldn't grasp Facebook. There was no way she would be able to explain YouTube or the concept of something going viral. And the temper tantrum that had started it all—the utter disappointment at having another relationship fail again? Her mother would never forgive her for being so rash. "I've really messed up this time."

Wasn't that the understatement of the year. Although the police had let her go with just a warning, she had spent a few humiliating hours in the police station in handcuffs and her landlord had kicked her out of her apartment. But those were things her parents didn't need to know.

Her father shook his head. "Beta, what did you do that was so bad?"

Layla shrugged. "It doesn't matter. I wasn't happy at my job and they knew it. I didn't like how they treated the people looking for work like they were inventory. They didn't care about their needs or their wants. It was all about keeping the corporate clients happy. I even told my boss I thought we could be just as successful if we paid as much attention to the people we placed as the companies that hired us, but she didn't agree. Things started going downhill after that. I have a feeling I was on my way out anyway, and what happened just gave them an excuse."

"So you have no job, no marriage prospects, no place to live . . ." Her mother shook her head. "What did we do wrong?"

"Don't worry, beta. I will fix everything." Her father smiled. "Your old dad is on the case. As long as I am alive, you never have to worry."

"She's a grown woman, Nasir. She isn't a little girl who broke a toy. She needs to fix this herself." Layla's mother crossed her arms. "So? What is your plan?"

Layla grimaced. "Well, I thought I'd live at home and help out at the restaurant for a bit, and I can look after the girls when Rhea is busy . . ."

"You need a job," her mother stated. "Or will you go back to school and get a different degree? Maybe doctor or engineer or even dentist? Your father has a sore tooth."

"This one." Her father pointed to one of his molars. "It hurts when I chew."

Scrambling to come up with a plan to appease her mother, she mentally ran through the last twenty-four hours searching for inspiration, until she remembered toying with an idea on the way home. "I saw one of my favorite movies, *Jerry Maguire*, on the plane. The hero is a sports agent who gets fired for having a conscience. He starts his own company and he only has Dorothy to help him."

"Who is this Dorothy?" her mother asked.

"She's his romantic love interest, but that's not the point. I'm Jerry." She gestured to herself, her enthusiasm growing as the idea formed in her mind. "I could start my own recruitment agency, but it would be different from other agencies because the focus would be on the people looking for work and not the employers. You've always told me how in the history of our family, the Patels have always been their own boss. Well, I want to be my own boss, too. I have a business degree. I have four years of recruitment experience. How hard can it be?"

"Very hard." Her mother sighed. "Do you think you can just show up one day and have a successful business? Your father and I started from nothing. We cooked meals on a two-burner hot plate in a tiny apartment. We sold them to friends in plastic containers. It took years to save the money to buy our first restaurant and more years and many hardships before it was a success."

"But we can help her, Jana," her father said. "What's the use of learning all the tricks of running your own business if you can't share them with your own daughter? We even have the empty office suite upstairs. She can work from there so I can be around—"

"Nasir, you sublet the office to a young man a few weeks ago. He's moving in next week."

Layla's heart sank, and she swallowed her disappointment. Of course. It had been too perfect. How had she even thought for a minute that it would be this easy to turn her life around?

"It's okay, Dad." She forced a smile. "Mom's right. You always fix my problems. I should do this myself."

"No." Her father's voice was uncharacteristically firm. "It's not okay. I'll call the tenant and tell him circumstances have changed. He hasn't even moved in so I am sure it won't be a problem." He smiled. "Everything is settled. You're home. You'll have a new business and work upstairs. Now, you just need a husband and I can die in peace."

"Don't you start talking about dying, too."

But he wasn't listening. Instead, he was clapping his hands to quiet the chatter. "I have an announcement. Our Layla is moving back home. She'll be running her own recruitment business from our office suite upstairs so if you know of employers looking for workers or people needing a job, send them to her."

Everyone cheered. Aunties pushed forward, shouting out the names of cousins, friends, and family they knew were looking for work. Layla's heart warmed. This is what she'd missed most in New York. Family. They were all the support she needed.

Her father thudded his fist against his chest. "Our family is together again. My heart is full—" He choked and doubled over, his arm sliding off Layla's shoulder.

"Dad? Are you okay?" She put out a hand to steady him, and he swayed.

"My heart . . ."

She grabbed his arm. "Dad? What's wrong?"

With a groan, he crumpled to the floor.

"I knew it," Lakshmi Auntie cried out as Layla dropped to her knees beside her father. "I felt it in my face."

Photo copyright Linda Mackie Photography

SARA DESAI has been a lawyer, radio DJ, marathon runner, historian, bouncer, and librarian. She lives on Vancouver Island with her husband, kids, and an assortment of forest creatures who think they are pets. Sara's romantic comedy and mystery books have appeared in *Entertainment Weekly*, *People*, *O, The Oprah Magazine*, *Marie Claire*, *The Washington Post*, PopSugar, Bustle, *USA Today*, *Woman's World*, *Hello! Canada*, and many more. When not laughing at her own jokes, Sara can be found eating nachos.

VISIT SARA DESAI ONLINE

SaraDesai.com

Ready to find
your next great read?

Let us help.

Visit prh.com/nextread

Penguin Random House